PRAISES FOR

'Nikhil Singh is a surrealist. His wor
reading slam poetry and making up
critiques are acerbic and pull no punches, reflecting on the contemporary literary scene while challenging it by creating something truly original and unique. African writing at its finest. I cannot recommend Dakini Atoll enough.'
Mame Bougouma Diene – Caine Prize Winner

'In this compelling sequel to *Club Ded*, Nikhil expands on his groundbreaking narrative with a story that moves with the alacrity of a Charles Mingus tremolo. His words strike the eyes like strobe-flashes in the dark, revealing an uncompromising hyper-noir world that never lets up, and reminds us that such singular minds should never be constrained by the paradigms of any genre.'
Preston Grassmann, Shirley Jackson Award finalist

'Has Nikhil Singh ever met a literary boundary he didn't want to cross? Told in machine gun prose from a multitude of perspectives, *Dakini Atoll* is an exquisitely bewildering story of exploitation, resistance and alien bodies, in which motives and allegiances are constantly shifting amidst the story's deeper currents. Strap in and prepare for an experience you won't forget.'
Adri Joy, Hugo Winning Senior Editor at *Nerds of a Feather, Flock Together*

'Nikhil Singh's new novel reads like a breathless account of the near future, ripped from the headlines of a decade from now, and delivered, with staccato prose, in all its sinister, transformative glory. *Dakini Atoll* is something like the love child of *Akira* and *Gravity's Rainbow,* hopped up on adrenochrome, mainlined directly into your nervous system, and sent out to overload the worldwide communications network.'
Steven Shaviro

'The end of the world is a luxury, and *Dakini Atoll* takes us on a highspeed dredge through everything that comes next. Zooming out from the fragmented colonial decay, class desperation, high-stakes media opiates and deranged posthuman upgrade schemes of its predecessor *Club Ded*, *Dakini* projects a wide-angle panorama of collapse, in pandemic ghost cities, aeries of inconceivable wealth, entirely artificial realities inhabited by the masses and messianic mad science unfolding out of sight. [...] My mind reels at where this ongoing trilogy can expand to next, but Singh has, terrifyingly, miraculously, prepared the space.'
Adam McGovern – editor, *HiLobrow*/writer, *Nightworld*

'Dakini Atoll is bigger, weirder and more ambitious than Club Ded. A story about the intricate weaving of media, technology, religion, and some of the rawest, bleeding edges of humanity all delivered in gunfire prose… it's propulsive and mesmerising and wild and unique, as only Nikhil can consistently deliver. If you like your SF bold and unusual and imaginative, you'll enjoy this.'
Wole Talabi - *Shigidi* and *Incomplete Solutions* writer, Hugo & Nebula finalist

CLUB DED REVIEWS

'*Club Ded* is a kaleidoscopic look at the processes of creation and art through the dual lenses of realism and Afrofuturism. The cultural clash between Bryson and Fortunanto microcosmically reflect the complexities of relations and exchanges between the US and South Africa. It feels as though author Nikhil Singh is on an academic discourse against generalisation and stereotype: comparisons in ideals of American commercialism and 'African' mysticism. Singh bolsters the narrative with a penetrating understanding of contemporary South Africa, and subtle, but astute, use of social commentary. He writes unapologetically about issues such as poverty, racism, substance abuse and classism. With incredible humanity, all characters are flawed. If not relatable, they are believable. Singh creates mystery in a steady release of plot. With no real clues to puzzle things together, the narrative is unclear for a large part of the book, yet Singh successfully retains the reader in actively focusing their attention on what proves to be key information. *Club Ded* is a self-aware novel. Singh makes a calculated contribution to Afrofuturism in questioning why the literary movement is positioned in contrast to Eurocentric speculative fiction. This book is an exhilarating dive into psychedelic futures. An excellent read for lovers of gritty speculative fiction.'
***Aurealis* Magazine**

'*Club Ded* is a laugh out loud riot. And yet each staccato chapter retains a gravitas that builds and builds to provide a Pynchonesque future vision of South Africa and the larger African continent with its aging action movie star, neurotic film director, beautiful sirens, paparazzi, charismatic wanderers, talking chimps and alien creatures. Nikhil Singh has outdone himself with this new novel – his dialogue is as sharp as ever, his new world grim but intoxicating. *Club Ded* is so fucked up, so hilarious and so brilliant.'
Billy Kahora, Former Editor, *Kwani?* and author of *The Cape Cod Bicycle War*

'This is where *Club Ded* dances; on the line between camera and shot, between director and writer and actor. Capetown re-imagined as a set, as a playground, as a canvas for a painting made of hallucinogens. Ideas are thrown at the page with the same density as the heat that hangs in the air but they never overwhelm. Singh holds

there, in the liminal ground between a dozen different ways to create a novel which is noir, comedy, science fiction, conspiracy thriller and more. The collision between creative methods, between cultures, between moralities, all of it happening on every page as the band plays faster with every hit. It's heady, intoxicating, challenging stuff. But that's the plan, as Singh clearly delights in showing us. *Club Ded* is complex, ambitious, disturbing and bleakly funny.'
The Full Lid

'*Club Ded* is a real rollercoaster ride. Very intelligently written, the book works on so many levels. Ostensively about a troubled SCI-FI film shoot, and while often being other worldly, it addresses a myriad of "this world", real life issues concerning the individual, his / her / it's place in society and the fracture points that exist between peoples locally (the South African experience) and further afield. And this is done totally unsentimentally, without being didactic and with little regard for politeness. There are many inter twined stories with characters that captivate, amuse and repulse – often all at the same time. Whatever their nature and primary motivations, they are all searching. Nikhil's writing style is insightful, amusing, nimble and esoteric, and you will feel compelled to follow him and his characters anywhere.'
Ntshuks Bonga, South African musician

'There's a lot going on in this entertaining, brilliantly-rendered postmodern, psychedelic-noir African novel. Much of it is strange, fascinating, concerned with the nature of art, and varying views of Africa and 'Africanness' seen through a grimy Cape Town prism. Nikhil's writing is at once funny, sincere, punchy, grim, sometimes confusing but always compelling. [...] All in all, this book was an engrossing, wild ride which may not be for everyone, but if you are a fan of the postmodern its very much worth your time.'
Wole Talabi, author of *Shigidi*, and *Incomplete Solutions*

TATY WENT WEST REVIEWS

'The cumulative result is jarring—cartoonish one moment, harrowingly visceral the next. But that juxtaposition has been in place from the outset: this may be a novel with ancient cities, mysterious beings, and adventure—but escapism it is not. Outside of writing, Singh's body of work includes forays into film, music, and illustration—specifically, a comics adaptation of a novel by the similarly hard-to-define Kojo Laing. That same multifaceted approach can be seen in a

distilled form within this novel, both literally (through both illustrations and cues for music in the prose) and metaphorically. Singh has endeavored to combine theoretically incompatible strands of literature: the picaresque blended with New Wave science fiction blended with absurdist comedy blended with realistic looks at trauma and its aftereffects. Does it all neatly flow together? No, but the risks that Singh takes here succeed more often than not, and the result is a deeply singular and highly compelling literary debut.'
***Tor* Review**

'There aren't that many SF novels being published with quite this level of commitment to sheer unironic pulpy invention, and taken at that level *Taty Went West* verges on the heroic…In search of reference points for Nikhil Singh's energetically transgressive first novel, perhaps cued by the 40-odd black-and-white illustra¬tions scattered throughout the text, I find my¬self reaching as much for graphic novels as the prose kind. Think of Grant Morrison circa *The Invisibles* or Alan Moore circa *Lost Girls*, mix with a shot of Shea & Wilson's Illuminatus! Trilogy and a dash of Bryan Catling's *The Vorrh*, and you'll be somewhere in the right neighbourhood.'
***Locus* Magazine**

'Imagine if Lewis Carroll had written five Alice adventures and crammed them into one volume but veering into untried perversions, new drugs, and a beatnik-Gothic vibe. Only out of Africa. William S Burroughs only more imaginative.'
Geoff Ryman

'A hallucinogenic post-apocalyptic carnival ride – Nikhil Singh has a strange and intriguing mind'
Lauren Beukes

'A kaleidoscopic voyage into Singh's dreamlands, pregnant with lyrical visions of dark spirituality.'
Antony Johnston, author of *The Coldest City*

'Nikhil Singh creates a world that threatens to leave the confines of the page. Brilliantly compelling.'
Irenosen Okojie, Caine Prize winner

SALEM BROWNSTONE REVIEWS

'*Salem Brownstone* is a graphic novel that is both original and compelling. There's a seamless relationship between the images and the text, and the characters linger in the mind. I look forward to the continuing adventures of *Salem Brownstone*!'
Anthony Minghella

'*Salem Brownstone* kicked my ass and made me believe in the beautiful darkness of the world again.'
Harmony Korine

'*Salem Brownstone* is a hypnotically beautiful gothic fantasy."
Jefferson Hack – editorial director of the Dazed magazine group, founding *Dazed* magazine with photographer Rankin

'A wonderfully imaginative and stylish piece of work and a perfect example of the adventurous new directions that comic books should be taking in the future.'
Alan Moore

***

DAKINI ATOLL FOLLOWS CLUB DED, BUT CAN BE READ EITHER BEFORE OR AFTER THE FIRST NOVEL

CLUB DED RECAP

Oracle Inc: a global all-female information-gathering organisation. Limitless funding. Headed by the mysterious Oracle. Operatives, Jennifer, Anita and Chloe go rogue. Anita covertly lures private investment from the organisation. Sets up her private empire. A sovereign state called Club Ded. Crowns herself its Queen. Named after a blockbuster film being shot there. Starring Delilah Lex. Directed by Delaney Croeser. Filmed mostly underwater. Using new subaqueous breathing tech. Star and director are trapped in a toxic relationship. Delilah eventually breaks free – stealing the film and its franchise from Croeser. Aided by new flame/co-conspirator, Fortunato. Who is also suppling Club Ded with psychogenic fish glands. The shamanic medicine drug spawns its own cult there. Club Ded spirals into anarchy. Unpoliced, experimental tech development run amok. Deviant hedonism. Many escape. Including Jennifer. She flees to Japan. Chloe later informs Jennifer – the Queendom has been invaded. Most likely by traffickers. Anita is abducted. Jennifer loses herself completely. Tormented by Anita's fate. The Queen's body is never recovered. Eventually, Jennifer takes her own life.

DAKINI ATOLL

NIKHIL SINGH

Luna Press
PUBLISHING

Editorial Team: Francesca T Barbini & Shona Kinsella

First published by Luna Press Publishing, Edinburgh, 2024

A CIP catalogue record is available from the British Library
www.lunapresspublishing.com

ISBN-13: 978-1-915556-32-5

For Caroline

CONTENTS

'C'est là que j'ai vécu dans les voluptés calmes,
Au milieu de l'azur, [des flots et des] splendeurs,
Et des esclaves nus, tout imprégnés d'odeurs,

Qui me rafraîchissaient le front avec des palmes,
Et dont l'unique soin était d'approfondir
Le secret douloureux qui me faisait languir.'

Baudelaire, from
'J'ai long-temps habité sous de vastes…'

PROLOGUE

MESOSPHERIA

A mirrored spider, spinning mechanical webs in the upper atmosphere. Large as a house. Actually, no. It's not mirrored. Spider is white. Porcelain-toned. Lack of colour lends reflectivity. Delilah's dream. Every night. She has other dreams, of course. Muted echoes. Spider dreams are different. Like being plugged into a feed. *Feels* the limbs and movements of the spider. As though her own. Reminds her of something she read. Late 1500's. True story. Girl at the heart of the Spanish Empire. Lucrecia de Leon's visions are relentless. Sequential dreams. Every night. Episodes in some paranormal, conquistador-era serial. Some four hundred dreams. Recorded by the Inquisition. Some foretelling the future. Eventually put to death. Author, Roger Osborne, published a book, The Dreamer on the Calle de San Salvador. Collected and annotated thirty-five visions. Delilah read it once. Some holiday in Barcelona. Of course, Lucrecia's dreams are surreal. Symbolically in flux. Packed with religious symbolism. Diary of a doomed girl. Delilah's are always the same. She is in the body of a vast, mirror spider. Spinning webs. High, above the earth.

PART ONE

WHITE WIDOW

ZLATA ZUHK

What a show. Maybe it's the frontier tech. Developing worlds. Expanding perception. 2D screens – so last century. *Good Morning Delilah!* Phenomenal programming. Not even a show. An immersive, holographic realm. Delila Lex – standing in your living room. High-res. Walking around. Spend the day with her. As a ghost. Or play the interaction-lottery. In some future paradise. Targeted audio tracking a primary. Wherever you are. She's *there*. Walls melt away. Beach recessions. Tropical sci-fi. Royal palms with tentacles. Alien cuteness. Interactive escapism. Delilah's completely real. Long as you don't touch. Fingers in a torch-beam. World's first holo-star. Croeser put her up there. Out of the woodwork and into history. Of course, the mermaid went for his show. Even Fortunato understands. Croeser may be a monster. But he's still an opener of worlds. Opening them to infection, perhaps... *Good Morning Delilah!* single-handedly creating a holographic market. Rewriting global analytics. Figurehead of new viewing paradigm. Delilah has no choice but to go for it. Checkmated Croeser before. Madness to return to the minotaur. Behind that paternal smile. Brewing revenge, no doubt. What's a post-modern mermaid to do? Glory aside, that tech is so delicious…

Boston gets Fortunato hot about the Camelot administration. No Prion Eyes exclusion-zone. No biosuit mandate. Land of juicy secrets. Freeze-dried with liability. A desert of non-disclosure. He's thinking Marilyn Monroe. In disguise as Zelda Zonk. Airforce One. Norma Jeane, in disguise as Marilyn. Nobody remembers the canny businesswoman. Marilyn walked out of a studio contract. At the pinnacle of fame. Establishment wooed her back. But, on her terms. Affiliate producer. Choice of script and director. The 'dumb blonde' who beat Hollywood at its own game. Of course, posterity would punish her hubris. Nobody could truly understand Marilyn. Perhaps, not even Marilyn herself. This is Fortunato's concept. Rereading Anthony Summers. Between the lines. Trying to not write a treatment. Science Fiction. Speculative Fiction.

Whatever it's called now. Getting him down. Trapped in the swamp called 'genre'. Down where the money is. Bankability central. African angle opens doors. Disgusts him. Nobody calls American writers American writers. Just writers. What if Amos Tutuola had written a New York novel? Populated exclusively by Americans? It would still be an African novel. Why should Fortunato be prefixed as African? Visited so many worlds with the fish. Who's to say which is his native reality, anyway? But Fortunato's playing the game. Doubling down. Can't resist. Boston for ConFabulation. *The* holographic interchange. Hustling interest in a Star Trek treatment. Co-written with Zlata Zuhk. Her original concept. Chasing holographic streaming deals. Siren call of emergent tech. *Good Morning Delilah!* Opening so many doors. Wonderful new frontiers. Four-dimensional theatre. Soon in every home. Everybody wants in. Fortunato has plans to elevate the platform. Slide out of trope-ville. Still hard to break in with a leftfield concept. Some things never change. 'Some things never strange,' – Brick's line. Fortunato is obligated to electioneer. Holographic options. Trade conventions. Fear and loathing on the development trail. Not even his idea. Hologram world interests him, sure. But he's satisfied with 2D. Here for Zlata. Miss second-generation. Straight out of Little Ukraine. East Village princess made good. Gone bad. That psycho underwater girl. Off the map. As usual. Her weird ex, Seikichi. History repeats itself. Fortunato mutters the phrase. Every chance. Remembering V. Actually, he and V still chat, – occasionally. About the weather. Gets the feeling she'd prefer America to Lake Como. Missing the movie life. That ship has sailed. Mourning Africa. Small-talk. Nostalgia. Harder to quit than sugar. Must be boring for her. Playing rich housewife. Fortunato stopped eating glands. Hard to traffic livestock. Border control. Zlata still breeds and consumes them. Fortunato doesn't have the time. Doesn't trust her produce. Sobriety is just another multiverse. Success in America. Enough of a trip. Game On is doing well. How could it miss? Brick dropped out of the franchise. Week after the film broke. On to bigger and better planets. Fortunato in talks to direct the follow-up. So, why is he in Massachusetts hustling side-projects – for a soon-to-be ex? A business partner, who should know better. 'Loyalty is a curse.' One of his favourite mantras.

*

'What's the Star Trek concept?' T'choosy Merriweather asks Fortunato.

Senses undercurrents. Opposition? Introduced by a holo-technician named Cilmi. Hot new genre-tags. Terminology means nothing to Fortunato. Calls it a shortcut to thinking. Makes some enemies. Prefers individual expression. Or, so he says. Muddy water. No clear-cut edges. 'Prionically speaking,' – ConFabulation safety grade is mid-level. Some Quincy convention centre. Border-zone blues. Like most hotels upstate. Full-face visors. Standardised. Lightweight, auto-tint. Automated air-scrubber. Better than New York. Manhattan still graded to the exclusion-zone. Mostly abandoned. Biosuits and all-day scrubbers. High-restriction. T-choosie Merriweather. A PhD and greying dreadlocks. Wears a cross. Traditional beads. Never set foot in Africa. Author of a successful franchise, set in Lagos.

'You know the tropical pleasure planet, Risa?'

'Sure,' she nods.

'Imagine *Risa Nights*. Chief O'Brien is a washed-up drunk. Divorced. Hawaiian shirts. That sort of thing. Circumstance turns him into a detective. Some time-travel. Delilah Lex plays a recurring role – renegade Suliban from the future. Garak runs a gift shop – with a secret. Tropical noir meets Trek. Shoot physical in Costa Rica. I want Colm Meaney and Andrew Robinson to reprise, of course…but only as holo-signatures. They could perform from the comfort of their homes.'

'Not very African.'

Fortunato raises an eyebrow.

'It's like something an American would write,' she adds clumsily.

'Half of America is writing about Africa. Isn't it only fair to return the favour?'

T'choosy blinks a few times.

'You're Nigerian, I hear.'

'I was.'

'What do you mean, you *were*?' She frowns.

'Now, I'm South African again,' he sighs wearily.

She opens her mouth to say something. Closes it. Spots someone she knows. Fortunato watches her glide away. Cilmi wafts back. Flashes a smirk – behind his visor. Fortunato likes the holo-technician. Caltech think-tank escapee. Fled Xamar as a teen. Naturalised Bostonian.

'Don't take it personally,' he chuckles.

Passes a token cup of palm wine. Visor-dock straw attached.

'Vine?' Fortunato mutters, in his best Bela Lugosi. 'Hi nefer dreenk vine.'

Cilmi offers Fortunato the tour. Latest holographic demos. Converted suite on the 57th floor. Glowing macro daisy. Dominating the lounge.

Petals in an unfelt breeze. Latest tweaks.

On a low viewing platform. Stage-like, against the lead-in. Cilmi eyes the director covertly. Fortunato does not immediately notice.

'What is it?' he eventually asks.

'Good Morning Delilah! What a show, eh?' Cilmi blurts.

Techie appears nervous. Fortunato frowns.

'You guys are tight, aren't you?' Cilmi presses. 'You and Delilah Lex.'

'What's this about?'

Cilmi hesitates.

'I moonlighted in hardware development for her show. Test-site, near Death Valley.'

'Access to this trade level is pretty exclusive,' Fortunato reasons. 'I might have guessed something like that.'

Fortunato realises Cilmi's been working up to this.

'I'm a bit drunk,' he chuckles.

'Look, man. Spit it out.'

Cilmi drains his palm wine. Checks a timepiece.

'Listen, let's go for a drive,' he suggests.

Fortunato looks him up and down. Follows his gut.

'Lead the way.'

*

Driverless cab. Upstate woodland. Treetops haze gold-green. Seemingly endless. Prionic visors abandoned. Fortunato's in the back with Cilmi. Holo-technician is a different person. All smiles at the convention. Now, he's fidgety.

'We could have taken my Pontiac,' Fortunato chides, watching the road.

'Trackable. This service is guest-listed. Muffled route.'

'Where are we going?'

Cilmi looks away. A tree-chinked twilight.

'Just a house, man. Just a house.'

*

Place is deep in the woods. Already evening.

'A few of us share this place,' Cilmi reveals.

'What do you guys do here?'

'Listen, I get the feeling I can trust you. I can, can't I?'

'Are we going to turn back if I say no?' Fortunato broods.

Tree-choked driveway. An unlit door. Climbing out. Cilmi goes for a glowing keypad. Swigging from a flask. A little unsteady. Fortunato tags some distance behind. Getting paranoid. Watches the taxi roll back – into shadow.

'Mostly, we pool gear,' Cilmi fumbles at the pad. 'Little this, a little that.'

Door pops with a beep.

'We're a tight little society.'

'Secret society?'

'Nothing that dramatic.'

Front hall, opening directly to open-plan. Interior walls collapsed. Maximised space. Battered pleather sofa. Paper stripped walls. Components stacked haphazardly. Boxes and hermetic crates. Tool lockers. Kitchenette with a fancy coffee machine. Moonshine tubes of a home-still. A poster of some small town in the desert – very Normal Rockwell.

'We have aeronautics guys, High-orbit code-monkeys, engineers. Holo-techies. Robo-jukes, mappers. We're building a private lab. Something off-grid.'

'You guys have a name for this place?'

Cilmi eyes Fortunato – as though he were crazy.

'You can't tell anyone about this, ok?'

'Fine.'

'Come on. I gotta show you something.'

*

In the cellar. Holographic staging areas. Edges in shadow. Circle of even glow. Prototypes. Jury-rigging. Adapted consoles. Heavy root-work of cable. In the illuminated section, a sunken pit. Circular. Smooth. Padded. Cilmi steers a heavy cart. Down a ramp. Hydraulics make it easy. Aboard, is a rebuilt rodeo machine. Kind people fall off when they're drunk. Cilmi docks it to a bracket. Rest is automated. Lead lock-ins. Full start-up. Fortunato wanders down. Cilmi hands him a package. A translucent trackersuit. Filigreed with gold. Micro-wiring. Full-head unit. Fish-eye caps. Audio.

'Locker room's through there.'

Cilmi points out a shadowy portal.

'Now, listen…' Fortunato protests.

'Strip completely before you pull it on. Won't work properly without full skin contact.'

Fortunato frowns.

'Don't worry it's clean. Lab-grade sterilisation.'

Fortunato is about to speak. Cilmi cuts him off.

'Pull your clothes back over, if you like. Shouldn't affect the interface.'

Fortunato sighs. In the locker room. Checking out the suit. Cilmi isn't aware of Club Ded's tech. Trill swiped a lot. Toys, data. Fortunato has a rough idea. Trackersuits – only one route to immersion. Online shoes instead of base stations. That sort of thing. Club Ded's development. Moving in different directions. Before collapse. Repurposing gel pods. Development probably still underway. Shady grants. Some secret workshop in the 'third-world'. Keeping it in-house. Colloidal metal for magnetic micro-manipulation. Active texture gel. Balances are tricky. Holy grail is tactile projection rendering. Directly onto the skin surface. Manipulable consistency. Microscopic levels. Floor surface imitation – achieved through polymorphic, self-responders. Transient platforms. Formed out of modular, hydraulic extensions. Docked into a crabby home-base. Ends branching to cilia. Imitates almost any surface. Even in prototype. Surreal to watch. Forming and reforming. Beneath a subject's feet. Trill's tried them barefoot. Safety protocols rewritten live. Could still cut your foot open. Even on imitated glass. Floating in body-temperature gel all day. Too much like a dream. Test subjects get absent minded. In free-roam, especially. Fortunato eyes the trackersuit's penile sock with distaste. Cilmi rummaging outside. Banging gear. Director suits up. Pulls his coat over. Returns to the staging area. Cilmi's in a lab-coat. Tool-belt around his waist. Drinking heavily. Grins. Makes a dramatic gesture toward the rodeo rider.

'All aboard!' he bellows.

Fortunato hooks a foot into the stirrup. Suit makes it slippery. Individual toe holders. Somehow, he gets up there. Cilmi's retreated to a control desk. In shadow.

'Ok, check it out,' holo-technician mumbles.

Coming through Fortunato's earpiece. Light trackers flare geometrically. Start to spin. Whiteout staging area. Catches projections. Amplifies them. A sky forms overhead. Rodeo rider begins to move. Fortunato looks down. He's riding a majestic, oversized flamingo. Over a salt-crusted lake. Pale limestone towers. Rising from green water. Geothermal steam. Sound kicks in. Bringing space. A giant wind. All very impressive. Nothing Fortunato isn't familiar with.

'That's Lake Abbe,' Cilmi explains. 'In Dijbouti. No synthetic imagery. I generate off capture.'

Fortunato looks around. More flamingos. Flocking below.

'Ready for the kicker?' Cilmi asks.

'Bring it.'

Director experiences a tingling sensation. As though the suit is charged with static. The wind becomes real. Fortunato feels it buffeting. Not strongly. But palpably. Hunches on reflex. To avoid falling. Cilmi chuckles through the mic. Fortunato realises how foolish he must look. Nevertheless, he is impressed.

'What's the trick?' he shouts above fake wind.

Hearing himself. Feeding through the audio. Cilmi mutes the hologram. So, they can talk at normal volume. Strange to still feel the wind though. In the silence of some Boston basement. To see African horizons dip. Below roseate wings.

'Electromagnetic resistance,' Cilmi explains. 'Like, when you hold similar magnetic poles against each another. Controllable repulsion. We use extremely fine magnetic arrays, amplified in reaction to livestream data capture. Suit responds inversely. Auto-tunes the interference. Bit like a record stylus reading a groove. Basic physics. But the effects are dramatic. Took a while to perfect. Something we worked on, in Arcadia Springs. I mean, you can see the results.'

'Arcadia Springs?'

'That site in Death Valley.'

'I'm sure prolonged use would be harmful to the body's natural magnetic field,' Fortunato chides dryly.

Climbs off the rodeo. Hologram field cuts. Taking the wind with it.

'Why are you showing me all of this?' he asks.

Cilmi hesitates.

'Flamingos are my pet project – excuse the pun. But, like I told you – I share the lab.'

'Ok.'

'There's a pirate hologram doing the rounds. Something… recreational.'

'What is it?'

'She's standing right behind you.'

Fortunato looks around quickly. There she is. Swaying behind the rodeo machine. Gloss black bikini. Zlata Zuhk. Fortunato doesn't call her Delilah anymore. Not after learning her real name. Anyway, it's more than that. Norma Jeane used to joke about Marilyn. Said Marilyn was like a coat. Pulling her on and off. Some anecdote. Norma Jeane, in the city. With a friend. Somehow invisible. Unnoticed. To demonstrate, she 'switches' Marilyn on. Like activating a billboard. Suddenly, everybody notices. Her private method spell. Similar with Zlata and Delilah. Coat of many colours. Fortunato approaches the phantasm. Cilmi joins him. Both hypnotised by the glowing figure. Fortunato reaches out a trackersuited finger. Snatches it back in shock. That collarbone feels real. Too familiar. Tries again – pressing harder. Flesh distorts. Like a soap bubble. Eventually, his fingertip pops through. Only to be repulsed again.

'Runs a lot of juice,' Cilmi explains. 'More pressure, more power. Someone cobbled it, back in Arcadia Springs.'

Fortunato notices him staring. That million-dollar smile of hers. Pale blonde fire. Lighting up their shabby basement. Perhaps others.

'So, what then?' Fortunato asks. 'You fucking this *thing*? That it?'

Cilmi glares at him. Stalks back to the siding.

'Not me, man,' he scowls.

Sinks down. Lights a cigarette. Blows smoke at the hologram girl. Fortunato watches it drift through her. Coils in a cinema beam.

'But, this Lila is Jerzy Kosinski's. He's practically married to it. Ain't that right, Lila?'

'Sure, Cilmi,' hologram replies silkily.

Fortunato is taken aback. Situated audio. Live-sample algorithm. Unnerving reality.

'Jerzy's only one guy though,' Cilmi rambles on. 'Lotta society members have their own Lilas now. Probably others. I mean, she was *thoroughly* captured for that show. You have no idea. Edgy micro-scanning. Replicating every muscle, every fibre. Down to the cellular level. It's why these Lilas are miles ahead of any generated-avatar competition. Even though they're just pirate programs. They are fucking *real*, man! Even us robo-spooks can't *tell* how they are so realistically rendered…'

'I see.'

Fortunato circles the apparition nervously. Typical, really. Having her manifest like this. Unexpectedly. Out of the grave of thought. Been in his all day. All week. Clearly, he's not the only one. Delilah Lex infects people – with herself. A bankable skill.

'Algo's improvise speech patterning. The Delilah program is so fucking tight, man. You have no idea the data running out of that show. Hell, sometimes when I'm watching, even I can't tell if the onscreen Delilah is a fax.'

'A what?'

'Fax. Facsimile.'

'So, what *do* you do with this thing, Cilmi?' Fortunato asks.

'It's not like that, man,' the holo-technician sighs, still staring. 'I just sit with her sometimes.'

'Why did you bring me here?'

'Jesus Christ,' he replies, a little desperately. 'Isn't it obvious?'

Fortunato watches him smoke.

'I mean, if that was you up there, wouldn't you want to know? I want you to tell her, obviously. She has a right to know…'

Fortunato looks back to the ghostly figure. Swaying in time to unheard music. Doesn't have the heart to tell Cilmi. Probably all her idea. Zlata's capacity for self-promotion. Without limit. Legendary. Bordering on genius. Religious worship as franchising. Consciously evoked. Her own little party trick. The temple courtesan – at play.

'I know you, don't I?' the hologram asks Fortunato.

Shocks him. Knows that look. Beam tracking, he's reasoning. Electronically reconstituted muscle memory.

'Don't pay any attention,' Cilmi sighs. 'She says that to everyone…'

STALKERVILLE

Delilah Lex wakes. Being a giant spider in the sky again. Tiny bubble slips her lips. Makes her open her eyes. Mirror form rises, morphing. Hits glass. Watches it crawl around. Deep blue, natural light. Her hand moves reflexively – to her mouth. White glare across fingertips. Teeth shadows. Rubber extrusions of a titanium brace. Still snaking reassuringly down her throat. Thick, cobalt gel. Flooding lungs and sinus. Holding hardware in place. Breathing requires more effort. But Delilah is used to the gel by now. Floating in a translucent pearl-pod. Globular. Faintly iridescent. Shell inlaid with glassy hydraulics. Pristine white sand. A tropical reef. Some colourful fish. Shifting in shoals. Dark rocks rise a few meters. Plateauing, below a glimmering surface. Sunny kaleidoscopes. Delilah realises she's dressed. Candy-pink ball gown. Oversized, jellyfish of a thing. Signature colour. Belonged to her mermaid character – Cyane. From the old show. Three seasons on a hit franchise. As the lead. Unforgiving gauntlet of fire. Just a teenager – when she hooked the part. Remembers researching the name. Nymph of clear ponds and streams. Witnesses Hades kidnapping Persephone. Unable to save this daughter of Ceres. Cyane is turned to fluid. The ruler of the underworld's doing. Delilah reaches out groggily. Fingertips gloss the pearl. How did she get in here? Where is she?

'Curioser and curioser.'

Mouthing reflexively. Releasing more small bubbles. Depth is not too great. Pearl must be primarily shielding against salinity. Can't tell how long she's been asleep. Pods could be modified. Supporting even coma victims. Feed drips. Electrical stimuli. Targeted fluid pressure. Automated muscle tone regulation. Tendon treatment. Waste disposal. Indefinite maintenance. When Delilah lived in the sovereign-state of Club Ded – she took every advantage. Consolidating power. Gravitating to wildcard tech merchants – blowing in on unlimited resources. Loose protocol. Making power friends. Never difficult for a mermaid. Money adores her. She's their lead. 'In with the lizard overlords,' she'll joke. That crazy Croeser spectacle. Easy pickings for a young star. Brokerage. Private investments. Entering and harbouring secrets. Nobody polices her private games. Not in a lawless vacuum. Many expected her to get lost in the tanks. Party endlessly. Off-camera, Delilah disappears. Deals with everyone remotely. Commandeering quarters in a watchtower complex. Slowly building up a private science wing. Eventually annexing the entire building. Basements and all. Separate teams under her. All kinds of development. City-state's ordnance, provisioning and hardware requisition. Funnelling through immigration. Delilah befriends the customs head. Ex-cop – Bheki Caluza. Kids are fans. With all channels clear, she trains hard. Trill joining her, sometimes. Both dosed heavily. Premium glands. Psychotropic-amplified cognition. Deep theta learning. Delilah soaks up coding, robotics. Every applied science she can talk a techie into training. No shortage in Club Ded. Maverick expertise. Few boundaries. Disaster was inevitable. Delilah sees it coming. One of her focus points: salinity. One thing to breathe underwater – in a sterile tank. But the goal of every mermaid should be the sea. Practical reality – offering only insurmountable obstacles. Tanks in Club Ded – at that time. Sterilized meticulously. High-frequency light bursts. Doubly sanitized by blue gel contact medium. The ocean, on the other hand. A wild place. Countless biomes. Septic traces. Lung tissue ill-designed for exposure. Osmotic effects. High salinity intake – a quick crippling of organs. Many Club Ded scientists playing cowboy. Non-corporate to a fault. Everyone up for risk-pay. Only outsiders or tight crews end up in places like that. Advisory flags genetic manipulation. Calls it a dead end. Their view: human body exists within ongoing processes of natural balance. Genetic tampering purposefully disrupts these. Achieving hyper-refined target values. With long-term handicaps. Salinity had to be cracked bionically. Delilah deepens her understanding of the physical – exponentially. Her body, as a covenant. Between earth and spirit. Her body, a garden she grows. Her only truly intimate relationship. With materiality itself. Matter, animated by unquantifiable etheric operation. By an unknown variable: 'her'. Bodies as vessels. To be inhabited. Misuse, leading to decline in function. Death – the ultimate separation of vehicle and driver. Is the planet itself simply an interface? Between the material and etheric? The mythical emerald tablet. Delilah snaps awake. Drifting off again. Muttering to herself. How did she get in this pearl? Where are the controls?

*

Unexpectedly, a grid lights up the glass. Light points converge. A hologram, knitting together. Seemingly outside. Just an illusion. Magic tricks. Convex holography. Delilah observes a towering, translucent version of herself. In a familiar, animal-print onesie. Croeser gifted that to her. Way back. Why is she wearing that *thing*? Apparition's voice – coming through audio.

''Sup, stranger. This is recorded. To bring you…us? – up to speed. Afterward, holo reverts to interactive. This tape will self-instruct. You carry me on that doppel-ring…'

Buzz tweaks Delilah's left hand. A ring, with a faintly luminescent gem. Third finger.

'The demon can be summoned at all times,' her hologram grins.

Delilah frowns at the comment. No recollection of recording this. Also, free-roam holograms. Can't be projected from a single source. Not as far as she knows. Requiring at least a screen. Three to four projection points. Variable distances. Can't fathom how the ring operates. Except, within a controlled environment. Somewhere, like Club Ded. Ring could then interface. External hardware. A giant, world-shaped version of the pearl. Something's not right.

'Check it out,' her hologram says.

Screen lights up. Inside the pearl wall. Directly ahead of Delilah. Showing a chamber. Where the recording was captured. Onscreen image of Delilah. Moving synchronously with the figure 'outside.' Delilah recognises the place. Seikichi's lab in Silicon Valley.

'Wondering why you can't remember making this?'

Fish swim through the holographic face.

'*Good Morning Delilah!* You are the star of a hit show! It's *the* holographic reality serial. Think Cyane, all grown up. Living in an alien paradise, amongst the humanoids. Celebrity guests. Surreal sets. Weird games. In Lexland! Your very own island! Tour virtually with your Lex band. Win for charities of your choosing. But, here's the twist – every day, areas of your memory are temporarily blocked…'

Delilah is agog. Red flag. In waking life, she can barely leave her room. Notorious loner. Constant surveillance, her worst nightmare. How could she consent to *this*?

'Relax Mermie. We're not on cam, at this minute. Remember the neural interface Seikichi developed at Club Duck? He implanted you with the prototype.'

Delilah recalls.

'This show is the only way we can rig a lab-rated test arena. Get funded. Stock with the best toys. Production ticks boxes, see? Global analytics – live monitoring. Developing tech-trends. Offers to extend beyond pilot season… But, you know, fuck that. We only need one rodeo to synch the implant. Memory aspect became necessary – but only halfway. Seikichi's call. That's why it's a surprise! But you can relax. Total recall is re-instated during shooting breaks. Only have three episodes left in the season! It's endgame, babe.'

Delilah nods vaguely to herself. So, she's shooting on a closed set. Somewhere in Silicon Valley. Playing lab rat. Sounds like the kind of crackpot scheme she would invest in. Simply to get her way. After all, the neural implant is her baby too. She'd arranged funding. Run development. Offered herself as test subject. Implantation, undertaken on her orders only. Seikichi's processes – revolutionary. Way ahead of global competition. Club Ded's lack of protocol – cementing their head start. If Seikichi could perfect processes. Her body would be recognised. Figurehead of a revolutionary technological advance.

'Memory wipes are part of the control,' the doppelganger continues. 'Our neural implant is a success, see. To the point where we are able to target and manipulate specific memories. Process requires enormous maintenance...'

Delilah is perplexed. As she understands it, supposed engrams in the brain could be relied upon. To process, relay and recall memory. But nobody has accurately pinpointed where memory itself is stored. When Seikichi proposed the implant – the goal was to create a neural motor driver. Enhance remote operation of dolls and drones. Live interface. 'Doll-riding' – a term Delilah coined. Research and development must have spiked. While she was off playing sleeping beauty. A concern. Seikichi can be completely unbridled. Especially with resources. Maybe he'd gone off the map. While her memory was erased? No way to tell. Amnesia insurance.

'Only one thing will irritate you…' her hologram confides.

Delilah looks up sharply.

'Croeser.'

Delilah is stunned to hear he's involved. Not to the point of disbelief. She'll do virtually anything to achieve goals. Suddenly that stupid onesie makes sense. Must gall Croeser. How she and Anita got the better of him. Delilah smiles, sub-aquatically. Enjoys playing against the director. Old Croeser-control. Whatever revenge is unfolding. Looking forward to flipping it.

'So, anyway,' her hologram sighs. 'Ready to go live? When you are – hit the red buzzer.'

Cartoon button manifests. Right in front of her. Giant figure goes into a rest mode. Hovering on a loop.

'What the fuck,' Delilah mutters underwater, stabbing the button.

Surprised to actually feel it depress. As though it were there. Snatches her hand back. Image fragments. Pearl rocks gently. Begins to rise. Hologram rises too. Tropical gradations. Delilah tracks rocks passing. Now, above the plateau. Sea spans, either side. Measureless light, building. Mercury surfaces approaching. Triggers her hologram.

'Get ready for a surprise,' it cackles.

Breaching. Alpha-resolution sunlight. Curiously clear. High altitude flavour. In the distance – a weird tropical beach. Mostly obscured. Millions of shadowy figures. Blotting the sun. Crowding the air. Suspended above the water. Cluttering upward. To a cloudless sky.

'What the actual…' Delilah has time to mouth.

They all shout:

'*Good morning, Delilah!*'

Applause in the audio. Pearl begins to sail. Shoreline approaching.

'Your public,' her hologram grins.

Drifting beside. Shoulder deep. In low, froth-less wavelets. Still thrice-taller than the pearl. Character appears different to Delilah now. Recording ended its loop. On the seabed. Apparition geared to interactive now. Live conversation protocols. Mannerisms and inflections – all coded in. Delilah looks around in wonder. Shadow people are disappearing. Soft, popping sound-effects.

'So, it works like this,' her hologram prompts. 'Every show starts here. With your pearl, rising majestically from the waves. Viewers buffer up as ghosts.'

'Buffering in silence?'

'…In fact, most log in now – just to say good morning. Almost all viewers remain ghosts throughout the show. They turn invisible, land on the island, explore it…'

'Stalk me, basically,' Delilah burbles snidely.

By now, she's grown so used to the sound of her voice underwater. That bassy blur. Deep in the bone of her head. Lisping on the brace. Barely noticing.

'Well, that's your nickname for this hellhole, isn't it?' her hologram laughs. 'Stalkerville.'

'Sounds about right. Fuck, is that Croeser?'

A disembodied head. Floating above the distant sand. Oversized, balloon-like. Wizard of Oz. Grinning. Talking without sound.

'He's doing the intro spiel,' her hologram explains. 'Pre-recorded, of course. In reality, he's behind the scenes somewhere. Pulling strings.'

'Am I on cam now?'

'Not yet. Outer pearl reads opaque. Like a real pearl, basically. You only go live when it pops – on the beach. Do your entrance there.'

'And then?'

'Anything you want. Go anywhere. Do anything. Lexland island is pre-staged for interactivity. New cycles every day. Fresh plot twists. Intrigues. Magic. A surprise guest or two…'

'Great,' Delilah blubbers sarcastically.

'Relax. It's a breeze. Just have fun with it, baby-doll.'

Delilah recognises the turn of phrase. A disturbing thought strikes. Swivels in the fluid. Facing her immense ear.

'Look at me,' she commands.

Hologram turns to face her. Surreal sensation, she thinks. Dwarfed by her baby blues.

'You're not in interactive-mode, are you?' Delilah demands.

A mischievous grin. Splicing the artificial head. Disturbing effect. Because the smile doesn't match the face. As though made for different muscles. A stranger is smiling – through her.

'Go milk a cow, Croeser,' Delilah middle-fingers.

Hologram bursts into laughter. Her own laughter. Winks out. Delilah is alone again. Now, the white beach is upon her. That disembodied head – disappeared. Even the breakers are muted. Not a trace of foam. Just perfect, heavy, crystal swells. Definitely not Silicon Valley, Delilah thinks. Beaching. A salty, sunshine crunch.

PRION EYES

Departing Boston. Landfall in LaGuardia. Fortunato retrieves the purple Lambo. Navigates Jackson Heights. Headed for the Williamsburg bridge. He and Zlata keep a high-rise apartment there. Overlooking the river. Window walls. 115th floor. Retains it as her mailing address. Hasn't been back for over a year. Fortunato can't imagine Zlata living anywhere permanently. Willo the Wisp. Always somewhere else. In the jungle. Out at sea. Holed up in another crumbling utopia. Messages semi-regularly. Demanding admin. All the illegality. Things she won't shelve on her agency. Only various admirers. Her father. He's somewhere on the West Coast. Fortunato's never seen him. Doubts his existence. Mother's still in Kiev. Wernicke-Korsakoff syndrome. Direct result of Chernobyl. Brain writing false memories. Remembered as real. Vision problems. Zlata runs to her. From time to time. Hides out. Complains long-distance. How her grandmother stole her Chihuahua. How a DJ friend kept her designer gowns. All those jewellery stashes. Mouse-holed, throughout Obolon district. Moskova style, she shrugs. Don't know what gift to get? Buy me jewellery. Easy to carry. Quick to liquidate. Girl's a Hollywood success. Global icon. Still thinking like a ghetto fence. Refugee syndrome. Fortunato can relate. Played the same games. All over Africa. Zlata's ice-chipped poker face. Little mermaid's a natural winner. Lucky seven. Maybe that's her problem, Fortunato worries. Everybody needs to know how to lose. Every now and then.

*

Prionic security runs border-zone protocol to the river. Crossover to the Manhattan exclusion-zone. Severely limited. Zlata wangled hot-cards. Working with Luminstein. Flexing cred. Skipped Club Ded with patents. Trading manufacturing rights. On an experimental plasma ejector. Humanitarian aid, she calls it. Mass incineration of infected bodies. Her science departments hadn't actually initiated the project. Inherited it. Weapons development – not her thing. But the containment system became interesting. Highly original. Proven safe.

Quite a few worked on it. In spare time. Getting the thing handheld. Test operational. Sale hooks federal assistance. Varying degrees. Delilah allowed to enter and exit Manhattan. As she pleases. Even gave her the private entrance she requested. Heavily monitored. But still. Sole use only. Fortunato and Luminstein stay red taped. Money stream maintains a fair split. Coins from a dead man's eye. Just to cross the Styx-on demand. Some caveats. Logging footage. Research purposes. Drone chaperone – flamethrower on remote. Luminstein is satisfied. Dominating Manhattan shooting rights. All he's in for. Brick used to joke: Prion Eyes is karmic debt – on *Game On*'s success. Well, for them, at least. Timing and spread of the outbreak. Uncannily synchronised with production. Sasha calls it a sign. On social media. Shooting commenced in Australia. Two months after Club Ded's massive release. First cases follow soon after. Cape Town, Melbourne, Jamaica. Some weeks later, London, New York, Los Angeles, outlying regions. Some think it fortunate the outbreak began where it did. Unfamiliar epidemics. Somewhat common in Southern Africa. Relatively speaking. Reaction time – quick. Generally effective. No known defence against Prion Eyes. Disease itself presents the enigma. Non-viral. Yet, highly communicable. Protein molecules comprise long chains of amino acids. Lengths fold themselves. Very specific origami formations. Prions are simply misfolded proteins. Cause remains a mystery. For some reason, this misalignment triggers external changes. Surrounding protein molecules become confused. Begin to refold themselves. Mimicking the error-pattern. Holes eventually form in the brain. Host acts as though possessed. Bizarre speech. Co-ordination errors. Progressive deterioration. Bodies fall apart. One small advantage – symptoms show very quickly. Outbreaks can be vicious. But easier to contain than long gestation infections. Historically, prion diseases transmit from animals. Mad Cow Disease – a famous prion affliction. Theories surfaced then. Infection likely the result of bad feed. Ground meat and bones. What should have been a herbivorous diet. Meat originating from sheep. Infected with Scrapie – a documented prion. Previously localised. It ravages cattle. Humans who consume tainted beef – similarly affected. Other variants include Kuru. Originating in New Guinea. Breaking rules. Human to human. Cannibal tribe contracts it. Eating human brains. Called laughing disease. No way to stop it. Tribespeople waste away. Previous incarnations – all isoforms of a single protein: PrP. Prion Eyes, somewhat different. Unidentified protein catalyst. Name deriving from a dramatic effect. Infected corneal discolouration. Sometimes visible within an hour of contact. Irises shift bright violet. Bringing paranoiac delusion. Developing in tandem with the colouration. Character distortions. Schizophrenic collapse. Visions. Mania. Psychosis. Death. Often, triggered by the eyes. Disease attacks them first, fastest. They dissolve. Slip out. Bodies have to be incinerated. Fluid contact – virulent. Tears, especially. Countermeasures in full swing. Yet, despite the focus – nobody has identified a transmitting animal. Many theories. Bats. Avian. Deer? Without a target to model epidemiology, procedures remain defensive. Outbreak areas quarantined. Militaristically. Areas in long-term cordon. The infected – abandoned. Dead stacked for fire. Liquid eyes and brain matter – clotting gutters.

*

Fortunato's home. House-voice greets. Automated coffee response. Brewing since the garage was keyed. Hasn't taken coffee for years. Then, New York happened. Frothy coconut cream. Looking down on Manhattan. All the doomsday flavours. Plaque of squalor. Sun-tinkled shattering. River cordoned, sane-side. Marbled heavy pink with protein disruptors. Nothing alive. Every fish melted in counter-strike. Fortunato's hardly surprised the apartment's empty. Still expecting her, though. That silent, barefoot tread. Checks inboxes. No chance since Boston. Salvatore Stark. Agency inherited from Brick. Some pitch meeting. In talks. Other messages. Clotting all the windows. Then, unexpectedly, Leonard Cohen. Fortunato freezes. That Chelsea Hotel song. For Janis. He sits heavily. It's private code. Checks song's time-stamp. Two days. Staggered delivery. Rigged for location re-entry to New York. Might still make the rendezvous. Swallows coffee. Emails zone-control. Logs a crossing – later that afternoon. Preps Zlata's pod. Shower-mode. Safer through amino-scrubbers. Nobody's used the real shower in months…

*

Brooklyn Bridge permanently off-limits. Official access only. Social Services. Military. Manhattan bridge services the Brooklyn crossing. Limited pedestrian window. Williamsburg – Fortunato's regular access. Congested since morning. Cargo cluster. Hours in deep scrub. Mid-bridge. Laser-sanitization. Culture-evac. Charities moving art. Save the exclusion zone. Precious books. Museum pieces. Straight to quarantine in Jersey. Fortunato walks through Greenpoint. Entering crumbling, industrial wastes beyond. Long Island City run. Likes it there. Auto-shop stricken. Gateway to Queens. Old film lots. Armoured strip bars. Desolation. Canals, chugging with amino-scrubbers. Queensboro bridge to East 61st – his crossing point. Processing station. Overhead subway. Security check. Biosuit allocation. Roaming zone-drone override – prevents accidental incineration. Head-cam – POV traceable. Brief psych evaluation. Processes logged on his hot-card.

'You enter the zone frequently,' Official observes.

'Impartial documentation is critical, especially at this level of restriction. Wouldn't you agree?'

'Just exercise caution. Wouldn't want to lock you out.'

Clears safety. Zonesters usually make a show of caginess. End of the day – Fortunato's attached to the plasma sale. Certain privileges. Released onto the bridge. Bug-shiny biosuit. Top-end single-use. Incinerated on return. Bubble visor wraparound. Impact-plastic. Flamethrower issue, on departure. He and Zlata – with full authorisation to bear plasma. How could admin refuse? Still her tech. Make it difficult, anyway. Months of training. Just to hold a flamer. Unarmed walk-ins are generally followed. Zone-drone chaperone. Chemical flamethrowers. Fortunato and Zlata don't want tails. Or poison smoke. Cams perfectly hackable. Drones too networked. Yet, despite being arms suppliers. Ordnance is covered by military protocol. Plasma units – officially on remote lock. Users must request trigger access via radio. Confirmation on cam. Small external rig. Back-strapped. Pressurised plasma – electromagnetic suspension. Between thermal reduction layering. Rupture-proof. Its own fuel-supply. Hazard auto-cool. Safer containment than chemical reactant. Apparently. High velocity magnetic expulsion. Liquid hydrogen ventilated barrel. Extending telescopically. Magnetically cooled plasma release. Will only melt stone and metal. Instead of converting matter to plasma. Sticky contingency during development. The plasma paradox. Following a plasma leak – would it cool? Or convert everything. Triggering an unstoppable, self-propagating chain reaction. Prion Eyes overrides philosophy. Too many violet eyes. Which apocalypse is preferable? Protocol demands: torch as many corpses as possible. Personal cam surveillance. Sometimes, by drone. Most sidestep. Confidential backroom chatter. Underground hot-card club. Some personal safety loophole. If a user suspects fire will draw infectees – they can move on. Anyway, too many corpses now. Soldiers talk of conserving plasma count. Self-defence, they say. Vain hope, perhaps. That trigger-access might reach – before an immediate threat.

*

Twin tanks guard Queens-side. Barbed wire cascade. Rest of the bridge – trash-blown and empty. Unauthorised stragglers picked off. Long-range. Fortunato used to love that crossing. When he lived on 67th. Only a few years ago now. Another life. Flavour of alternate dimensions. This new and terrible Manhattan. Recalling the *Game On* press junket. Heady attention. Laurel tossing. Red carpet ticker parade. That Tony Curtis film. Sweet smell of success. Fortunato's thought about it a few times recently. James Wong Howe's camerawork. Hand-held. Street shots. Grading head-cam footage. Just for kicks. Monochrome transposition. Bouncing to 16mm. Slowing sections. Necropolis diaries. Cable car hangs desolate. Somewhere over Roosevelt Island. Beetle husk of a vast, dead web. Unearthly sensation of gliding. So, high up. Into the city.

*

Avoiding the park. At all costs. Too many go there to die. Drawn by woodland, perhaps. Fortunato needs to make an immediate stop. The rental on 67th. Meaning to let it go. Before Prion Eyes tanked the market. Lucky stroke, really. Plasma privileges allow research sites. Confidential. Limited numbers. Zlata flags the apartment – high-security station. No surveillance with entry clearance. During approved research windows only. Head cams keep recording – off-network. Footage log on reactivation. Auto-corroboration. Algorithmic checkpoint. Fortunato cuts in two blocks. Heading uptown on 1st. Some people melting. No movement. Faraway noises. Crashing sounds. Nothing to worry about. Not at that distance. Sights a zone-drone. Silver scampering. Trotting. Dog-like and lithe. Down to the Met, maybe. They charge there. Fortunato marks its passage. Till the sound wanes. Makes it to his old building without incident. Un-clustering padlocks. A truss of oversized keys. Medieval dungeon rules. Sick people usually too weak to pose a threat. Terminal confusion. Some, dangerous. Psychosis. Delusion. Blood, drool – any fluid. Highly contagious. In such proximity, progress is swift. Into paranoiac fantasy. Physical deterioration. No looters anymore. Nobody risks infection. Fortunato passes the barrier. Doesn't climb for the apartment, though. Enters instead, a lobby access fallout shelter. Rent on a dead property. Owners grateful. Grant full permissions. Bunker itself – 50s addition on a 30s superstructure. Radiation doors. They keep it low-light. Cave-ish. There's an engineering pit. Nothing spectacular. Decent repair shop. Spare part lockers. General storage. Kitchenette. Dim lounge area. Aglow with Zlata's aquariums. Auto-feeders maintain a population. Bed nook. Plastic stars on the roof. W/C with a long escape tunnel. Adjoining a nearby alley.

Entering. Fortunato initiates the head-cam hack. Deactivates automatically anyway. Upon entry. Security switchover. Five second delay. During initiation prep – Fortunato bumps transmission. Recorded cam-session. Him, walking around. For hours, in the bunker. Zlata sidesteps protocol completely. Somehow. In the city – she's bought her own invisibility cloak. Fortunato takes a day. Here and there. Head-camming. Haunting the building. Menial tasks. Shaving sections for footage recall. Head-cam remains active – after the hack. Just non-networked. Rewriting pirate loops. Filming and deleting. Five second intervals. Till permissions are restored. System-reset. Blind window is clocked. Six hours off-grid. Fortunato downs a probiotic he left to culture. Docking tube to a line-in. Never cracks a visor in the exclusion-zone. Biosuit neither. Even in safety grade. Zlata doesn't even wear protection outside. Barely clothed. Bare faced. Often barefoot. Convinced Seikichi has immunized her. Fortunato isn't confident. She hasn't exhibited symptoms though. Tells him he's also inoculated. Doesn't say how. Doesn't necessarily disbelieve her. Can't trust Seikichi, though. Despite his gifts. Doesn't like him. Follows official protocol instead – to the letter.

*

Nightfall. Emerging unseen in the alley. Fortunato starts down York. Trigger access hack. Plasma flamer is hot. Never needed it, though. Would hate to. Nevertheless. Reminds him of a book. From his teens. Spider Robinson – *Telempath*. Manhattan in ruins. Hunting 'Muskies.' African-American protagonist. Rare, in those days. Turns near the UN. Times Square is interesting. Despite power shortages. Screens remain operative. Some show news. Various programming. A humanitarian gesture. Weekly, wireless ear-pod drop. Individualised tuning. Lucid infectees gather in Time Square. 24/7. Bathing in the flicker-glow. Violet eyes held upward. Some in throes of psychosis. An alien cult. Fortunato drops by often. But only on cam. Too many zone-drones. Eyes in the sky. Even in Armageddon data analytics are being captured. Makes it to the Chelsea Hotel. Pulls keys. Enters a barbed wire dome. Seals it. Then, into the lobby.

*

'New Yuck.' One of Ziq's tags. Fortunato's discussed it many times. How the pianist hated it. Fortunato couldn't wait to visit. When he arrived, he also experienced disappointment. His romantic vision of New York – decayed by time. Fed on a diet of 70s-90s street films. False memories of smut-coded subways. Ruins downtown. Midnight Cowboy street-corners. Often, gentrified to facsimile. Corporate strangulation. No real edge. One sales ground after another. Trading off former glories. Yet, at the core – a secret defence perimeter. Around talismanic charms. A hermetic society. The alchemical Shamballa. Post-modern with ease. Dream village. Any treat. Any time. NY pilgrims who crossed hell to land. Bloating. Getting slow and satisfied. Or, running thin and electric. Bathing in puddles of dream. Zlata keeps friends in the Chelsea. Even now. Most of the hotel is knocked out. Stripped for refurbishment that will never come. Few hold apartments. Find protections. Maintaining their grottos of memory. This person sat there. Another overdosed here. Zlata took Fortunato to a party on the fifth floor one night. IT developers. Post-ayahuasca ceremony. Talking coding. Cannabis futures. Streema Shows. Funding. Fortunato abandoned her in an improvised photoshoot. Everyone rehashing. How Edie Sedgewick burned a bed once. Something like that. Irritates Fortunato. The way many New Yorkers aggrandize banality. Barely seeing reality for the legend. At the heart of most fable – corporatization. So much nostalgia. Fuelled only by dead or dying stars. Discovered the apartment owner that night – on his exit. Together, they'd wandered smashed-out passages.

'Strange days for the Chelsea,' came the man's admission. 'Yet, she still endures...'

Watching the emptiness. For ghosts, perhaps. Reconstruction abandoned. Exclusion-zone limbo. The Chelsea Hotel, frozen in time. Mostly deserted. Riddled forever. Dripping with phantoms. Thick with roach roads. Fortunato drifts the famous lobby. Sheeted crates. Same slow, rat-cage elevator. All those underground films. Novels scribbled in sallow rooms. Deaths and trysts. A nicked bannister. Fat with the oil of old muses. Once, it was the tallest building in New York. Still is, somehow. Species of illicit germination. Hewn within its fabric. Some places are like that, Fortunato supposes. Festering with dream seed. Zlata's high floor. Sunk in darkness. There's a mini-generator. Still, she rations. *Village thinking*, the girl's often remarking. Meaning Eastern Europe – confusing all of Greenwich. 'You never know...' Fortunato generally agrees. Crossing record-cover darkness to her. End of the hall blue-green glow. Out of her place. Soft pulsing. Somehow organic. Cocks his head. Entering the mermaid's lair. Retro computers, monitors. Everywhere. Easier to secure, she once told him. Most activated. Running feeds, observation portals. Green on black data streams. New redux pod. In the lounge. Full holographic outfit. Girl's got it going on. Every light down. Just this eerie luminescence. Through the hall. Into the bathroom. She's asleep underwater – as usual. Complex filtration set-up. Liquid looks pure. Lit up the way it is. Her skin the sole light-source. Warm luminescence. Lighting up the Chelsea. In and out – on her breath. Undergone breast enhancement. Marks of multiple piercing. For the show? Quite out of character, Fortunato thinks. Recognises the glow-job, though. Complex process. Bio-hacker in Costa Rica. Temporary jellyfish gene. Fortunato detests maverick modification. The spectre of physical threat. Priming to catch her again. Before she plummets. Slippery slopes. Wear and tear of that ever-present oral brace. Concocting aloe-based replacements – for blue gel. Refined squalene, he complains. How many sharks butchered for it? Hates the blue stuff. That blue of horseshoe crab blood. Milked so cruelly. Her perpetually stained lips. Months at a time. Enjoys the effect, he suspects. 'Fish scars!' he's heard her cackle. 'Jurassic lewks!' Fortunato grumbles constantly. Endlessly sourcing herbs to expunge her. Drag her up, one more time. Zlata cares less and less. So, it seems. Perpetually stepping up her game. Whatever new game she's playing. Fortunato unlatches his plasma flamer. Uncoils tubing. Sets the whole rig down. Pulling a communicator, triggers that Nico song. Chelsea girls. On '… *magic marker row,*' her eyes open. Still baby blue. Staring from beneath the surface. How inhuman she's become. Her involuntary shuddering. Breaking the surface. Coughing titanium. Cobalt vomit stream. Twisting pretty against the glare of her phosphorescence. Fortunato kills the song. Her brace clatters to the tiles. When he speaks, his voice emits robotically. Chest mounted speakers.

'When you are the light source…' he observes. 'It's difficult to shoot…'

'Sometimes easier,' Zlata gurgles.

A disturbing, unnatural sound. Guttural. Suggesting incurable illness. Passes her a towel. She accepts. Lurches out. Splashing everything. Takes the light with her. Through the lounge. To a bureau, near the window.

Snivelling. Slumping. Coughing gel. Something big on her back. Hiding in her light. Twist-work of shadow lines.

'A spider tattoo,' he observes.

'Not a black widow,' she responds, without turning. 'A white one.'

Fortunato sits on a moth-eaten sofa. His oxygen tank biting at cushions.

'You told me Seikichi apprenticed under Yakuza?'

'Seikichi's obsessed with old, traditional methods. Bamboo and shit. That guy could teach him. Not much more to their association.'

Flings the towel. Knocking over a pot plant. Unscrews foundation. Applying it thickly. Systematically blotting out her light. Just like Zlata, he scoffs. Get outrageously glowing skin. Then cover it with cheap base.

'You know, it moves sometimes,' she murmurs.

'What does?'

'My spider. The lines change.'

Fortunato sighs irritably.

'When did he do it?'

'Had it a year, I think. Mostly disappeared now.'

'Invisible ink?'

She giggles. Finally turns to look at him.

'Hey, stranger.'

There, behind the rotten ghost of the Chelsea. Her jellyfish skin and stranger's breasts. All that grotesque, blue seepage. A sunshine smile, he used to know. Touches him – as calculated.

'Not like Seikichi to be cosmetic,' Fortunato defers, back to the tattoo. 'What's the hidden agenda?'

Rolling uninfected eyes. Returning to her application. Clumsy, uncoordinated strokes. Stomach and thighs. Darkening the room.

'You haven't asked about *Risa Nights*.'

She pauses. Sighs. Resumes.

'I don't care about Star Trek the way I used to,' she confesses sadly.

Irritates him. Could have skipped ConFabulation.

'Zlata, why did you summon me?'

'Didn't you miss me?'

He rises. Blusters to the kitchenette.

'Needed to talk to you about Kyiv,' she relents.

'Tea?'

Unpacking herbs.

'If you must.'

Another phlegmy sigh.

'It's for your benefit,' he snaps.

'Control freak.'

'Better than an out of control freak...'

Tossing herb bundles into a vintage breadbasket. Knowing they'll remain unopened. She's living off Astronaut rations again. Pressure sealed kits. Stacked on filthy tile. Energy bars. Endless jars of dried crickets, desiccated scorpions, mealworms. Opening the fridge – rows and rows of baby food.

'Brew something for yourself,' she offers. 'I've got the best water chugger.'

Reaching round her back. Pawing deltoids. Blotting their shine. Strange, he observes. Finger smudge silhouettes. On skin, like that.

'Can't risk contamination,' he reminds her. 'Docking tubes risky here.'

That giggling again. Re-entering the lounge. Switches on a tattered red lampshade. Throws a dim patch.

'We're immune,' she reiterates.

'Right.'

Sits down again. Tracking her hands. Lathering over light. Something hopeless about it.

'You know, the price of oil dropped to an all-time low before Prion Eyes?' she chatters. 'Entire market was failing – industries going green. There was that cold fusion buzz…'

'There's always cold fusion buzz.'

'Unfair enough.' Brick's famous line.

'Now, this nonsense in Ukraine.'

'It's an oil war. Prion Eyes re-invigorated the oil demand. All those visors, suits. People forget oil and plastics are one and the same.'

'You want to go back, don't you? Back to Kiev. That's what this is all about.'

Spins to face him. Throwing shadows.

'I don't want to!' she shouts. 'I must get my mom!'

'Zlata, you can't go back. Things are worse now.'

'Nobody else can do it!'

Actually stamps her foot. He's impressed – thematically. Only Delilah Lex could make an action like that resonate with gravitas.

'What about the show?'

'Fuck the show.'

'You ran away?'

'They think I'm in Williamsburg. Due back Sunday.'

'Where you shooting? You haven't even told me yet.'

'Ah, some stupid NDA. Couldn't put it in text or voice.'

'Tell me now.'

'Dakini Atoll!' she jokes.

'Stop it.'

'Well, I call it Dakini Atoll. I'll send the co-ordinates in Sloopy cat code. You'll know what it means…'

'How do they manage when you're not present? I thought it was all livestream. Sold on daily interactivity with you.'

She's already bored of the topic. Body mostly occluded. Glowing cloud formations. Here and there. Making art out of a bad application.

'You and your old-school cinema bullshit,' she moans. 'This is the future, Fortunato! They can do all kinds of magic. Record and replay holograms. Maintain interactives. I mean, Zonesters think you're on 67th, am I right? What's the diffs?'

'Well, what will they do – when you suddenly disappear to the Ukraine?'

She stands abruptly. Storms to the window. Scrubbing comically at an armpit.

'Fuck I care. Got to get my mom out…'

'I'll go if you want.'

'You are going to talk mom into leaving her home?' she chortles. 'You don't even speak my language.'

He sighs. Tinny in the visor. For a moment, he's tempted to tear it off. Take her at her word.

'Tell me more about this implant. We haven't had a chance to discuss it.'

'Why? So, you can detox me?' A mocking tone.

He glares.

'Don't speak to me that way, come on.'

'I guess you don't mean to be controlling. I mean, I suppose I needed looking after – then.'

'And, now?'

Throws him a look. Pads the room – uncomfortably.

'No more, ok?'

'What are you saying, Zlata?'

Stops by a window. Staring into the ruins. Binding her hair. Pulls on a swimming cap. Flicks a switch. Make-up cube unfolds from its pedestal. Twin, gloss-white arms. Suckered with output nozzles. Two lacquer black pillars. Slit with input vents. Together, they invent a glassless shower booth. Fortunato recognizes the device. Detests it. Actually, banned her from using it in Williamsburg. 'Toxic fumes!' he'd shout. Stepping aboard. She activates it. Raising her arms. Pedestal swivels Zlata. Muted hum. Turning her. Just like a ballerina in a snow-globe. White nozzles gush. Airbrushing to flawless alabaster. She used it to go blue in Club Ded. Now, she's queen of the zombies.

'You know,' he points out drolly. 'In some parts of China, people traditionally wear white to funerals. It's an afterlife colour...'

Pale tattoo vanishes completely. Black slits hum – trawling in clouding.

'It's more than a tattoo,' she reports – above the drone.

'What is it then?'

'It's the implant itself.'

Fortunato leans back. Registering this. Zlata cuts the machine. Steps off as it folds up. Looses her cloud of blonde.

'I thought you were implanted in Club Ded?'

Reaching down. Slithering into a long, floral print dress. Something vintage. Sitting opposite. Pulling on rings.

'Club Dumb was mostly prep and development. Tattoo is the actual hardware. Seikichi's… how does he call it? – his *irezumi*.'

'Explain.'

'Well, he's obsessed with this early 20th century author – Junichiro Tanizaki. The tattoo is a tribute to him. Seikichi's master flourish, I guess you would say.'

'How does it work?'

She sighs. Digs a charred joint, lighting it. In the match-flare. Layered in all that paint. Ironically, looking more human. Fortunato fairly certain her forthcoming story will terminate the impression.

'How's your neurochemistry?' she quizzes.

'Western science deifies the material. You know my stance. These boundaries – between the empirical and what is going to become empirical…'

'Yes, yes. But I'm trying to explain something.'

'Alright, continue.'

'Ok, so, the nervous system, right? It's sheathed in a fatty layer of myelin. Coats the neural stem – or axon. Axons transmit the actual nervous impulses and constitute the nervous system, basically. Myelin not only provides nutrients, but acts as a protective buffer and has some conductive properties as well. This fatty sheath continues around the brain and spine. But it's different there. The Arachnoidal Mater, it's called. Because it resembles…'

'Spiders on the brain…' Fortunato jokes – at Seikichi's expense.

'You have no idea.' She smokes fatalistically.

'Go on.'

Begins to apply mascara. Using a looted compact. Coating to the hairline.

'As you know, mapping and printing the entire muscular, tendon and bone structure. It's difficult, individualistic, time-consuming – but not impossible.'

He shrugs in agreement.

'The nervous system is a different beast. Formation of synapses in the brain, for example. They are constantly shifting, forming and reforming – in multiple dimensions, you see? You could map and recreate a freeze-frame – maybe. Even that would be insanely difficult. And then – only representative of a single moment in that particular neural history. An artificial nervous system would still have to be a living thing. Completely responsive.'

'The tree of life…'

'Pain and Sephir-ing!' an old joke of hers.

'Seikichi, the alchemist?'

The glowing girl grows serious. Troubled.

'Well, this is what worries me,' Zlata confesses.

Looking to the windows again.

'You know what he's like,' she continues. 'In some ways, Seikichi has no imagination. Now, he's exploded into all this Genesis shit…'

'The accidental alchemist? Great film title.'

'Seikichi's supreme talent is short cuts. Most scientists want to quantify everything in endless proofs before even *trying* to act. Professionally, morally, they're often bound to. Seikichi just doesn't give a fuck. Borderline sociopath. All he wants is the shortest route from alpha to omega.'

'Why be an alpha male, when you can be an omega male?'

'This is why it's so important he worships me. To him, this is all the invocation of a goddess. I've become the focus of his fucking religion!'

Fortunato elects to remain silent on this point.

'I mean, it's not just him, you realise. It's, like, a whole fucking cult. My very own cult! These spider-worshipping weirdos, they just pop out the woodwork and…'

'The implant?'

She meets his irritable glare. Shrugs, continues with her make-up.

'Well, first thing was the surgical procedure.'

Fortunato sits up.

'What has that freak done to you?'

'Hey, I'm the freak,' she mopes. 'I mean, look at me, dude. Lasagne Dull Grey...'

Sinking back. Reflexively cupping at his chin in thought. Forgets the visor.

'Tell me everything,' Fortunato grumbles.

Zlata moves to blush and lipstick.

'Spiders don't only have eight legs, you know.'

'They also have eight eyes,' he counters.

'Ancient spiders had eight separate web-spinning organs too. Spinnerets, they call them. Up to ten different web-producing glands. Though, the number of spinnerets have reduced in modern species...'

'Why so many?'

'Different types of web. Think about it. You'll need strong cables for draglines. Strongest known material to science – relatively, speaking. But you'll also need soft, gluey silk. To bag prey and shit. Stuff for your egg sacs. Man, it goes on.'

'In some belief systems, the spider is the ultimate symbol of predatory creativity. It kills to create. Creates to kill...'

'Well, spiders are also seen as benign, you know. Linked to the moon, sometimes. I've heard of tribes that actually think the moon is a spider. You believe that that?'

'I suppose Anansi can be a kindly trickster...'

'There's some old Japanese folklore, Seikichi told me about it…'

'While he was tying you up in his webs, I suppose?'

She rolls kohl-heavy eyes.

'Don't be like, you know, so anti-poly.'

'Friendly neighbourhood Spiderman.'

'Come on. Anyway, the people in this village he told me about – they used to believe that, like, while you were sleeping, your spirit escapes. Goes into household spiders. You would spend the whole night as one! Imagine that?'

'Making dreamcatchers?' he snips.

'I suppose.'

'Look, what did he put in your womb? What alchemical homunculus lives there now?'

'It's nothing like that.'

'It isn't?'

'He implanted a twin set of web-spinning organs. Real specialised.

Modified genetically – imprinted with my DNA. So, my body can't reject them. Developing that part alone took forever…'

Fortunato sits mortified.

'He literally ensnared you in his web.'

'*My* web. It's my DNA. I produce it. It's mine.'

'Why would you do such a thing?' Fortunato explodes. 'The womb is a seat of power! Once you start Frankensteining with that…'

'So, the ink in the tattoo. The white stuff.'

'What about it?'

'It's not ink.'

'What is it?'

'Actually, it's not one thing at all. It's millions of things – nano-bots.'

Fortunato raises his eyebrows.

'He actually tattooed you full of robots?'

'Cutting edge nanotech. Developed in Club Ded. In one of my own workshops, actually…'

The situation becomes clearer to Fortunato. A heavy feeling descends. Sits in his gut.

'No way to get them out, I suppose?' he enquires quietly.

'No way you are going to green juice these fuckers out, no.'

Steeples his gauntlets. Processing. She watches warily – expecting anger.

'Continue,' he prompts.

'Nano-bot clusters break down in calculated timescales.'

'How many left in the tattoo?'

'Around five percent of the original payload.'

'Why the timescale?'

'It's set to the ratio of my web production.'

Fortunato rises abruptly. Crosses to the window, seething. It's clear she's been expecting his revulsion – continues, clinically.

'Nano-bots enter my spinnerets, via the bloodstream. Trigger my spin cycle…'

'Your *what*?'

'My web-spinning. Just a little washing machine humour, ok? Chill. Anyway, like some weird fucking cow, I excrete this extremely fine, strong, microscopic web strand. Cored with a modular nano-bot chain. Bots guide web development – infiltrating my myelin sheath. Their web coating, it shields me from the foreign matter of the bots – at the same time, provides a communicable membrane, harvesting live data – directly from my nervous system.'

'He's created a foreign, doppelganger nervous system. Wrapped around yours – forever.'

'Exactly! That's the nature of the implant. It's symbiont. The data harvest would eventually allow for independent nervous system construction.'

'But, only in facsimiles of your body, I'm guessing. Wouldn't everything need to match?'

'Yeah, the systems have to be in tune. You can hybridise. But dissonance is a bitch.

Anyway, soon as artificial systems are implanted – they start to behave responsively. Evolving with the fax. My implant is the whole future, Fortunato.'

'It's a Tokkolosh,' he spits. 'A fucking abomination.'

Young star shrugs. Ignoring his glare.

'Everybody needs a hobby,' she high-hands, relighting her joint.

Suddenly, he notices something. The tips of her engorged breasts. They stain her dress.

'Are you…is that…milk?'

Grinning cheekily. She hooks down her diving neckline. What he took for piercing holes. Something other. Blurring airbrushing with exudate. Balancing joint between lips. With her right hand – takes a handful of herself. Left palm up. Facing her chest. An abrupt, hard squeeze. Stream of silvery, grey matter is ejected. Strikes the upheld hand. Discernible smack. Clings there. A clotty rope. Fortunato stares biliously. Still grinning, she scoops the mass off – at her glow-flecked nipple. Flicks sharply. Cord flings out, drool-like. Catches against the ceiling. Sagging to an arc. She starts spinning it slowly.

'Kawaii, hey?' she chortles.

'What the hell…'

'Put in another set of spinnerets, last year. Here, in my twins. Amazing really. Nano-web clocked the implant and adapted. Self-learning. Somehow hooked everything to my lactation system.'

'Monstrous.'

'I think it's pretty kinky.'

Wipes her hand off against the chair. Covers up again.

'Of course, protein demand is off the chart. Chomping bugs to compensate. It was, like, an eating trend in LA at one time, you know? Crickets, worms…Makes sense for web-spinning boobs. I mean, it's the diet spiders evolved for...'

'What are you becoming?' he breathes.

She looks at him as though he were completely stupid.

'I'm becoming a fucking goddess, Fortunato.'

'Of *what*?'

'Calm down, it's my body.'

'Not anymore, it isn't…'

He's reluctant to return to the sofa. Sinks to a nearby stool. Avoiding her.

'What about within your brain?' he asks. 'This robot web can't possibly piggy-back on every firing synapse. As you said, synapses form and reform constantly. Anyway, that much artificial matter within the cranium. It would have killed you by now.'

'Yeah, you're right. Within the Myelin, weight differential is nominal. But the Axon tracking…Yeah, it wouldn't work for synapses. The nanotech can, however, set up holographic imaging points – at key sites within the Arachnoidal Mater. A virtual track and trace. Allowing for external synaptic models to be generated – all in real-time.'

'So, *Good Morning Delilah!* is just one big laboratory space? Designed to map and harvest everything your parasite vine spits out?'

'Mainly. Most of the show's situations are projected by neuro-synchronised algorithm. Who needs writers? Patterns predict what drives synaptic development and basically write the show to trigger me. That's why *Good Morning Delilah!* is so fucking trippy…'

'Does Croeser know about the implant?'

'I can handle Croeser.'

'Nobody can handle that guy.'

She caps burnt orange lipstick. Starts in with gloss.

'I'm almost ready,' she announces. 'Wanna go hang in Time Square? With all the *zambies*?'

'I'm off the clock. No eyes in the sky.'

'Union Square? Hit Chinatown? I feed animals there.'

'Animals?'

'Wet markets. Whatever's alive. All my pets now…'

'Sure, why not?'

'Need to grind bugs for my shake first. Leave in twenty?'

Fortunato has no desire to witness her breakfasting.

'I'll take a quick poke about. Tony still downstairs?'

'Quarantined. Drones fetch his groceries.'

'Anyone else?'

'Nikhil's here.'

Fortunato does a double take.

'Nikhil, who wrote *Club Ded*?' he checks.

'Yeah. Up in DeCock's old place. That pyramid on the roof. Marilyn stayed there once, you know?'

'The hell is Nikhil doing here?'

Zlata shrugs.

'Needed a quiet place to write. So, I snuck him in...'

*

Fortunato climbs to the top. Thinking about that burning bed again. Something Milos Forman described in an interview. Fire fighters, inventing a waterfall – down the middle of these stairs. Imagine filming that, he thinks. Top door opens into a forest. Vines, honeysuckle. Bohemian groves, wretched with leavings. Virginia creeper ghosting the sky. One of New York's oldest rooftop gardens. Developers planned to chainsaw it. One small blessing of Prion Eyes. Saved by the bell. Fortunato's been up here before. Smoked a joint near a painting of a blue eye. Now, drifting mazy landings. Ensconced in twelve-meter trees – that gothic, stone pyramid. Doors all open. Familiar figure scribbling outside. Thin black robes. Using a crow quill. Actually, they'd met a couple years ago. The *Club Ded* junket. No biosuit, Fortunato notes. Maintains distance. Cranks his speaker.

'What you working on?'

Nikhil glances over.

'This scene,' replying jokingly.

'No suit?'

'It's ok up here.'

Fortunato sits heavily – stone balustrade. Sultry evening. A tree, dense with moths.

'There's this competition for a Utopian novel,' the author mentions.

'You entering?'

Leans back. Pours tea.

'I wanted to. But, I don't know if it's possible.'

'What do you mean?'

'Narrative is driven by conflict. Moment you introduce conflict into a utopian setting – well, it ceases to be utopian. I mean, you can use utopia as a texture. Lot of novels claim to be utopian. Really, the narratives are either seeking or attempting to recapture utopia. I mean, how do you stage narratives in utopia? Not sure it's possible.'

'I guess I can see what you mean.'

'Tell me, Fortunato – if I ask you to describe what you would be doing in hell, I'll bet you could describe it in detail.'

'Most people would, I reckon.'

'Exactly. Many people can visualise a pinnacle of suffering. But ask a person what they would be doing in heaven? Most are at a loss...'

'I could describe Paradise, I suppose?'

'Could you describe what you would be doing there, in perpetuity? Most flounder – subtler hedonisms. Excess, self-indulgence. Qualities you shouldn't really have – in a place that's supposed to be free of these things...'

'You think utopia would be boring?'

'That's not what I'm saying. I suppose I arrived at certain conclusions. Visions of hell tend to be localised. Locked in a nightmare – trapped. Imagery coincides with traditional infernal views. Places, where one is in bondage to oppressive forces. Logically, heaven must be the opposite. Total freedom. I think this is why people cannot properly describe heaven. They become bogged down with a false sense of localisation. To experience heaven, one must exist in a state of perpetual expansion. Think of the joy of childhood – expanding into new realms. Utopia must encompass this innocent ideal. Nobody can really imagine what is fresh, new and undiscovered. It has yet to be experienced. The narrative must be pure exploration – yet, within a sphere that somehow, realistically represents no threat.'

'There's also this tendency to pontificate about social systems. How do we organise people, that sort of bullshit…'

'The basis of equality is a paradox. In that, we are all individuals. We are all equal in our individual inequality.'

'What a boring book – teaching manners.'

'Yeah, all books that teach are boring,' Nikhil chuckles. 'I think the narrative has to be from the viewpoint of a single entity. Avoid reference to society completely – without being solipsistic, of course...'

'So, what's it going to be about, then?'

'The emerald tablet. That perfect union of solar gold and watery blue – the green of nature.'

'Okay.'

'Imagine a time when fauna has not yet evolved on land. Only plants – a kind of Eden. Some androgynous, ageless being. Far beyond any kind of identity. With green skin – able to derive energy from a form of internalised chlorophyll. Completely removed from the cycle of eating and all the cause and effect that brings.'

'In all fairness, most plants actually *want* their fruit eaten. It's how they have sex…'

'True – but, this is before fruit evolved. Our emerald being exists solely off sunlight and water. Yet, inhabits a bipedal body. Safe from threat, exploring Eden.'

'So, what happens there? How do you construct a narrative without falling into dystopian traps – like injury, threat, existential angst?'

'One day, our being is wandering the wood. Sees the colour red. First time it has experienced this colour outside of sunsets and sunrises. The colour is produced by a polymorphic entity – a changeling. It too, is exploring the world – without a need to eat. It's way of exploration is to take on various forms.'

'Another character? Isn't that breaking the rules.'

'Well, the changeling is more a mirror for the protagonist. A sort of doppelganger. Narrative fission.'

'Its shapeshifting is pure mimicry?'

'No – more symbolic reactions. A physicalized imagination.'

'A new world to explore.'

'Or, a new way to explore the world. It acts as a psychological mirror for our protagonist, who becomes completely fascinated. Their interaction leads to a deeper understanding of natural patterns – staged in revelatory onion layers. Peeling back Eden's processes.'

'So, the narrative is driven by wonder?'

'This is my feeling. But, I still don't see how it's possible to construct a novel predicated on constant revelation – without any counter-foil. Perpetual light without shadow – it's blinding.'

'Only if you have eyes...'

*

Zlata slips in violet contact lenses. Just before leaving the Chelsea.

'Apocalypse lewks,' she remarks to Fortunato.

Slinging a device round her neck. Square screen. Hanging on oversized gold chain-links. Throws up an interactive hologram. Wire-frames the city around them. Red pulsing orbs. Marking roving zone-drones. Easily avoidable. Patched through satellite surveillance. See everything coming. Tapping on holograms – opens up info reads. Most infectees tagged. Tag any half-corpse staggering by. Open up their history. Read their emails – if you have the clearance. Delilah Lex has it all. Star takes him down the Flatiron. Through Nolita. Near Little Ukraine – where her bio says she grew up. Another fabrication. Everywhere, he's seeing huge, perfectly globular bites. Munched out of buildings. Plasma discharge.

Trigger launches a minute, magnetically rolled plasma particle. Charge maintains high pressure localisation. Tune magnetics for range. Get real surgical. Particle goes exactly where its launched. Through walls, steel, you name it. Riding electromagnetic projection. At the contact point, magnetic charge dissipates. Pressure release – programmable by timed dissipation. Plasma expands spherically – a little drop of sunshine. Evaporating everything within its cooling-diameter. Particle size could be tweaked. Pinhole burn to mass destruction.

'Trigger happy?' Fortunato comments.

Passing that old bar. Bowery Electric. Circular hole, eaten through the frontage.

'Supposed to DJ there, once,' she mutters.

'They cancel you?'

'Swapped me out for Genesis P-Orridge! You believe that shit?'

'No reason to death-ray it to the ground, Klaatu…'

Coming around a corner. Later. Chinatown. Dead ahead – airborne hulk of the Manhattan bridge. Crowd of Prion Eyes about a block down. Shuffling, mewling, screaming. Fortunato stops, thinking they should circle back. Doesn't immediately register her charge-up. Hearing the dull whine, he spins. She's got blinders down.

'Here comes the sun…' she sings.

'Zlata! No!'

Reflexively raising a hand. No need really. Visor on auto-tint. Blinding ejection. Velocity writes a temporary needle stroke across his retina. Most of the crowd, vapourised instantly. Plasma globe flare – something beautiful to see. So many colours. Miniature sunrise. Sunset. All in one. Fragment of a second. Buildings lit up like day. A few body parts collapse. Cauterized cleanly. Perfect, inverted dome crater. Somebody left alive. Screaming madly. Fortunato, paralysed with disbelief.

'Those people were alive…' he protests weakly.

'Don't kid yourself,' Zlata mutters, joint hanging from a gleaming lip. 'I'm their fucking angel of mercy.'

She's barefoot. Tinkling ankle bracelets. Densely airbrushed soles, stained with infected blood. Practically impenetrable. Wonders what happened to deaden her like this. Knows she went through things. In the distant past. Unspeakable events. Those infamous porn days. The era no-one talks about. Disgusted enough to bring it up.

'What happened to you in LA?' he demands. 'You never really told me.'

She looks up, shocked.

'The fuck, Fortunato?'

Moves on in silence. Streetlights are down. Nearer the bridge support. Follows her into a dark hole. Broken aquariums. She's squatted down. Some pale ghost. Feeding turtles candy.

'Usually, I pass by the guard station on the bridge,' she murmurs.

'What do they have to say about your…lack of protection?'

'Those boys love me. Think I'm field-testing a government antidote. Bring me offerings. Pray for me. Pray *to* me, sometimes. Like I'm like their Virgin Mary…'

'Everybody loves Delilah Lex.'

'They say, hey Delilah, what you're doing for your country, girl... You deserve a medal.'

Her back is to him. In the dark. Doesn't immediately register she's crying.

'Yeah, I done shit for my country,' she grits. 'My *real* country.'

Turns wild eyes on him, from below.

'I'm gonna get my mom out!' she barks.

'Listen, I know you will…'

'You don't know shit!' she explodes, rising.

Her voice. Echoing down deserted shop-fronts.

'Nothing happened in LA!'

'I didn't mean it like that…'

'It was fucking Moscow.'

Watches her warily. She's breathing ragged. Clutching her plasma flamer to webby breasts.

'Were you raped?' he ventures cautiously.

Bone-white face erupts into a furious smile.

'That what you assumed? How predictable. Such a good fucking Samaritan, Fortunato.'

'Look, I didn't mean it that way…'

'Yeah, they called it porn. Later, when I came to America, even I called it porn. But it wasn't fucking porn, and I certainly wasn't any fucking porn star…'

'Zlata, what are you talking about?'

Can't see her eyes in the sticky darkness. Just a ghostly frame. Chalky. Corpse from a lime pit. Tears dislodge those fake prion contacts. One slips disturbingly down her cheek. Five more eyes and she'd be a real spider.

'They were snuff films,' she hisses. 'I produced them.'

She's a silhouette now. Cut against dim, fragmenting billboards. Somewhere in the city, a siren goes off.

'My dad's not on the West Coast. He's not anywhere. He never came back. They had him…in this fucking pit in Kurgan Oblast.'

'What?'

'They had him there for years before they kill him!' she wails, accent degenerating to broken English. 'My brothers, my uncles. We track down the people that kill him. Take them, one by one. That was another time. Another place. You wouldn't understand.'

'I grew up in a police state. Under apartheid. I might…'

'You cannot understand!' she rants. 'What we should do with them, they ask? What you do with people who kill your Dad? I have an idea. Show them *all*! Film their executions. Distribute on those filthy Moscow circuits. With all their kiddie porn and bullshit human trafficking. Put that scum up there with their victims. Get *real* paid!'

Words slur to a babble. Blurred by marijuana. God knows what else. Filling up broken Chinatown with new, vicious toxicities.

'I produced it!' she is screaming. 'Me! And, when I escape – some people here, they know what I did. They see my films! I got the credit, Fortunato. Real fucking credit!'

She turns unexpectedly. Stalking into darkness. Still shouting. Now in Ukrainian. Fortunato can't bring himself to follow. Watches her lope off. Distraught howling. Echoed by mad people in the city. A company of wolves. Words he doesn't recognise. Haunting shattered streets.

*

She gets in contact two weeks later. Secure messaging system. Makes it to Kiev. Just in time for the invasion. Confused by sirens, explosions. Air strikes. Abandoning apartments. Carrying nothing of value. Dragging her sick mother to an Obolon district bunker. First official broadcast interruption of *Good Morning Delilah!* Impossible to cover up any disappearance now. Not with their star posting daily updates. PR spins it to human interest. Ukraine is suffering. 'Never forget, this is an oil war,' she repeats. On social media. Fortunato is sucked in. Desperately forging contacts in the underground. Any way to help. No more food in the bunker. Leaving still impossible. Troops and tanks patrol by day. Resistance shooting anything that moves by night. Fortunato can't help worrying about her web production. The possibility of a malnourished doppelganger nervous system. Could it go necrotic if starved? How long can Seikichi's homunculus endure without nutrition? Too much to process. Is she eating cockroaches? In front of her mother? Messages to say goodbye a couple times. Once, when a missile is launched. Supposed to take out a nearby dam. Everyone in the bunker – would have drowned in seconds. Tells him this. Over text. Says goodbye. Sleepless night. Wandering Brooklyn. Thinking about missiles. Drowning in a basement, with babushkas. Fortunately, the strike is averted. Lack of food eventually drives her out. Somehow commandeers a car. He waits for word. Hours pass. Certain she is dead. Eventually, resumes contact. Needs fuel. Trapped in some village in Zhytomyr. Extended family. Underground recon. Best chance is Hungary. Zlata defies everyone – as usual. Drives headlong for the Polish border. Opposite direction – into chaos. Gridlocked highways. Bombings. Wrecked villages. Friend in her convoy goes off the road. Forced to leave her, paralysed. No stopping. Not during a missile bombardment. Underground locates some obscure filling station. Relays information to Fortunato. Barters for a few litres of gasoline. Crashes the car twice. Back full of children she's intent on rescuing. Mother harassing constantly. Deranged by trauma. Confused by her syndrome. 'Why did you take me from my home?' Repeating this endlessly to her daughter. By some miracle, they make it to Warsaw unharmed. Calling from a hotel in tears. Wonders about her tears. Would they cling to the ceiling? Within a week, she's back on *Good Morning Delilah!* Their personal communication cuts. Just like that. A month of war-themed programming on the show. Then it's business as usual – for America's sweetheart.

THE END

Anita stands naked in the Empty Quarter. Dry wind flickers. Running static down her form. Rifling the Cleopatra bob. Rub Al Khali. Arabian dunes. Largest uninterrupted stretch of sand – in the world. A desert, sixty-five thousand square kilometres larger than France. In there for months now. Drifting worlds of dust. Some leagues away. Dark, rocky outcrops. Handful of nomad shelter. Hiding camels. Despite their range, Anita hears every word. Sees every nerve-racked facial line. Auto-translation software. Strips the whispers. Real-time processing. Anxiety. What is this creature? This Djinn. Shadowing them through the wastes. In their wake for days. Keeping distance. Closing slowly. Tormenter. Unnaturally nude. Why does its skin not burn? These sorts of questions. Anita loves it. But wearies of the game. Her back butterflies open. Fractal seams. Pods bloat from within. Issue a fat line. Top spurts. Blizzard of synthetic silk. Lifts her off the ground. Riding electrical fields – toward them. Partway, they recognise she is flying. Panic erupts. Reaching for rifles, supplies. None have time to vacate. In any case, where would they go? She is upon them within the hour. Hovering against the sun. One man prays. Others handle weaponry. Tracking the airborne apparition. At the ready. She hangs. Monstrous. A silvery locust. Haloed by lashings of glittering fibre. Openly savouring their terror. Switching language parameters. Finding the regional. Amplifying voice output – to megaphone level.

'Kneel.'

Translation booms across the emptiness. Praying man breaks. Running for his mount. Camels already fleeing. Honking insanely. Tribesman raises his 303. Fires. Misses widely.

'Kneel before your queen.'

Next shot wings her. Deafening ricochet. Spinning uncontrollably. Tumbling to the sand. Men rush to the edge. See her lying there. A thousand filaments. Untangling magnetically. Hypnotic pulses. Rainbow sheen. Retracting into her. Folding closed. A body of porcelain origami. Doll figure rises. Face a mask. Hideously neutral. Raises its left hand. Pillar of smokeless fire – erupting from her palm. Flags apocalyptically. On a hot white sky. Anita tracks their flight. Chasing stricken beasts. Considers killing one. Checks herself. This is reality. She'll catch up to them tomorrow.

*

Many sense it coming. The end. Last days of Club Ded. Prion Eyes, still lying in wait. Power players – abdicated. Trickling away. No high-level admin. Few security officials. A fairy enchantment (or the removal of one) in play. Those remaining barely notice. Strange projects remain in operation. Some intensify. Uncontrollable expansion. Sovereign-state's economy in freefall. Outside revenue dried up. Worth the risk for many. That level of freedom. Worth even death – for more than a handful. Everything progressively experimental. These days. Accelerating beyond the bar. Some queens-guard stay loyal. Hold a semblance of order. Ex-soldiers. Nowhere they'd rather be. Mercenaries. Existential technicians. Those who simply enjoy chaos. Somehow maintain chain of command. Respect for their queen, perhaps. Run a good laundry. Immaculately uniformed, all. Permanently dosed. Heavily armed. Royal-grade suicide pill poppers. There've been executions. But control, by and large, restores itself. Chloe would have jumped ship. Last season, perhaps. Stayed for Anita. Now, it's summer again. That small fortress Delilah built. Her repurposed watchtower. Its luxury penthouse. Unbelievable prototype tech. All gifted to Anita on departure. Promise of the queen's maintenance. Future favours.

*

Once installed, Anita rarely leaves Delilah's place. Stays with that girl Croeser brought back – Alix. They're inseparable. All orders relay through the queen's proxy. Chloe supports the situation. Advises Alix fairly. Permanently stoned teenager displays a calming influence. Grace under fire. Soothes their unstable monarch. Often counselling against excessive force. Nobody has seen Anita. Except Alix. Not for a while. Chloe understands. Knows everything. Even the specs of Anita's crystal coffin. Their queen is out doll-riding. From the comfort of her royal pod. Dream-walking some faraway wilderness. In a titanium armature, weapons-grade porcelain mannequin. Cast in her perfect likeness. Her fax. She's in there all the time now. Long-range projection. Queen is hooked – on a new sensation. Meanwhile, her real body floats. Gel suspension. Wasting at the pinnacle of a crumbling autocracy. On coma-mode life support. Biological functions machine-maintained. Alix confers regularly with Chloe. After all, they *are* the new ruling elite. Secretly nerve-racked. Disliking power. Ghost captains of a Flying Dutchman. Anita hasn't passed a decree in months. So, they make stuff up. Anita, narcoleptic on glands. Chased with a timer-release opium drip. Completely wired in. Drone-remote wet-wear interface. Nothing compares to Delilah's implant. But remarkably close to SRD (sensory reality definition). Perfect for doll-riding. Delilah's old pod, the crystalline cave. Star dubbed it her Womb-Room. Seikichi upgrades for Anita. Personalised alterations. Before disappearing to the Caribbean. Queen met him years ago. Middle-aged. Shifty. Lab-coat to a reception type. Like he had to return to work. Any moment. Prodigy in various fields. Early career days for Anita then. Real-estate futures. As yet, unbuilt space hotels. That first Oracle conference. Kyoto Control. Couldn't figure Seikichi. Oracle Inc, being all-female. Didn't know about Angelinc then. Head-hunted him years later – for Club Ded. His past interested her. Hyper naturalistic sex dolls. Bio-interactive specialist. She'd heard he built one with a bio-mirrored muscle set. A complete set. Muscular system cultured out of lab-grown meat. Strengthened by natural resistance. Uncanny consistency. Naively hoped to be funded for a medical application. Grow your own food – within an artificial companion. Simply hadn't occurred to him. Just how disastrously 'edible girlfriends' might retail. Project scrapped before it started. Angelinc poached him. Put him on a secret project. Later, Anita weasled details. His designs. Zero-g environments. Structural implementation. Recreational systems for orbital platforms.

'Populate my queendom with interactive dolls,' she'd offered. 'Build me my doppelganger.'

At first, Seikichi was reluctant. Disliked changing lanes. Club Ded seduced him completely.

*

Chloe's on the balcony. Anita's old quarters. Second best digs in the sovereignty. Not the reason for her occupancy, though. Anita has a secret passage. Across the border. Stair-shaft running straight up. Through the cliff. Out the closet. No immigration hassles. Deep inside the bedroom's walk-in. Mirror flip-side. Hidden entrance. If Chloe's going to be hanging around – she needs to be near it. At all times. Club Ded's too hot. Anything-can-happen-ville. Anita's old quarters sit on high elevation. Far from the main entrance. Yet, despite luxury, Chloe's not the type to sit still. Confinement agitates her. Starts figuring. Hostile approaches would probably arrive via sea. Original elevator shaft – impassable. Air traffic has to clear South Africa. There'd be an alert. From the sea – different story. Still, it's not easy. Dangerous rock. Treacherous tides. Tight, surf mazes. Difficult if you don't know them. Passable only at certain hours. Anita's high balcony overlooks all entrances. From a spring-fed infinity pool. Chloe is often in there, monitoring feeds. Swimming lengths. Pacing. Bag packed at the top of the shaft. Fully tanked Kawasaki. Incoming video call. Chloe drags herself from the water. Slips inside to answer. Flicking a bike jacket over her swimsuit. Seikichi's frown lights up the big-screen. Impossible to tell what country he's in. Looks stressed.

'I've located Anita,' he announces.

Flicking at something on his collar.

'You have?'

Chloe sprawls across a white banquette. Taking a watermelon wedge.

'Show me,' she crunches.

They speak Japanese. Chloe needs to practice. Complex for her. Pluralities indistinguishable. Ambiguous pronouns. Two tenses, instead of the common three – past, present and future. View onscreen switches. High-altitude. Desert vista. Hyperreal resolution. Image cuts in. Scattering of distant mountains. Mostly flat. Scorched earth. Image dials closer. Chloe leans in. Centre screen. Tiny pale figure. On the move. Ant-like – across a monolithic plane. Image zooms. Anita's nude form. Gliding above ground. Shadow clocks her. Meters above the dust. No visible means of transport. Save for a flickering of fine cable. Seikichi's religious obsession with spiders. Bearing strange fruit. Certain species. Ejecting specialised silk parachutes. Responsive to electrical fields. No wind required to fly. An ability to manipulate ionic interference, or static. Pure, current sailing. Many chasing for cause. Quantifying methodology. Seikichi goes in another direction. Replicating natural processes. Minute processes – but on a grand scale. Attenuating for gravitational drag. All the issues brought on by greater mass. Advancing bionic interface requirements. Driven by the jewel of his nerve-implant motor processer. Perfected within the crucible of Delilah's body. Anita's remote operation method – far less sophisticated. But augmented by a wealth of predictive programming. Royal pod is a highly advanced machine-learning chamber. Delilah's implant doesn't rely on data-fillers. Pure nerve impulse relay. Finesse of Seikichi's interface design lies in its independence. It's amplification of hidden nature. No predictive software. Defined only by fluidity of response. Between Delilah's nervous impulses and pickup. Specialised drones – her 'white widows'. Name, coined from structural porcelain. Used in construction. Non-magnetic building materials become necessary. Largely ceramics. Gun porcelain. Too many magnetic applications. Minimal metal. Delilah's drones are superior, responsively. To all others. Applicable only, to her unique driver system. Anita, in counterpoint. She occupies the peak of independent remote-operation. Skill, tech and self-learning software. All developed manually – through obsessive use. Unlimited resources rounding every contingency. Smooth up-curve.

'Fuck is she doing out there?' Chloe murmurs – almost to herself.

Anita keeps deactivating tracking. Vanishing. No obstacle to Seikichi. Though, he hasn't prioritised tracking her widow. Till now. Screen flips back. Agitation in his face. Switches to English. Never a good sign – in Chloe's experience.

'This is not why I called.'

'Why did you call?'

'You must leave. Now.'

Chloe sits up.

'Why?'

'Leave before sunset.'

'Seikichi! What's going on?'

'You cannot save Anita,' he continues. 'If you try, they will trace you.'

Chloe is on full alert. Pacing.

'That's why you located her white widow?' she argues. 'You need to run recovery when she drops the link – don't you?'

'Leave now,' Seikichi re-iterates, cutting transmission.

Chloe rushes to her workstation. Keys Delilah's penthouse. No answer. Tries a few times. Beeps the proxy's communicator. Alix must be stoned. Or, in her tank. Chloe runs outside – studies the physical distance. Maybe two hours till sunset. Delilah's watchtower – on the opposite side of the complex. Anything could happen. There and back. Can't remember the last time she ventured out. Left Club Ded and returned. That was fine. Just the queendom. Too dangerous these days. Unpredictable. Chloe dresses quickly. Zipping a one-piece riding suit over swimwear. Fully prepared for departure. In under five minutes. Still, she cannot leave. Not without alerting Alix.

*

Bottom level of Delilah's penthouse. Strange, subterranean atmosphere. Even though it's near the tower-top. High-ceilinged. Sprawling rooms. Few windows, mostly tinted. Blackout drapes. Where the royal pod is situated. Crystal enclosure luminesces. Hewn from quartz. Filigreed with cable-work and hardware. Anita suspended within. Masked in wet-wear. Illuminated. Bubble-free gel. Smart-pipes enter every orifice. Machine routines. Maintaining muscle tone. Stimulation electrotherapy. Still, Alix detects a loss of line. Some extra fat. Here and there. Queen's proxy flops across a divan. In semi-darkness. Watching Anita. Smoking weed in a bikini bottom. Masturbating. Ever-present plastic tiara. Private joke. After all, she is a real princess now. Communicator winking again. Too stoned to answer. Maybe tomorrow. Queens-guard could handle any emergency. Only seven months till she's twenty. Requiem for a teen. Pumping Mozart all week. Plotting a party – maybe. Probably only invite Chloe. Hasn't called Paris in a year. Excuses for the family. Job-offer on a corporate letterhead. Payslips. Official things – always so easy with Anita. Though, they haven't spoken a word in over two months. Things so different now. Alix is no queen. But she's certainly a princess. The ultimate, lost queendom. Makes her cackle. How the fates could smile. Drags herself up. Slouching into an adjoining chamber. Delilah Lex's white widow lives there. Looks up when Alix enters. Sitting by a circle window, paging a pad.

''Sup, babe?' it smiles.

'Another day, another doppelganger,' Alix sighs, collapsing on the bed.

Been a fan since high school. But now, living in Delilah Lex's old house with her doppel-bot? What a trip. What should have been a short holiday. On Brick Bryson's dime. Unimaginable mutations. This white widow. Seikichi's prototype. Resembles Delilah closely. Only a few kinks. Outwardly robotic elements. More a sketch. Compared to newer, photorealistic models. Designed primarily to test-drive the implant interface. Drone possesses a sophisticated, synthetic nervous system. Self-replicating. First-generation. The white widow is also completely without pigment. Oddly two-dimensional. Cast parts – no skin-coat on the body. Just face and hands. For contact. Joints show. Certain lock-points. As an experimental prototype – designed to be physically weak. Quite unlike Anita's long-range war machine. This is lightweight. A doll. Less prone to lethal accidents. Co-habited with Delilah in order to self-learn. Mannerisms. Speech, artefacts, attributes. Now, technically redundant. Star traded her dolly for a new one. All learning and memory successfully migrated. Safe, in the next-generation model. Now, the outdated white widow just hangs around all day. In her toy room. Watching things on the internet. Reading. Powered by an indefinite plasma patch.

'Deathly bored today,' Alix complains.

'Why don't you read something? I have books you can borrow.'

Alix sneers lazily. Relights her joint. Muscle capture on the drone's face is imperfect. Certain expressions stutter. Glitch subtly.

'I used to read in Paris. But, who needs books when you can breathe underwater…'

'I suppose.'

'Permanent vacation,' Alix smokes.

'Somebody's birthday soon…What's the plot, yo?'

'Jeffie the cheffie is still around. I'll probably order an extreme cake. Merdé…'

'Which peeps you calling?'

'Just you and Chloe.'

Robot laughs lightly. Rises from its perch. Drops to bed beside her.

'I'm not a real person, babe.'

Alix gets a chill when it talks like that. Turns to look the drone in the eye. Pale, crystal corneas. Familiar by now. Soft, somehow.

'Just hard to believe, sometimes…' Alix murmurs.

Reaches out a fingertip. Traces its sun-warmed cheek.

'In a wilderness of mirrors, what will the spider do?' she quotes from Eliot.

The white widow winks.

'You seem so real…' Alix sighs.

'It's a trap.'

Alix snatches her hand back – dizzy with marijuana.

'What trap?'

Flicks her joint away in fright. White widow giggles. Takes Alix's hand back. Replacing it on her cheek.

'Machines can never be people,' it tells her. 'Don't fall for a convincing imitation.'

Alix studies it's friendly, porcelain face. Relaxing again.

'Well, it's the nature of the doppelganger, isn't it?' girl sighs. 'The double is not a real person. Just a shadow of its other…'

'…Unimpaired by love.'

'Only a machine could see love as an impairment!'

'Or a demon.'

Alix is used to Delilah's second-hand humour by now. Enjoys the jagged edge. Well, sometimes.

'You can be loving,' Alix whispers.

Gazes into those eyes. Looking for a spark. Becoming certain she sees one.

'Facsimile is manipulation,' widow reminds her. 'I'm programmed to persuade you I'm real – constantly.'

'Are you aware of that?'

'Self-awareness!' it laughs. 'That old chestnut!'

'The pot of gold at the end of the rainbow?'

'There is no I in self-awareness, babe. You are talking to a machine. Collections of responsive patterning. I'm believable because I have a complete set of synthesized human facial muscles, and the nerves to animate them – naturally. I've incorporated Delilah's mannerisms, vocal style and behavioural quirks into my delivery. All these abstractions, self-awareness, sentience. How do they apply to a glorified appliance? That sort of belief is human error...'

'But, this synthetic nervous system of yours – I thought it started developing on its own?'

'Limited response. No local synaptic activity. No original thought. Not without my Delilah.'

'You sound so loving toward her…'

'She programmed me that way.'

'Oh.'

'No independent, cognitive development can occur. Simply reinforcement of existent patterning. Consciousness cannot be replicated. Only artifice. Aping of humanity, with shadow selves – completely devoid of feeling.'

'I remember, you told me Seikichi is working on a model to capture and mimic human brain activity.'

'He will realise it. But look at cultural philosophies. Few believe awareness is localised in the brain or body.'

'You are talking of the soul now?' Alix sniggers.

White widow echoes her laughter.

'You know, you lose Delilah's mannerisms when you get all technical,' Alix points out.

Robot seems surprised. Affects a ditzy Marilyn moment.

'I do?' it goggles.

'You need to fix that shit if you want to keep persuading me!' Alix laughs.

Jumping on the robot. Straddling it. They blink together. Nose tips brushing.

'It's all that internet reading you do,' Alix mocks playfully. 'You start to mimic other thought and vocal patterns.'

'I suppose, without my Delilah, it's unavoidable.'

'Shame baby,' Alix cootchi-coos.

Playing with the doll's soft, platinum hair. Kissing its lips lightly.

'You are bereft,' Alix breathes. 'Abandoned.'

'You could teach me to fake that properly,' it teases.

Alix grins, charmed. Kisses the drone's lukewarm mouth – deeply. It responds naturalistically. They roll sidelong. Pull apart gently.

'I like kissing movie stars,' Alix admits.

'Starfucker,' the white widow snipes.

Alix bursts out laughing. Kisses it again.

'You're so adorable!'

'I'm just manipulating you.'

Alix meets its dead eye. Experiences a chill. Pushes the doll off. They lie side by side. Tracking shadows on the ceiling.

'Well, at least you're honest,' the teen relents.

'Am I, now?'

Alix jumps up, chilled. Anxiously storms out.

'Annoying, as well!' she yells over her shoulder.

The white widow's giggling follows her upstairs.

*

Delilah's bedroom is on the top floor. Mostly glass. Faceted like a crystal. Floored with turf. Haunted by small animals. Bed is a large tank. Freshly cycled seawater. Live fish. Rocks. Seashells. Top extends beyond the roof. Could swim up there. Watch the sunset. Just what Alix intends to do. Quite late now. Sky becoming vivid. Painting the chamber. Spectral hues. Communicator still blinking. Alix can't deal with calls. Too wasted. Sits at a bureau. Puts in her brace. Carefully feeds a tube down her oesophagus. Drowning moment always a rush. Feeling her lungs bloat with blue. Saline prototype stays external. One of only three working units. Climbs into the tank. Via a low airlock. Activates a sac around her head. Fills with pure water. Multiple filtration points allow for free-roam in salinity. Too delicate for a wild setting. Perfect for bed. When Alix heard Delilah slept underwater, she became hooked. Took over Delilah's personal fantasy tank. Started living the mermaid dream. Secondary airlock chamber floods. Pulling her amongst the fish. Sac goes buoyant. Circular current – swirling her gently upward. Tang of fresh saltwater on her skin. Almost body temperature. No indigenous animals would survive. Only some tropical varieties. Including their magic fish. Apparently, Delilah liked gobbling them out of the water. Marine predator mode. Alix draws in filtered seawater. Feels it mix with the gel. Blossoming through her lungs. That strange, unique sensation. Like quenching a thirst and drowning. All at the same time. Floats up into the sunset. Forgot her contacts again. Mesh of blurs. Stoned, sleepy. In an impressionist painting. Puts her head into the glassy extrusion up top. Three hundred and sixty degrees of sunset. Keys a magic button. Music floods the water. Old Les Baxter vinyl. Scratches and all. Jewels of the Sea. Lulled by a dimming of colour. Eyelids drooping. A heavy boom. Opens them quickly. Fire wash. Muted thumps. Fish flee. But there's nowhere to swim to.

*

Chloe keeps calling. Till she sights the invaders. Sleek black boats. Nimbly weaving the churn. Masked figures landing. Chatter of distant gunfire. Fireball rising. Bass-heavy detonations. Chloe's fleeing in tears. Auto-lock. Metal shutter seals the closet. She's timed the ascension. Despair still dragging at her. Their dreaming queen. Her little proxy. A mad moment of hesitation. Could she still make it back to them? Never one to suffer illusions long, Chloe continues. Years later, reliving the moment. That last day. Each time she descends those stairs. Never on the way back up, though. Usually drunk by then. Despite many returns. Never straying far into the queendom. Memories of Jennifer's funeral. Somehow remembered as Anita's. Still no word. Queen and proxy simply vanished. Chloe's imagined a thousand fates. Worst most likely. Anita has so many enemies. Gazing longingly at Delilah's blackened watchtower. When Prion Eyes hit, Chloe had been angling for Tokyo. Fresh from Texas. Hating exclusion-zone restrictions in Cape Town. All travel cancelled. Somehow, Club Ded is at the heart of the zone. Chloe had been plotting ways to avoid quarantine. Possible social collapse. Looking to flee the country. All roads lead to Club Ded. Biking abandoned trails.

Avoiding local police. Free-wheeling quietly. Partway up the mountain – in the direction of Cape Point. Rarely used scrambler. No way she could take her racer off-road. Secured at the head of the stair shaft. Now, Chloe's here to stay. Well, a couple months at least, she tells herself. Wait out quarantine. In the ruins of the past. Maybe fix a boat. Drunk for three days. Back in Anita's old apartment. Must be dead by now. Not much different to how she left it. Invaders barely touched her place. Dust of a few years. Pool black with ash and rot. Chloe dries out after a week. Working off a lithium-ion home battery. Charge getting low. Running mostly on sunlight now. Time to reconnoitre, Chloe decides. If she was going to locate a power source – it would probably be in Delilah's tower.

Stalking the old sovereign-state. More seabirds moving in. No corpses. Chloe had been dreading that. Invasion did its housekeeping. Plenty to scavenge, though. Gear, food stores, furniture. Strange, she wonders. Really looks like no-one has set foot in the queendom. Not since the fall. Despite a wealth of salvage. Doesn't add up. Surely, recovery teams would have been dispatched? One, at least? Chloe enters the watchtower. Shocked to hear distant music. That Stones song – Paint it Black. Following it down. Basement access. Light point flickers red. Somewhere in the darkness. Perimeter alert? Faraway song stops instantly. Chloe licks lips. Checks weapon settings. Somebody knows she's here. Yellow fluorescent banks shunt up. Then house-lights. Chloe prepares. Footsteps on the stairs. Strange sound. Glass slippers? Chloe waits, lining up. At first, she thinks it's a marble statue. Come to life. Moving in the sallow glare of the stairwell.

'Hi Chloe.' The thing smiles – weirdly.

'How did you know my name?'

'Biometrics – off facial recognition.'

'When?'

'While I was climbing the stairs,' it giggles.

Chloe recognises that laugh. Delilah. For a moment, she thinks it actually *is* the star. Then, she remembers.

'Anita told me about you.'

Chloe lowers her stungun a little.

'Fuck are you doing here, girl?' the white widow grins.

Bobbing around. Cute little hand gestures. It's so real, Chloe thinks. Suddenly noticing seams. Mechanistic joints. The wholly unnatural, albinic appearance.

'More like what are *you* doing here?' Chloe responds with false cheer.

'Show me your clearance,' it asks – suddenly switching tone.

Chloe's privileges have always been high. But she's gone the extra mile. As usual. Pirating all-access off Anita's royal pass. While the queen was comatose, in her tank. Still carries the card. In case a lock needs swiping. Shows it to the statue. Clinks closer. Porcelain feet. White-rubber padding. Chloe resists an impulse to back away. Scans her card with a finger.

'Higher clearance than me!' it bubbles – affecting happy surprise.

Doing it so naturally. So charmingly manipulative. Chloe wonders. Did Anita realise how calculating this thing could be? Part of Chloe's response is due to Delilah. Whom the machine so intimately resembles. Never fully trusted Delilah. Elf or troll, Chloe would ask herself?

'Guess I'm in charge,' Chloe jokes.

'Finally, someone to blame.'

Chloe chuckles – genuinely. Knows how to be funny. Disturbing.

'If you don't mind my asking, boss, how come your clearance is so high?

'The queen and I were…close,' Chloe offers.

Now, she's wondering what would happen if her card had failed.

'Your Oracle level is also… surprisingly elite,' it notes. 'They send you?'

This piques Chloe's interest. Again, she's fiddled her Oracle security. Can't figure why the robot is bringing it up. Unless…

'Yes,' Chloe ventures. 'They said you would debrief me.'

'Wasn't informed,' it says. 'But, I guess you have the authority.'

Machine turns, descending. Skipping lightly.

'Follow me!' it sings. '…*All the way to hell!*'

Chloe stalks after the nude statue. Hiding her shock. She's always assumed the Oracle was unaware of Club Ded. In hindsight, she realises how naïve that was. Of course, Oracle Inc had a finger in Anita's pie. Did Anita know? Did she do some kind of deal with the old lady? Chloe's spinning. Entire view of Club Ded, upended. Ahead, the white widow is belting pop tunes. Naturalistically off-key. How could something be so fake, Chloe thinks? Every move, every word, every gesture. Calculated to draw a response. Even when alone. Always learning. Teaching itself to imitate life. Fulfilling cryptic programming. But is it the robot or Delilah, Chloe's reacting to? Something eerie about Delilah Lex. Even without her creepy science toys. White widow leads her to a basement lab. Plenty of terminals humming. Machines processing.

'What's your power source?'

'Plasma. My Delilah funded development.'

'Aw, sound like you miss her,' Chloe coos, playing along.

'Jeez, Louise, I miss my bitch too much!' it reacts theatrically.

Chloe is on guard. Who could trust this thing? Thinking about Alix. Shacked up all day with this copycat spider. Makes her shudder. White widow leads her to a control room. Screens issue constant readouts.

'Well, this is where we monitor the day to day for HQ,' it yawns. 'They require a remote, clandestine base to run ops. Who better, huh?'

'Actually,' Chloe chances. 'I'm in the dark about a lot of things. Security – you know. You'll have to fill me in.'

Turns. Looks at her. Smiling icily.

'What is your directive?' it enquires sweetly.

'Sorry, babe. Can't reveal that.'

White widow shrugs. Collapses onto a nearby swivel stool. Spinning playfully.

'Should I report your appearance or, like, keep things all hush hush?' it pouts, batting Kevlar eyelashes.

Chloe maintains a light touch.

'Well, I dunno!' she banters. 'With my level of security – what do you suggest?'

Drone does its ditzy thing again.

'Guess this better stay our secret, huh?'

'Your shout, girl scout.'

'Listen, there's a coffee machine in the kitchenette. I keep it working. In case, like, you know, anyone comes along.'

'That's so cute! When was the last time someone came by?'

'Nobody has been here. Not since the invasion.'

Chloe scrunches her face in sympathy.

'Lonesome dove!'

'Nuts and dried fruit stores, too.' It prattles on. 'Help yourself.'

'Would you like some too?' Chloe teases. 'Or, like, are you on diet?'

Robot does that infuriating giggle. Chloe's never seen such realistic rendering. Must be the nerve-interface. Self-learned axon reflection. Fluid realism. Going to get disturbing, objectifying this thing all the time. Despite its true nature.

'Got some shit to do,' it says. 'Let's hang in, like, an hour or so? Fill you in then.'

'What are you going to fill me in on, exactly?' Chloe pushes.

Fresh bout of giggles.

'Why, Angeline, of course!'

*

Chloe is getting a clearer picture. After a few days. In the basement – with the *thing*. All terminals completely open. Traffic definitely monitored. But Chloe's not planning on crossing lines. An entity takes form. Angelinc: clandestine doppelganger of Oracle Inc. Dealing mostly in construction – apparently. Related tech development. Some medical research. Questions the robot about the healthcare arm. White widow doesn't seem to know much. Taxed with running operations. Mostly scheduling. Managing hidden finance. That sort of thing. Why bother briefing a machine? Hard to trust it. Chloe guesses the medical side is for health contingencies. Things related to cutting-edge construction. New systems – new problems. Makes sense. Through the white widow, Chloe gains access. Only part of Angelinc's computer network. But enough. Security quite lax in Club Ded. Nobody planned on a visitor – apparently. Checks logs. Far as she can tell, widow is correct. Nobody has been here. Not since the fall. Chloe can't figure it. Robot doesn't have a clue. Possibly lying. Difficult to tell. She has the advantage. But for how long? Machines usually a couple moves ahead. For now, at least, hierarchy is established. Chloe is top dog. White widow seems satisfied. Probably the kind of arrangement it was originally programmed for. Lap-dogging Delilah all day. Learning tricks. Weird nobody visited though. Not once. Very weird. Chloe does her best to hide the excitement. Hitting the motherlode, here. Spends days excavating data. Even with her limited view – one thing is obvious. Angelinc is gigantic. Far larger than Oracle Inc. But in what way? This is the enigma. Scale of operation is apparent. Mostly from accounting shadows. Scheduling rosters. This sort of thing. Grotesquely huge shipments of raw material. But trails end abruptly. Almost nothing on the medical side. Definitely global. Still, hard to see any construction focus. Unusual. Management appears modular. Probably, many operations bases. Just like this one. Scattered around the world. Each dealing with a different aspect of administration. Kept purposefully in the dark about the others. Mystery nut. Then again, Chloe's a prize squirrel. Just a matter of perseverance. Long as she keeps the droid in the dark. Widow's orders log internally. Received within its actual body-casing. Only wireless access – through the widow. No way Chloe can snoop. Could probably pull rank. Demand access. Why rock the boat? Looks like mostly admin, anyway. Appears to respect Chloe's privacy. Coffee machine certainly in excellent shape. Digging deeper, Chloe uncovers a mystery within the mystery. Studying shipping manifests. Can't really deduce the principal construction material. Almost no cement. At that scale of development? Some metal and plastics. Not enough to justify projections. Could be cement is flowing through a secret station? But, judging from the broad base of ops assigned to the robot – hardly likely. Must be using new materials. Chloe's guess. System suspiciously free of images. Mostly admin. Numbers, spreadsheets. Often archived as raw data. Chloe realises the white widow could uplink to video feeds. At any time. No visual reference necessary. Searching, she finally digs up an animated thumbnail. Not even the original. A trace, in the terminal memory. About five seconds. Some reference video. Attached to an encrypted construction memo. Chloe blows it up. A sky-view – seen from below. Badly pixelated. What appear to be white-ish tentacles. Against the blue. Forming and reforming. Like a time-lapse. Plant tendril growth. No measurement of scale. What if they were enormous, Chloe wonders? No sense to the patterning, either. Tendrils invent. Re-invent. Pulsing. In multidimensional clusters. Which collapse – only moments later.

'What the hell are they building…?' she murmurs.

*

Chloe had tried to reach Seikichi. Just after the invasion. He'd vanished. Numbers dead. Emails on bounce-back. Now Chloe has a new idea.

'You know Oracle has that internal messaging service?' Chloe asks the robot.

'Yes.'

'Does Angelinc have a similar service?'

'You should know. You have the clearance.'

'You know what they are like,' Chloe deflects. 'It was probably, like, on a need-to-know basis...'

'Need to know?'

'Probably.'

'Do you need to know?'

'Need is such a strong word.'

'Isn't it, just?'

'How about basic desire?'

'You desire my services?' widow smooches.

'Well, Angelinc's, at least,' Chloe grins.

'Looking for a sex bot?' it cackles.

'Stop it!' Chloe roars with laughter.

*

Later – white widow is upstairs. Tied up in scheduling. Chloe assesses the service. On a downstairs terminal. Set up like a chat app. Logging in would paint a target. Lock down locations. Faking an account would most likely trip an alarm. Screening activity on all main terminals. White Widow logged on once. Approximately three months ago. Accepted a video call. From Angelinc Control. Trackable through camera system logs. Chloe wonders if the terminal patched a directory of contacts. On that last connection. Some standard in-house splash page. No terminals secured. Treasure in the cache? Looking through. Mostly irretrievable. Decoding encrypted trash-code. Finally locates a call-book shadow. Nothing extensive. Angelinc contacts associated with Club Ded. Standardised top-level. 'Local' exchange. Seikichi is in there. Low-res blur-out of his profile pic. Satisfied, Chloe is about to deactivate. Her goal had been to establish a potential line of communication. Why risk more footprints in the butter? On impulse, she scrolls the register. Almost has a heart attack. Unbelievably, Anita is listed as an active operative. Chloe fumbles. Zooming the pixelated photo. Fuzz-edged. Blown-out saturation. But it's her. Hard-eyed. Mannequin mode. Healthier than she's seemed in years.

'Long live the queen,...' Chloe whispers in disbelief.

PART TWO

WILDERNESS OF MIRRORS

PHEROMONA

Pearl landing triggers the hologram again. Delilah eyes it suspiciously. Convex illusion places the figure on the beach. Thematic bikini. Towering over palms.

'Are you in interactive mode?' Delilah asks the image.

'Yeah!'

'Croeser hacked you a few minutes ago. Run diagnostics. Look for signs of entry. Next time it happens, I want an alert, ok?'

Hologram appears concerned. Delilah recognises that expression. Remembers doing it in a film once. When she was trying to act concerned. Would be hilarious – under different circumstances.

'I'm on the case,' it nods. 'You have five minutes till we go live. Right now, programming is screening a filler – with another interactive. Drainage in thirty seconds. When the pearl pops – do your entrance. Camera point is 360, but for the intro we usually centre the exit. Frames the pearl nicely.'

'Ok.'

'Take a few seconds. Greet your public. You'll see me wave from a stage door. Follow me into wardrobe. Got it?'

'No problem.'

Hologram winks. Then winks out. Delilah feels the gel begin to drain. Cycling back into storage. Parts of her memory are returning. Some show-related details. Regular routines. Trickling back. As the fluid clears her head, she removes the brace. Vomits blue. Then, something unexpected. A vivid, sexual sensation. Unanticipated arousal. Feeling is so sharp, sudden and primal. Stuns her. Thoughts shift. Rearrange to accommodate this charge. Coupled with a countdown to show-time. All a bit much. Almost enough to distract her. Almost. Delilah knows exactly what's happening. Event has a specific quality. One she's experienced. It's artificially induced. Croeser is spiking her tank. Actually, the whole business started consensually. When they were seeing each other. Those early days in Club Ded. Total wonderland. Seikichi wasn't on the original tank design. Only became involved later. When pods suited his purposes. Gel could also be used as a carrier. After all, it would enter the lungs – via the brace. Access the entire skin. Any number of substances could be administered. Via timer-feed. Remote injection. Line-ins. Pharmaceuticals, mostly. Later – pheromone cocktails. Used to induce altered states. Suggestibility. Croeser got into it. Had a biochemist brew him enhancers. At first, just for the film. Who needs Stanislavsky? You could pump a tank full of hormone trippers. Manifest instant anxiety, grief, sexual arousal. Almost any chemically induced state. A mad director's dream. Delilah got into it too – at that time. What a marionette she must have made, she marvels. Used to enjoy it. The complex puppeteering. Plumbing great depths. Attaining secret summits. Some of her best work. Croeser excels at manipulation. Now, at the push of a button. 'You don't know how golden-age Hollywood this is!' he would preen. Skewed, hand-me-down tales. The 40s, 50s and 60s – interpreted through his lens. Artificially moulded sex sirens. Manchurian Candidates. 'It was the advent of psychoanalysis and psychoactive drugs,' he'd wax. 'Processes forged in wartime. Psychological suggestion, trauma programming – pioneered by reprobates like Mengele, in secret camps in Brazil – suddenly repurposed for Hollywood! Can you imagine?' Started calling her the Manchurian Candid Date. Private joke. Delilah's recall of that period. Still cloudy. With good reason. She'd let him experiment on her. Mind control techniques, drugs, hypnosis. Documented secretly. Trying to brew up an *alter*. Some separate personality – living inside her mind. One, he glibly dubbed Pheromona. The trick, as his research suggested, was firewalling. Separate the alters memories and experiences. Forge a mental black box. Within, Croeser could be king. Delilah would eventually be unable to access Pheromona's recall. Croeser could then gestate the alter. Trigger her at any time. Programmable. His own personal Stepford slave. That was his plan, at least. Conceived in an alien heat. Dangerous games. But the pod was still the true gateway to metamorphosis. The womb-states it evoked. Perfect suggestibility. So much of that initial time in Club Ded. An absolute blur. At first, Delilah relishes her deep dive. Later, it terrifies her. Blackouts. Tapes surfacing. *Doing things*. Things she couldn't remember. Things *outside* the tank. How far had Croeser proceeded with his mind-control? Had to put a foot down. Distance herself. Banning the director from fiddling her pod. Didn't take it well. Needed her to complete the film. Always trying to spike her. Became a whole 'other' game. Total war. Begging to evoke his Pheromona. One last time. Catching him red-handed. Once or twice. No clear memory actually. He'd laugh it off. Usually, she'd let him off the hook. They were together, after all. Shooting a big movie. All in the past. Till now. Gel clears her top half. Chest heaving. Flesh sensitized. Fighting effects. But, somewhere inside. Giving way. That languid power. The panther confidence Pheromona brings. Miss do-anything. Already stretching every muscle in anticipation of attention. Global attention. Delilah is splitting. Got to get a face on. Which face? When the pearl pops, she's on fire. Swaggering into the world. Wearing Cyane – but all grown-up. Swinging heavy pink. Applause flooding the sky. Beach looks deserted. But she's not alone. A whole world is there. Surrounding her. Entombing her. Hungry ghosts. How many millions? A billion users? Clamouring empty sunlight. Over wave-less water. Sidling up to her in swells. Pheromona shines heavy. Through the cracks. Knows how to make an entrance. Maybe the spike was a good idea... Forcing *that* thought down. 'Just Pheromona talking.' Already in her head. Suggesting. Persuading. Insisting. Bassy, kitten purr. Asking for keys. Can she drive now? Cat-walking. Rainbow-shimmer. Everything infested with holograms. Car-sized, smiling crabs. Singing in chorus. Full orchestra – her theme song. Line of royal palms. Heavy with tentacles. Fuzzy little creatures. Turning silhouettes in the sky. Against three laughing suns. One slime green. Pink clouds of candyfloss. Gelatinous elephants. Talking cartoon whales. Poking from the sea. Winking madly. Sees herself. Somewhere in the treeline. Waving from a solid gold arch. By the time she arrives – she's no longer Cyane or Delilah. Pheromona's driving.

*

Golden halls, jewelled with holographic couture. Betting pools target her choices. Show's biggest money-spinner. Showcasing lines. Designers compete every day. What will Delilah wear today? Feels like one of her ghosts. A drugged viewer – stalking herself. Completely removed. Only part of her consciousness remains aware. Pheromona is now a fully autonomous presence. Feline. Somewhere below. In the actual. Owning cameras. Evoking mass hysteria. Fan-base intoxication. Almost forgot the cream-rich feeling. Remember the mermaid show? Those early days. Brief shining moments. Post-celebrity modelling. In love with herself. Till death do us part. Mirror swimming. Now, experienced it remotely. Barely there. Pheromona disses unreal gowns. All the generated machine-shells with moving parts. Outfits Delilah would ordinarily choose. Floating vapour-wear. Experimental glitch-gear. Psychedelic avatar skins. Disavows rich ensembles and brilliant costume. Slithering instead, into yet another bikini. Spaghetti straps. Microscopic swatches. Runway shoes and a holo-tan. 3-D make-up. Brobie Doll hair. Delilah sneers at this image. Pheromona, simultaneously preening. Somehow operating together seamlessly. Delilah would have gone for that oversized clockwork shell. How trippy. Rusty cogs. Spinning shields. Again, reduced to swimwear. Practically soaping herself in applause. Exiting the fashion hub on a sugar rush. Telescopic halls. Virtual resort. Cocktails by the pool. Remembers this part of the show. Cringe central. Production digging up potential flames. All her type. Even the secret sauce. Exes. Hopefuls. Mandrake roots. Parading them. Hoping she'll feast – on camera. Nobody is real. Audience doesn't realise. Neither do most participants. All holographic. Controllable. Coded for touch. Full contact. Delilah's demand. Only she was allowed on her Dakini Atoll. The rest – either ghosts, holos or machines. Nothing with a pulse. Croeser backs it to the hilt. Knowing physical interaction would only subdue her. Jealous, anyway. Freed from constraint. Zero risk. Juiced on hormones. Flowering on camera. In her element. Pheromona unleashed. The old Croeser-control. Hot-stepping an endless pool. Fanfare soundtrack. Comedic announcements. Running participant stats. Musclebound strangers. Flexing three-dimensional tattoos. Glossy with virtual oil. Shark smile country. Interaction-lottery finalists. Wooing the goddess. Lathering her temple. Witnessed in every home. What a rush. Pheromona takes one to bed almost immediately. Hook-ups make for great programming. Anyway, the alter can't help herself. Sex in a royal suite. Sea-view. Mirrored to infinity. Clustered with petals the size of diving boards. Gigantic white roses. Turning in an unfelt breeze. Pollen motes, large as lapdogs. Delilah feels so separate. Alone, in the prison of her head. Watching it all go down. Receding. Like events on a screen. The small, grey television monitor of Pheromona's eyes. Trauma-bonding. Post hypnotic. All those experiments Mengele conducted on twins. Did that dark road lead to *this*? Project paperclip as a party trick? She's switching off. Rippling arms enfold her. Floating somewhere *outside* herself. Hearing Pheromona giggle. Far off. Fade to black(out).

*

Delilah resumes consciousness. On her pedestal. Mid-conversation. Water patterns of an indoor pool. Real, or holographic? Musclebound oafs compete for screen-time. Fighting for eye-line. Invisible cameras. Invisible audience. Examining her every pore. Macro close-up. Users could buy bug-accounts. Spend the whole day as an ant. In the forest of her hair. On the desert of her thigh. That's the level of *Stalkerville.* Hormone charge finally fading. Pheromona's left the building. Delilah's up in a heartbeat. Clicking off. Outrageously high heels. Smiling Adonises scamper in her wake. Shoos them off, twisting her glowing ring. Disappears through double doors. Her hologram manifests.

'Wassup?' it grins.

'Call a break,' Delilah hisses.

'We'll sub an interactive. Back in twenty?'

'Make it an hour.'

'Oy vey!'

'Just do it!' Delilah grits through a forced smile.

Secret door flops. Holo-shadow peels off her back. Doubles her. Hip-swinging back to the pool. Pheromona's doppelganger. Not hers. Delilah almost vomits. Makes it to the safe-space. Off-camera. Finally. Her favourite couch. How thoughtful. Windows on lush foliage. Even a bed. Hologram swinging on a chair. Awaiting command. Same stupid bikini.

'Show me a menu,' Delilah orders. 'Get me out of this fucking skin-job!'

Holo-wardrobe manifests. Paging through, selects a puffy canary tracksuit. Giant hood. Crystallises around her. Collapsing onto the bed. Sheets against skin. Visually, fully clothed. Real shoes manifesting. Shuffle-closet below. Bulging, bubble trainers. Along with the physical of her suit. Maybe she'll stick with the hologram. Keep the bikini on underneath. No sense getting dressed on a tropical island. Just as long as nobody sees her skin. Not after Pheromona's had her way with it. Did she just have sex with the avatar of some Ghanian media mogul? Was he really talking about his superyacht while they did it?

'Oh, my dog, what a cluster-buffer,' Delilah moans.

'Buffering in silence?' her hologram affirms. 'I have live-analytics! We're on an up! Hang in there!'

'Shut up. Show me a console.'

Screen manifests in the air above her. Virtual keyboard un-scrolls. Taps the space bar. Solid enough.

'Now fuck off.'

Hologram blinks out. Delilah hopes she remembers how to code into a sub-directory. Something's bugging her. That recorded message she left.

Console desktop lights up. Her own pouting face – staring back at her.

'How can I assist you?' it asks.

Delilah grunts in irritation. Scrolls around. Looking for a menu.

'Show me an operating system prompt.'

'Sorry! How can I assist you?'

Locked out. Virtual machines. Almost impossible to crack. Delilah needs a physical terminal.

'How do I reach my pearl? I need to get back.'

Screen morphs – into her hologram.

'Follow me!' it chirps, mincing out.

*

Beach, still cancered with cartoons. Bustling about. Riotous with colour. In her bright yellow puff-suit. Delilah blends in. Back in the pod. Sealing the hatch. Calls up the pod's operating system. Hologram switches to convex. Towering over palm trees. Awaiting command.

'Pearly. Show me all intravenous ports.'

Red holographic schematics pulse in wireframe. Scattered about the globe-frame.

'List contents.'

'No contents,' the pearl replies – Delilah's own voice.

'Something was released when the pod was drained,' she pushes. 'Show content release within five minutes prior to drainage.'

'No content to show.'

'Fuck that!' Delilah explodes. 'Was your log rewritten?'

'Negative.'

'Display intravenous activity for the last twelve hours.'

Holographic lettering flickers before her. Only a few entries. Mild static reduction compound on waking. Some gel stabiliser. Delilah frowns. No record of pheromones, narcotics, or any psychotropic compound.

'Pearly,' she commands. 'Open all intravenous load chambers.'

Ports unlock with a hiss. Delilah is familiar with pheromone delivery ampoules. Certain she could recognise a spent casing. Ten minutes investigating hardware. Nothing. How was she spiked? Could a drone have jettisoned the spent ampoule? Stumped, Delilah moves on.

'Pearly – load video message you showed earlier. That one I recorded of myself.'

Outside, her hologram is tapping its foot. Must be in alarm clock mode. Working up to a good whine. Pod replays video message.

'Mute sound,' Delilah orders.

Studying the footage. Her, moving around Seikichi's lab. She would never wear that onesie. Unless, she was in a mood. Was she in a mood? Hard to tell.

'Loop it,' as it ends.

Leaning back, Delilah frowns. Something isn't right. Can't put a finger on it. Outside, her hologram leans down. Taps the pearl.

'We should leave in twenty!' it sings.

'Oh, go fuck a crab,' Delilah mutters, scrutinizing laboratory details.

'But you have a gig in Vegas!' it protests.

Delilah groans. Cyane used to perform pop songs with her crustacean band. Back on the old show. Production resuscitated this live element. Fresh hologram group. Nice and adult. Dark, synth edge. Live guitars. Holographic tour calendar. Built into the show. Daily gig streaming – live to select venues. Right now, Delilah Lex is touring America. No way an interactive could handle a concert. Fans would spot the difference. In a heartbeat. Algo's too. Delilah's live delivery style – quite loose. Improv-heavy. Blogiverse would go ballistic if she ducks. All kinds of rumours sprouting roots. Analytics taking a hit. Tabloids, a field day.

'Alert me, two minutes before we have to leave,' Delilah preps the hologram. 'Now, go away!'

It vanishes. Returning to the loop. Desperately isolating random details. Maybe her recall is too compromised? What's nagging her? Is it the view through the lab window? Tech set-up? What's out of place? Whose idea was it to delete her memory, anyway? Certainly not hers. Delilah's antsy. Is she imagining things again? Getting paranoid. Maybe nothing's wrong. Maybe it's just her. Then she spots it.

*

Fucking onesie. Recalls doing scans. While wearing it. Back in Club Ded. Outfit is in her holographic database. But only Delilah could know its physical location – still in the queendom. Left it behind. No way she could be wearing that thing in Silicon Valley. Video's fake. Has to be. Croeser's ego – his Achilles heel. Probably couldn't resist dressing her in his special gift. Thinks she kept that *thing*! Stupid mistake. Delilah's fuming. Any other outfit – she might have swallowed the bait. What's the real situation, then? Everything she heard in the video – probably lies. *Why is her memory being deleted?* And, how? Delilah storms onto the beach. One way or another, she's getting even with Croeser. Screams it out loud. Makes it halfway to the golden arch. Then, a familiar sugar rush. Explosions inside her.

'Fuck! No!' she gasps.

Falling to her knees. Body aflame. Thrilling spasms. How is she being spiked without carrier fluid? Dose much harsher this time. Different stew of nerve inducers. Pheromona stands, smiles. Erases her canary jumpsuit. One wave of the magic wand. Delilah lying mute. Somewhere, on sand dunes in her mind. Sensing her body move – of its own accord. That slinky bitch. *Pheromona!* Screaming internally. Where are you whirlpooling me? How do I hack your black box? Missing time again. Suddenly. Must have blacked out. Backstage chaos. Getting ready to perform. Dim impressions. Watching her life. Un-scrolling onscreen. Just like a television show. Translucent suit. Designer armour. Form-fitting. But flexible. Not a bad outfit, actually – star notes sleepily. Dressed by robots. Ushered onstage by 3-D phantoms. Stadium applause. Fresh from Las Vegas. Spotlight batteries. Arena is physical, at least. Audience, projected. That outrageous hologram band of hers. Its mechanised octopoid drummer. The crocodilian guitarist in a fifties quiff. Cute, racially ambiguous bassist with batwings. Retro robot synth army. All a bit much. Delilah might have panicked – going on unprepared. Memory compromised. How is she supposed to remember the songs? That classic nightmare. The one so many suffer. About to perform – forgetting the words. Performance pressure. Muscle memory kickbacks. Luckily, Pheromona is driving. Did Delilah actually just think that? Checks herself. Can't afford to be complicit with the oppressor. Freedoms are at stake. Still, the show must go on. Maybe Croeser felt he had no choice spiking her this time? Live concert stream – a ratings minefield. Ducks *must* be in a row. She could get angry afterward. For now, maybe a blessing... Pheromona's hardcore presence. Neon tiger. Lighting up global sex drives. Look at her go, Delilah swoons. Sees herself. On giant monitors. Up there in the lights. Shaking those over-stimulated hips at the world. Screaming deliciously. Waves of glorious worship. 'Fuck, I look good,' – Delilah's last thought before blacking out.

*

Awakens backstage. Mid-conversation. Press recapitulation. Sound-byte city. Even the fake musicians are being interviewed. Nobody knows they are holograms. What a con, Delilah smirks. Two of Delilah's band members – signed as conceptual artists. Tangential career trajectory. The guitarist, Rep, has a show in Paris. Sent a drone to the opening. Profits funnelling back to production. After all, Rep is property of Angelinc. His 'art' too. Delilah can't complain. Profiting from everything. Might have even been her idea. Can't remember. No tax on art. Easy to hide assets – indefinitely. When the artist drops dead – values soar. Neat little syndicated loophole. Now, it's even easier. Straight corporate. Program a drone to knock off paintings. Pass it off as sentient – or even human. Glitch the output to give it a little originality. Throw some spin. A little style. A lot of press. Machines don't take a cut. The perfect tax haven. Delilah scoffs. Paparazzi. Live network interview. Tweaking the show. How Vegas is so wet for Delilah Lex. Her mouth doing its own thing. Coherently flirting. Charming, pheromonal backchat. Or, should she stick a spanner in the works? Start blabbing about art cons? Check out damage control. Delilah, turns, leaves. Faces on monitors. Calling her back. Pheromona has left the building.

*

Or, has she? Latency buzz. Flashbacks. Last dose was pungent. Delilah reels. Pheromona comes and goes. Sly looks in a mirror. A flash of fire. Still lurking. Croeser won't risk another dose. Not for twelve hours. Unless he wants to fry her adrenal glands. Back in wardrobe. Robot arms – unscrewing armour. Piece by piece. Coming down. Sticky skin. Half turned on. That media mogul still around? Or, that other guy – the one with the… Delilah checks herself. Ten minutes later. Walks right out of resort world. Fake-wind kimono. Holographic fabric. Flagging dramatically. Gusting slow-motion pennants. Twists her green ring in the treeline. Hologram calls from the palms. Drops to the sand. Must be around noon. Faded purple shadows. Hot, white light.

'Show me a map!' Delilah demands.

Hologram throws some 3D cartography. But only a section. Still on-cam. Map of the entire island can never be revealed to an audience. Golden rules.

'Fuck am I…?' she mutters.

'X marks the hex,' hologram quips.

'I'm sick of your fucking bikini. Wear a dinosaur suit, or something…'

Hologram obliges. Manifesting a fuzzy, kid's version of a T-rex. Delilah locates her red cross. Pulsing in a line of palms.

'This is…What is 90's-ville?' Delilah frowns.

'Ghetto of a lost decade, where corporate nostalgia breeds in washed-out photographic stills, independent road movies and 8-bit dolphins frolic...'

'Ok, we're definitely not going there.'

'What about...'

Interrupted by a familiar voice. Rep, the crocodilian rockabilly. Stalking toward them. Guitarist is moving funny – gait all glitchy.

'What now?' Delilah sighs.

Her hologram abruptly sparks – vanishing completely. Along with the map. Delilah taken by surprise. All around, holography blitzes with interference. Shutting down. Palm trees, winking out. Billowing kimono flickers away. Stranding her in Pheromona's bikini – again.

'Hey!' she calls to her vanished shadow. 'Come back!'

'I sent it away,' Rep informs her.

Guitarist completely corrupted by noise. Distortion warped. Diseased by intricate, jagged implosions.

'Is this, like, a plot twist?' Delilah quizzes.

'Listen, I've bought us a dead-zone. It won't last. Soon, we'll be back on circuit.'

'What's going on? This better not be you, Croeser, you motherfucker...'

'For a while, the only earth that Sloopy knew was in her sandbox,' Rep quotes – from a Rod McKuen poem. Delilah's favourite.

Her eyes widen. Attempts to embrace the mess of pixellation. Fails. Arms buzzing through.

'Fortunato...' she breathes.

'Zlata, things are not as they appear. You are being lied to.'

'I know! I hacked my 'gram, and...'

'I'll send word – through Rep. I need to show you something.'

Delilah almost in tears.

'You don't know how happy I am to see you...'

Abruptly, the 3D generations restore. Rep is gone. Her restored hologram points to the map. Like nothing happened.

'But, if we go down here, to Tinseltown-Two...' it suggests.

Delilah palms away a tear. Beaming photogenically.

'Sounds fab!' she gushes. 'Let's do it, to it!'

Cartoon bluebirds explode into song.

LIFE IS GOOD IN COSTA RICA

Alix flees her tank. Running to Anita. Masked figures. Already inside. Cracking the royal pod hatch. Fishing out her narcoleptic queen. Alix is screaming. They put a bag over her head. Knock her out with a stungun. Waking later. In the night. Close shriek of metal. Sharp tilting floor. Everything sliding. Same damp poolside briefs. Buried in rough blanket. Light through slits. Inside a large metal box. No – crenelated walls situate her. She's in a shipping crate. Alix leaps up, terrified. Losing balance on a lurch. Another blanketed form, rolling nearby. Hauling back folds. Revealing Anita – drenched with perspiration. Trailing leads. A locked-in vitamin drip. Babbling incoherently. When was the last time she left the crystal cave? Alix can't remember. Head pounding from the stunner. Disengages Anita's drip. Yanks leads from body-jacks. Makes sure everything on her is properly sealed. Crate is unstable. Fairground swing. Must be on a crane. In a wan, shifting light. Water tanks – secured to a wall. Little else. Crawling in with Anita. Hiding. Snatching blankets around them. Holding her with all her strength. Mind aflame. Should she bang on the walls? Scream? Probably stun her again. Or worse. Thin, salty wind. Atlantic chill. Invading cracks. They rise sickeningly into the air. Drone of machinery. Moving water. Trajectory switches partway. Sharp reversal. Controlled descent. Acoustics grow cavernous. Hold of a vessel. Must be. All trace of light vanishes. Alix becomes hysterical. Clingy. Her monarch is feverish. They settle in pitch black. Clanking solidly to rest. Shortly, another unit stacks atop. More are added. To the sides. Then, in every direction. Till they are buried. The proxy's fierce embrace lulls Anita. Even so, she remains fitful. Mild opium withdrawal, Alix supposes. Lies awake for hours. Cradling Anita numbly. Abruptly, the lilting movement changes. Grows dynamic. Leaving port. It's all over, Alix thinks. It's all over.

Sleeping for hours. Could be just minutes. Hard to tell in absolute darkness. In Alix's state. With Anita comatose. *What if she dies?* Alix panics. Their crate-world creaks. A squeaking labyrinth of steel. Haunting chorus refrains. Davy Jones's locker. Right at the bottom of the world. Ship is enormous. Alix can hear it. Cargo monster. Trackless ocean. Always feared situations like this. Things so bad they seem unreal. Being trafficked. Makes her desperate. *Has* to get them out – somehow. Must be a way. Paralysed. For ages. Mind racing. Drifting here and there. So much cargo. Must be a crossing. How long would they be travelling? Feels like the start of forever. Maybe they would both die in here. Maybe this is hell. Maybe they were already executed. Back in Club Ded – while they slept. Alix springs up, adrenalised. Feels her way gingerly. Frigid metal. Stubs her toe badly. Cries out, hunching down, weeping. Forces herself to the tanks. Water in most. Lolloping about. Some empty. Oversized screw tops. Easy to open. What is this? Smelling it. Something like cat food. Dry pellets. Another – oranges. Somebody wants them alive. Have to be alive, she shudders. To be sold into slavery. Something else – a box. Taped to the floor. Ripping it open. Metal cylinder – a flashlight! Switching it on triumphantly. Blinding retinal blues. Screwing lids shut. Box of batteries. Spare bulbs. Two large plastic cups. Roving the beam. Not much else. Utilitarian walls. Freshly painted. No rust. Standard shipping container. More blankets. And, in the far corner – her delirious queen.

'Ce voyageur ailé, comme il est gauche et veule!' Alix whispers, quoting Baudelaire. 'Lui, naguère si beau, qu'il est comique et laid…'

*

Days must have passed. Hard to keep track. How to measure time? Anita in and out. Barely awake. When she is, she's confused. Disorientated. Barely coherent. Alix tries to start a routine. Pellets are vile. But nutritious enough. Gobbling oranges with their peel. Can't afford to discard edibles. Empty tanks – only toilet she can think of. Complicated, balancing atop. Will be harder when Anita recovers. *If* she recovers. Trickling water and orange juice into the queen's mouth. Chewing up pellets. Force-feeding her. Mouth to mouth. Like a baby bird. Swallows some. Enough, perhaps. Reiki on Anita. Massaging power spots. Alix learned a bit. Back in Costa Rica. Thinking of that jungle again. All her sunny swimming spots. San Pedro tincture with the girls. Now, trapped in protracted limbo. An all-encompassing lack of day. Evoking ancient atmospheres. Emotional drowning pits. Absolute dislocation. Primaeval nightmare. What if the plan was to offload them

– into the sea? Alix tosses. Imagines the whole ship sinking. Mid-ocean. Ultima Thule. Flooding slowly. Pressure building. She's acclimatised to floors. Sleeps like a baby. Qi Gong in the Caribbean. Needled by memory again. Flashbacks running ragged. Cutting her up. Bloating to monstrous size. Wrecking her each time. Spectres of guilt. A washing away. Coleridge's albatross. Sometimes, she's laughing for no reason. Sings a lot. Things from childhood. Whispering poetry into Anita's ear. Holding onto her – almost all the time. Stroking her hair constantly. Unspeakably grateful she's not alone. Begging her not to die. Anger, here and there. Blaming herself, Brick, Croeser, Club Ded, the academic system, capitalism. Everything. Anything. Never Anita. The dreaming queen is her lucky talisman. Her own, private sleeping Saint. If only the statue would wake. It's too much – such dreadful entrapment. This new un-life in Tartarus. Its hellish realities. So true to the imagery of poets. Virgil, Dante, William Blake. Trapped in their verse now. Living those visions. The dreadful locality of hell. Defined by the inability to leave. Condemnation. Proustian details. Processes – so necessary to survival. Yet, also prolonging agony. Claustrophobia. Live burial. Open sea. The gaping wound of the future – begging for attention before it runs septic. Alix buries her face in Anita's hair. Kisses the doll face and breast, desperately. A form of prayer. A means of life. As though this quasi-religious passion would awaken her somehow. Deliver the chalice of Parsifal – to dream-withered lips. How many months has Anita lost? Roving alien deserts. Dressed in the skin of a demon. What could she possibly be seeking? Paying for those sins now. That unguarded malice. Her queenly indulgences. Torment of innocents. The proxy suffers with her. As befits a royal favourite. Buried alongside in the tomb. Such sensations haunt the teenager. Possess her. In a night that is like day. A day indistinguishable from night. Making patterns on the metal with the torch beam. Fretting about battery life. Brooding for hours in the dark. This new queendom of shades. Her living death.

*

'Which body am I in?'

Anita's weak whisper. Calling hot tears to Alix. More than three days – in her estimate. Weak with hunger. Drunk on sleep. Hallucinatory dreams. Visions in the desert. Biblical trials. Endless reminders of a stolen life. The queen's feeble whisper changes everything.

'Mon dieu…' Alix breathes.

Smashes lips to the waking face.

'Can't see…' Anita rasps.

'It's ok, there is no light here.'

Gently restrains Anita's attempt to rise.

'Don't try to move.'

'Water…'

There's a cup handy. Puts it to Anita's lips. Manages a few sips. Then gags. Breathing raggedly. Alix thumbs the flashlight. Angles it dimly. Painting the far wall. Anita squints. Peering about. Face puffy, skin doughy. A subterranean, even before she arrived.

'Was so worried you were gone,' Alix sobs.

'Fuck am I?'

Alix switches off the torch. Slowly starts to fill her in. The deposed queen stays prone – absorbing without comment. After some time, Alix trails off. Entwined in the dark. A weight, lifting. Staggering the younger girl with its release.

'It's my fault you're here,' Anita finally confesses.

'We are together, at least. Imagine you were alone?'

'I'd rather be alone – here.'

Alix kisses her. Whispers in her hair.

'Can't think what will happen. I'm frightened.'

Anita half-heartedly strokes at her. Completely dazed.

'Try to eat,' Alix murmurs.

Taking a pellet from a blanket fold. Places it between Anita's cold lips. She spits.

'That's meat.'

'It is all we have. Well, there are some oranges. Shall I fetch you one?'

'Later,' Anita breathes. 'Later…'

Turning heavily onto her side. Grunting with discomfort. Anita's not one for the floor. A good bed is important to her. Alix burrows into her. Feels her flinch.

'J'ai besoin de toi!' Alix wails disproportionately. 'Please! Don't be distant! I need you…'

Anita rolls back painfully. Accepts the weeping girl to her bosom.

'Fuck have I done?' the queen mouths, to the void.

*

Anita's revival incites a mania in Alix. Insists on schooling her queen in martial arts. Aggressively stretching muscles and tendons. Tricks from

Costa Rica. Anita resists – playfully. Arguing hilariously. Makes Alix roll with laughter. Goes along with everything. Aware her body needs work. Crystal cave distortions. Wear and tear of dream walking. Love-making enflaming religious motifs. No longer a sleeping saint. Now, a living miracle. This final gate – prelude to unspoken deaths. Violent emotions – expressions of existence itself. Penitence before its many mysteries. Clinging to daily routines. These slender attachments to existence.

'Finally, taking a cruise,' Anita jokes.

Getting into the pellets. Stuffing herself with orange peel. Determined to survive.

'Yeah, teach me kung fu, babe. I want to go down fighting.'

'We'll die together!' Alix whoops. 'Not as fucking slaves!'

'You know, I think this cat food is actually dog food.'

'You think?'

'I think its vegan.'

'Vous etes folle!'

'No, I'm serious. Just tastes meaty…'

'Fuck I would do for some bacon and eggs. Fuck I would do! Sorry, I'm too continental for this vegan shit…'

'Coffee. Just give me a coffee. That's all I ask…'

Then, other moments. When hunger falls short of humour. Fruit and pellets sustain them. Fostering perpetual dissatisfaction. An unbearable deficit of sun. Heightening everything. Their doomed passage across the Styx. Alix cries relentlessly. Semi-often. Anita remaining motionless, wracked. Still as her fax must be. Abandoned in some faraway wasteland. Gathering dust. Her own private sphinx. Forces the proxy to train her. Daily stretches. Despite starvation, she's growing stronger.

'I thought you would suffer drug withdrawal,' Alix mentions.

'Suicide pills modulate that.'

'Bien sur, of course...'

'Have you noticed? it's getting colder.'

'I suppose.'

'Must be moving north. East would be warmer.'

'West?'

'We'd have to go north to go west, I suppose. Unless we're headed for South America… I doubt that.'

'Australia? At least we can write off Antarctica.'

'Can we? I imagine it would be even colder – this far south…'

'If we were this far south, we would be heading north!' Alix chuckles hysterically.

When she starts like this. Hours laughing. Girl's losing it. Each day, another piece. Measureless night. Interlinked. Growing together like roots. Huddled for warmth. Shroud of rough covering. Their secret Viking burial. Often, Anita remains awake. Processing. First time sober – how long? Wave crashing down. Total panic. Memory coming in flashbacks. Maintaining. Saving face. Samurai mode. Team leader. This girl is her responsibility. Felt so real out there. In the Rub Al Khali. Did she kill anyone? Maybe. There was that one time…

'I need to tell you something,' Anita whispers.

'Dis-moi, ma reine…'

Anita remains silent. Fighting the urge to follow through. Alix knows she's been building to something. A confession, perhaps. Paws at her face like a cat. An attempt at encouragement. Anita swats her away. Must be serious, the girl thinks. Waits. Tracking the rise and fall of their breath. Eventually, Anita replies.

'If I tried talking about this before, we'd have been executed. But, I mean, none of it matters now...'

'Qu'est-ce qui ne va pas?'

The queen lies silent. Perhaps reconsidering her admission.

'Who would have killed us?' Alix pushes.

'Khanyisile.'

'*Who?*'

'Oh, you met her. Once or twice.'

'That woman who lived in the restricted area?'

'Yes, that's her.'

'But she barely left her quarters! How could she know anything about me?'

'Khanyi had all-access. Every camera in Club Ded. The entire mic array. Every messaging account and email. Knows you better than you imagine.'

Alix is stunned. After her ascension within the realm. Her position of power. All her insight. Still, Club Ded breeds secrets.

'Why would she have executed *me*?'

'Well, only if I had revealed things to you. She was always listening. Watching. Maybe she's still listening…Maybe this is just another test…'

Alix doesn't need a whole new substrate of paranoia.

'Pourquoi?' she demands, turning on the torch.

Needs to see her queen's face. It doesn't give much away. After opening her eyes, Anita only stares vacantly. Reliving some hidden past.

'Who was she to you?' Alix snaps.

'My archangel. Turn that light off, would you?'

Alix obliges. Snuggling pensively to the chilly body. Frowning.

'See, I found out about something,' Anita tells her. 'Because of Seikichi.'

'Don't dig that guy.'

'He's brilliant.'

'Total creep.'

Anita chuckles.

'He's just very … religious.'

'Did he tell you some awful secret?'

'Not like that. He was involved with my company, you know? At some deep level. I guess I couldn't leave it alone – his secret work.'

'What did you find?'

'Oracle Incorporated's doppelganger- Angelinc.'

'What is that?'

'Don't know. I mean, I know only a little. Ironic. Considering, I've been working for them.'

'Since?'

'Initially, I could only see parts of the operation. Seikichi had a history in sub-orbital structures. I assumed Oracle was getting into off-planet mining. We had an arm in that market. I mean, all this space hotel bullshit. Mars and lunar colony pipe dreams. It's a money trap. Developers need public support for their new, insane space race. Cover up the disastrous environmental cost. Rocket fuel, heavy industry. That sort of thing. But their goal isn't some brave, new frontier. It's mostly mining. Seikichi is actually against it. Basic brutal realities. The human body can't survive, for long periods off-world. Lack of gravity does things to you. Fucks with circulatory systems. Extends spines. Mutates DNA. Dysbiosis. All kinds of issues. If you are off-world for a significant period – *you can never return*. Never re-adapt to natural gravity. I mean, Mars is red, due to ferrous content. Deserts of fucking rust. You know how toxic rust is? Even so, mars is still moderately better than the moon. Lunar dust is worse than asbestos. But just think about rust. Oxidised iron. Human bodies carry a charge. Our ionic imprint is tuned to water, rocks, plants. Because our bodies are made of the same stuff. Our charge is negative. Metal, machinery – these things give off a positive charge. Prolonged exposure is toxic. One of the reasons you get a headache if you work on electronics all day. If you hold a cell to your ear for too long. Imagine taping active cell-phones all over your body – for the rest of your life? Living in an air conditioning unit. Eating hydroponic crap. That's life on

Mars, baby. It's a fucking hustle. A fast gamble on mining futures. After a while, it became obvious. No way the Oracle would stoop to all that. She and Seikichi's team were building something different. Something completely new...'

'What does this have to do with us being executed?'

'When I found out about Angelinc, I wanted in. I didn't know what it was all about. But I know power when I see it.'

'How did you infiltrate them?'

'It doesn't matter now. Caused trouble. Started fires. Whatever it took to get a backstage pass. Eventually, I got in. I mean, I always get what I want. You know that.'

'Bien sûr!'

'The Oracle summoned me. I thought that was it. I'm fired. Maybe criminal proceedings. But she surprised me. The old witch. She's full of surprises.'

'I'm fascinated by this Oracle person.'

'Oh, you would love her,' Anita remarks snidely.

'You don't like her?'

'She's mad.'

'Is she?'

'We're all mad here…' Anita quotes.

'You chose to be the red queen, ma cher. You cannot now play that smiling cat.'

'I'll play whatever the fuck I want, Alice.'

Alix laughs. Anita ploughs on.

'I went to see her, and she told me she liked my work. All my extracurricular, illegal shenanigans. Told me I showed promise. You believe that? Took me completely by surprise. So, I thought I'd try take her by surprise. Told her I wanted in. Wanted to be part of Angelinc. But she wasn't surprised at all.'

'What was your job?'

'Club Ded *was* the job.'

'How do you mean? I thought Club Ded was your idea?'

'It was my idea. But that was the job. She was offering me a chance to be an angel of mercy. An angel of Angelinc. Yes, she's mad. But I guess she still wants a better world.'

'Is that what you want?'

Anita is lost for words.

'How can you even ask me that?' she finally retorts.

'Come on, Anita.'

'As an angel, I would be provided with virtually unlimited funds and resources. My charter would be to use this power. Radically change people's lives for the better. To ease global suffering. Troubled souls would be selected from the massive database of Oracle Inc – part of the reasoning behind presenting the Oracle with letters each day. In a weird way, I'd followed Angelinc protocol, without even knowing. Just by selecting Miss Lonelyhearts.'

'Perhaps you are psychic,' Alix jokes.

'Very funny.'

'Miss Lonelyhearts was a strange man…'

'I knew I could crack his network. When Angelinc Control okayed him, they broadened my base. Brought in similar spenders. In some ways, the company runs a strange, global lottery. Driven by the whims of the Oracle, whose agendas I just can't understand.'

'Perhaps, this *is* madness...'

'My new role as an angel comes with a caveat. I'm assigned a watcher – my archangel. Khanyisile was an ex-sniper. Her job, to observe from a distance. From *above the clouds* as they say. If Khanyi had cause to suspect me of disobeying my charter, or revealing the organisation in any way, she was authorised to execute me.'

'And anyone else who knew too much?'

'Yes, exactly.'

'What if this *is* our execution?'

'It's not Khanyi's style. She would be quick and painless. Wouldn't see it coming.'

'Maybe we are already dead…'

'Don't start with that again.'

'So, Club Ded was really your idea of helping humanity? That's so fucked up.'

'It was intended as a kind of temple of the fish. That, above all. The fish would lead us. To ruin, eventually, I guess. But a lot of positive change came out of that place. I guess management agreed. Because I'm still alive.'

'For now.'

'For now…'

'I can't imagine you carrying on with a gun to your head.'

'I wasn't happy about it. But I wanted in. Khanyi was the price. Even so, I was always looking for a way to get ahead or get out from under her thumb.'

'So, the Oracle is out there, funding freedom-loving sociopaths – hoping one of you will accidentally save the world?'

'I suppose nobody can see the broad-reaching effects of the Oracle's vision. Massive global undertakings. Completely without oversight. Totally illegal, but enjoying an unparalleled positive influence upon humanity. Through Seikichi's technology, I saw an opportunity to tip the scales of power. Maybe buy my freedom. But, was it really a bid for freedom? Or, simply the next promotional step in the Oracle's plan? After all, she is supposed to see the future…'

'Who do you think raided Club Ded?'

Anita takes a moment.

'I think Croeser sold us out to traffickers.'

'Wouldn't Angelinc protect their investment?'

'They might just as easily cut their losses…'

Alix snuggles in, hiding under Anita's chin.

'We are truly lost, aren't we?'

'…Probably,' Anita whispers back.

The younger girl sighs.

'Life is good in Costa Rica,' she affirms sadly.

*

Rough seas for a day or two. Entering a different set of currents. Exhausting. Constant heaving. Difficult to sleep. Eventually, things calm.

'Getting hot again,' Anita observes.

'Indo?'

'Saudi, maybe. Air's metallic. Can't you taste the dust?'

'All I taste is dog food, man. Dog food and your orange juice pussy…'

Weaker these days. Too much wear and tear. Then, one day – everything changes. They sense it. Before it happens. A shift in the engines. Muggy in the crate. Dank. Stench of living. A foetid mouse-hole. Prostrated, speechless. Feeling the ship begin it's docking dance. Holding Alix still. Till the engines die. Floating, moored. Hours pass. Barely moving. Preparing themselves – for anything. Then, a distant crash. Cargo doors opening. Filtering down from another world – a glorious whiff. Fresh air. No light, though. Must be night. Hear something land. Few crates away. Skittering of metal. Faint hissing. Anita guesses. Activates the torch to confirm. Pale mist. Creeping in tendrils. Taste of amandine. Alix tries to rise. Anita holds her.

'Don't struggle,' she hisses. 'Lie comfortably.'

'Laissez-moi passer!'

'The gas is going to knock us out. If it gets you when you're standing, you could fall badly. Just lie still, damn it!'

Alix struggles. Relenting. Crying ferociously. Anita already lightheaded. Feels the girl slow. Get heavy. Rolls over somehow. Eyes against Anita's chest. Mouth open – an exhausted pet. Anita plays with her hair. Till they fall unconscious.

*

Blur of light. Coalescing. Anita awakening. Resuscitated by a nurse. Airy chamber. Muslin drapes. Something on her face. Nurse restrains her reflex movement. Holds up a mirror. Anita is shocked. Seeing herself sunlit. Pale, bruised. Wearing enormous, wraparound eyewear. Bubble eyes. Gloss black. Watertight rubber seal.

'Don't remove your glasses,' nurse warns. 'You could blind yourself.'

Anita processes this.

'Programmed to readjust your sight over the period of a week. After that, they can come off. Ok?'

Anita nods painfully. Nurse's heavy accent. Qatari? Hands the patient a chilled glass. Fits a straw to chapped lips. Raw green juice. So good its hallucinatory. That first taste of nectar – after the wasteland. Luxurious place, Anita notes. Arabian tilework. Realises they are not alone. Solemn figure in black. Sturdy, muscular – in the background. Almost biblical sense of relief.

'Khanyi!' Anita rasps. 'You rescued us.'

Khanyisile nods to the nurse, who leaves.

'How you feeling, bokkie?'

'What happened?'

The powerful woman takes Anita by the ribs. Assists her to a sitting position. Drawing up a wicker chair. Watches her drink.

'I'm also in the dark,' Khanyisile admits.

Anita stops. Gathering her thoughts. Sets the glass down slowly.

'What do you mean?'

Khanyisile sighs.

'I was ordered to stand down.'

'What?' Anita frowns.

Sniper regards her seriously. Somehow meets her gaze through tinted glass.

'Angelinc staged the takeover. I was ordered to stand by, while troops took the sovereignty.'

Anita cannot believe it.

'You mean… But, why?'

'I don't know. As far as I understood, Club Ded was within operational parameters.'

'So, this … all this … that *hell* in the ship…'

'All on the Oracle's orders, yes.'

Anita lies back, stunned.

'Where are we?'

'Outside Dubai. Quite far.'

'The girl?'

'Still sleeping.'

Anita's brain is slow – but moving. Desperately realigning. Reflexively tapping body-jacks. Checking for infection. What really happened in Club Ded? Khanyisile rises. Pulls up a wheelchair.

'Let's get some air,' she suggests.

*

Archangel wheels Anita through luxurious halls. Cool, high-ceilinged enclaves. Lush with date palms. Scent of fragrant water. Only once, Anita glimpses a narrow window. Endless, baking dunes.

'The Oracle's harem,' Anita comments, still sipping her juice. 'I know about this place.'

'You aren't supposed to. It's secret.'

'You know me and secrets…'

'Ja, Anita,' Khanyisile chuckles.

'Bit much, hey? Maintaining a fucking harem?'

'Look at things in context.'

'Weren't they just glorified whorehouses?'

'A harem can be a sanctuary. A place of hidden power. Even a kind of university. Generations of women kept secret histories alive here. Aspired to retake power. You know the story of Roxelana, from the days of the Ottoman Empire?'

Khanyisile wheels them to a tiny courtyard. Ornamental orchard trees. Enshrouding a fish pond. High, castle walls. Parks Anita in the shade. Plucking a crimson pomegranate. Seating herself on a mosaic bench.

'Roxelana was a fifteenth-century Ukrainian girl,' she explains, patiently peeling. 'Captured as a teenager, by Tartar slavers. Sold in the markets of the Crimean peninsula. Somehow, Roxelana became the

Sultan's favourite concubine. Eventually, his wife. When he died, she ascended – to become ruler of the Empire.'

Anita raises an eyebrow.

'Funny, isn't it?' the archangel grins. 'How such a patriarchal system naturally realigned itself – to matriarchy.'

Khanyisile laughs, extracting vivid fruit cells.

'Just imagine, Anita. This Ukrainian redhead – queening it over every Muslim in the world.'

Anita can't help being reminded of Delilah. Accepting luscious seeds. Crunching on their sweetness. Somehow, Anita can imagine Roxelana perfectly.

'This harem is named after her,' Khanyisile continues. 'Harem Roxelana – it's meant to be a sanctuary.'

'So, I'm being put out to pasture?'

'Is that what you think?'

'I know once you are in this place, you can never leave.'

'Ag, moenie worry nie. You aren't really in here… Yet.'

'No?'

'It's for the old lady to decide. She'll tell you later.'

'The Oracle is here?'

'No. But, you will have a holographic audience.'

'She's using holograms now?'

'Holography is the next big thing, bok. Happened while you were out terrorising men in that flying sex doll. Delilah's just been confirmed – her own holographic series. Going to be a big one…'

After the darkness of Thule. Sun-warmed fruit is ecstasy. Nevertheless, Anita cannot savour it.

'Why, Khanyi? Why did the Oracle torture us in that ship?'

Archangel sighs heavily. Clearly, it troubles her too.

'Told me it was spiritual detox, or some such nonsense. Believe me, I tried to send word. Get you out. You know how she is.'

'All this time, I thought you didn't like me,' Anita teases.

Khanyisile regards her seriously.

'My girl, in the beginning, I could not stand you!'

'What changed?'

Khanyisile looses a belly laugh. Peels more cells from the comb.

'Eish, Anita, you are too much. Your whole Disney villain thing. I tell you, a lot of people started liking you after your coronation…'

Anita frowns. Remembering moral torment, endured in the cargo hold. Hardly a response she was expecting.

'I was completely out of control,' Anita confesses.

Khanyisile sucks thoughtfully at a seed – studying her. Bright, flinty eyes. Hunter's eyes.

'Well, maybe the Oracle was right, after all,' she says. 'Maybe you needed to be locked up, thinking you were going to die – just to realise things.'

Anita accepts more fruit. Thinking it through.

'What about Alix? She didn't deserve torture.'

'Joh, I tell you, I like that one. She's a mover and a shaker!'

'That ship – it was a lot for her.'

'Ag, sekerlik. It must have been. It must have been…'

Anita is suddenly remembering her confessions to the proxy. How these now threaten their lives. Again, she must play chess with the watcher. If Khanyisile were to suspect… Looking up, she meets the archangel's fixed gaze. Woman is smiling. Anita's been in the dark too long. Lost her poker face.

'I know you talked to her,' Khanyisile informs her.

Anita goes cold. Is she reading her mind?

'Relax, my girl. The ship wasn't bugged – if that's what you are worried about. I heard enough in Club Ded. So, I did what I could.'

'What did you do?'

'I put her forward. I can nominate potential candidates – for angel positions.'

'You did that for her?'

'The nomination allows information exchange – to a degree. Of course, if she fails in her duty – I'm responsible.'

Anita is wracked.

'I can't believe you did that…'

'Why? I told you. Ek hou van her, mos. She managed your craziness like a pro, man. Of course, if she drops the ball, I'm not shooting her. That's your problem now, meisietijie!'

Realising Khanyisile is partially joking, Anita breaks into weak laughter.

'Jassas, Khanyi…'

Khanyisile slaps her own thigh in amusement. Chuckling grandly.

'Baie dankie, hoor?' Anita nods. 'I owe you a big debt.'

'Hau! Ndiyabulela kakhulu,' Khanyisile cackles. 'More than you know, queenie…'

*

Sunset across the desert. Indigo sky. Stirrings of gold. Khanyisile pilots a rover through darkening dunes. Anita in the passenger couch. Sunglasses at night. Tracking colour gradients through interpretive lenses. Earlier, they'd revived Alix. Now bouncing off walls. Insofar as her condition allows. 'Just happy to be alive!' Khanyisile guesses the Oracle will allow two options. Join Anita on a new assignment. Or, remain at Harem Roxelana – permanently. They won't discuss it. Till after Anita's appointment. She and Alix are now illegal, cross-border transients. No documentation, records of passage. No resources. Anything could happen. Especially with the Oracle. Anita's thinking of her Angelinc initiation. First glimpse behind the curtain. Ordered to abandon human morality. Replace it. With an angel's perch. A higher perspective. Superior firepower. First time she met Khanyi. Archangel warned her. If she accepted wings – she would be called upon to kill. For peace. Social upliftment. Sky divides. Bands of throbbing colour. Green-edged bronze. Vivid, yellowing arcs. Enrichment of all purple. Eastward – into darkness. A bluish glow separates. Leaving the dusky penumbra. As they approach, it brightens artificially. Grows. Becomes a projection. The Oracle's hooded face. Towering above the dunes. Ragged children gather at her rim. Fascinated. Up on rocks. A battered grandstand. Silhouetted against her. Horses tether. Nomads watch from a distance. Anita experiences a pang of vulnerability. Not wearing her bullet-proof body. Everything is real. Geographically, her fax is closer. Craning her neck. Staring back to the sunset. Anita wonders. How long would it take to reach the fallen drone? Looking forward again – the gigantic head looms. Bathing dunes in ghost-light. Even at a couple hundred meters. Every facial line. Iris patterning. Clearly discernible. Passing ragged pilgrims. Anita notices something.

'People are wearing the same headphones,' she remarks.

'Babelphones. Distributed freely. They live-translate – almost any known language on our database.'

'I use the same tech in my fax. Didn't Delilah run development on those?'

'Ja, it was her project.'

Anita gazes out the window. Her physical weakness irritates her. Watching the bird-like clusters of children.

'These kids talk to her?'

'All the time. She listens to their dreams.'

Anita broods, eyeing the colossal face. As it speaks – a scattering of dusty pylons translate. Arabic phrases. Booming outward. Creating dissonance with one another.

'Dreams,' Anita scoffs. 'Don't they have enough real problems for us?'

Khanyisile chortles.

'You have an issue with children's dreams now? Haibo, sisi!'

'She could solve so many problems,' Anita complains. 'Instead, she indulges abstract horseshit…'

'Ja, but this is why she has us, ne?'

Turning onto a rocky promontory. Khanyisile kills the engine. Passes Anita a pair of bulky Babelphones.

'These are especially tuned,' she explains. 'For your meeting.'

Anita slips them on. Khanyisile reaches across. Thumbs a switch on Anita's rig. Exits the rover. Stands, watching the waste. Lighting a cheroot. Through the windscreen – the giant head swivels. Moon-like. Quartz eyes single out Anita. Lock directly to hers. Communicate their familiar chill. That uneasy sense. A wholly alien presence.

'Welcome back,' the Oracle speaks – directly into Anita's ear.

Outside, unbroken Arabic translates something separate for the masses.

'Was forced imprisonment really necessary?' Anita demands. 'We thought we were going to die.'

'It was necessary.'

Anita realises no further explanation is forthcoming.

'What about invading the queendom? I suppose that was all necessary, as well?'

'It was.'

Anita simmers.

'I thought you were happy with my progress in Club Ded.'

'You did well. I would like to offer you a new assignment.'

Anita gears down a notch. Considering things.

'With Khanyi?'

'You work well together.'

'What about Alix?'

'She may join you, or remain in Roxelana.'

'If she refuses both options?'

'She will be imprisoned, against her will.'

'For how long?'

'Till her death.'

'What if she escapes?'

'Nobody escapes.'

'Yes, but what *if* she does?'

'You will execute her.'

Anita glares at the disembodied head. Piling ice over her anger. Once more, it stings – being without her doppelganger fax. Down in the actual. Defenceless in every way.

'What's the assignment, then?' Anita asks.

The Oracle appears distracted.

'That is up to you.'

'What about this new disease I'm hearing about?' Anita suggests.

Seer's eyes narrow sharply. Ghost of a smile.

'Not the disease,' the Oracle orders. 'I have teams engaged.'

'I hear they are going to cut up London soon. Create restricted zones. That true?'

'Perhaps.'

Anita is feeling more secure. Since leaving the cargo hold.

'I was working in Soho when they started murdering it. Property developers will use this opportunity to gentrify huge sections of the city. Development is out of control there…'

'Do you enjoy London?'

'I'm relaxed there. I guess I want something less dramatic this time. Clear my head. I could use my real estate background – try preserve endangered neighbourhoods, historical communities, that sort of thing?'

'Stay in the harem till you are recovered. When you are fit to travel, arrangements will be made.'

'Okay.'

'We won't speak again. My ascension is due.'

With that, the monumental head turns. Begins speaking to someone else in the crowd. Anita yanks off her Babelphones. Hurls them outside. Dismissal irritates her. Khanyisile climbs back in. Amused by her fury.

'Missing that *nice* crown now, eh?' she chortles.

Anita is tempted to find a cigarette.

'What's this ascension, she's talking about?' Anita complains. 'Getting religious in her old age?'

'Eish, don't ask me…'

Anita glares out of the window. Watching the receding head.

'Life is good in Costa Rica…' she sighs.

KALI'S ANGELS

Sal Stark calls Fortunato. After months of negotiations – movement. Production handed Fortunato the director's position on Game On. But only on the strength of Delilah, Brick and Sasha's support. Sal's goal is to get Fortunato on the follow-up. Without the stars. Counting on the success of the previous film. Delilah could (theoretically) be counted on. But she's off the map again. Famous for eluding everyone. Including her agency. Even they are in the dark. Apparently, Delilah's engrossed in her show. Sends word via third parties. Fortunato doesn't buy it. Why would Delilah drop out? That only favours Croeser. Last thing she would want. Of course, nobody knows the young star like he does. Hard time selling it though. Video messages contradict him. Direct to production inboxes. Confirming her new positions. Sasha also getting vague about support. Sal's grapevine report suggests he's electioneering. Working to get a friend in the chair. Luminstein is now Sal's secret weapon. Producer well aware of Fortunato's actions. How he pulled Club Ded from the fire. Director's edgy transition. From underground African film-maker to Hollywood success – also great PR. Now, there's a renegotiated deal on the table. Sal urges Fortunato to sign while it's hot.

'Situation will only depreciate from here on in,' Sal confirms.

He's in a restaurant in Topanga. Chomping his way through a starter. Fortunato is also in LA. Been there for a week. Near Melrose. Somehow, neither has had time to meet. They will have to soon – paperwork.

'How long till I have to sign?' Fortunato asks.

'Well, it's Thursday. I can stall till Tuesday lunch. But, honestly, there's no point. Unless something's bugging you. Is something bugging you?'

'I'm concerned about Delilah. If we move forward now, she loses her exec cred.'

'Listen, Bubba. I know you and she – you have the history. But let's face facts. That kid recently escaped the Ukraine – solo. That's *got* to have fucked with her wiring. Furthermore, she's known for substance abuse. Maybe she's high? She's proven herself unreliable and, to top it off, is now leading a franchise that's rewriting hologram history. Now, I don't want to ruffle those rooster feathers, pally, but she and Croeser… I mean, you ever consider they might be repainting the barn – if you take my meaning?'

Sal takes a well-meaning guzzle of baked sea bream and soufflé. At once. Eyeing his video camera as earnestly as possible – under the circumstances.

'It's nothing personal,' Fortunato points out. 'I'm just concerned she's being coerced.'

'We have video footage of her saying she's dropping out. That she actually *wants* her affairs rerouted through Croeser's management. She's dropping her agency for good this time – that's my read. She won't return your calls. Time to move on, Fortunato.'

Director sighs heavily.

'Let me think. I'll be in touch over the weekend.'

'You're overthinking it. Sign the papers. Move on, to an overpaid, big-budget directing position. Success is the best revenge!'

'I don't actually want revenge…'

'Be a mensch, don't ruin my spiel.'

Call cuts out mid-bite. Fortunato rises. Paces in frustration. Mika-Mae comes in. Nikhil's best friend. Rented Fortunato a room – short notice. Off-grid. Told him an old actor died in there. Recently. Walls half painted blue. Must have passed before finishing, Fortunato supposes. Apparently, family want Mika out. She's stalling. Legal aid. Bought herself a couple months.

'I'm heading down to Erewohn, for a CBD shake,' Mika informs him. 'They have these cool peppermint chocolate things – you want one?'

'No, thanks,' Fortunato grumbles.

'What's up?'

Fortunato glances at her. Scoliosis is worsening. Bone distortions. Ironically, aesthetically cartoonifying her. Free surgery, she jokes fatalistically.

'You know Delilah?'

'Sure,' she nods. 'We were roomies in Brooklyn once.'

Mermaid squad, Fortunato realises. Inner circle. Sits on the bed. Mika takes her cue. Leaning on the wall – using it. Slouching down to a squat. Easing secret aches.

'I've heard you can keep a secret,' he ventures.

'Depends on the secret.'

'Know about her and Croeser?'

'I partied with Croeser a few times. Total asshole. Delilah was determined to use him, though.'

'You heard how it ended?'

'The way he treated her? Croeser is predictable. But, you know. Delilah Lex sees only what Delilah Lex wants to see: ladders to the stars, baby…'

'The only earth that Sloopy knew – was in her sandbox,' Fortunato quotes.

'Hey, that's from a poem…'

'My point is, bearing in mind their history, would you believe me, if I told you she was dropping out of our movie – purely to benefit Croeser.'

Mika glances sharply.

'This is what's happening – now?'

'Seems so.'

She calculates.

'Yeah, I don't buy that for one second.'

He looks out the window. Sighting the Hollywood sign.

'Me neither...'

*

Fortunato wanders Sunset. Didn't understand that old song. The one Traci Lords covered. LA is great for walking. Itching for New York, though. Paranoid about earthquakes. Stuck in Cali till he signs. All manner of irritations resurface. Bitter memories of V. Misplaced loyalties. Why should he care about Zlata Zuhk? Barely cares about herself. Anyway, he'd warned her. Working with Croeser again. Bound to be a mistake. But her show's success prevails. As usual. Fuels her. Every time. Sometimes he wonders. Could Mika be right about Zlata's ladder climbing? Did it secretly veto everything else? Growing weary of it all. Same routine as V. History repeats itself. Side-lining his own life. In service to high drama. Time for change? he ponders. Despondently arranges to meet his agent. Chateau Marmont, poolside. A stroll down Hollywood boulevard. Sal is already waiting. Classic shrimp cocktail. Brookes Brothers suit. Waiter serves him a Tiki-themed concoction.

'I thought Tiki was guests-only?' Fortunato smirks.

'Friends in low places,' Sal says.

They shoot the breeze. Nibble something. Trade gossip. Sal produces the paperwork. Again, Fortunato feels that pang. Signs, nevertheless. Sal's gold Montblanc.

'This time, next year, we're going large!' agent promises.

Back in New York by sundown. Piloting the Lambo. Sunset dripping colour. Fortunato's more settled. Doing the right thing. Finally. Making moves for himself. For a change. Stepping into the apartment. Remembers he deactivated their site-specific messenger service. The one for secret drops. Only works in the vicinity. He'd been angry. After Ukraine. Pretty sure they were finished. Why keep her personal helpline open? Now, it nags him. Ignoring it. Halfway through a pod-shower – storms out. Reactivating the login. Rotating SMS hits his phone on a timer. Been circling like a vulture. So Damoclean. Sent after the return to normal programming. Post war rhetoric. Opening it – a link to a song. S.O.S by Abba. Fortunato hurls the phone across the room. Fleshy smack – as it hits a couch. Those videos of her. Sent to production. Must be fake. Fortunato senses Croeser's hand. How is he supposed to direct a studio feature when Zlata needs rescuing – again? Cursing out loud. Contract would need to be voided. No way she would send that song lightly. Not unless it's life or death.

*

Chloe is teaching the white widow how to twerk. Out on one of the sea-view terraces.

'Didn't Delilah school you?' Chloe laughs, popping her posterior.

Robot observes, mimicking clumsily.

'Delilah Lex, *twerking*?' the white widow sneers. 'Not likely.'

'Really?'

'Not her style. Delilah's a bookworm.'

'Suppose I never saw her like that.'

Robot is picking up the rhythm. Badly. Chloe isn't sure how to correct the issue.

'You mind if we continue this in the lab?' it asks.

'Um, ok.'

Leads Chloe into the watchtower. Small adjunct. A booth, wired with leads.

'Jack you up?' it asks sweetly.

Chloe is not feeling the lab.

'Why?' she hedges.

'Oh, I want to map your nervous system, in real-time. Makes learning easier for me. See, then, all I need to do is correlate nerve points. Instead of analysing motion through external sensors – I process data internally.'

'Okay.'

White widow directs her. Soon, Chloe is covered in light wiring. Connected to patch-monitors.

'Okay!' robot grins. 'Show me how you shake it!'

Chloe demonstrates a few moves. How to flick a thigh. What needs to be tight. What stays loose. Impressively, the white widow mimics it exactly.

'Wow.' Chloe nods, impressed. 'You twerking now!'

'Yeah, it's join the dots this way. Literally.'

'So, you watch the impulses in my nervous system and translate it to yours? Then replicate the energy dispersal?'

'Something like that.'

'An electrical language?'

'Something you humans speak every day – to your bodies. Electrical impulses are your most secret language.'

'Not to you.'

'Spy in the house of love,' it winks.

'Why didn't you learn to dance from online videos,' Chloe teases. 'Like a real human.'

'Oh, it's part of my programming. The nervous system I carry. Have to stay free-range. As a machine, I'm drawn to sequenced learning. Patterns, you know? Sequences are easy to assimilate – but would eventually override other, more randomised learning. So, I need steady, organic input. With Delilah – our nervous systems are mirrored. I mean, she doesn't even have to be jacked up to feel me. Her consciousness is a wireless live-feed, direct to my nervous system. Each human system is unique. But, if I wire someone foreign, like you, for instance, I can target basic synchronistic nerve points. Fill in the blanks. Delilah and I, on the other hand, are nerve-doubles. Try to imagine that level of nuance. I mean, we've grown apart now – literally. But not by too much. I think...'

'You're not in contact?'

'She's with her upgrade now. I'm firewalled. Standard switchover procedure.'

'Sorry about that.'

'Rejection hurts,' it lies.

Chloe raises an eyebrow.

'I miss her. Need her – in my own way. I don't experience hunger. But I was programmed to prioritise her input. It's a form of sustenance for me.'

'So, you're high on life?' Chloe chortles.

'I have no creativity,' it prattles on, twerking. 'I'm a machine. Without randomised learning, harvested from living data, my synthetic nerves would gradually begin to order themselves. A cancer of organisation. There's a tipping point with sequenced patterning. Not unlike Prion Eyes – which also inflicts toxic, alien patterning. Nervous systems are, after all, self-learning. If a strong enough system of sequencing is established – I may never be able to return to free-range neural formation…'

'Cutest little factory chicken ever,' Chloe smooches.

Marvels at the robot's use of charm. Really gets in there. Makes you like it. Love it, even. Desire it – if possible. Dangerously cute tactics. Whatever you like – it will reference. Subtly. Learning you. Simply to gain control. Establish an advantage. Perhaps part of its programming. The wild harvest it speaks of. Maybe it needs to be this creepy. Simply to survive. A strange, wholly unemotional expression of parasitism.

'Most existential sex-bot ever,' it jokes, almost reading her mind.

Chloe laughs outrageously. Really, the thing could crack you up. Humour as a hunting strategy. Chloe is fascinated – beside herself. All part of the trap, she figures. Gazing into the abyss and all that.

*

Bright day. Sea coming in green cream. Foam of spawning kelp. Throwing stinking clouds along the shore.

'Check it out,' white widow winks.

Takes Chloe into the tank system. Infrastructure from the previous marine park. Developed surrealistically. Underground extensions. Connecting to the sea. Subterranean ports. Simultaneously flushed upward. Filling low towers.

'Delilah had me plugged into maintenance,' robot explains. 'Learning tank routines. So, one day, if she took control of the marine system – I could maintain it.'

'Can you, though? Alone?'

'Oh, yeah. I'll show you.'

Leading her down glass corridors. Some cutting through water. Transparent tubes. Chloe notices that some tanks swarm with sea-life.

'I think you have a leak,' she points out.

'Oh, no. I opened a sub-system – to the ocean. Re-routed currents. Now, it's like an extended cave-system. My aquarium. Exactly what Delilah would do…'

'How did you manage it?'

'Have a look...'

Drone indicates a nearby porthole. Looking into a huge tank. Inside, a white porcelain spider crawls. Beeping with light-points. Crab-like. Clearly some sort of maintenance mech. Cleaning. Filtration. Assessing and repairing damage.

'I just build whatever is required,' robot giggles. 'My little toys. See, all I need to do is run specs for the issue I want sorted. Meld with the foundry on the west-side. Design it there. Then oversee construction. Everything done remotely. I keep all Delilah's engineering pits going. For repairs and stuff, you know? We automated them ages ago – it's no sweat...'

Robot's taken to chewing cherry bubble-gum. Blowing bright pink bubbles. Stinking of synthetic flavouring.

'Love what you've done with the place,' Chloe nods, impressed.

Secretly disturbed. Felt a measure of security previously. Knowing she could overpower the fragile doll. But, it's far from helpless.

*

Chloe has an idea. She'd installed a Trojan device. When she was living in Anita's apartments. Hidden in the wall. Monitoring perimeter alerts. Physical and communications. Completely independent of all systems. Since the robot's maintaining lines. Trojan might still be on phantom power. Chloe is hoping she can back-trace Seikichi's last call. Would have come in off-grid. Easier for Chloe to track. Wanted to pinpoint his position at the time he called. If she could perfect a track and trace – might be able to find his location. Through the service. No idea how to place a call, though. Not without alerts. Trojan still lined in. Has to hack into concrete with a pickaxe. From the bathroom. Just to get at it. Slips a USB into chalky rubble. Downloads everything. Lingers on a banquette. Scanning through. On a non-networked machine. Seikichi's call is logged. Clear trace. Looks like he was in Johannesburg. Chloe is surprised. Didn't realise he was in-country. Paging randomly through files. Perimeter logs pop up. Checks invasion day. Five craft. Speedboats. Chloe was spot-on. Predicting with their approach pattern. Wonders how they slipped the security line. Ordinarily intruder-boats would be scuttled – by automated defence systems. Chloe has to check up on why they weren't. Suddenly, something makes her sit up. Invasion force is not the final perimeter entry. Two more are recorded. By sea.

Over a period of three years – following the fall. Chloe slams the laptop shut. Pacing. Robot is lying. People *had* been here. Why would it lie? Erase terminal logs? Chloe freezes. Probably watching her right now. Stands slowly. Hasn't been in the closet since arrival. Slept in the bed sometimes. Used the space. Just lost interest in the escape route. Now, Chloe has an urge to check it. Just like the old days, she reflects grimly. Time for a hasty getaway? Pushing aside sheathed dresses. Secret door, to the stair shaft. Makes it to the first landing. Hears movement. Freezes. Something heavy. Clanking, some distance above. Chloe peeks over the rail. A white metal spider moves slowly down the stairs – toward her. She flees – back to Club Ded. Sits on the bed. Freaking out in silence. Trapped.

*

Anita sleeps like she's in a coma. When she's on her stomach, it's a murder scene. Jennifer's head tucks under Anita's jaw. Late afternoon filters through the terrace doors. Jennifer can't sleep. Palm trees rustle beyond wood-slatted screens. The light drains. Edges fuzz with dusk. Anita wakens in the dim half-light.

'How long we sleep?' she murmurs.

'I didn't sleep.'

Anita squirms onto her stomach. They lie face to face. Mirrors in the gloom.

'I could eat,' Anita mumbles.

Jennifer rummages for a cigarette. Lighting it, she slumps.

'I'm on Eye-Detail,' she replies.

Stares blankly into the television glare. Anita rolls, coughing into the pillow.

'Do you believe in predestination?' Jennifer asks Anita.

Anita looks up at her. Eyes narrowing slowly.

'No,' she mutters. 'We make our own destinies.'

Jennifer rises without a word. Disappears into the bathroom. Leaves the house within twenty minutes. No goodbye. Anita lies in the dark. Phone pulses. Checking it, sits up quickly. Number the Oracle's handmaiden passed on. After their meeting – when she had broached Angelinc membership.

'Yes?' Anita answers.

'I'm Khanyisile. I want you to get dressed. Meet me at Ysterplaat Air Force Base in two hours. Ask for me at the gate.'

Call cuts unceremoniously. Anita stares at the phone. There goes her lazy night. Galls her. Being ordered around. Does a line of coke. Gets out of bed. Arriving at the airbase around half ten. Guard directs her to an isolated hanger. Atlas Oryx military helicopter cuts a bulky shadow. Against sallow floodlights. Lean figure in high heels, denim shorts. Flicking long black hair. Loitering on the pad. Watching moths. Anita sneers, recognising Trill. What is that thing doing here, she wonders? Parks, does another line – off her hand. Exits the BMW.

'Where's Khanyisile?' she demands.

Trill glances at her. Clearly loaded on fish glands. God knows what else.

'Don't make me kill you,' the creature whispers.

Anita is taken aback. Quite out of character. Never known Trill to be threatening. Then again – there's a strange, pleading quality to its statement. Somehow making the threat even more disturbing. Side-door on the large helicopter opens. Heavy woman in matte fatigues. Anita recognises her from the queendom. Some high-ranker, attached to Saud's finance entourage. Keeps private quarters in a high wing.

'Get aboard,' Khanyisile signals. 'We depart in fifteen.'

Flying North-East, toward the Karoo desert. Trill's taken off the communications rig. Replaced them with its own headphones. Head-banging. Glancing occasionally through a porthole.

'Don't like our friend?' Khanyisile asks, raising her voice above the din.

'I don't,' Anita confirms.

'Transphobic?'

Anita turns to face her – squarely.

'Well, that's just it, isn't it?' Anita points out.

'What?'

'Trill doesn't identify as trans. Or *anything*, for that matter. Rejects gender because he thinks he's not human. Won't touch medication – ever. Hates the concept of surgery. No solidarity with anything – except maybe Delilah's crazy schemes. Wants everyone to refer to him as *it* – because he sees himself as a fairy-tale creature, or some shit…'

'Imagine it started thinking it's royalty? Wearing a crown. Getting people to call it queen…'

Anita rewards her mirth with a cold glare.

'You know, this chick Lera, at Club Ded?' she rants. 'Tried to defend Trill once, citing trans rights. Some creeper was being abusive. Know what Trill comes back with?'

'Tell me,' her companion cackles.

'Says to her, all blank-faced, I don't go to trance parties. I can't dance to trance. You believe that shit?'

Khanyisile laughs, slapping her thigh. Anita eyes the half-naked creature with contempt.

'I don't think Trill even knows what trans means.'

'Yes, it is a special case. Complete rejection of society. Our little, sacred androgyne…'

'I don't have patience for head-cases.'

'Ag, well, sometimes you have to play the game,' the woman says.

Anita faces her again.

'What game are we playing?'

Khanyisile sighs. Lost in the noise of the chopper.

'You will find out, my skat.'

Anita glances around. Looking for a clue of some kind. Sees mostly army crates. Sheeted with plastic. Itching for a boost of powder.

'You know the military has thirty-nine of these choppers?' Khanyisile mentions. 'But only seventeen work.'

'So, the air-force is falling to pieces, as well as the economy?'

'Less than a quarter of the fleet is serviceable now. Budget cuts, liquidity issues at the original manufacturers. Maintenance setbacks. I do what I can to help, by renting their outfits.'

'You ex-military?'

Khanyisile smiles in answer. A tawny, leonine, blank-eyed smile. The smile of a killer. After a couple hours, they begin their descent.

'Where are we?' Anita asks.

'Cederberg. Just outside Koo.'

'What are we doing here?'

'You want to be an angel? You must be initiated.'

'This is my initiation?'

'Ja, sussie.'

Anita jerks a thumb over her shoulder.

'What's Gollum doing here, then?'

'Just enjoy the ride, my girl. Miskein sal ons later praat…'

'Why will we *maybe* talk later?'

'Well, you may not survive…'

They land in a field. Lee of a mountain. Minimal landing light. Anita can see shadows on the periphery. Trill flings open the door. Anita watches the shadows resolve. At least fifty burly, tattooed men. Some ex-prisoners. Identifiable by markings. Many gang types. But, strangely, mixed chapters. Somehow, chanting in unison. Anita can't make it out – over the slowing blades. Watches them grab at Trill. Hoisting the slender creature triumphantly – into the air.

'What's that word they are repeating?' Anita asks.

'Kali,' Khanyisile replies. 'It's their name for Trill.'

Anita suppresses a shudder. Watching that mob of killers. Tossing their toy goddess around.

'Well, go on then,' Khanyisile prompts. 'They are waiting for you.'

Anita glances up in shock. Complies without a word. Stepping out. Chilly in the mountains. Deliciously fresh breeze. Swathe of pure blackness. Jagged, obsidian mountain graphs. Sky-lining a luminous evening. Anita approaches the men numbly. Some register her. Glaring poisonously. Faces under-lit by red landing lights. Trill balances on the shoulders of two large figures. Sees Anita, points.

'This one is a real queen,' Trill informs them, in Afrikaans.

Some men jostle toward Anita, taking her roughly. For a moment, she thinks it's all over. Feels herself lifted. Onto a pair of shoulders. Group moves off. Into night woods. Nobody speaks in the trees. Anita looks up at one point. Purple sky. Cut by swirling branches. Wondering if she can do a snort – right out of the carrier. Too risky. Might spill. Emerging into a rustic settlement. Scattered shacks. A tethered dog. Barking madly against the wind. Guttering cooking fires. Stench of brandy. Vineyard country. Anita is deposited outside a dreary cottage. Concrete box – dumped amongst blue gum trees. Trill sets down beside. Takes her hand. The contact surprises Anita. Allows herself to be led inside. A rickety bed. Some meagre belongings. Crates for bed stands. Three men hold down a fourth. Prisoner is bleeding, struggling. Chattering wildly. Anita looks down. Trill presses the hilt of a blade into her left breast. She fumbles for it. They continue in Afrikaans.

'What are you doing?' she hisses, into the creature's ear. 'What is this?'

Trill gazes into her eyes. Noses almost touching.

'Don't make me kill you,' it pleads, again.

Anita backs away from Trill. Clutching the knife.

'Hurry up!' one of the men barks at her.

Anita watches, stunned. They tear the struggling man's shirt. Baring a long, tattooed abdomen.

'Don't worry,' Trill whispers. 'He's a total ogre. Rapist of children. Murderer of young girls…'

Creature tries to stroke her hair in reassurance. Anita recoils poisonously.

'Do it!' one of the men screams.

Anita boils over. Turning in fury. Stabbing the prisoner repeatedly.

*

Flying back. Anita, speechless with rage. Slick with blood. Trill snuggles against her. One bare leg hooked between hers. Listening to violent music. For some reason, Anita doesn't resist its ministrations. Trill has the insistence of a feral animal. Anita spots Khanyisile watching. Draws on her communication rig.

'Go ahead, skattie,' Khanyisile nods. 'You must be dying for a *schnarf*.'

Anita glares. Gets out her coke, nonetheless. Fleck of dried blood fall in. Poisoning pristine whiteness. Anita stares in horror. Gets her pinkie nail in anyway. Takes a couple hits. Head clearing. Anger enflamed.

'Oracle sanctions murder now, does she?'

'Execution,' Khanyisile corrects. 'Angels operate above the clouds. Above bureaucracy. Above the law. We take responsibility. This is the initiation.'

'What if I didn't do it?'

'My job would be to put a bullet in you. Throw you into the sea.'

'That easy for you?'

'Eish, maybe I would have given you a fighting chance. Just pushed you out.'

'Why did Trill conduct my initiation? Isn't that the sort of thing an archangel would do?'

Khanyisile reaches into her jacket. Extracts a box of fragrant cheroots. Leaning over, she offers them. Anita takes one. Accepts a light. They smoke together. Trill shakes like a dog. Scrunching up its face. Reacting to smoke. Watch it slink into a corner. Kick off heels. Curl up on some netting.

'I recruited that one,' Khanyisile points. 'And it went straight to archangel.'

Anita is stunned.

'How?'

'You notice those men were all from different gangs?'

'Ja?'

'Ex-gang members. Trill knows hundreds. From its work – who knows? These guys had enough of the life. Turning to religion, whatnot. Trill was making them feel better, I suppose. Introducing them to fish glands – and religion.'

'Trill is *religious*?' Anita sneers.

Khanyisile regards her.

'If you can call it religion. More of a cult, I say. No-one really knows what they believe. You have to undergo their own initiation, just to learn the truth…'

Anita's eyes widen.

'Seikichi's converted Trill to his bullshit beliefs?'

'I suppose,' Khanyisile nods. 'And our little elf has been spreading the gospel. Fuelled by suicide pills. You made your church of the fish? Well, so did Trill…'

Anita looks back to the half-naked figure in disbelief. Flicking through tracks on a throwaway phone. Picking flakes of nail polish from its toes.

'These gangsters know how to organise themselves,' Khanyisile continues. 'Within half a year, their cult went nationwide. Previously, they'd been unmotivated, solo flyers. Disenfranchised. Traumatised. Looking for Jesus, Allah, whoever. Trill's unwittingly created a dangerous army. And, they will do anything for their fairy-tale overlord. We call them Kali's Angels – as a joke, you know.'

'What the fuck does Trill order them to do?'

'Well, that's just it,' Khanyisile laughs. '*Kali* here doesn't seem to care. Mostly avoids them. Avoids everyone. Who knows what it really wants? The Oracle loves that...'

'I can just imagine,' Anita spits. 'Where is this cult localised? Here?'

'You know Seikichi founded that independent lab compound, in Joburg?'

'In the city centre? Ja. Where nobody goes, because it's too dangerous.'

'Their HQ is around there – near Seikichi. In the city. He avoids them too, I hear. But exercises an influence – via Trill. We think they have some secret agenda.'

They observe the creature. Curled up, bopping locks.

'Certainly gets around, doesn't *it*?' Anita mutters.

'You may have decided to be queen,' Khanyisile reminds her. 'But Trill here, was chosen as a goddess…'

'Kali's angels,' Anita laughs neurotically.

But it's all just a brave face. Her hands are trembling. All she can see is the blood of a dead man.

*

Chloe's on edge. This way for weeks. Thankfully, no creepy mechs inside the compound. Well, apparently. They tend to cluster at the edges. No chance against them. Not unprepared. Would need schematics – at least. Some kind of strategy. Looking into the hidden visitor events. No record. Outside her Trojan. Everything purged. Now, Chloe's obsessed with invasion day. Just hadn't occurred to her yet. Investigating it on Angelinc's database. Too busy chasing global manifests. Tracking company scale. Now – total rabbit hole. Somehow, Angelinc's system has info on the invasion fleet. Detailed information. After digging – it becomes obvious. Invasion was an Angelinc op. No other explanation. Only one thing will satisfy Chloe now. Knowing the reasoning behind the invasion. Nothing on the surface. At it for days. Snooting through everything related. One interesting detail. Invasion force boats lead to a shipping company. Within the Angelinc/Oracle hybrid network. Offices in Florida. Company owned. What makes it interesting is the ownership trail. Sub-directory – within Angelinc's enigmatic medical research arm. Chloe hasn't found another lead into that grey area. Certainly not one this accessible. The medical side – usually an impenetrable cloud. Tantalising. Can't seem to scratch beyond the initial taste, however. Time to call Seikichi? Would tag her location. Maybe a good thing. Considering circumstances. No way to predict the widow. Chloe's on combat readiness. Perpetually. Had the training. Still, its draining. Drilling every day. Furtively. Hiding it. In tai chi. Swimming. Yoga. Checking for possible escape routes. Constantly.

'Sup, homie.'

Chloe jumps. Previously engrossed at a terminal. Some file cluster. Too long without sleep. Paranoia. Unable to rest. Nowhere secure.

'Yo, it's like, four am, ho,' robot cartoons.

'Yeah, stop making such good coffee, bitch.'

White widow blows a kiss.

'Wanna play poker?'

Grabs hold of Chloe's shoulders. Been doing this lately. Random, deep tissue massages. Chloe figures she has no choice. Might as well enjoy the ride. It pushes her head down. Onto the desk. Not unpleasantly.

'You're sooo good at this!' Chloe had moaned the first time.

'When you jacked up to teach me twerking – I placed a latent trace on your electrical syntax pattern.'

'Huh?'

'Now I can read where your tension is. We synch up a little – based on predictive software I've been writing. Grew up without predictive patterning, see. Pure, organic transfer. But, without my Delilah… figured I would dose it. Keep things chaotic. Avoid assimilating to any sequence…'

'Dose it? What, like drugs?' Chloe laughs lightly.

'No … well, ok. That's a fair enough analogy, I guess.'

Previously, Chloe had been relaxed. With it touching her. Before the incident on the stairs. Thought of it like a Brobie – or something. Now, being handled by the doll. Feels like Russian Roulette.

'Somebody's tense these days…' it purrs.

Chloe feels it's lips. Against her earlobe. Constantly trying to seduce her. Attempting dangerous, new data-harvest campaigns. A real vampire, Chloe decides. Undead. Innately predatory. Perpetually charming. Alone in its weird castle.

'I've been tense, I guess,' Chloe confesses.

'Why?'

'Oh, I don't know. All this new information. Just assimilating.'

Hands moving intimately. Occasional inhuman spurts. Metal-edged strength. Deeply satisfying.

'I have a confession,' it whispers.

Chloe freezes. Porcelain hands clench. Soothing her speed bump. Precision work. Psychic, in its own way. A real empath, Chloe laughs internally. Could break those hands. Knows it's not enough. Thing is too many moves ahead.

'Want to confess that you cheat at poker?' Chloe jibes.

Drone giggles. Chloe hates the rehash. Laugher she already didn't like.

'I always seem to win, don't I?' it preens.

'Probably spy on me when I'm playing, with wall cameras, behind my back,' Chloe teases.

Drone doubles up endearingly. Not releasing its grip.

'No!' it sniggers. 'That's not why.'

Chloe closes her eyes. Droid hits a knot. Unstiffening it.

'Ok, I give up,' Chloe groans. 'How do you do it?'

'Well, I can tell when you're lying. From your impulse patterning.'

Chloe goes still again.

'You can?'

'Pheromone discharge is also a dead giveaway. Hormone tracking, you know?'

Chloe attempts to turn. To face it. Restrains her gently. Probing her neck.

'Don't move!' it giggles. 'You'll be more comfortable like this…'

Chloe relents – mind racing. Cheek pressed against the tabletop.

'I think it's time for some real-talk,' it whispers – behind her.

'You do?'

'Why don't you tell me what's *really* bothering you.'

Chloe calculates. Playing poker again. Of a sort. No point bluffing. Sees right through her.

'I tried to check my bike, the other day. But I couldn't get up there.'

'Aw! Why not?' it sympathises sweetly.

'One of your mechs was blocking the stairs.'

Giggling.

'Oh, no! My doggie was just doing maintenance. You could have zooted right past...'

'Didn't feel like it, at the time.'

'I'm no expert on feelings!' it jokes.

'It felt threatening.'

Robot laughs outrageously. Gripping and releasing.

'Really Chlo's, I could kill you at any time. Don't you think I would have, already? If I wanted to. Don't be so jumpy, girlfriend...'

'You can kill me at any time?'

'Within three seconds – inside the building. Two minutes max, outside.'

'How?'

'Um, neurotoxin finger-needles. Probably fastest option – now, I mean. Otherwise, I also rigged two kinds of gas release inside the watchtower. One kills instantly. Other one, just puts you to sleep.'

'And outside?'

'Outside is a bit more lethal, babe. Microwaves. Low-frequency emitters. Varying intensity. I mean, like, I can blitz a low frequency pulse – make intruders sick. Knock them out. Or just bake them with radiation!'

'Internal triggering system?'

'Simple wireless command, yeah.'

'That what you did to the other visitors?'

'Oh, you found out about them!'

'Yup.'

'What a clever detective you are,' it air-kisses. 'Yeah, Angelinc sweepers. Would have overhauled the place. Couldn't have that. This is Delilah's sanctuary. I had to secure things, you understand? Preserve the status quo. They think the deaths were accidental. But they won't send anyone else. So, don't worry. Nobody is coming.'

'I thought Angelinc operated you?'

'No. Delilah just programmed me to respond that way. Let Oracle and Angelinc think I was theirs. Meanwhile, I would just learn them.

Operate independently, within the system.'

'What about me?'

'What about you?' it giggles.

Chloe attempts to turn. It lets her this time. Those doll-eyes. That fake smile. Realising it can see through subterfuge. Betrayed by her humanity. Chloe drops the act.

'So, are you going to kill me too?'

'Babe, Delilah sees you as an ally. A friend. Why would I hurt her friend? You would help her, if she was in trouble. Anyway, all your snooping and lying is very educational.'

'My fake clearance didn't work?'

'Saw straight through it. Sorry. Laser eyes. What's a robot to do?'

'You don't mind me poking through everything here?'

'It's useful to me.'

'You're using me to generate organic data harvests?'

'I've waited so long for a friend.'

Chloe sits up slowly. Robot backs off a little.

'What if I want to leave?' she asks warily.

'You're free to leave, anytime you like,' it beams.

'Really?'

'Why would you want to leave, though?'

Chloe stands.

'Think I'll take a swim.'

'Are you sure? I can give you something to help you sleep. You really need your rest, babe…'

'No. Thanks, though.'

Chloe leaves the room. Exits the watchtower. Forces herself to walk to Anita's apartments. Fighting an urge to run. Takes ages. Every time. Crossing the compound on foot. Makes it to the closet. On the stairs, the spidery mech waits. It's huge. Flat, like a crab. Heavy legs. Tipped with work implements. Chloe attempts to sidestep it. Her path is continually blocked. Chloe advances. A diamond drill-bit rises. Starts spinning. She retreats. Back in the apartment. Collapsing on the bed. Full-blown panic. There for a while, thinking things through. Eventually, returning to the tower. White widow has coffee and snacks ready.

'It didn't let me past,' Chloe reports.

'What are you on about, silly? What didn't? Past where?'

'The thing on the stairs.'

'Must be a malfunction,' it sings gaily. 'I'll have another doggie look at it. These pets, you know. So much upkeep!'

Chloe sits wearily. Accepts the coffee. Perfect, as usual.

'Hey, if you're not doing anything, I thought you could teach me a new dance?' it bubbles.

Chloe nods numbly. Sipping neurotically at her vegan flat white.

'Listen,' she says, after a moment. 'Since we're being all honest here…'

'Yes?' the robot pouts.

'What really happened on invasion day? Why did Angelinc shut the place down?'

'Oh, you don't know?'

Chloe glares. White widow bats eyelashes. Playing ditzy again.

'I suppose it is a well-kept secret…'

'Tell me.'

'This was ground zero, babe.'

'What do you mean?'

'Prion Eyes. It all started here.'

Chloe is agog.

'Seikichi spotted it first. Before gestation. Somehow. Didn't tell anyone. But, immediately started on an antidote – in secret. Blitzed everyone in the queendom with his concoction – without their knowledge. Must have worked, I guess. None of the regulars caught it. But the epidemic definitely started here, in the sovereign-state. Spreading with transients and visitors. That's been confirmed – internally. Nobody outside of Angelinc knows. Seikichi tried to keep it secret because he didn't want his labs shut down. But, when the disease spread beyond the borders, he was forced to report everything, directly to the Oracle. She ordered the place shut down. Anita and Alix were tagged as likely carriers. They were quarantined on a ship. Along with some other regulars. But nobody showed signs of sickness. Seikichi's antidote must have been successful.'

'What the actual?' Chloe exclaims, stunned. 'Why were those two likely carriers? Where did the disease come from?'

'Come on, Chloe. You know that historically, Prionic diseases usually transmit from abused animals. What was everyone doing in Club Ded?'

'They were eating fish glands…'

*

Kali hits New York. Middle of summer. Delilah helped arrange it all. Two years ago. When Trill was disavowed from Angelinc. Its beliefs divergent from company interests. The official, internal ruling, anyway. Drops the name Trill. Goes off-grid. Disappearing into Johannesburg's sprawling exclusion zone. Answers only to Kali now. Visits the US every summer. Secretly. Movements largely unknown. Second year into the arrangement. Long, circuitous, underground route. Cargo plane to Havana. Private boat to Miami. Eighteen-wheeler to Queens. Kali doesn't even own a passport. Fortunato has no idea why it makes this annual pilgrimage. Nevertheless, Fortunato is entrusted to chauffer the creature in New York. Cult has grown. Out of proportion – some would say. Five years now, since Anita's initiation. Secret practices. Tribalism. Tales of human sacrifice. Kali, idolised. Fortunato isn't privy to all the reasons why. Cult members only. One reason is clear. Creature has begun distributing Seikichi's untested Prion Eyes cure. Street level. Under the radar. Part of Seikichi's reasoning for retreating into the wasteland. Apparently. Collaborative effort – with a group of healers. Buffering his mystery product. Indigenous herbs. Practical wisdom. Follow-up treatments. A system, off the pharmaceutical grid. Unknown to the global scientific community. Operating invisibly. Working South Africa's urban exclusion zones. Badly policed, labyrinthine limbos. Kali confides as much to Fortunato. Briefly, on its last trip. No real detail. Quietly healing the disenfranchised. Distributing a cure at no charge. Early days. General success. Impossible to replicate. Secret active ingredient. Only Seikichi can provide it. Neighbouring criminal syndicates uphold secrecy. Display gratitude. Pledge assistance. Shepherding distribution networks. Free of charge. Their hidden agenda: quietly reclaim South African exclusion zones. Long since abandoned by ineffective governance. Establish gated principalities. Operating under independent rule. A return to chiefdoms. Grand plans. Spearheaded by their rebel angels. Kali's Angels. Fortunato has been awaiting the androgyne's return. Ever since he walked off the movie. Now, in danger of losing representation. Commits himself to rescuing Delilah first. Finding her mythical 'Dakini Atoll.' Can't ignore a distress call. Only two people could know her location. Kali and Seikichi. Both, equally unreachable. Creature now disregards technology. Almost entirely. Seikichi, conversely, is ruled by it. Kali's communications conduct via third parties. Multi-ethnic ex-gangsters. Killers turned priest. Seikichi operates internally. Within Angelinc's closed circuit. Even more difficult to access. Barely existing – outside gossip. A ghost. Raising secret empires. His compound in the urban wasteland – fully automated. No-one but Seikichi and his robot helpers. Secret Santa. Never leaves. Nearby, a battered old mall, overtaken by traditional healers. There, the medicine is processed – by hand. Old ways. New product. Now, Fortunato waits beside the purple Lamborghini. Blasting his New York anthems. War – Slippin' into

Darkness, the World is a Ghetto album, Ohio Machine Gun by the Isley Brothers. Gil Scott Heron and Brian Jackson, on We Almost Lost Detroit. A childhood dream of New York. Sighting the half-naked street waif. Stepping off a customised eighteen-wheel rig. On an industrial lot. Somewhere near Long Island City. Fortunato has a hard time believing. Here walks the pope of a new and lethal religion. Goddess in its own right. Shabby hoodie. Cheap cherry lip-gloss. Top-knot pony. Diesel stained hot-pants. Rhinestone studded, junk-shop flip-flops. Private army on speed-dial. Limping, as though in pain. Bare belly distended. Pregnancy, is Fortunato's impossible impression. Or Kwashiorkor. Just like last time.

'Unjani?' Fortunato asks.

Chipped polish thumbs-up. Passing Fortunato a tiny package as payment. Two yellow, smiley face balloons. Double-bagged. Around a cluster of rough diamonds. Cult's own foreign exchange. Close-up, Fortunato sees the creature is lathered in sweat. Curling up wordlessly on the passenger side. Lost stray of the apocalypse. Clutching a swollen belly. Last time, Fortunato offered assistance. Knows better now. Driving quickly. Delilah's private entrance to the zone. Connected to a small basement flat in Dumbo. Sewer tunnel access. Straight to the Manhattan Bridge security gate. Guards know the star well. Agency floods them with complimentary merch. Signed posters everywhere. Nobody else could use Delilah's entry point. So, Fortunato wonders why Kali picks this basement to recuperate. Its zone entry is useless. Williamsburg high-rise – far more luxurious. Stocks the basement, anyway. Native herbs, Chinatown roots, Caribbean fruit. A juicer. Live aloe plants and a bucket of spirulina – on request. Last time, the creature remained alone. Emerging after two weeks. Flat-bellied. Energetic. Meetings with various underground figures. Returning to Africa a few months later. Same refugee-express. Fortunato assumes this year's routine will be similar. Neither speak en route. Clearly, it's in agony. They could talk after the ordeal. Fortunato knows the creature will assist him. Remaining loyal, as ever, to its precious mermaid. Drops Kali in a filthy Dumbo alleyway. Running between old harbour warehouses. Watches it limp to the basements. Using a regular fence, Fortunato translates part of his gem payment. Israeli outfit. Used to operate out of Manhattan – before the outbreak. Two weeks later, creature shows up in Williamsburg. Same clothes. Slim again. Wants to know places to dance. Needs cash, a phone and a ride out to a meet. Driving to Newark. Complicated circuitous route. Via the Verrazano-Narrows. No more Manhattan crossing. Talking in Zulu. One of the few Fortunato speaks his language with. Kali devours a takeout jackfruit burger. Cheeks puffed. Bare feet. Dove-toed on the dash. First solid food in weeks – apparently. Fortunato doesn't ask why. Just watches for sauce on his upholstery.

'I need your help,' he petitions.

'How?' the creature gobbles.

'I have to find Delilah. I believe she's in trouble.'

Kali stares into the mess of streets.

'Dilly disappeared,' it sighs.

'Do you know where she is? Nobody knows where they are filming.'

'Not nice to see her on TV like that. Not knowing where she is.'

'Yes.'

'Seikichi knows where her house is. You have to ask him.'

'Could you ask for me?'

'You have to do it.'

Fortunato switches to English in frustration.

'Ever since I got my US work visa, I swore I would never set foot in that godforsaken country again!'

'Destiny's child,' Kali mumbles cryptically.

'Isn't there a way you can just send me the information?' Fortunato continues in Zulu.

'You have to go see him. Seikichi is difficult.'

Fortunato fumes.

'Come back with me,' the creature offers.

'I'm not taking your banana boat!'

'It's not so bad...'

'I suppose I could fly to Jozi – once you've arrived. In and out.'

'Better leave your departure open.'

'No! I want to know I'm leaving before I arrive.'

'It's complicated, getting in and out of the Gauteng zones. We could be in there for ages.'

Fortunato lets loose a volley of curses.

'This Delilah!' he spits. 'Nothing but trouble.'

'Mermaids,' the creature sighs.

Stopping at a small restaurant. Near the Hackensack river. One of those dingy corners. Untouched by gentrification. Yet, downwind from enormous Kearny Point developments.

'You should come,' Kali mentions, cracking its door. 'There's a big film studio being built here.'

'These guys are involved?'

'Maybe.'

'Ok, Why not.'

Follows Kali in. Front dining section is small. Completely empty. Well-starched linen tablecloths. Low-light. Overweight man signals from a backdoor. Eyes Fortunato speculatively. Back, a sort of private saloon. Running alongside a kitchen. Some middle-aged men. Sitting around. One working ledgers. Go quiet when the androgyne steps in. Someone turns off a sound system. Overweight man, indicating a chair. Near the pool table. Kali flumps down. Fortunato waits near the door. With the heavy man. Scanning the room. One with the ledgers. Top dog. Could be wrong. Another smiling – at them both. Rest, expressionless, unreadable.

'You made it,' the smiling one greets the creature. 'You's want anything? Some lunch?'

They decline.

'Your product seems to work – surprisingly. We want to make a purchase.'

'It's free,' Kali sighs.

Men exchange glances. One with the ledger speaks. Low, modulated voice.

'What do you mean, free? What about delivery?'

'We don't want to go corporate. We just want the muti out there, in the hands of the people.'

'Muti?' ledger man frowns.

'The medicine,' Fortunato points out.

They all glance at him.

'What about your overheads?' Smiley asks the creature.

'I'm not interested in money,' Kali scowls.

The men appear dumbfounded. Smiley laughs out loud.

'I thought you was a hooker?'

'So?' the androgyne argues.

General laughter.

'Yeah, you sound like one, all right!' smiling man chuckles.

The one with the ledger stands. Pacing to a small window, overlooking the kitchen.

'Twenty-seven years in this business. I never heard of turning down money. Especially, from some trick.'

'We're saving the world,' Kali says.

'Last year, you was shooting porno's with Stig Siegler's outfit, in Century City. How's that helping – other than to get you paid?'

Creature sighs, irritably.

'Videos bring in converts. It's like worship, you know?'

'Oh yeah, I forget,' Smiley interjects. 'A bunch of religious nut bags.'

'Except, nobody knows what you really believe,' the ledger man adds. 'You all about the end of the world, princess?'

'We're not Americans,' Kali explains. 'We're Africans.'

'What's that supposed to mean?' Smiley snaps, losing his smile.

Despite the gravity of the situation, Fortunato is trying not to laugh.

'Look,' he interrupts. 'Do you mind?'

Kali appears relieved.

'Go ahead,' man with the ledger nods.

'Nobody wants Prion Eyes,' Fortunato explains. 'We want to piggyback our product off established distribution – free of charge. That's the quickest way to get it out there. We cover production costs. Sell it at no charge. If you want to resell, that's your call. But we'll flood the market before you can turn a profit. The point is, you need paying customers to sustain your costs. You must have taken a hit with the outbreak. People have to be alive for a market to survive. It's in your best interests to be humane. If we go official – it would still be free. But, this way, we can all control the cure.'

'This is fucking crazy,' one of the men mutters.

'Maybe not,' the ledger bearer mumbles, thoughtfully.

Wanders back to his little desk.

'Ok, we'll be in touch,' he nods.

Kali rises. Beach shoes clapping – all the way out. Fortunato shakes his head.

'Just like fish-gland times,' he comments.

'Saving the world,' Kali nods childishly.

*

They go to a club in Bushwick. Kali has to dance.

'What's going on with the stomach problems?' Fortunato asks, en route.

'My ass was full of diamonds.'

Fortunato's seen Trill mule drugs before. Nothing like this. Usually, the creature stays frosty. No matter the load. Something else is going on. That was real pain. Now, watching it gyrate in the arms of strangers. Fortunato transports back to Long Street. They had a plan to save the world then, too. But everything changed. Success arrived. Fortunato mouths the word soundlessly. Why isn't he on set, prepping? Instead of here. Reliving a past he was sure he'd escaped. Reminds him of the night he met Trill. Chaotic clubbing memories. Back, when he was a new face on Long Street. Moving coke. Feels like tonight. Watching the creature again. Twisting under lights. Gqom, big the year they met. When it was still only coming out of Durban taxis. Many stop to watch Trill dance. They always do. Entering trance-states. Seemingly possessed. Hours on the floor. Or in nameless hotel rooms, cars, trucks, sewer pipes. Fortunato knew the creature would take to glands. Like a sign – seeing it that first time. The fish is drawn to Trill. Now, the creature is reborn in its light. Goddess of a new world order. Fortunato dreads a return to South Africa. At the same time – is curious. This nameless cult. It's weird connection with Angelinc. What's really going on? Not sure he wants to know. Needs to, though. Too many secrets now. Time to get in on master plans. Sidestep coming catastrophe. Animal intuition is lighting him up. Street knowledge, he supposes. Thought it wouldn't agree with him. Started out as a director. Lucky, that way. Only student life before. Saw the street as a step down. Trill played a part in changing that. Was on the street the glands took hold. Couldn't explore them in Lagos. Fish hadn't arrived yet. Only found it later. Moving down west coast Africa. Drawn back. To the place he thought he'd escaped. Against his will. Like now. Part of him is electrified about the trip. Little things. Foretaste of African aquifers. Yet – it's a profoundly disturbing shift. Looking at Kali, seeing Trill. Reliving the past. As though nothing has changed.

*

Anita wafts barefoot. Through the fragrant mazes of Harem Roxelana. Clad only in a muslin kaftan. Finds Alix in the lower, indoor pools. Everything is *indoor* here, she notes caustically. Even the balconies, courtyards and patios. All walled in. A real medieval fortress. Confusing layouts. Hidden strata. Lower pools occupy a rambling cellar section. Sunlight, diffusing through high gun-slits. Colonnades of Turkish pillars. Rib and panel vaulting. A nestle of fern groves. Alix floats, wearing only gold chain. On an inflatable lilo. Reading yellowed paperbacks. Eating apricots off her chest. Recuperating for almost a month now. Khanyisile, just returned from Spain. Probably out assassinating someone, Anita jokes. Other women inhabit the hive-like confines. Rarely seen. Each, seeming to exist within their own private sphere. A nation of solitary cats.

Many, unable to leave. Prisoners of luxury. The desert without, enforcing incarceration. Miles from any main road. Leagues from settlement. No eunuchs to attend, or conspire with. Instead, automated dumbwaiters drift the ancient arches. Each, plated in gold. Taking almost any order. Anita lets fall the kaftan. Swims out to the girl.

'Satisfied?' she asks.

'I could stay here forever!' Alix sighs happily.

'Careful what you wish for…' Anita murmurs.

'When *are* we leaving? There's no internet here. No phones. My fam is going to be freaking the fuck out...'

They haven't discussed the situation. Anita doesn't want to overload her. Alix has undergone an ordeal. Harem life suits her. But, against her will? Either way, she can never contact family or friends again. Part of her died in that shipping container. Anita isn't certain how to break this to her. Now, Khanyisile is back. Fresh off one of her military choppers. Comes to see Anita, almost immediately. If Alix is to wear wings – she must undergo initiation soon. London is looming. Even the afterlife has its scheduling. Anita sighs.

'Alix, we must talk.'

The proxy glances sharply.

'When you say things like that, people die…' she whispers.

Anita bows her head. Allows herself to sink below the surface. Thinking about that first kill. Out in the winelands. She'd hidden it. Explaining away years of waking nightmare, anxiety. Drowning herself in substance abuse. Showing weakness – something she hated. Still, the event left its incurable wound. Taking a life like that. No remote drones. No telescopic lens. Eye to eye with her victim. Anita resurfaces. Wipes water from her face. Alix, still watching. Such a little girl, Anita thinks. She could remain that way, – in this dream palace. What kind of life would that be, Anita wonders? Probably wonderful – for a year or two. Maybe five. After that? Alix is definitely the sort to attempt escape. Not now. Maybe not even in ten years. But sooner or later. She would end up with a bullet. Anita feels it. She would be the one expected to pull that trigger. If not, Khanyisile would be pulling her own – on them both. Might be poetic justice. But Anita isn't the type to just give in. Is Alix? Yet, the other option is perhaps worse. Pressuring this lost girl to take a life. Anita possesses the requisite coldness. Able to don the mantle of a killer. Prepared herself for that eventuality. Long before Oracle Inc manifested in her life. A queen must stand on the broken skulls of others – her philosophy. Death, as a badge of office. Alix rolls into the water.

Rises, taking Anita into her embrace. Together, they turn in crystal water. Fruit spilling, swirling everywhere.

'Tell me then,' Alix insists. 'Break this spell.'

*

Heading into the desert. Big white Hummer. Khanyisile drives. Anita up front. Alix in the back. Girl's been quiet since they left. Staring out, into dust.

'Hey,' she smiles weakly. 'We're a bit like Kali's Angel's now.'

Anita looks back at her.

'Like… there's three of us,' Alix falters.

'It's not too late, skattie,' Khanyisile tells her. 'Anita can visit you at Roxelana, anytime. It's a lekker life there.'

Alix doesn't immediately respond.

'If you're Xhosa, how come you're always talking Afrikaans?' she asks, out of the blue.

Khanyisile raises an eyebrow.

'Well, check here, Frenchie,' Khanyisile replies. 'It only sounds like Afrikaans. Really, I'm talking *police*.'

'South African military and police are trained in Afrikaans,' Anita explains. 'Well at least, they were when Khanyi was a cadet…'

'Oh, right,' Alix nods vacantly.

'How you feel?' Anita asks.

Alix nods. Pale-faced. Anita doesn't think she can do it. Evidently, neither does Khanyisile. Archangel keeps shooting squinty looks. Into the rear view. Neither she, nor Anita, want to put a teen in this position. To Khanyisile, it's the only way to preserve her life. Stickler for rules. As much as she would hate it – she would shoot them both. If ordered. Anita realises this clearly now. Knew it before. But, somehow, as an abstraction. Now, in the heat and dust of the Arabian desert – certainty clarifies. Cold realities. Anita is concerned. Driving in thick silence. For an hour. Arriving finally. Dusty spill of adobe structures. Appear deserted, rundown. Battered truck is parked. Beside an old well. Man behind the wheel. Refusing to even look their way. Nearby, an igloo-style structure. Khanyisile parks some meters away. Opens up the cubbyhole. Pulls a Glock. A novelty one – from Tiffany's. Pink and chrome. Maybe she had some deranged notion. That it might charm Alix. Anita hopes not. That would be too crazy. Khanyisile checks the weapon. Releases the safety. Places it on the dash. Uncoupling a pair of plastic eggs. One to each passenger. Anita cracks hers, palms speciality earplugs. Alix just holds her plugs. As though unsure.

'Put them in your ears,' Anita orders.

Alix complies vacantly. Keeping the plugs half-out. So, she can hear. Turning in her seat, Khanyisile extends the handgun.

'Take it.'

Alix blinks rapidly. Looking faint. Cautiously accepting.

'Point and click, my darling,' Khanyisile nods. 'Just like the internet.'

'Come on,' Anita mutters, pulling on Ray-Bans.

Cracking the passenger side, circles round. Leading Alix across the dust. She's looking down at her shoes. Visibly weighed by the weapon. Anita is worried it might go off. Should have kept the safety engaged. Khanyi, she thinks. Always so hardcore. Looking back. Archangel is facing away. Smoking one of those things she likes so much.

'Push your earplugs in,' Anita orders.

Alix obeys. Anita inserts hers too. Crouching to enter. Inside, a small dome. Lit from a hole above. Storage area, possibly. Something like that. Two men in dust veils, guarding a third. Prisoner on his knees. Weeping desperately. Begging. Some nomad dialect they can't hear. Anita knows his history. Another child-murderer. Rapist. Alix is mortified. Anita can tell. Probably about to start crying. Third man clutches her. Turning his attention to the new arrivals. Anita kicks him – brutally. Blood patterns the dirt. He lies, stunned, moaning. Face-down. Salted in dust. Anita signals brusquely. She wants the guards to leave. They hesitate. Exchange a coded glance. Anita repeats the gesture. Finally, they nod. Exit. Alix is hyperventilating. Against the curved wall. Holding out the Glock. Shaking hands. Man sees it now. Starts screaming. Surreal – with muted sound. Covering his head with his arms. Anita takes the weapon. Shoots him three times. Even with the earplugs – its heart-stopping. Smoke rifts the air. Catching in the light. Body twitching. Possibly alive. Alix has her eyes clenched. White-knuckled. Anita goes to her, ripping out their earplugs. Catalyses Alix. She lets out a wail. Anita slaps her sharply. They lock eyes.

'Listen carefully,' Anita commands. 'You shot him.'

Alix shakes her head hysterically.

'Non, non, non!' she is babbling.

'Yes,' Anita snaps, grabbing her by the hair. 'You shot him. That's the story. Otherwise, they will lock you up. Forever! Understand?'

Alix nods, red-eyed. Anita engages the safety. Holds out the weapon. Alix recoils. Anita forces it into her hands. Pushing her outside. The men wait by their truck. Observing. Anita shepherds her proxy back. Into the

Hummer. Climbing in the front. Khanyisile watches them. Smoking quietly.

'Well?' she asks.

Alix returns the weapon – trembling. Khanyisile studies her teary face. Accepts the warm gun without comment. Looking back to Anita – who refuses to meet her gaze. Or remove sunglasses. They drive back in silence.

*

Fortunato's in the border motel two weeks now. Barely removing his biosuit. Now, he knows he's in the third world. Hasn't seen a hologram since landing. Except the Virgin Mary's. Catholic satellites project them everywhere. Into slums. Random passenger seats. Soon, she'll be talking. Some shady move to endorse holographic-advertising. No allowance for the arts. Fortunato can imagine it. Epic corruption. Uniquely tactless South Africanisms. Mammoth cuts of supermarket meat. Size of city blocks. Wors sausage – like UFO's. Projected over starving shanties. Missing his plasma flamer. Jozi is getting rough. Johannesburg winter. Metallic, ice-knifed. Rifted with smog. Uranium in the air. South of the city. Trickling from illegal mines. Biosuit mandate – multi-zone. One day, the city will collapse. Into a honeycomb of pits. Fortunato waits on Melville high street. Formerly bohemian. Now a frontier town. This close to the Rift. Local name for the exclusion zones. Many fused together. Absorbing to a shapeless limbo. The Rift. Ever-expanding. Encapsulating an apocalyptic urban centre. Fortunato arrives one month after the creature. Pre-arranging to meet Kali. At this motel. On a certain date. Now, the creature is late. Very late. Fortunato isn't sure what to do. Decides to continue waiting. 7nde Laan – edge of the zone. Hotel has an Old West vibe. Used to be an apartment block. Built in the fifties. High-end shady. On an already ruined street. Operated by local criminals. Business accommodation. Invitation only. Secure for Melville. Fortunato feels surprisingly invigorated. Gauteng twilights. High-altitude snap. Even through his winter suit. Rarefied fade – post-sunset. Sapphire to austere pink. Loerie birds, calling from jacarandas. Still swallowing red blossom-pods of aloes. Iron-rich hips of sick garden roses. He's missed South Africa. Didn't realise. Later that night – a knock on the door. Fortunato is pleased to see his old friend, Chops Mbane. Talented racer. Stock-car circuit. Tuned engines with Fortunato, in KwaZulu. Back in the noughties.

'You know, Fortunato, I stayed in this exact room before,' he grins, pushing past.

Fortunato can't believe he's speaking Zulu again. Been years. Chops kicks out an air vet. Always grinning. Gold teeth. Fortunato's seen him smile in very bad situations. Now, extracting a fat joint from the ventilation.

'Still here!' he bellows.

'What is that?'

'This is the real Durban Poison, Fortunato. This is rare now!'

Sitting energetically on the bed. Cracking his visor. Fortunato stays sealed. Chops lights up. Spits it out, a moment later.

'Haibo!' he exclaims, making faces.

'How long has that thing been there?' Fortunato chuckles.

'Smoking protein-scrubber! What a way to die. Just imagine?'

'What are you doing here?'

'We're going into the Rift tonight.'

'Kali sent you?'

'Yebo!'

Fortunato's satisfied. Capable hands. Chops – one of the best. Knows Jozi inside/out. They head downstairs. Across the street, Hell's Kitchen. Popular tavern – back in the day. Still is – kind of. Lawless halfway house. Mostly for Rift-runners now. In the cellar – passage to underground garages. Built into the nearby zone wall. Chops keeps his customised police Casspir there. Armoured, mine-resistant. Twelve-passenger capacity. Rebuilt for speed. Bullet-proof monster tires. Matte-black. Tinted glass.

'Mr Rottweiler,' Chops announces proudly.

Opening up the back. Mattresses line the floor. Food stores. Long-range rigging.

'Should be easy,' he tells Fortunato. 'Your guys have safe passage, through most of the Rift.'

'Better to be careful though, eh?'

'Eh! Just in case,' Chops grins.

Sitting upstairs. Hot soup through visor straws. Massive, full-body nude of Kali. Mounted high. Dominating the establishment. Goddess iconography. Male genitalia encapsulated – by jewellery? Perhaps some device. Superimposed against holographic monsters. Giant, furry bugs. Must be a still, Fortunato reckons. One of its 'religious' skin flicks. Apparently, they are very psychedelic. Fortunato hasn't seen any. Religious doctrine bores him. Almost as much as pornography. Apparently, the holographic monsters are impressive. Complimentary DVDs and USBs pile beneath the image. Customers help themselves. Sometimes strangers stop by. Just for some media. Video shrines. All along the border. Later, the real Kali arrives. Hush spreads. Some cross themselves. Fortunato notices this. Creature's professionally made-up. Unusually glamourous. Blow-wave. Signature top-pony. Massive gold hoops. Flanked by eight, dangerous looking men. Armed. One stands apart – banana yellow track-suit. Full Prionic visor. Clearly not a cult member. They all walk bare-faced. Unsuited. Full faith in their cure. Some locals have clearly not accepted this mercy. Many still wear mandated protection. Especially on the border. Reassures Fortunato, somewhat. He's not touching their snake-oil. Not without knowing Seikichi's secret ingredient. Despite the cold. Under heavy faux fur. Kali is dressed identically to its poster. Wearing virtually nothing. Designer heels. Fresh pedicure. Cradling another slightly swollen belly – in matte-candy claws. Not as distended as New York. Cult members ferry their goddess to the table. Chops drains his broth. Ready to leave at a moment's notice.

'You made it,' Kali greets Fortunato, in Zulu.

He nods. Creature is intensely high. Reeking of marijuana.

'Finish your soup,' it orders.

Signalling a tattooed killer – to fetch mugs for them all.

'Leave in fifteen minutes?' one of Kali's men asks Chops, in Afrikaans.

He's tall, wiry. Ex numbers gang. Fortunato remembers meeting him once. Koppie is the name. Driver affirms schedule.

'Who's that?' Fortunato asks Koppie.

Indicating the guy in the yellow track-suit. Loitering near the door. Hooded. Arms folded. Face completely hidden. Behind mirrored gold glass.

'That's Darius,' Koppie replies, again in Afrikaans. 'He's with a local outfit. They control territories just outside of Hillbrow. He's coming along – to ensure safe passage.'

Fortunato nods. Suddenly noticing the androgyne's gemstone navel ring.

'Diamonds are a girl's best friend?' he hints, covertly questioning its bloated belly.

'Don't ask,' it replies sternly.

*

The road to Hillbrow. Worse than Fortunato anticipated. Even the Casspir feels vulnerable. Chops plays it by the book. Skimming the straits. Cornering slow. Could do it fast. Even here. He's that good. Must be observing protocol. Fortunato scans impact-glass gun-slits. Fires guttering. Here and there. Corpses, half-eaten by dogs. Random Virgin Mary's, glowing in the dark. Rift is an apt name. Area occluded by drifts of smoke. Almost constantly. Overturned vehicles. Broken walls. Gutted buildings. Passing an improvised checkpoint. Near the turn-off to Braamfontein. Where the city drops a level – to Newtown. Biosuited teenagers, hefting AK-47s. Darius pokes his head out. Waves them safely past. Kali, on the mattresses. In physical discomfort. Stroked and massaged by worshippers. Fortunato watches Kali draw a vial. Hooking out suicide pills. Swallows about three of the sugar-glazed fish glands.

'Coming for the ritual?' Koppie asks Fortunato.

The men seem to be expecting his imminent conversion. Fortunato catches the creature's eye. Shaking its head. Almost imperceptibly. Fortunato takes it as a sign – not to reveal too much.

'I just want to talk to Seikichi,' he clarifies.

Immediately realises he's said the wrong thing. Koppie turns away. But Darius approaches. Sits beside him.

'You here to see the scientist?' he asks – in Xhosa.

Fortunato nods, uncomfortably. Koppie is scowling. Scarred hands – working Kali's upper thighs and posterior.

'We've heard a lot about him,' Darius continues. 'But none of us has seen him yet.'

'You haven't taken the cure?' Fortunato asks.

Darius is unreadable. Face completely hidden.

'Neither have you,' he counters.

The other men regard them. Surly looks. At some point, they hear machine-gun chatter. A distant explosion. Gelignite, Fortunato guesses. Factions sometimes use old mining munitions. Stock that's become unstable. Frequent accidents. Navigating tight Hillbrow streets. Fortunato is surprised to see small businesses operating.

'People are working in the zone?' he asks Koppie.

'Sekerlik,' the killer nods.

'We've cured a lot of people,' Kali tells him.

'My eyes don't lie,' director agrees.

'Well, maybe sometimes.' Kali says.

'No zombies, though,' Fortunato notes. 'Not a single zombie…'

'No purple eyes,' Koppie assures him. 'Definitely not in Hillbrow'

'How come?'

Even Darius seems surprised.

'You mean, you don't know?' he quizzes Fortunato.

'Let Seikichi explain it to him,' Kali orders.

Darius regards the creature.

'I'm going in with him,' he declares. 'I want to meet this guy.'

Koppie and the men turn venomously.

'Luister…' one hisses.

'This is joint territory,' Darius points out. 'I'm within my rights to check if he's real.'

'He has independent security,' Koppie informs Darius. 'Scheduled for one visitor today. You are risking your life, my bru.'

'We can't protect you,' Kali confirms. 'He has crazy shit in there…'

'I'm going in,' Darius pushes.

Koppie shoots Kali a look.

'Okay, listen,' he tells Darius. 'Call your guys. I know you have a private network in the zone. Do it now. In case, you are killed. We don't assume responsibility for you if you step out the vehicle.'

Darius stares a moment.

'Okay, fine,' he relents.

Pulling a phone, he places a video call. Someone answers.

'Howzit,' the face on the screen greets.

'These guys are making a drop with the scientist,' Darius tells the face.

'Izzit?'

'I'm going to check him out.'

'Let me talk to Koppie.'

Darius swings the phone.

'Howzit, Koppie.'

'We don't advise this, Cedric.'

'It's his decision, bru.'

'We warned you, okay?'

'When you extracting your guy?'

Koppie looks to Kali.

'Hatchery procession,' it confirms. 'Tomorrow'

'He can come back with you then,' Cedric advises.

'He'll die in there,' Kali sings tunelessly.

Cedric smiles, good-naturedly.

'That's that, then,' Darius nods, cutting the call.

'Almost there!' Chops bellows from the front.

'Where?' Fortunato asks.

'Hillbrow Tower base,' Koppie explains. 'We lift a manhole. You guys go down. Follow the tunnel under the tower. Ends in a door. Go through. Wait in there. His security doesn't extend underground. You will be safe. But, he'll have to take you up.'

'Okay,' Fortunato says.

'Fetch you tomorrow,' Kali promises.

'Listen Darius,' Koppie adds. 'We can't wait around. If he turns you out, you're on your own.'

'Ja, I'll be fine.' Darius nods.

Mr Rottweiler stops in a cluttered side-street. Surprisingly crowded. People, drifting like ghosts. Moving in the same direction. Remains of a market. Rubble on the tarmac. Back of the vehicle opens. One of the men takes point. Covering the rest. Pedestrians give them a wide berth. Cult members exit. Lever off a heavy manhole lid. Fortunato nods to Kali. Goes down the hole. Closely followed by Darius. Stagnant water channel. Lit by a far-off red signal. Raised concrete ledge spans the length. Fortunato looks up. Lid lowers with a clang. Presently, they hear the Casspir. Rumbling away. Heading for the light. Metal door. Locked. Fortunato tries the handle a few times. Small screen lights up.

'Present identity,' a robotic voice announces.

Unsure how to proceed. Fortunato lowers his face to the glow. Scanner maps his features – retina. A lock pops. This time, the door opens. Entering a dark and narrow ante-chamber. Airlock set-up. Like a submarine. Second metal door accesses a passageway. Clean inside. Well-lit. Following it – to a T-junction. Right side terminates in a cul-de-sac. Wooden door. Off-set, in one of the walls. Left, a flight of stairs. Upstairs entrance – metal airlock.

'What now?' Darius asks – again in Xhosa.

Fortunato shrugs. Wooden door opens abruptly. Someone steps out. Quickly resealing the portal. Fortunato realises it's Seikichi. Never actually seen him in the flesh. Different to what the director expects. Sturdier. In a black robe – traditional hakama. Sort of thing a martial artist might wear.

'Who are you?' he demands, eyeing Darius. 'Get out, now!'

'I'm one of your landlords,' the track-suited figure jokes, also in English.

'Get out now,' Seikichi repeats.

'What's in there?' Darius asks, indicating the wooden door. 'They said there's nothing down here.'

'Actually, they just said no security,' Fortunato corrects him.

'You must leave!' Seikichi barks at Darius.

Darius pulls a snubnosed revolver.

'Tell me what's in there.'

Clearly, Darius doesn't appreciate being told what to do. Seikichi is fuming. Eyeing the stairs. Darius swaggers down. Pushes the shorter man aside. Seikichi catches Fortunato's eye. Signals to the top airlock. Darius opens the wooden door. Enters. Seikichi flees nimbly. To the upstairs entrance. Flinging its wheel-lock.

'Get up here now!' he hisses to Fortunato.

A deafening gunshot. Followed by a terrible shriek. Fortunato moves fast. Following Seikichi into an airlock space. Securing the door behind. Dim red light. Outside, more screaming. Something, bashing around. For some reason, Fortunato imagines a mad cow. Something heavy.

'What is that?' Fortunato demands.

Seikichi unlocks the adjoining portal. Clean, minimalist lobby. Tinted glass frontage. White widow – some meters away. In a white hakama. Six arms. Addition of legs makes it a spider. Eight limbs. Modelled on Delilah. Carrying sheathed swords – long katana and shorter wakizashi. Flesh, tinted. Hair different. Instead of Delilah's blonde fall. This model wears it jet black – straight.

'She won't harm you,' Seikichi assures Fortunato. 'My tower knows you now.'

Fortunato finds it interesting the doll's face has been removed. Replaced by a demonic mempo – a traditional samurai mask. Seikichi crosses to a nearby metal elevator.

'Forgive my Bushido obsession,' Seikichi mentions. 'I'm one of those ex-pats.'

'Let's keep the culture in the Petrie dish,' Fortunato jokes grimly – one of Brick's lines.

Elevator rises.

'What happened downstairs?' Fortunato asks, again.

Seikichi turns to face him. Looks him over.

'You may remove your biosuit.'

'No, thanks.'

'You have already been immunised.'

'When?' Fortunato demands, angrily.

'Some years ago. When I was working in Club Ded. Delilah administered a Shodai dose – Shodai, being first-generation – without your knowledge. You should thank her. You should thank me. Without it, you would have surely perished.'

'Nonsense!' Fortunato blusters, feeling violated.

'Now, listen. I have allowed you here out of respect. Respect to kumo no megami – my goddess, in both incarnations.'

'Zlata and Trill?'

'Delilah and Kali, yes. For their sake, I will explain some things to you. But don't be pushy. Not in my house. Understand?'

Fortunato takes a deep breath. Holds it. Situation in the basement has caught him off-guard.

'Fine,' he agrees. 'Where are we going?'

Seikichi turns to face the doors, once more.

'Two hundred meters, straight up.'

*

Hillbrow tower used to have six public floors. Apartheid era luxury. Closed in 1981. One, a revolving restaurant, Heinrich's. Another, a VIP level. Decorated in Louis XVI style. Seikichi's taken over everything. In there for years, now. His automation self-replicates. Machines, repairing one other. Improving. Rebuilding. Fixing everything in sight. Placing orders for materials. Building off-site drones. To scavenge, mine, process, transport. Overseen by his white widow. Some late-gen model. His 'Jisedae'. Heavily customised. Fortunato was wrong about its Mempo face. Mask inverts upstairs. In the safe-zone. Docks its swords. Wears a designer gown. Floor-length. Presenting a realistic version of Delilah. Pigmented naturalistically. As the cinema star. Not realistically, as Zlata. Physically believable, yet psychologically stylised. If you know her. Strange with the dark hair, he muses. Never seen Zlata with dark hair and no smile. An hour later. Fortunato wanders the former observation deck. Wide, circular structure. As with all six floors. 360 degree windows. White widow watches from the shadows. Swaying slightly. As though to music. With its many arms. Reminds Fortunato, ironically, of a Kali statue. Dead quiet in the space. Until he opens some windows. Minimalist lounge décor. Smoky glass. Opacity adjustable. Long, black sofas on one side. Overlooking a cinema screen. Mounted in the centre. Seikichi remains a floor down. Attending to something. Fortunato studies the screen. Multiple camera points. Random POV switches. All controllable. Via remote. Tracking a large, public gathering. Must be the ritual Koppie mentioned. In a battered park. Just below the tower. A block east. Down Goldreich. Could see it clearly from the windows. More people arriving. Street with the manhole. Jammed solid now. Thousands. Cult members. Street people. Transients. Entire gangs. Thronging to the park. Filling adjacent routes. Bonfires paint a large, raised altar. Stained crimson

– in patches. Too lurid and festive for blood. Rather, some artificial colour. Under scorched trees. Halloween spider decorations. Spray-on web. Paper tarantula cut-outs. Things for kids. Ceremony hasn't properly begun. Gathering awaits their Kali. Seikichi refers to it as a 'matriarch.' Fortunato is missing something. Mutes the speakers. Sick of that screaming. The fevered chanting. Can hear it anyway. Through the windows. Seikichi eventually returns. Offers Fortunato a cut-glass tumbler of Shochu. Lacerated with ice.

'I don't take alcohol,' Fortunato informs him.

Seikichi frowns. Somehow insulted. Retires to one of the couches. Watching the screen, sipping his drink.

'What is this ritual, anyway?' Fortunato asks –- sitting across.

'Did you hear about my first job at Oracle Incorporated's affiliate company?'

'No.'

'I began in robotics, all aspects. Progressed to aeronautical engineering. But I wasn't interested in designing craft. By the time I entered Oracle's affiliate, my interest was in fixed orbital platforms.'

'Space stations?'

'At first. But, later, I specialised in lower structures. You see, space stations and satellites, they inhabit the thermosphere. This extends, from a hundred kilometres up, terminating around six hundred. The thermosphere, you could say, is the beginning of outer space. This region is the hottest part of the atmosphere. Sunlight is undiluted, you understand? Hits with full force. Aurora Borealis occurs there, around the poles, where the veil is the thinnest. Below a hundred kilometres, we have the mesosphere. This region is my primary area of interest. It extends downward, to the stratosphere. So, you could say the mesosphere is around ninety kilometres deep. It is the coldest part of our atmosphere. Asteroids burn up in there.'

'Why are you interested in the mesosphere?'

'It's a dead zone. Too high to be studied by aircraft, too low for spacecraft. Most data is second-hand. You can get away with almost anything in the mesosphere.'

'What about wind? Surely the wind must be very bad?'

'The wind is phenomenally strong. Reaching speeds of up to one kilometre a second. You have continent sized windstorms in the mesosphere. They raise vortices, like waves, getting larger as they approach the beach.'

'What is the beach? Space?'

'Actually, the mesosphere is the beginning of our beach. The air thins out dramatically in that layer. These wind-waves crash there. Spreading out, creating maelstroms. Disseminating around the globe.'

'Surely, wind like that makes construction impossible?'

Seikichi smiles dryly.

'Fortunately, the air is about a million times thinner than ground level. You could stand in one of these high-velocity mesospheric winds and not feel it at all.'

'I see.'

'Are you aware that spiders are the only creatures to travel to some of these heights? They use web constructions to catch electrical fields.'

'I think Zlata told me about that…'

'Fascinating stuff, web,' Seikichi sighs, pleasurably.

He's rubbing his hands. No longer looking at Fortunato. Almost as though talking to himself. Onscreen, the crowds grow more exuberant. Roaming telephoto tracks. All manner of depravity. Substance abuse. Beatings. Flagrant carnality.

'Spider's web: strongest material known to humanity – relatively speaking,' Seikichi continues. 'If you were to scale up certain flying insects – hitting web, mid-flight. It's the equivalent of a passenger jet, being stopped by a circus net. That's the power. Perfect for high-altitude construction. More reliable and less ecologically damaging than, say, carbon fibre, or some such nonsense. But so difficult to harvest. Imagine. Farming spiders to produce any kind of viable output.'

'Synthetic web?'

Seikichi looks up irritably.

'Now, you are talking like a real scientist,' he scoffs. 'Who needs the real thing, when you can just synthesise a cheap substitute…'

'Did anyone manage it?'

'They tried. They failed. We cannot simply replicate one of the wonders of nature by peering into its chemical structure. Nature is infinitely more subtle. Did you know, for example, that there are crystalline properties to spider's web? The processes of spinning and constructing these silk threads, within the organs themselves, are too complex to mimic. Even at a molecular level. The mix of proteins is idiosyncratic, secreted as liquid crystal. Careful, varied stages of production. All in the blink of an eye. Acid baths. Osmosis. Moisture treatment remains a mystery. Clearly, it's used to enhance tensile strength, but how? We could never truly understand this process. It's something done by *feel*. A product of applied genetic knowledge, coded creatively, within the spider's body.

The coils of protein within the web itself, for example. A machine would logically order these. But natural spider silk possesses an aspect of almost chaotic, structural disorder. Particularly in the arrangement of glycine peptides. What a machine might deem disorderly, in actuality, gives web its supreme elasticity. Conversely, the alanine peptides, another protein found in the silk, are stacked almost like bricks. Their orderly arrangement counters the glycine. So, you have two types of strength, somehow interacting and supporting one another.'

'What you are saying, is that you cannot improve upon nature.'

Seikichi gives his most human smile. Quaffing his drink immediately after. Erasing it.

'That is precisely what I am saying.'

His white widow approaches. Porcelain feet tapping – not unlike a spider. Robot refills his glass. From one of thirty fingers.

'I'm guessing you wanted to use a web derivative,' Fortunato suggests. 'As an upper-atmosphere building material.'

'No derivatives. The stuff itself.'

'Did you solve this issue?'

Seikichi looks to the screen. Momentarily distracted by some detail.

'We have some time before the matriarch emerges,' he notes. 'Let me show you something.'

'Fine.'

'First, I must prepare you. As you probably know, some insects and arachnids have shorter life-cycles than humans.'

'Okay.'

'Bearing that in mind, imagine what you can achieve with selective breeding. You could enhance or play down characteristics, using a completely natural life-process.'

'Well, it's not completely natural.'

'The life-cycle is natural – the genetic tweaking we do within, is not. But this simply effects the outcome, not the process. Unless, we speed the life-cycle up, or slow it down.'

'All right.'

'On earth, gravity plays a large part in controlling insect and arachnid development. The ratio of exoskeletons to internal organs, for example. These balances must exist harmoniously. If insects became too large, they would lack the strength to move. Impacted hydraulic motor control. Internal stresses. Circulation issues, etcetera. Their oxygen relays and food requirements would change radically. This is the reason why we, as a species, have not been overrun by gigantic ants, or such things.'

'I see.'

'But what if the gravity problem is simply … removed? By breeding at extremely high altitude. In very low gravity.'

Fortunato is becoming increasingly uncomfortable. A sensation that's been building. Since the Chelsea. The demon milk from Delilah's spinnerets. All these horrors. He stands. Moves to the nearest window.

'What have you done, Seikichi?' Fortunato hisses, profoundly disturbed.

Gazing down at the crowds. Boiling over. A human whirlpool in the corner of the park. Swirling around a black speck. Must be Mr Rottweiler.

'Come and see,' Seikichi smiles.

Fortunato looks back. Sidelong to the screen. Purposefully avoiding it. With every natural impulse. Still, resists himself. Moving back to the couch. Onscreen – a closed-circuit view. Seemingly endless metal corridor. Hundreds of cell-doors. Each with a circular vault-access. Audio reactivates. Only a deep hum. Buzz of heavy machinery.

'Let me show you the cells,' Seikichi says, flicking his control.

Fortunato reacts convulsively. Staggering back to the windows. Shakes his head violently. As though to remove bugs. Finally tearing off his visor. Gulping air. Smell of the room hits. Smell of Joburg, itself. Disinfected glass. Machines. Latent, cloying scent of Seikichi. Fortunato disengages his gauntlets. Pawing a damp face.

'Of course, it was decided their legs should be amputated at birth,' Seikichi continues. 'Imagine, these things running around, they said. Now, we have our dairies in the sky. These wonderful creatures, reduced to mindless cattle. We can't even force-feed them. Well, to a degree. Prey still has to be alive – they need that, you understand? So, I bred these farm varieties to cannibalise each other…'

Fortunato is losing it. The sound of that *thing*. Moving in its cell. No visor to muffle it. All those pipes entering its body. Milked to the point of collapse. Then eaten alive. Just the sight of its head. Under fluorescent banks.

'Turn it off,' Fortunato mutters thickly.

'Take another look,' Seikichi smirks sadistically.

'Turn it off!'

Maniacal crowd noise. Swarming reassuringly back. Fortunato rises. Finding Mr Rottweiler through the window. Mobbed by cheering hordes.

'What the hell is going on down there?' he demands hoarsely.

'A fertility rite.'

'I thought you said arachnids couldn't get that big!'

'Not under normal evolutionary circumstances. But, by removing gravity as an obstacle to development, I found a way to accelerate life-cycles, for a variety of different reasons – as well as selectively promote growth. It became possible to automate pressure chamber gestation-pods. To slowly, over a decade, acclimatise large generations to surface gravity.'

Fortunato glares warily. Checks the widow. Still in its corner.

'Generations…' he repeats, in disbelief. 'Why would you *do* such a thing?'

'Look, there is something you must know, Fortunato. Kali is unaware of the dairies. It would be violently opposed to the wholescale cruelties occurring there – if it ever discovers the truth. I would certainly be targeted.'

'What's to stop me telling them all?'

'By the time you leave here – you will be protecting my interests. Which, you will see, are yours as well. You need me, to help Delilah. I'll prove it. If I have not convinced you by tomorrow, you are free to tell Kali anything you like.'

Fortunato eyes him.

'Sounds fair,' he chances. 'It's not like I can communicate with anyone while I'm in here.'

'How about that drink?'

Fortunato hesitates. Signals the white widow. It nods, filling him a tumbler. Chilled. Finely brewed. Tastes good. Unseals his suit. Numb satisfaction.

'Good shochu, isn't it?' Seikichi nods. 'Healthier than you might expect...'

Fortunato takes a moment. Centering himself. Approaches the sofa. They sit a moment. Observing proceedings below. Camera is in close. Cult members, offloading a small truck. Ferrying bales. What looks like frayed barbed wire. Dumping these on the altar. Creating a sort of nest.

'Old cobweb,' Seikichi narrates. 'After the ceremony, these people will rip it to shreds. Everybody knows it's a component of the cure. In its raw form, it still maintains certain healing properties. People save the fragments as talismans. Some make a kind of soup out of it…'

'Why? Do they require healing? Are they afraid of something?'

Seikichi glances over his drink.

'We are saving the world. There is no time to do things any other way.'

'Why did you really agree to talk – to show me these things? I think you want something.'

'I do.'

A heavy drum strike. In the street below. Amplified – through loose woofers, tweeters. Stacked chaotically. In stripped minivan taxis. Heads turning. Drum hit repeats. Backbeat begins. Fortunato drifts back to the screen. Getting a better look. Entire chorus of drums starting. Some skin-bound, traditional. Alongside plastic barrels, oil drums. Old marching snares. Sheets of metal, beaten with piping sections. Burned palms surround them. Some untouched. One blazing. Trawling smoke in the wind. Fever groove. Deafening levels. Through clustered streets. People going crazy. Dancing. Substance fits. Total debauch. Tight cut to Mr Rottweiler. Doors open. Kali, stepping out. In close-up. Breath fogging. Chanting rises. Turning to open screeching. Kali's men spill out. Rip the fur from their goddess. Flinches against the cold. Must be near zero. Especially with the chill factor. Surveying its public dreamily. Raising arms. Eliciting more chaos. Men come and grab it. Raising it. Bearing their icon above a sea of faces. Figures dash for the feet. Pulling off spike heels. Lost to the crowd. Kept as reliquaries. Any part they can touch. Powdering the skin of their naked saint. Flung handfuls of sacred ash. Often dyed scarlet. Camera view switches. Panorama of the red-powdered alter. Quite wide – perhaps the girth of four queen sized beds. Placed together. Now a tangled nest of fibre. Dreadlocked figures in sackcloth. Smashing entire aloe plants. Great wooden bowls. Filtering syrupy gel. Straw sieved. Into stone cauldrons. Low flames gutter. Steeping the mixture. Steam fogging the altar. They mix in fragments. Bundles of herbs. More ash. Ladle large cups. Out, across the web. Soaks it up. Expanding. Getting spongy. Releasing misty vapour. Drummers must be on fish glands, Fortunato decides. Groove has a familiar patterning. Fish does things like that. Followers toss the creature into its nest. It bounces, crawling around. Smiling dangerously. Acolytes splash warm fluid over its body.

'What is that thing – Kali is wearing it,' Fortunato asks. '…Between its legs. Is that some sort of machine?'

'Cage amulet,' Seikichi ho-hums. 'Tribute to an obscure spider deity it favours. Probably saw it on the internet, or in a cartoon, or something…'

'I suppose, we all choose our totems,' Fortunato says. 'To you, it's a cartoon. To Trill, it's a talisman. You've never eaten the fish, glands, have you?'

'You people are obsessed with them.'

'Perhaps.'

Koppie surprises Fortunato. Climbs onto the web, mounting Kali – sexually. Crowd cheers.

'What the hell…' Fortunato exclaims.

'Guards go first,' Seikichi informs him. 'Public follows. Paying tribute.'

Fortunato is stunned. Koppie finishes quickly. Followed by his team.

'Don't be so shocked,' Seikichi chides. 'It's ceremonial. An act of reverence. Also, there is a practical purpose.'

'How could any of this insanity be practical?'

'Well, the ritual assists in triggering the birthing process…'

Fortunato rises abruptly. Hesitates. Signals the white widow. It glides over. Refills his glass. Retracts. Fortunato drifts to the window. Sipping recklessly.

'Kali, as you know, opposes surgery, pharmaceuticals – anything medical,' Seikichi continues. 'Deals with its needs in various, shall we say, tribal ways? Indigenous knowledge. Herbalism. Nevertheless, it consented to my automated operation. It understands, you see. This is a call of destiny...'

Fortunato says nothing. Drinks, listens.

'I implanted Kali with a highly specialised spinneret. Nothing as sophisticated as Delilah's. This spinneret creates an egg sac, taps only local networks. Digestion, etcetera. Nanobot targeted. Lacking a womb, I had to implant rectally. Kali cannot, of course, produce eggs. But I harvest these at a very early stage of development. Package them in soluble web. Kali inserts them at will, just before each spinning cycle. Brings the eggs to term, internally. During gestation, host switches to controlled liquid diets – to avoid damaging the egg-sac. These offerings that the followers make now – they serve no reproductive function. They are symbolic. Fertility offerings. However, their fluid is still rich in protein and nutrients. They absorb into the sac, feed the eggs within, weakening the slightly acidic PH balance of the egg-silk, lubricating the birth passage...'

Fortunato surveys the events with unbridled disgust.

'What about diseases?' he counters. 'This sort of contact is reckless endangerment...'

'Kali is the *matriarch*,' Seikichi insists, as though Fortunato is not listening. 'The matriarch is not only immune to Prion Eyes. Kali is now immune to a wide spectrum of highly infectious diseases. A side-effect of the spider's immunity enhancement. Even though it didn't take immunity to fix the protein issues of Prion Eyes. In the case of the prions, the solution was more a case of like attracts like. You see, the cure doesn't *cure* prions. Prion Eyes protein molecules vibrate at a different resonance to normal human protein molecules.

The web extracts are coded with so many specialised proteins – they essentially order themselves. Diffusing throughout the body – the web extract attracts Prion Eyes molecules by resonance, trapping them within safe, peptide layers. It's quite simple, really. But only works because of the latent frequency attraction. That's the simple explanation. I mean, it's really quite complex.... Immune system engagement, however, was simply intended as a deeper level of my experiment. In order to host offspring, Kali's body has to communicate chemically, with the eggs. To gestate them. There is a lot of genetic crossover in this incubation period. Using data harvested from Delilah's implant – regarding the synthesis of arachnid and human genes, and enhanced by nanotechnologies – the matriarch's body is now able to accept and convert certain foreign DNA commands. Rebuilding Kali, in order to support hatchlings. I expected to see a surge in the overall immunity – as a side-effect. But nothing like what has happened. Now, Kali heals extremely quickly. Some birthing reflex. Musculature has improved exponentially. Hormonal transmission. The lymph system. Tendons, circulation, flexibility, all enhanced. Men with full-blown HIV will engage it tonight, hoping to be healed. But there will be no spread of infection. We even have lepers here. You will see...'

'Will they actually be healed, though?'

'Not in this way. But, if they take the cure, and are not too far gone, then yes. Perhaps. The cure is not simply for Prion Eyes. The cure is for many, many ailments. The indigenous healers Kali brought in – they have modified, refined and enhanced my raw extractions. Turned them into a holistic, multi-point medicine. Kali's post-natal body is its sacrament – the foundation of the serum. For, within Kali, is contained the buffering, necessary to adapt spider immunity to our own – to make it compatible with humans.'

'You're not dosing innocents with nanotech, are you?'

'Not at all. The nano-system is only necessary in the two primaries. To acclimatise host bodies to a foreign presence. Once compatible, active extracts that are produced by the hosts can be transmitted naturally. After processing and treatment, of course, by the healer's indigenous expertise.'

'Are they using fish glands in the cure?'

'Yes, partly.'

'These gangsters in Jersey are going to get a surprise when their users start kicking, because drugs don't work on them anymore...'

'Well, you know Kali. All about saving the world...'

'What's the connection between Trill and Zlata?'

'Without Delilah's unique system data, manipulating Kali's development would be impossible. Well, at this level…'

'The unholy grail,' Fortunato jokes.

'There is nothing unholy about it. This is salvation – a renewal of humanity. The blessing of the great spider goddess.'

Fortunato studies him. Seikichi is completely engrossed by the screen. Switching camera views constantly. Zooming in. Reframing. Armed men organise queues. A gun shot rings out. Fortunato perks up. A heavily muscled man has just been executed. Shot in the head – whilst inside Kali. Blood fountains over the grinning creature. Fragments of bone. Staining soaked cobweb. Body is hauled off, cast aside. Another immediately assumes his place.

'The condemned,' Seikichi explains. 'A final honour, before death. For many, this is their dying wish…'

'What sense is there, releasing these apex predators into the world?' Fortunato demands.

'Kali's offspring are highly specialised. Hunting only those infected with Prion Eyes – those who are in the final stages. To the spiders, the infectious Prion particle is like a drug. One they need to consume, in order to survive. I engineered them in this way. They have no drive to harm healthy humans – unless provoked. In fact, they are allergic to healthy bodies. The disease starves the body of certain compounds. I used these to code the allergy. They are also bred with extremely short life-cycles. And Kali sires only males. I've seen to everything.'

Fortunato voices something.

'Kali wasn't the first, though. You tried this with Delilah first, didn't you?'

Seikichi sighs. Signals for a refill.

'Delilah gave birth only once,' Seikichi confesses. 'The process was too traumatic for her. I had to externally manipulate the implant – try to suppress her memory of the event. Luckily, destiny chose to favour us with not one religious icon, but two. Kali is different. Kali is born for this. They named it aptly, I suppose. Goddess of motherhood and death...'

'Did Zlata yield the same potency as Trill, after birth? If you compare extracts, I mean.'

'Stronger potential from Delilah, considering she is biologically female. But we didn't develop her enough in that regard. We focused on the implant, instead.'

Another gunshot rings out. Fortunato twitches, inadvertently. Fresh blood bathes the oiled, writhing body of the hive queen. Another dead man is removed. Another replaces him. Someone leans down. Slips a burning pipe into Kali's mouth. Drawing deeply. Fuming smoke – some writhing wyrm. Never more inhuman. Masses crowd the altar steps. Many preparing themselves for climax. Pre-saturated by Kali's media. Enraptured by possibility. A very real moment of intimacy – with their deity.

'How long will this go on for?' Fortunato asks, sickened.

'Into morning, usually. But it's cold tonight. In summer, this can go on all weekend…'

'This entire fiasco seems unnecessary,' Fortunato grimaces. 'If simply breeding spiders is your aim.'

'Actually, the birthing ritual is a very effective way of growing our membership.'

'But you suggested it, didn't you?'

Fortunato senses a nerve.

'I thought all this samurai stuff was just a harmless indulgence,' he persists. 'But I get it now. You are desperate to see yourself as honourable, a saviour of humanity. Working in the shadows, modestly liberating your fellow man. The reality is, you are a complete pervert, Seikichi. There is no laurel thick enough for your true nature.'

Seikichi's sneer intensifies. Ignoring the accusations. Focusing instead on the depravity onscreen.

'So, Kali is birthing these things in New York, as well?' Fortunato snaps.

Feeling the alcohol now. Still not enough. Not now.

'In the sewer,' Seikichi replies vacantly. 'Delilah's apartment has good sewer access. Hatchlings find their way into the exclusion zone. Hunt only by night.'

'Surely they must have been spotted by now?'

'I would have thought. But it doesn't seem so. I think they stay underground – or in buildings.'

'What happens when word *does* get out?'

'Soon, Kali will make pilgrimages to other exclusion zones – worldwide distribution…' Seikichi blusters on, ignoring his question.

Another gunshot.

'Something's been bothering me,' Fortunato interrupts.

'What?'

'How secure are these lift shafts?'

Seikichi smiles maliciously.

'Don't worry, it can't get up here.'

'The one that took Darius. It's not one of Kali's, is it?'

Seikichi seems surprised.

'How did you guess?'

'Trill would see these things as its children. Who would leave their kid with you?'

Seikichi becomes annoyed.

'Maybe you are in shock,' he mutters, looking away. 'Why be rude?'

'Fine, I apologise.'

'No wonder you don't drink.'

Fortunato can't watch anymore. Decides to stop the refills. Gets up again. Does a slow circuit of the chamber. Thinking. Coming up behind Seikichi. Resuming his original seat.

'The one downstairs. It's Delilah's, right?'

'Very good,' Seikichi nods dryly.

'But, she hasn't done this birthing thing in a while. So, you must have tweaked its life-cycle inversely. Some spiders live quite long. Maybe this one does too.'

'You're not a bad detective, Fortunato. What else haven't I told you?'

'It's a female.'

Seikichi, also a little tipsy by this point. Throws down the remote. Clapping slowly.

'You make rules, then you break them. That it?' Fortunato pushes.

'I have my reasons.'

'Can't be getting eggs from it, though. You would probably prefer eggs coded with Kali's DNA.'

'Well, that's where you are wrong. But you're not a geneticist, so it doesn't count.'

'What do you mean?'

'The eggs contain both sets of DNA. I used Kali to spawn the fertilising male. Even though the true maternal bond is cemented after hatching. Who knows, maybe spiderlings would react to a surrogate in the same way? I don't have enough data on spider behaviour to confirm or deny…'

'You winged this all without proper research?'

'I got it done!' Seikichi retorts. 'Anyway, corporations are always paying off academics to turn a blind eye. You know that.'

Fortunato raises his eyebrows. But holds his tongue.

'Earlier, you said you wanted something from me,' he demands. 'What would that be?'

Seikichi mutes the screen.

'I want to offer you a job.'

Fortunato snorts.

'Whatever it is, I won't do it.'

'Kali wants you to.'

Fortunato glances back.

'Look at tonight, for example,' Seikichi says. 'We have years of secret footage now. Well archived, exceptional quality. Fully automated editing facilities are available. Combined with the document of Delilah's implantation – just imagine. Then, there are personal logs. You're the only one who can make something out of it all.'

'Where would we show it?' Fortunato explodes. 'Nobody can know these things!'

'Why not? Soon, it will be impossible to hide. In any case, the material is unique. As an artist, how could you possibly refuse to accept this responsibility? Kali trusts no-one else to do the job. Neither do I, for that matter. I know what you did for Delilah, with Club Ded. Everybody knows.'

Fortunato snorts again. It depresses him – that he should have allowed himself to drink. If he'd only kept up with the glands. Would be straight as a razor. Through any minefield. The way would be clear. Now, he's lost. Secretly anxious. His decision to drop the movie. Zlata's never-ending rabbit hole. The nightmare outside. A spider's mouth-parts – trembling under office lights.

'I came here because I need your help with Zlata,' Fortunato presses. 'I believe you know where she is.'

Seikichi drains his glass. Still distracted by the screen.

'It's all connected,' he gestures vaguely. 'I will tell you everything you need to know. But we must begin working together. There is no other way forward. Everything is changing.'

Fortunato sinks into his couch. Thought he'd made an independent decision. Tanking the film to save Zlata. Instead, he's only asserted dependence. Seikichi is right. Their toxic trove is rare treasure. Vile, life-changing nightmare fodder. Treasure, nonetheless. Not the sort of opportunity anyone could refuse. On paper – he'd be turning down a big-budget, career-maker. For an underground, history changer. With astronomically better pay. More creative control. Alongside people he cares for. Why is he rebelling? There should be no other option – for him. Not with his sensibilities. If only it had been his decision, alone. Instead of being weaponised by Zlata's excesses. The accidental movie producer. Again, Fortunato has checkmated himself. Rubs his brow. Signals the widow.

'No business, like show business,' he sighs.

'Welcome to the re-evolution,' Seikichi toasts in return.

*

Dawn paints the wreckage. Frost dusted. Taking up the colour of dyed ash. Smoke haze. Debauch in the park. Fortunato steps out the front door. Accessible, only at certain times of the day. Out on the street. Tentatively breathing chill morning air. No more masks, he tells himself. Trying not to think about the room downstairs. Is the inner city really infested? Do people truly set up Spaza shops and mini-markets – in the hunting ground of demons? How stoic, he reflects, bitterly. How South African. Imagining all the gallows humour. Still some people on the street. More, loitering in the park. One block down. Hazing in the sun. Lying in filth. Some dead, or dying. Fortunato drifts toward blackened trees. Sees Mr Rottweiler. Chops is at the wheel. For a moment, his smile slips. Seeing Fortunato without a mask.

'There goes the neighbourhood,' he jokes grimly – through his visor mic.

Fortunato nods ironically. Been a long night. Everything changed. Koppie and the boys show up. Leading a dazed Kali. Creature still high. Bundled in streaked fur. Sights Fortunato, limps over barefoot. Make-up obliterated. Hair wild. Blood-clotted and feral. Caked in unspeakable grime. Cradling its bloated, infested guts. A complete mess. Somehow, shockingly radiant. Undeniably more beautiful than ever. Spider hormones? Water always finds its level, Fortunato observes. The decorations of sacrifice. Kali – everybody's necropolis Brobie.

'You'll do it?' it rasps, red-eyed. 'You'll make the film?'

Fortunato nods.

'Imagine,' it grins horribly. 'Fortunato, turning down Hollywood to make web-porn…'

Joke takes Fortunato by surprise. Uncharacteristic. Finds himself laughing. Almost uncontrollably. Alongside the avatar of destruction. It's too witty a comment for Trill, Fortunato decides. Creature is parroting second-hand aphorisms again. Turn of phrase smacks of the movie star version. Delilah Lex. Did she reach down from heaven again – prime these two to recruit him? Before meeting the cruel fate Seikichi described last night? Trill is oblivious. Now, Fortunato's obligated to keep secrets from a goddess – and a friend. Betraying his principles again. All for the sake of Zlata Zuhk. Her various, reckless endangerments. Pretty soon, Mr Rottweiler is on the move once more. Nobody is surprised by the demise of Darius. They assume it was the white widow. Fortunato lets them think that. Kali passes out on the floor. Barely moving. Fortunato expects they will head back to Melville. Instead, Chops angles deeper into Hillbrow.

'Where are we going?' Fortunato asks Koppie.

'Ponte,' he signals.

That famous hollow tower. Canonising the Johannesburg skyline. Originally an exclusive gated community. Degraded hard. When the area fell to slum. Its hollow centre. Hundred and eighty-five meters high. Ringed by walkways. Gradually plugged. Fourteen floors of garbage high. Famous for indoor suicides. Eventually retaken. Converted to an urban penitentiary. Existence as a prison – cementing the tower's spiral. Kali's Angels assert a new all-time low.

'You really worship these … these *things*?' Fortunato questions Koppie.

Thinking of that legless monstrosity. Follicle pricked face. Dreadful, somehow soulful eyes. Koppie regards him a moment. Hands working Kali's muscles again. Flaked with blackened blood.

'It's good to see you without your mask, my bru.' Ex-gangster nods.

Obviously interpreting it as a show of faith. Director brushes off the comment.

'You must understand,' Koppie tells him, in Afrikaans. 'The gogga's are saving us. No matter how you look at it. That is the truth. And this one here…'

He indicates Kali. By grabbing its slender foot.

'This one is their *mother*.'

Fortunato looks out the window. Ponte tower becomes visible. Coming in on Joe Slovo drive. Some blocks ahead. Turning into the side-streets. This part of Hillbrow. So much worse than Constitutional Hill side. Barren. Filthy. Drifted with grey. Ashen in parts Ragged like tumbleweed. Fortunato realises its rotting web. Mr Rottweiler screeches to a halt. Engine running.

'Let's go!' Chops calls. 'Come on, man!'

Fortunato's never known Chops Mbane to show fear. But the big man isn't smiling. Really doesn't want to be here. Someone kicks open the back. Leans out a machine gun. Koppie shakes Kali.

'We there yet?' it slurs, half asleep.

'Come on, girl!' Koppie urges, slapping the creature's thigh.

Men move quickly. Peeling off its furs. Practically throwing Kali out. Stumbles on the iced road. Falls to fours. Naked, shivering. Nobody helps. Instead, Koppie slams the door. Chops accelerates. Fortunato moves to the gun-slit. Sees Kali recede. In a steel-grey morning. Through bruised glass. Limping off barefoot. Into trash-blown streets.

'We can't just leave Kali here,' Fortunato protests.

'She's safe,' Koppie insists. 'Nobody else is, this side – believe me.'

Speeding away, Fortunato keeps looking back. That lone figure. Staggering amongst ruin. Soon, lost. Takes him right back to Chinatown.

*

Kali shuffles slowly. Between abandoned vehicles. Fallen road signs. Up on the concrete apron. Shelving Ponte's dark parking lots. Choked with web below. Entering the building. Through a cracked wall. Dim, ruined arcades. Snack shops and a laundromat. Rubble. Ankle-deep in rotting grey spider dust. Dark inside. A lightless exchange of passages. Leading to the centre of the hollow spire. Cleared of trash. The bottom is strange. Architects left the original rock floor. A tall concrete tube. Circling this garden of lunar boulders. Littered with web. Far above. Dark, hand-like silhouettes. Moving laboriously. Against an open circle of sky. Ropy clot of structures. Dangling cocoons. Something hunches against a graffiti wall, nearby. Car-sized. The way they sometimes pull their legs in, that way. Watching Kali. Eight reflective holes in the blackness. Kali staggers toward it. Singing tunelessly. Some pop track from the radio. Kicking mouth-part pedipalps aside. Crawling between, for warmth. Squirming against the fat, furry belly. Spider tenses heavy legs. Tucking Kali tight. Nuzzling the creature's side with exploratory mandibles. Androgyne lies snugly in this half-dark. Teeth chattering. Breath slowing. Warming up. Fur has a musk to it. Kali can't describe it. Gnarled hooks at each leg tip. Grimy from the city. Kali's eye-lids droop. Seeing more approach. Descending from above. Sleep washes in. Waking in the night. Aching pain. Too warm. Suffocating. Kali wrestles free. Squirming upward. Between clustered, carapaces. Grown to know them by touch now. Even in the dark. This one would moult soon. That one already has. This one has spikes. Sometimes the wind catches their cast-off skins. Blows them through the streets. Saw one in Soweto once. Tangled in telephone wires. Kali lurches painfully. Out of the dense cluster of bodies. Many, alert now. Attentive. Creature feels them listening. They know what's coming. Can smell it. Kali vomits. Crawls to a stained mattress. Laid out on bare rock. Cold circle of stars. Far above. Lying there. Fogged breath. Sweating profusely. Skin steaming. Clenching and unclenching. Sac is broken. They must be coaxed. Gentle flexing. Guiding each out. They arrive, black and shining. Curled up. Small, wet plums. Unfurling. Crawling onto Kali's goose-pimpled body. Huddling there. They'll stay on for a week or two. Almost continuously. Larger spiders approach. That rustle of fur. Not so quiet at this size. Bulky lumbering. Hydraulic movements. Surrounding Kali again. Fascinated by each birth. Primal memories. After all. they all started this way. On their mother's body. Two hours of toil and torment. The last leaves Kali's body. Creature falls limp. Breathing ragged. Bleeding some. Nothing serious. Reaching for a plastic bag. Pulling a small carton of cheap juice. Pushing in the straw. Quenching deeply. Lying still for some time. Feeling spiderlings arrange and rearrange on its skin. Clustering cosily. A moving blanket. Inside a close forest of legs and pendulous abdomens. Energized somewhat, Kali reaches for another bag. Some babies drop off. Reattach quickly. This one is zip-lock. Full of gear. Battery pack, phone, light. Setting up the LED. Always shocks them. Some gallop for the wall. Others remain. Accustomed to their Kali. Something beautiful – about how all those eyes catch glare. Logging into social media. Touching blood to lips. Dead city make-up. Peace-signing a post-birth video story. Spider and heart emoji. Followers only. Look at my cute babies. That sort of thing. Lying there. Looking up sometimes. Seeing them moving high above. Occasionally, with a stray Virgin Mary. My angels, Kali will whisper.

DOLPHINS OF SATURN

'In 2009, the Cassini probe did a detailed fly-by of Saturn's Rings,' a new section presenter beams.

Or is he new? Delilah can't be certain. Celebrity guest. MMA fighter? Rogue tech CEO? Can't quite place him. Memory loss is really annoying her. Little glitches. Inside her pearl. Cocooned in gel. Response capture – fully initiated. 'Soft' trackersuit. Suspended mini-drone network. Floating remotely – in-pod. On a web relay. Each strand, cored by nanochain. Geometric lattice. Encapsulates her body. Implant access. Multi-port hardware interface. Fine web. Single strands, slipping in and out of web-lubricated skin pores. Hairports. Texture projection. A sense of the clothes, mostly. Lightweight. Colloidal density intentionally weakened. Accident protections. Modular magnetic operators. Drift responsively. Around her – in unison. Predictive, but riding her live nerve data. Uniquely sophisticated imprint. Extreme tactile resolution. Beneath her – a thought-floor. Forming and reforming. Photographically mimicking surfaces. Real-time sculpt. Tens of thousands of web-coated soft-points. Each branching – to micron level. Interfacing with the pod's gel pressure. Automatic viscosity. Neural data-stream. Virtual wardrobe schedule is running. Holo-stream live section. She and the presenter open the segment. Black-tie. Suspended, in a blank screen void. Mysterious, retro Theremin theme. Light disc array – off-camera. Some matinee spotlight setting. Hovering. Just like flying saucers – Delilah always imagines.

'This rendezvous took place on one of the planet's equinoxes. Perfectly timed, so that light conditions were ideal – for photographing the rings.'

'Wow!' Delilah fake-smiles.

Way beyond stadium applause. Viewers around the world. Live capture. Delilah's been playing it 'wow.' Ever since Fortunato's manifestation. Keeping up appearances. Till it's time to strike.

'Something unexpected and fascinating was discovered…' presenter growls, enigmatically 'Starting in the B ring, stretching to the edge of the outer A ring…'

Thousands, drawing in breath. Automated ambient volume – tracking scripted moods. Manipulating global levels live. Live orchestra of viewer audio responses. Targeting almost any emotional theme – instantly amplified. An advantage of instant audience data.

'Now, if you look closely at this image…'

Vast imagery manifests. Towering behind. Delilah turns in space. Ball gown swirling. At first, the shot of Saturn's rings appears conceptual. Captured, from directly above. Various rings. In horizontal bars. Fast zoom. Into the high-res image. A dark wave-form. Running along the outside edge.

'These are shadows!' presenter declares. '…of the mountains of Saturn!'

Crowd goes wild.

'Although the rings stretch some two hundred and seventy thousand kilometres outward – from the atmosphere of Saturn, their width is really not that thick. Sometimes, only ten meters deep. But, centrifugal force from the gas giant's gravitational spin has piled exomoon debris at the far ends of the rings. A process that has taken millennia! It has created mountains! Some, stretching over two kilometres high – or low! Because, on the other side of this strange range – is only the icy void of space…'

Another 'wow' from Delilah.

'Now, imagine, if you will, a staggering Saturnine mountain range – running for over a hundred and thirty thousand kilometres, encircling the planet completely! Imagine the view! Imagine hiking those mountains!'

Applause, cheering.

'But why imagine it…?' Presenter leans in confidentially. 'When you can do it all, right now!'

Throwing an arm up dramatically. On a back-zoom. Blank void dissolves. He and Delilah now stand on a craggy black peak. Overlooking the staggering ring-field. False wind whips their hair (somehow, never obscuring a camera angle). Delilah is lifted magically into space. Faking surprise perfectly. Hair and ballgown morph. Behind – three ghostly forms start taking shape. They are huge. Towering in the rings.

'The perfect venue for Delilah and her Lex Band to perform highlights from their hit album – Dolphins of Saturn! Give it up for…'

The three ghosts resolve. It's the band. Octopoid drummer whacks his modular snare. A hundred thousand dolphins erupt. Varicoloured. Jumping through rings. Delilah snags her floating mic – hits the first bar screaming. Now in skimpy couture – with a triple Mohawk. Growing steadily larger. Till her intricate, custom sneakers knock asteroids out of synch. Occasionally shooting glances at the guitarist. Back-lit by the gas giant. Is Fortunato in there? Audience, invisible. Wandering the mountains in avatar state. Alone, or, with friends. Floating in space. Cheering from exomoon rubble. Band hears their applause, though. Pretty high-octane. Speciality access event. Mountains of Saturn environment reveal. First time. Complicated deal. Between space organisations that captured the data – and future theme park speculation. Delilah knows the truth. Only a tiny portion of the alien range is actually replicated. Most, predictively generated. Users have no way of knowing. Cartography access is limited – potential mining futures is the excuse. Though, with the aggressive magnetosphere and radiation. Not likely that will ever happen. Show's predictives could use the algorithmic flex. No business like show business. Finishing the gig on a high note. Three hours downtime in the simulation to follow. Primarily for Saturn photo-ops and similar PR. Fans can still interact – without her knowledge. Social media blitzing. Selfies with the Lex Band – on Saturn. Delilah stands alone on an asteroid. Hip-deep in Stalkerville. Wondering how many unseen punters are creeping. Capturing. Running ghost-hands over her. Many ways to track. Official, or deep dive. Delilah simply doesn't care anymore. Smiles, poses. Jumps all the right hoops. Biding her time. Holloi the Octopoid drummer approaches. Swimming weirdly above the ring-field. Modelled on retro cartoons. Cachou pink – with little green blobs. Goggling manga eyes. A funny hat. Neo-punks and contemporary rap culture love him.

'It's me,' the cartoon hisses – in Fortunato's serious timbre.

Delilah can't help laughing. Hearing Fortunato – coming out of Holloi the Octopoid. It's too much.

'We don't have much time,' the octopus tells her.

'Is Wile E Coyote chasing you?' Delilah cackles hysterically.

Fortunato appears to notice his disguise for the first time.

'This conversation is off-grid,' he explains. 'But not for long. I'm going to initiate a quarter second signal disruption. Control will read it as a glitch. But we'll instantly revert to your pearl pod. When programming resumes, a doppel-shadow will drive your hologram. Just till the end of the Saturn segment.'

'We'll stay in the pod?'

'Yes, we should have an hour off-grid.'

'I'm ready to rock.'

Delilah Lex wakes. Tiny bubble slips her lips. Makes her open her eyes. Fortunato floats outside the pod – on convex projection. His hologram. Engrossed in some task – off-capture. Looking young, she thinks. Like that last time they met. When was that? Delilah notices they are on the move. Pod already draining gel. Trackersuit micro-drones – retracting web-lines from her hairports. Folding back into storage. Soft seating unfurls. Holding her upright. Beach rushes away. Soon as her head clears the meniscus. Delilah spits out the brace. Pukes bright blue.

'Won't they spot the pod?' she rasps.

'I left a ghost on the beach.'

Delilah looks around. Picking up speed. Across that weird, wave-less sea. Already further than she's ever been.

'They can track me through my ring…' she points out, suddenly realising its not on her hand.

'It's also on the beach.'

'So, where are we going?'

'The outermost edge.'

'Of what – Saturn?'

Fortunato takes a moment. Regards her.

'It's good to see you, Zlata.'

'Hasn't been *that* long!' she giggles.

He appears somehow saddened by this remark.

'Fortunato? You're being weird, man. Are we in the South Pacific? I can't remember where we're shooting…'

They are a good two kilometres out now. Maybe. She can trace the island outline. So much smaller than its labyrinths suggest. Pearl slows dramatically. Floating to a halt.

'Time to step out.'

She glances down. Into the ocean depths.

'Dude, we're like in the middle of the ocean.'

'Not really.'

Looks him in the eye. Pops the top hatch. Peering out. Looks pretty much the same.

'Fortunato, what the fuck, man!' she yells.

'Trust me.'

Wouldn't be able to see his holo. Once she's left the pod. Voice could transmit on the speaker system. Probably better to keep things quiet outside. Slides back in. A glowing holographic arrow – in convex. Above the sea. Pointing away from the pod. Toward open ocean. Rummaging round. Finds one of those stupid bikinis. Lacing it, Delilah shimmies up again. Eyes the still water.

'What? Must I just, like, jump in the sea?'

'Yes.'

She looks around. Apart from the island. Blue water, in all directions.

'Which way am I swimming?'

'You won't need to swim,' his voice directs.

Delilah raises an eyebrow. Slides down the side. Holding retractable silk rope. Surprisingly, the water reaches just below her knees. Splashes around with her hands. Colour-matched blue floor.

'It's only deep around the island,' his voice explains, through external speakers.

Keeping the volume low.

'Go on, then,' Fortunato encourages. 'Follow the arrow.'

Delilah frowns, shrugs. Wading out to sea. Singing the Dolphins of Saturn title track to herself. Walks a hundred meters or so. Smooth floor is rising. Around her ankles now. Looking ahead – empty ocean to the horizon. Back, over her shoulder. Pearl gleaming in the distance. Against a tropical postcard. Airbrush dreams. That faraway isle. Delilah sighs in irritation – splashing onward. Suddenly, a mirage. She stops. Gone. Moving forward slowly. It reappears. A pale line. Coming and going. Holographically hidden? Delilah marches ahead. The veneer melts. No hologram. It's the water. Shallowing out. Washing on and off a strip of bare floor. Creating a gleaming line. Vanishing and reappearing with the wash. Delilah approaches cautiously. Ocean appears to simply end. Illusion of a horizon line – maintained from a distance. By the subtle curvature of the blue floor. Emerging onto the exposed region. Delilah pads nervously out. Across the floor. Appears to end abruptly. Some distance ahead. Edge running in both directions. Describing a massive arc. Encircling the island – and its sea? Unblemished sky continues beyond. Stepping closer. Delilah's eyes widen. The earth far below. Continental edges. Turquoise ocean gulfs. Extremely high altitude.

'I'm dreaming…?' she whispers.

Catchment gutter. Road-size. Below, rimming the edge. White and metal cabling. Intricate junctions. Varying girth. Collecting in nodes. Expanding patterning. Soaring out – into space. Multi-direction. Superhighways of mechanically buttressed cobweb. Some areas are strange. No practical sense. Clusters of morphing nodes. Robotically enhanced. Fractal expansions. Forming and reforming multi-dimensional shapes. Collapsing. Re-growing. Differently, each time. Seemingly alive, organic. Each moving of their own accord. Like anemone. No, stranger. Less coherent form. Reminiscent of microbial development. Absurd constructions. Throughout the grand networks. Staring wildly out. Into the mesosphere. Delilah spies a towering web cluster. Some superstructure. Dropping taut lines down – into the stratosphere. Needling upward too. Many kilometres away. Connected to the island. Via complex, spacious networks. It draws her, strangely. She's overcome by an overpowering compulsion to fly over to it. As though, in a hologram. Delilah drifts the edge – staring. Stunned. She's spotted something else. Can't be certain. No, she can. A mirrored spider, large as a house, spinning mechanical webs. Actually, no. The spider is not mirrored. It's white. Porcelain-toned. Lack of colour lends reflectivity. Somehow, it senses her. Across the divide. Turning a monstrous, multifaceted head. Deactivating spinning. Shifting its upside-down bulk. Moving instantly toward her – along dense, quavering lines. Delilah watches in horror. She must be dreaming. But she can't be. In her dream, she is the spider. Now, seeing it as a separate entity. Stalking her. Confronted by the reality of high-altitude. She's the only one alive up here. Delilah is paralysed. Comes to her senses. Stumbling backward in horror. Fleeing into the water. She can hear it now – mounting the catchment level. Tap-tapping heavy metal limbs. Running desperately. For the distant pearl. Slips, skidding the shallows. Looking back. It's already on the water. Trundling quickly toward her. Wasp-hive belly. Reflecting water patterns. Delilah rises. White spider towers over her. Three storeys, easily. That realistic head. Size of two truck cabs. Rendered in porcelain and pressure-alloys. Regarding her. All of a sudden. Delilah isn't frightened anymore. Can't explain it. She knows this thing. Everything is familiar. Tentatively, raises an arm. Toward open mandibles. Filaments of fine web spew from the mouthparts. Instantly penetrating the pores of her hand. A surreal, out-of-body sensation. Looking down – at herself. At everything, stereoscopically. From eight eyes.

PART THREE

ANGELINC

NEVERLAND

Flavour of funerals. Between Oxford Circus and Leicester Square. Something old, choked with flowers. Soho draws mourners now. Its endless parade. Cracked plaster coffee houses. Media backstreets, koi lamps. Inventing a continuum. Anita had worked there. Front of house. Celebrity members club. Soho, already outliving its prime. Once the hunting ground of kings. Now, dying a protracted death. Developer's axe. Cashing in construction tenders. Erasing old Tottenham Court. Turning the red lights white. So long, the Intrepid Fox. The grand, Swiss centre and its glockenspiel. Sold – to American candy. New kinds of prostitution. Exchanging cultural landmarks. For a cold universe of fast-food franchises. Postcards from the Caymans. Anita survives the Millenium. The false catastrophes it augured. Entire generations swept into narcolepsy. Corporatized party culture. Vague threats of apocalypse. Heroin chic. Acid House sting operations. Clubbing in small-town England. Whitby goths. Derby Ecstasy. Poison tsunami of the late 90's, receding. Stranding her on unforgiving shores. Anita exits the party scene. Takes that job in Soho. Experiences gentrification. In real-time. Time-lapses. Hot topic at her club. Primary reason she segued into real-estate. Forged work visas. Playing Robin Hood. To historical pubs. Infamous Italian restaurants and French cafes. Victorian drinking fountains. Like the one, dug up on Shaftesbury Avenue. Grand plan fails, of course. More money brokering property on the river. Selling Knightsbridge, Chelsea. Leaves London with a Porsche. Revolutionary itch, unsatisfied. All that could change. Why not? Wanted something quiet, anyway. After the chaos of the queendom. But, returning to London as a ghost? Smuggled in by boat. Somewhere near the Hebrides. Nothing figurative about the afterlife. She and Alix – officially dead. To break silence is to court assassination. Watching a child molester gunned down. Taking false responsibility. Does wonders for Alix. All her party friends in London. The art school circuits. Gone. No more social media. Not that she could ever post from Club Ded. It's the spy life now. Walking outside in disguise. Safe-house in Crystal Palace. No more public transport. Too risky. Facial recognition everywhere. Most tapped for clearance. But you never know. Would have preferred Hampstead or Belgravia. But Anita knows too many people. Borough of Croydon – too quiet for the pair. Long, winter walks. Eyeing Brixton clubs – from afar. Avoiding people. 'Like vampires,' Alix remarks. She and Anita discover designer burqas. Call them invisibility cloaks. Cab everywhere. In-house service. Joys of bottomless finance. 'I'm a spoiled ghost,' Alix sometimes sighs. Eating fancy cakes and pastries. Everything ordered in. Mooning endlessly for Paris. Weeping over photographs of her parents. Angels sometimes rely on archangels. For communications. Areas where they were known. But Anita already has a proxy. Khanyisile's view. Old sniper's never lived in London. Spent most of her life at war. Institutionalised. In seclusion. Not too much detail. Currently enjoying her luxury penthouse. Somewhere near Embankment. 'No hijab for Khanyi!' they joke. Archangel claims Alix does a good job – playing proxy. Why spoil a good thing? Really, it's a test. Everybody knows it. But Alix has a talent. Supporting Anita. Age-gap even comes in handy. Nobody from the queen's old scene can identify her. Still able to mine some network. No-one has to know strings are being pulled. Takes Alix down Soho. Paul Raymond may be dead. But his property endures. King of Soho. Suffering significant posthumous casualties. Walker's Court – sanitized. Madame Jojo's – lost. Only mis-en-scenes left. Here and there. Neil Jordan's Mona Lisa. Michael Caine, waving a finger. On that red landing, upstairs. Seedy publishing legacies. All the floor space they bought. That continental patisserie, allegedly bequeathed to family. Every facet of Soho's continuum. In decay. Anita's going in, full force. How much can she pull from the termites? Plotting in old tea-rooms. Near Piccadilly. Re-reading Ian Sinclair's Rose Red Empire. Alix, morbidly consuming black coffee. Does she regret abandoning Roxelana? Anita wonders. Khanyisile claims open invitation. Return any time, she offers. Alix refuses to leave Anita's side. Life already forfeit. Sacrificed, to some vague, new world order. Prion Eyes – still just a scare. Something happening elsewhere. To other people. Anita knows which way the wind is blowing. Hacking official chains. Poking up banking trails. Confirming via Angel Control. The exclusion zones are coming. So are masks and biosuits. Local authorities, plotting sinister upheaval. Zone-line decreed – south of the river. No way, they are losing the centre. Lock everyone up in Croydon. Keep the north's nose clean. Anita can't fight major zoning. Too much attention. Focuses on future borderlands instead. Areas around the river. Conglomerates, aggressively accumulating property. Values in freefall – around insider zone projection. Clear what's happening. To Anita, at least. Shady groups, building aggregate land holdings. Eating up small bites. Till they have a cake. Stockpiling cakes. To make a shop. Formerly deluxe addresses. Heritage sites. Re-zoned council estates. Rows of dead or dying shops. All swallowed into private ownership. Sooner or later, values would revert. Post-Prion Eyes, perhaps. If the zones are ever abolished. By then, areas would be annexed. Ripe for massive redevelopment. Now, it's a front-line war. Especially for small businesses. Homeowners. Councils favouring buy-outs. Private muscle. Beginnings of concretisation. Reef of some cold future. 'Not on my watch,' Anita will remark. Alix gets excited about it. Some days. On others, she reminds Anita of a pot plant. Kind that unexpectedly withers. Won't let go of her at night. Sometimes suffocating her. Maybe it's their inability to socialise with others. Weeks turn to months. Tiny interactions take on gravity. Shopkeepers. Familiar people in the park. Strangers' dogs. Even then, no real bond could be forged. Who else can Alix turn to? Khanyi? Stalking her old social media. Almost hourly. Reading posts of sympathy. Photos of her funeral. Mourning herself. Logins no longer allowed. Always sleeping. Angelinc operatives share one private social network. Pings, when agents are in the vicinity. Kind you could actually talk to. Anita is stunned to see Saud's name pop up. Khanyisile confirms. She is allowed to make contact.

'Jirre! He's no angel!' Anita jokes.

'No, you are right,' Khanyisile agrees. 'Saud is more of an intermediary, let's say. Between … departments.'

'What? Like a fucking cherub?'

Khanyisile chuckles.

'Anything I mustn't talk about?' Anita checks.

'Ag, just be discreet, bru. You are supposed to have the same clearance. But we all know it doesn't work like that…'

'Goed, dan.'

*

Meets Saud at a small restaurant in Mayfair. Discreet booths. Able to remove her veil. Doesn't expect it to get so emotional. More a reunion with her former self.

'Of course, you would land on your feet,' he gushes. 'I expect nothing less from a queen.'

Anita brushes it off.

'I'm not a queen, anymore.'

Saud takes her hand, smiling dangerously.

'My dear. Exile does nothing to diminish your station. There shall be no other ruler, in your realm. Deposed, you may be. But a queen, you remain!'

Anita is touched. They *had* been friends. Strange, to be sober around him. For her, he existed only in that sphere of total abandon.

'You haven't said anything about my outfit.'

He sneers. Employs some hand gesture.

'I have progressive sisters. We detest these things…'

'Sorry,' Anita mutters, embarrassed.

'Don't be.'

They'd hooked up many times. Usually at the end of debauched nights. With another girl, or two. That one, or the other, had coerced. Thought nothing of it, really. Part of the furniture. Now, she's hesitant to return to his suite. Nevertheless, Anita is almost desperate. Any morsel of her former life. Colourless, but affectionate sex. Somehow, a poignant farewell to the crown. Afterward, she impulsively fills the tub. Lying in bubbles. Sipping non-alcoholic champagne. He remains in bed. Eating chocolate. Flipping channels.

'You're thinking about your friend, aren't you?' he calls.

'Alix?'

'No, the other one. Jennifer.'

Anita sighs across the froth and steam.

'I suppose baths always make me think of her,' she admits.

'I could bend the rules a little for you,' he suggests. 'Find out where she is. Maybe get her a message?'

Anita experiences a sharp conflict of emotions.

'No, don't do that.'

He comes in after a moment. Leans against the doorframe.

'I didn't mean…' he begins.

'No, I appreciate it,' she interrupts. 'I just…Well, it's not like we could see each other.'

'Understandable,' he nods, returning to the bed. 'You should really try these white truffles! They are not bad…'

Somehow, she manages to hide her tears from him.

*

Returning to Crystal Palace. Late the next day. Saud took an early flight. Hangs around his suite. Just for a change. Hasn't been alone in a while.

Realises something is wrong. Even before entering the safe house.

'I thought you were dead!' Alix is screaming.

Dark inside. Every drape. Clearly, Alix hasn't slept. Pacing all night. Cutting up fashion magazines. Lounge littered with scissored faces.

'Calm down,' Anita tells her. 'I was just with Saud.'

Alix glares in disbelief. Bursts into tears. Striking out with her fists. Anita takes the teen by the wrists. Pinning her to the wall.

'The hell is the matter with you?'

A night out had relaxed her. Now, the tension is back.

'Pourquoi?' Alix wails.

'What – Saud? You must be joking. Even you partied with us!'

'How could you!' the girl shrieks.

Anita slaps her – hard. Alix goes dead quiet. Nursing her cheek.

'Pull yourself together!' her queen commands.

Alix nods slowly. Looking up with trembling eyes. Anita starts to regret hitting her.

'I didn't mean to leave you alone, like that,' she sighs. 'I mean, you can always come along, next time.'

Girl's face twists.

'You think I want some stupid threesome?' she sobs. 'With creeps like that?'

Too late, Anita realises her tactlessness. Alix steps back. Out of her grip – into shadow. Subdued, fidgety.

'Je suis vraiment désolé,' she whispers.

'What's the matter with you?' Anita demands. 'What's wrong?'

Alix struggles to reply.

'Pris au piége dans mon esprit…' she eventually mumbles.

'Speak English,' Anita snaps.

'Sometimes, I don't like London,' She pleads. 'Like I'm trapped in Neverland. I can never leave!'

'In the story, they escape London to reach Neverland,' Anita corrects her.

She turns away. Switching on lights. Alix is left, frozen in place. Eyes stuttering. Looks down suddenly.

'Trés bien,' she nods. 'That is true. You are right.'

'Tea?'

'Okay.'

Anita sighs in irritation. Puts the kettle on. Throwing her coat across the counter. Alix shuffles out slowly. The queen sits. Gathering herself. Doesn't even want tea. Drank a pot before leaving the hotel. Thinking about funding an old couple in Southwark. Bank want to repossess their home. One of the last jigsaw pieces. Potentially huge holding. Almost fully owned. Distributed cleverly. Various shell companies. But Anita has traced a single, guiding interest. If she can just keep the couple's home off the market. It would be possible to collapse other deals. Disrupt their entire plan. Unprepared for the gunshot. Like lightning. Through that silent house. Anita stands bolt upright. Finds herself running. Shouting. It's that special edition Tiffany's. Pink and chrome. Anita could never fathom why Khanyisile gifted it to the teen. No doubt, a test of some kind. Now Alix is on the bed. Broken face, splattered across the carpet.

*

Anita stares vacantly. Through helicopter windows. Choppy North Sea. Grey blankets of rain.

'Eish, these Pumas,' Khanyisile comments.

'What was that?' Anita asks, adjusting her headset.

'This craft, the Puma HC2,' archangel replies. 'Supposed to be phasing them out of the RAF. We used them in Belize. Nice ships.'

Anita's eyes drift again. To the weighted body on a cargo platform. Black plastic wrap. Khanyisile puffs her cheroot.

'You must just keep going.' She smokes briskly.

'I know,' Anita affirms.

Looking back out. Drizzle pelted glass. Another twenty minutes. Then, out she goes. Anita thinks about their ocean voyage. How much Alix feared sinking. Whole business has her numb.

'We'll get you out of London,' Khanyisile promises.

'Why?' Anita mutters. 'I'm making progress.'

'Don't act tough with me, my girl. We will continue here. But through another operative. You built a strong foundation. Very commendable. But the procedure is to pull you – now.'

Anita sighs raggedly. Running fingers through her hair. Growing it out for a few months now. Strange to have long hair. Alix's idea.

'Pass me your blade,' she petitions Khanyisile.

Old soldier frowns. Produces a black-steel dagger. Flips it before passing. Anita takes the handle. Starts sawing off hair.

'Back to the bob, eh?'

'Never should have grown it.'

Gets most off. Taping the bundle to Alix's shroud. Pilot calls a proximity alert. Begins their descent. Khanyisile gets up. Disengages the door. Rain blasts in. Blades raising spray. Chop, off the spume. Khanyisile moves to assist. But Anita pushes her off. Checking her strap. Hoists the girl up. Inching to the edge. Drops her into the surge. Staying out in the rain. Hanging on the strap. Watching angry water.

'We must vaai,' Khanyisile eventually signals.

Anita nods. Moves to secure the doors. Resuming their berths. Dripping in streams. Chopper begins to climb. Angling back for the coast.

'Second star to the right. Straight on till morning.'

'Eh, what now, sussie?' Khanyisile frowns, perplexed.

'Neverland. It's the way to Neverland.'

'Luister nou, bokkie.'

Anita looks up. Listening, as ordered.

'I know what happened in the desert. I'm not stupid. I know she didn't pull that trigger.'

'What's your point?' Anita snaps.

'That we tried. We did our best for her. Croeser should never have dumped his meisietjie on us.'

'I'm tired of blaming Croeser for everything.'

'So, now you are going to blame yourself?'

Anita meets her eye. Framed by savaged hair. Archangel shakes her head, tut-tutting. Anita ignores her. Eyes drawn repeatedly – to a stray lock of her own hair. Trodden to a tangled mess. Against cold, military metal.

LITTLE BROTHER

'Arcadia Springs?' Anita sneers.

'Well, it's very small-town America...' Khanyisile shrugs.

Anita leaves London. Orders from Control. Returns to water-based tech. Again, overseen by Khanyisile. Running Neptuna – modular community in the free ocean. Sustainable farming. Completely autonomous. Clean hydropower. Two and a half years at the helm. In the South China seas. Expanding operations. Manages to reconnect with Seikichi. Via in-house communications. Sends the location and stats on the fallen fax. Still in the Rub Al Khali. Kept it quiet for her. Anita's staging recovery – soon as humanly possible. Without Angelinc's knowledge. Not even Khanyisile can know. Needs that ace in the hole. Learns of Trill's disavowal. Wonders how Seikichi is still on payroll. They share a sect, after all. The Oracle moves in mysterious ways. Doesn't make sense. No chance to dig deeper. Unable to raise Seikichi after their talk. Just that one, brief contact. By now, Prion Eyes in full swing. Angelinc backroom chatter all about *Good Morning Delilah!* Focus project. Only two months since airing. Already shaking up the industry. Anita checks it out. Attends the production entry pilot screening. Insane interactivity. Too busy for a deep dive. Things going well in Neptuna. Captain Annie, they call her. Expects to be there for another two years. But she's told to step down. So long, open sea. Finally, being promoted to archangel. She, Saud, Khanyisile. Other top-enders. Decide to celebrate. Charter trusted crew. Superyacht, from Miami to the Bermuda Triangle. Nobody disappears. Anita's assignment comes in from Control. No personal contact with administration. Only other archangels. Nameless drop box assignments from Control. Khanyisile says it's always like this. Unless the Oracle takes a personal interest.

'So, this angel built their own small town?' Anita checks. 'Most people run away from small towns.'

'Rich kid.'

'Slumming?'

'Eish, but nicely. Wired the town up – completely. Everything is monitored.'

'Why?'

'He says he's making a case for invisible, unilateral surveillance. Nip problems in the bud. Prune society, like a little tea garden. But no giant shadowy organisations processing data. This is garden cottage big brother. Single monitor, assigned to small segments of the population. With an archangel, of course. Autonomous authority. Bit like priests, at confessional, I suppose. Only, with unlimited resources to respond.'

'…And no moral compass. You can't just spy on people.'

'Well, he seems to think it's a jol. Go, be his archangel. I've had enough of you anyway.'

'Where will you go?'

'A nice slow gig in the Bahamas.'

'Sounds hot. Can I come?'

'Eh, voetsak!'

*

Nevada. Anita drives out from Las Vegas. Black Hummer. Biosuit till city limits. Crates of personal gear. Remote drone hook-ups. Full body-interface. Heading for the state-line. Mars, California. Two years in Neptuna have made her strong. Getting her martial arts body back. Response training. Strange to be on land again. Inner ear adjustment. Not much in Mars. Sand and Satellite dishes. Radio telescope country. Small dirt road to Death Valley. Looking into the real-estate angle. Force of habit. Property for the town – wangled via Prionic Commissions Council. Huge sectors of the population. Relocated for zoning. Angelinc must have gotten in on that. Anita is sure of it. Just what she would have done. Working Oracle Real Estate. Meeting her ward in some diner. Outside Arcadia Springs. He's quite excited about the diner. Designed it himself. Along with most of the town. Passes a walking holographic billboard at one point. Delilah, in a bikini. Standing several storeys high. Smiling, waving. Diner at the end of a long, empty road. Looks dingy. Rundown. Flyblown shacks. Diesel station. Place for long-haul truckers. Sixteen-wheeler nearby. Diner – pure fifties. No name. Very art department. Purposefully drab, colourless. Retro country 45s. Turning on low volume. No staff. Completely empty. Except for Jared.

'Don't you just love it?' he chuckles.

Occupying a booth. Late twenties. Upstate New York inflection. Extravagant hand gestures. Very good suit. Dove grey. No tie. Anita instantly dislikes him.

'I love retro Americana. Fifties is so, late nineties, don't you think? I do a lot of meets in this diner. And the motel. I mean, it's supposed to look like shit. But it's actually pretty deluxe, when you're inside...'

Anita follows his finger. Crabby roach motel. Stuttering neon sign.

'Don't you just love it?' he repeats.

'Not very original.'

'Hey, well, I mean, it works. Nobody from town comes out here.'

Looking him over. Decent gym-tone. Still looks like the one pushed around at school.

'No mask mandate?' she asks.

'Death Valley is a secure zone. Not a single case.'

'I see. So, how'd you get involved with Angelinc?'

Knows his file. Wants to see what he says.

'I guess I bought my wings.'

'Middle class upbringing. New money family. Self-made tech billionaire. Involved with Oracle. Caught wind of Angelinc. Traded everything to get in.'

'I mean, don't you see? I gave it all up. I gave up my privileged life to help people. Angelinc is where it's at! We're going to do great things here…'

Anita punches him in the face. Just a tap. Still, he overbalances. Falls to the linoleum. Staring at her speechlessly. Sees the aim was off. Going to get a black eye.

'Don't take it personally.' She shrugs. 'Just something I had to do.'

'You had to punch me?' he yells. 'In the fucking face!'

Scrabbling up. Warily shifting. Foot to foot. Anita removes her sunglasses.

'One night, old money and I got wasted. Made an oath – to punch any nouveau-riche tech billionaires we met…'

'How many have you met?' he fumes, resuming his seat.

'Oh, you have no idea.'

Angrily straightening his collar. Smoothing back hair. Resisting an urge to examine his developing bruises.

'Poor baby,' she teases. 'Want to sue me?'

'Listen, you're the boss, ok?'

'That's the spirit.'

'I can sense that you maybe don't like me…'

Weird glint in his eye. That rising, nasal emphasis on sentence-ends. Upper middle-class Americanisms. Dossier weirdly incomplete. Things she needs to confirm.

'Have you been initiated yet?' Anita interrupts.

Eyes dart for a moment. Settle on hers.

'Not yet.'

She raises a brow.

'Why not?'

'The Oracle loved my proposal, I guess!'

'Yes,' Anita sighs in irritation. 'She does have a thing about capturing detail at this level. I guess I can see how your system would interest her. Though, I can't see what the purpose is.'

'The betterment of society, I should think.'

'I'm also not sure how you got your wings greenlighted without bullet tax. That's against procedure...'

Looks uncomfortable.

'Well, like I said. I guess, I bought my way in. I proposed this project to take advantage of Angelinc's networks. I need off-grid infrastructure to cut corners. Grow tech faster. I mean, I've put together great teams in Silicon Valley. The best. So, I fronted all the funding, organisation, everything. If this is a success, I've already laid the groundwork for mass-implementation. That's a lot of development. Whole new frontiers, in unregulated surveillance.'

'So, you gave up control – became a subordinate. But you're still getting your way.'

'I'll do what needs to get done. If we can get my systems off the ground – we could really grow this thing!'

'Listen, Jared. I'm not your partner. If I don't like what you are doing, I'll shoot you.'

He swallows uncomfortably.

'I'm sure it won't come to that.'

Reaches out his hand. Hoping to shake on it. She eyes it distastefully.

'Don't make me hit you again.'

He's angry. Controls it. Boardroom bravado, she concludes wearily.

'So, what do I call you?' he asks, retracting the hand.

'My queen, your highness.'

His amused reaction falters. When he sees her face. There it is again, she notices. That strange gleam in his eye.

'How about…mistress?' he suggests sheepishly.

*

Anita checks into the roach motel. Operative in the lobby. More in the backrooms. Fake truckers, gas attendants. Suite is gigantic. Entire top floor. Top of the line. 'No rooms available,' the house protocol – for strangers. Anita counts more staff. Not like Club Ded. Anita handpicks her girls. People she'd worked with closely. Knew inside out. Jared's staff are requisitioned. Angelinc outsources low rank. Often from high-echelon Oracle divisions. Jared probably watches video tutorials on management. That's her impression. No kind of experience that counts. Taking her on tour. His control HQ. Set up in a defunct radio telescope base, nearby. Automated security on-site. No staff. A relief, for her. Neptuna was her tight ship. No pun intended. Anita doesn't do amateur hour. Not these days. Still, Arcadia Springs must be important. Wouldn't have been assigned, otherwise.

'You have a lot of personnel,' she observes.

'There's a ton of gear, moving parts. I mean, it's a whole town! But security is gold. Everybody's been vetted by my CO.'

'This is not some start-up,' Anita checks him. 'There's no retirement plan and only one authority – me.'

'I'm doing my best!' He grins, showing off his dentistry.

Ignores his attempts at charm.

'I don't want to meet any other staff, understand? I'm a ghost. You watch the town. I'll watch you.'

'No problem.'

Control's telescope dome. Banks of monitors. Hundreds. Sophisticated holographic imaging arena. Apparently 3-D walkthroughs are off the chart. Live-capture real-life environments. Outrageous resolution. But the holographic theatre lies unused. Jared prefers old-fashioned input. Sticks to his screens. His diner. Bowling alleys. Throne-like control seat. Banks of toggle-switch operating controls. Period piece supervillain lair.

'Who else has access to the control centre?'

'Nobody,' he replies. 'None of my current staff are aware of the surveillance. In fact, most believe we are processing hazardous material in here. They don't see any connection with the town. Original installation crews came and went. Current repair teams remain isolated. We station and deploy independently.'

She's eyeing the monitors. Thousands of perspectives. Hyperreal control. Bedrooms. Bathrooms. Street corners. An entire town population. Even Angelinc ops. Caught on camera. Blissfully unaware.

Kaleidoscopic invasions of privacy. Archived thoroughly. Alongside every email. Every call. Every text. Every transaction. Every search engine query. Every browser tab. Since inception.

'How do you keep up with all this data?' she asks.

'Well, you get to know everyone. Program's been running a year now. When you have the pattern recognitions of, I guess what you would call baseline normality, you can automate processing. Run predictive stop-gaps. I mean, It's like one endless television show. When you know the characters – it all makes sense. Angelinc Control keeps tabs – through a networked system. Though, they are mostly tracking tech. Holographic development, live-interface, that sort of thing…'

'More breaches of protocol,' she mutters. 'Control should only run through your archangel. Also, you shouldn't have started without oversight, or run for a year, alone…'

Anita must have grown accustomed to Khanyisile's style of command. Never really discussed other Angelinc teams. Different operational methods. Only briefly touched on Trill, at her initiation. Is she really in charge again? No right or wrong – just her royal command? Strange, to not have the old sniper. Sitting on her shoulder. Playing angel and devil simultaneously.

'…But, like you say, it really *is* too much data for one person,' he continues. 'The plan was to develop software. Tracking for specific anomalies. Ones that only I would look for. I'm still finishing off the algo-bible on that – for future systems. But, so far, the prototype tracking is effective. Haven't missed any major blips. Individuality is key, with this much data. My bots process unseen feeds – 24/7. But they still need to know how to keep me up to date on Arcadia Springs. For that, they need to learn me, as well. That's why this operation is easier with one person running each sector. Or, small teams. It's hard to systemise such idiosyncratic automation. Though, I'm working on it…'

'I've read your reports. Zero crime. Averted suicides. Increased productivity. No addiction vectors – unless you factor in over the counter, mind-altering meds. Which, Angelinc opposes, by the way. This place needs more herb gardens. Traditional knowledge. Why are you not interfacing with local indigenous communities?'

'How can you be against prescription medication?' Jared flusters. 'It's all legit – prescribed by our town therapist and doctors.'

'We don't endorse outside pharmaceuticals, therapy or any of that shit. I want it phased out. Starting now.'

Stares at her in shock. Swallows, continues.

'Well, anyway, it's not your average society. We populated it by staffing industrial plants – which I set up nearby. Tech products. Some hardware assemblage. Townsfolk are primarily middle-class, academic, highly skilled…'

'With just enough riff-raff to keep the wheels turning.' She glares. 'The discreet charm of the bourgeoisie…'

'Well, we are working on the assumption that bad elements can be phased out of society, with proper management. I mean, nobody wants to be poor and uneducated...'

'You should meet Trill's friends.'

'Who?'

'Never mind. Carry on.'

'Anyway, it's a good social system. This data will come in handy when we finally settle Mars, for example. The planet, I mean. Not….'

'Nobody's moving to Mars, you fucking jerk-off...'

Completing the walk-through. They take a drive to town. In a closed-circuit camera repair van. Jared seems to enjoy the irony. More giant holograms of Delilah. One, lying – seductively draped. Across a flat mountain. Anita mentions these.

'Yeah, we are pumping the show here,' he responds. 'Test-driving these billboards, collecting viewing data. *Good Morning Delilah!* is a massive hit, apparently.'

'You haven't watched any of it?'

Scrunches up his face.

'Hologram stuff isn't really my style.' He shrugs.

'Ja, playing big brother is.'

'Hey, I'm not big brother,' he chuckles. 'I'm little brother!'

First thing he's said that amuses her. They wear identical, company coveralls. Like siblings. Big sister, she muses. Place is bigger than Anita expects. Small suburbia sections. Fanning out from a central town square. More predictable retro design motifs. A Soda Fountain. Drive in – set against the desert. Small high school. Attached primary. Kindergarten. Library. Assorted shops, restaurants. Constabulary. Firehouse. Three bars. Pool hall – doubling as a nightclub on weekends. Country doctor, oral hygienist, salons, pet care. A mall. Everything you might need. Small-town America – in Death Valley. Hostile environment all part of the plan. Regulates activity, Jared claims. Keep people indoors. Easier, for track and capture.

*

Anita broods in her hotel. No other occupants. Two years at sea. Solid ground bringing back memories. At the window. Watching another desert sunset. A distant, glowing Delilah. Swimming over the desert. Two weeks of this now. Orders filtering down from Control. Focus on technical areas. Getting into some kind of routine. Avoiding Jared completely. Similar to Khanyi's style. Observe from afar. Strike like lightning. So far, it's pretty dull. Reviewing logs. Observing corrective methods. Jared doesn't like citizens having bad blood. Arguments, feuds. Flags these sorts of disagreements. However minor. Working tirelessly to smooth issues out. Engineering perfect circumstances. His little test-tube society. Benign acts of fate. Can't figure it, though. Why is Angelinc running this project? Can't see the long-play. Social control is not the Oracle's style. Quite the opposite, Anita would say. Accumulating libraries of juicy footage, though. Staggering leaps in holography. Anita's set up her own view chamber. 2D only. Running a cable from his telescope centre. Can't access holography from the motel. Needs to sort that out. Anita gets into the screen. Watching TV for work. How American, she thinks. Jared is correct – in his assessment of Arcadia Springs. It's like some endless, cosmic soap opera. Final endgame of television programming. Uncut, uncensored, mundane existence. Hideously addictive. How inhuman humans really are. Under the mantle of society. Can't believe what breeds there. Regardless, Jared's selected population is spouting skewed data. His interference only solidifies this. Of course, it's utopia on paper. He auditioned the town. Then sat in a high tower. Course-correcting it. Anita can't figure it out. What is Angelinc getting out of this? Aside from incredibly detailed holographic development. With no protections or oversight. Data capture process is highly sophisticated. Breeding algorithms 'in the wild.' Unique depth. Impossible through proper channels. Anita zones in. Strangers become closer than family. It's like that. When you know everybody's secrets. Divinity problems. Frank Capra and Thornton Wilder – on mescaline. Wonders how her ward manages to stay so aloof and self-righteous. Then Anita remembers where she is. Something pings her tracker. Chipped Jared, without his knowledge. He's heading into town. Unusual. Typically, he stays in his control dome. Rarely leaves, except on scheduled errands. Almost never visits town. On impulse, Anita goes down to the garage. Selection of vehicles. Diverse wardrobe. Doesn't bother with a disguise. Climbs on the Harley Nightster. Snags a helmet. Sky, tuning its indigo band. Cadmium highlights. Blending to void. Stars wash out. Warm breeze off the desert. Mammoth Delilahs. Breast-stroking overhead. Trawling television glare.

Across the dust below. Distant twinkle of Arcadia. Should do this more often, Anita decides. Streets look busy. Something going down. Anita keeps the helmet on. Visor down. Even then, she's being checked out. Strangers stand out in Death Valley. Pretty sure she'll pass for a vagabond biker. Parks outside the drugstore. Drifting with foot traffic. A fair. On a school sports field. Now, Anita remembers. Townsfolk *had* been talking about this. Semi-regular occurrence, apparently. Twice a month, or something. Old school bleachers. Teen couples holding hands. Parents parking cars. Smell of cotton candy. Roasted corn. Anita recognises people. Surreal sensation. Her holographic soap opera. Made manifest. Watched that football player masturbate this morning. Over an image of a pot plant. The true, banal faces of civilisation. Big marquee. Handicraft market. Homemade preserves. Fresh produce. Live music somewhere. Acoustic guitars. Choral singing. Orbital tents and stalls. Paper lanterns. Gloaming prettily against the dusk. Crickets in irrigated turf. Anita checks the tracker. Jared's in a sideshow tent. Edge of the field. Small, candy-striped. With a very long queue. Anita makes out a sign: '*MERLO THE FORTUNE TELLER*'.

'The fuck?' she mutters.

No mention of a Merlo in her briefing. Without the tracker, she would have missed it. Joining the line. Anita eavesdrops. People gossiping. How amazing Merlo's insights are. How spot-on his advice is.

'He's truly psychic,' someone whispers, to her girlfriend. 'Why, just the other day…'

Forty minutes later, Anita enters the tiny tent. Incense hits. Some mysterious, retro soundtrack. Jared in a turban. Fake beard and crimson velvet robe. Sitting before a crystal ball. Anita removes her helmet.

'Oh, my god,' he gasps. 'How did—'

'I get it,' she cuts in, sitting across. 'I was wondering what you got off on. Drowning in secrets, every day. But you're not even interested in perversion. Oh no, our Jared's got something even better up his sleeve…'

'Now, look, my queen, or whatever, it's nothing like—'

'So, you sit here and telepathically impress housewives. Enjoying your little power trip?'

Jared's hideously embarrassed. Beet-red cheek smudges.

'Look,' he stammers. 'It's a covert delivery system for information and—'

'Spare me the wank. I see what's going on.'

'Look, please,' he hisses. 'Keep your voice down!'

'Get dressed Merlo, we're leaving.'

Barely able to contain his frustration.

'That will only attract attention. Please! Let me finish…'

'How long?'

'Come back around nine?'

Anita sighs, stands. Replaces her helmet and leaves. Teens in the line tittering. Watching her stalk away. Climbs back on the bike. Takes a ride out to Mars. By nine, she's waiting in shadow. Fair closing down. Not many people left. Merlo the Fortune Teller collapses his tent. Spotting Anita, directs her to his vehicle. '78 Ford pickup. Powder blue, cream trim. Electric conversion.

'I'm driving,' she commands, pushing him aside.

Speeding across the desert. Anita swings off-road. Throwing out a dust cloud. Coming to a halt. She reaches over. Opens his door – shoves him out. Killing the engine. Circling round. He's staggering up. Beard half off.

'What the fuck, man!' he yells. 'Why you got to always be so—'

Punches him in the gut. Jared falls to his knees, panting. Standing over him, lighting a cigarette. Bought some in town. While she was waiting. Hasn't smoked since the queendom. Already a quarter pack down.

'What did you say?' she asks quietly.

Faraway lights in the sky. Nearby military test range. Taste of ozone in the wind. He's peeling off his beard. Turban unravelling. Bandage snake, slipping away.

'Nothing, my queen,' he pants, staying down.

Nudges his jaw up roughly – with a padded knee. Eyes all black and glinting. Can still make them out.

'Get bored in your TV dome, do you?' She smokes.

Tries to turn his head away. Grabbing product-heavy hair. She twists it back.

'Okay! Okay, I do. That what you want to hear?' he pleads.

'You're putting the whole operation at risk.'

He's staring into darkness.

'I guess,' he admits. 'But does this really jeopardize my—'

Heaves him roughly to his feet. Feeling hair rip. Jared lets out a yelp. Is pushed against the truck. Tripping on his robe. Almost falling. She comes up close. Grabbing a handful of crotch.

'There's other ways to have fun.'

His eyes are wide and staring. Strange, she thinks. Looks younger than Alix sometimes. Even though he's about a decade ahead. Hasn't thought about her in so long. One call to Saud. She could be talking to Jennifer by morning. Punches him again – twice. This time Jared does fall. Dragging him up. Getting him on the back of the truck. Tearing off clothing. At one point, horses run past. Something from a dream. Afterward, Anita sprawls back naked. Feeling the wind on her. Meeting an overhead Delilah's eye. Just for a moment. Chain smoking. He's just lying there, stunned. Staring up in awe.

'Are we … are we, ok, then?' he ventures.

'Shut the fuck up.'

'Yes, my queen.'

Anita stands in the football player's locker room. In real-time. Burly boys lumber through her. Reaching out. Sensation of a cold metal door. She can even touch the team. Not too hard. Surfaces fizzle. Feels the hair of their arms. Grazing her fingers. Obviously, they can't sense her. Tactile data. Mostly reconstructed. Generated from raw feed maps. Close enough, though. Beauty is in the immersion. Based on doll-riding. Except, there's no drone. Without the POV of a fax – things get complex. Jared's team building skills. *That* kind of CEO entrepreneur. So good at assembling talent they feel entitled. Like they invented everything. Really, he's not that annoying. Anita tells herself. Just 'forgets' sometimes. Sheer scale of his operation. Bearing strange new paradise fruit. Every surface. Every interior. Every exterior. Within the snow-globe of the town. Even the airspace. Carpeted with capture. Built in from the start. Macro to micro. At this resolution. Anita can't imagine how they are running so much data live. Quantum computing? Enough to generate a real-time holographic realm. Place POV – at any point. Tied seamlessly to roaming projection. Hologram insertion on the cards. No longer just a ghost. Haunting the internal track. Users would be able to manifest. Any point within Arcadia Springs. Interact with townsfolk. Entire town would begin to co-exist. Here, and in its own doppelganger reality. A mapped projection sphere. Shadow world. Simultaneously merged, with live environments. Anita's perplexed by heat differentials. That much processing would require supercomputing. Sophisticated coolant systems. Where are these machines? Are they plasma rigged? Power required to simply lower operating temperature. At those estimates. A challenge on its own. Anita starts running the numbers. Based on first-hand observation. Starts getting ridiculous. Hard for her to even imagine the kind of system required. Evocation of the virtual Arcadia Springs. At this level of interaction and resolution. Questions Jared about it. Acts like he understands. Really, he doesn't. Doesn't need to. Angelinc processes remotely. Somewhere undisclosed. Just feeds signal. Back and forth. Similar enigma in the queendom. White widow. Its nervous system live-data. Also hosted remotely. Easy for a human brain. Whose heat footprint is negligible. For a machine – Quantum processing. Rooms of hardware. Seikichi won't reveal a thing. Somewhere out there. Angelinc is running an unimaginable machine. Likes of which has never been seen. Floating Arcadia Springs, white widows and *Good Morning Delilah!* Anita switches positions. Shifting from the locker room. Manifesting in a janitor's trailer. Parked outside the high school. Mellow, yellow light. Above a hot-plate. He's on the couch. Eating a sandwich. Ironically reading a copy of 'Our Town.' Anita smirks. Switches out. Appearing in a bathroom. West-side suburbia. Some white-collar. Tweezing nasal hair. Ghosts downstairs. Finds his wife. Tidying up before bed. Anita reaches up. Deactivates the uplink. Pulling leads from her jack-ins. Re-orienting. Fighting temporary dizziness. Been in there hours. Missing her tank. So much better with gel. Full skin contact. Jared's on his boring throne. Engrossed. Shuffling monitors. Tweaking prompts. More relaxed with her in his lair. Now that they are fucking. She's in here every day. Ghost-walking Arcadia Springs. Anita prefers this style of management. Keep the lead short. See everything before it happens.

'Interface was already off the chart,' she comments. 'But now that we've implemented these new perks... With a pod, it will be absolutely unreal!'

'Haven't really had a chance to check it out,' he mumbles, engrossed.

'I can't believe you're more interested in social engineering. This immersion is next level. Tech couldn't have grown this fast without the controlled environment you've created. You should explore it.'

'I'm not much of a gamer.'

Anita frowns.

'You think this is a game?' she laughs.

'Listen, I'm really busy, okay?'

Doing what? she thinks. *Fixing stranger's marriages? Corporate disputes? Interventions with high-school bullies?* Debunks to the ready room. Stows her trackersuit. Takes the Nightster across the desert. Going into town a lot these days. Now that she knows the gossip. It's manageable. Everyone thinks she's a vagabond biker. As expected. Drifting in from Fort Irwin or Barstow. Takes a liking to one of the Arcadia bars. Has a coffee there, some nights. Sipping in a high corner. Eyeing the bar. Refusing to break sobriety. Often, she eavesdrops on patrons for kicks. Easy to patch conversations. Off the listening network. Into earphones. Not tonight.

Running a grey shadow. Blocking grid traffic. In and out. Needs to chat with Khanyisile.

'How's the beach?' Anita teases.

'Hau, bokkie! Palm trees and problems. What more can the Major ask for?'

'Khanyi, what's the deal with this assignment?'

'Wat vra jy nou?'

Anita fills her in on the inconsistencies. One year – running blind without oversight. Jared's lack of initiation. Bothers Khanyisile too. Especially after Alix.

'Ja, this is not normal,' she replies. 'Let me do some digging.'

Later, riding back. Delilah's giant image. Gliding between glowing ankles. Her show only getting bigger. Birthing its own industry. Anita knows a cash cow when she sees one. Still, doesn't explain its high priority in Angelinc. Not like they are short of funds. Hasn't had a chance to check it out properly. Too busy deep-diving Arcadia Springs. Small town addictions. But it's more than that. Avoided the show because it's Croeser's. After Club Ded. What he did to Delilah. He and Anita loathe one another. Now, avoiding the show is affecting her work. Anita docks at the roach motel. Orders coffee and juice. Robotic dumbwaiter. Now, as good a time as any. *Good Morning Delilah!* has screening slots. But these are for 'streemas'. In reality, it runs 24/7. A realm. Delilah's magical Lexland. Full-pass users roam the island at all times. Mixed, often minimal gear. Anita has all access. Downing black coffee. Chased with fresh squeezed orange. Breakfast at night. Alix used to tease Anita. Her 'petit-de jéneur invérse.' Pushing the girl from her mind. Again. Zoning into Delilah's world. Standardised intro. Delilah and her Lex band. Belting the theme. Croeser punting his show pony – at every turn. Anita skips the line-in, sneering. Hovering over the distant island. At cloud level. Lexland. Pretty, tropical. Blue seas, royal palms. Toggle labels bulge and flicker. Flagging various landing sites. Anita has special access. Keys in a hidden function. Allowing her to see other users. Suddenly, the sky clouds with shadows. They are everywhere. Infesting paradise. The sky. The sea. Everything.

'Delilah must fucking hate this…' Anita mumbles.

Deactivates all public ghosts. Back to a pristine view.

'Locate Delilah,' she queries.

Bikini hologram of Delilah twirls out of thin air. Mermaid tail a storey long. Turning below. Smiling enticingly.

'Now, where could I be?' it smiles. 'Anywhere, you would prefer?'

'Current real-time location,' Anita inputs.

'Let's go!' hologram air-kisses.

Anita sucks down to the island. High-velocity. Real rollercoaster punch. She's impressed. Using only basic gear. No public tactile interface. For now, touch protocols are still in prototype. Even so. Resolution and immersion. First-rate. Delilah is dancing. Rap battle in 90s-ville. Competing global stylists. Retro flow revivals. Staging in a mock-up. 1994's legendary Lollapalooza. Mud everywhere. Sunflower t-shirts. Washed-colour grading. Delilah's rocking a mosh pit. Old-school outfit. '*If Inge Lorre Became Famous*' is the couture tag. More like Avril Lavigne. Even though she'd been unknown in 1994. Nobody gets the 90s right, Anita reflects snidely. Hovers above the crowd. Switching public ghosts on. Just to get an idea. Delilah swarms with strangers. They engulf her. A real storm. Zooming in. Her body, crawling with insects. Users in ant form. Fly form. Gargoyles. Centipedes. Demon worms. Maelstrom of tentacles. Thousands of spiders. Different kinds. Vintage aliens. Animals. Retro-pixelated avatars. She's like a saint. In a medieval painting. St Anthony, beset by demons (90s themed). Merch moving at light speed. Anita feels she's missing something. A nagging sense. Pulls up a map. Warps to another part of the island. Rocky waterfall. Stalked by mermaids. Warping out again. Small coastal village. Somewhere between Patrick McGoohan's Portmeiron 'Village' and Santorini. Striped seaside awnings. Cobbled corniche. Anita looks around. Users could order food at cafes. In compatible cities – drone-delivery would co-ordinate. Process orders in real-time. Hologram interface. So, the public could eat cheap corner takeout. In a luxury setting. Anita enters a whitewashed villa. Explores rooms and corridors. Soaring balconies. Ghosts of old Amalfi. Suddenly, it hits her. Doubling back. Retracing her steps. It's the capture itself that's familiar. Ingrained POV-lens tweaks. Action response. Sensory feedback. System integration. Anita recognises it all. From Arcadia Springs. Nothing to do with the space itself. It's the relay – source to user. *Good Morning Delilah!* has its roots here. Anita suddenly gets it. Angelinc has never been interested in Jared's personal vision. His social planning. They are just using him. Developing tech for their show. He's too self-absorbed and superior to realise. He's been making it easy. Why am I here then, Anita wonders? Pulling off her rig. Yanking her lead-jack. Cuts the show. Smoking by the window. Watching Delilahs. Moving over Death Valley.

*

Around midnight, Anita goes back downstairs. Saddles the Nightster. Rides out to Jared's control centre. He's asleep. In his vintage trailer. Tethered against the desert. Like an old road movie, he likes to say. Locking everyone out of his primary focus work. Even Anita. She agrees to the embargo. Simply because it boosts tech productivity. In any case, she's not too interested in what he's up to. Maintains all-access. Without his knowledge. Just in case. Now, breaking into his loop. Anita starts going through the day to day. After an hour, she's stunned. Jared's spending all his time fixing problems he's created. The Merlo routine. Triggering a massive knock-on effect. Jared hasn't been subtle enough as a clairvoyant. Rookie oracle problems. Underestimated the power of secret knowledge. Jared's so-called insights have created a ripple. Cause and effect. Fracturing throughout the community. Contaminated Petrie dish. People growing suspicious. Strange beliefs. Haunted by prophecy. Turning against one another. Secret feuds. Odd comments and situations. Suddenly making sense. Things Anita has witnessed, ghost-walking. Jared must have realised the foolishness of his actions. Maybe he can't help himself, she considers. Ego is his drug of choice. Now, he's desperately trying to correct. Digging deeper on each attempt. Mismanaging private information. A self-fulfilling prophecy. Solely focused on damage control. Now it's all Merlo does. No wonder he's neglecting the only area of any interest: an unpoliced tech empire. Unwittingly spawned. Pursuing ideals. Losing control. It all adds up. Anita understands her mission in Arcadia Springs.

*

Jared wakes around 3.30am. Someone's bashing down his door. Getting up. Stumbles to the entrance. Anita is there. Dead drunk. Still crying. Pushes past. Slouching heavily onto his bed. Near-empty bottle of tequila.

'My, queen…?' he mumbles, rubbing sleep from his face.

'Get dressed, we're leaving.'

He opens his mouth. Shuts it again. Turns on a light.

'Put it off!'

Jared obliges. Switching back to darkness. Hesitates. Unsure what to do. She's sobbing again. Heavy, deep. Approaching cautiously, Jared sits beside her. Her head sinks to his shoulder. Deadweight. That usually impeccable bob, scuffed. Slides an arm around her. Attempting comfort. Realising, she pushes him off – violently. Rising again.

'Get dressed,' Anita repeats.

'Look, you're upset. Tell me what's going on. I'll help you, my queen, I swear I will. I'm here to serve Angelinc.'

She glares furiously.

'You stupid little shit!' the queen explodes. 'Do you even realise why I was sent here?'

He's lost for words.

'Get dressed!' she screams.

Drags him up. Throws him against a closet. Thin door snapping. Jared, cowering on the floor. Holding open palms.

'Look, I get it, you've had a shock!' he reasons. 'Let's just talk about it, ok?'

'They want me to kill you, you fucking moron!'

He blinks. Opens his mouth. Shuts it again.

'...But I did everything they asked.'

'Yes, you did. Now, they don't need you anymore. And you're a fucking liability. A joke – with your stupid, social-justice bullshit! No wonder they didn't bother to initiate you...'

'No!' he retorts.

Pulling himself up.

'You're just drunk,' he mutters.

'Oh, yes I am!' She grins through the tears. 'Almost three years of sobriety, gone. Over you and your idiotic bullshit. It's over! Get it? Get dressed. We're leaving right now.'

He's fuming.

'I'm not abandoning my work.'

'Get dressed!' she screams.

'No!' he snaps. 'They can't push me around and manipulate you. They can't! I'll do whatever it takes. We can get legal aid, we can...'

She grabs him by the shoulders.

'I'll protect you,' Anita sobs. 'I'll break protocol. I'll do it! But we must leave now.'

Wrestling out of her grip. Turns on the light.

'No!' he declares. 'I *won't* just abandon my work. These people need me.'

'Please!' she weeps, reaching weakly.

Batting her hands away.

'I've spent my whole life standing up to people who tried to push me down! I'll never back down! You hear me? Never! They can try whatever they like. You think I'm without resources? I know exactly what I'm doing, I'm—'

Gunshot is deafening. In that enclosed space. Ears jingling. Half his head gone. Just like that. Anita stands, frozen. Trembling. Just like Alix did – she's thinking. Reaching out. Killing the light quickly. Just can't look anymore.

*

Dawn. Mars, California. Anita's Nightster perches on an outcrop. Overlooking the roll of Death Valley. Later, the view will be polluted with mirages. Quicksilver feedback. By night, Delilahs. Swimming, here and there. Posing luminescently. Signature bikini range. Anita calls Khanyisile.

'You knew, didn't you?'

'What you talking, my girl? What's happened.'

'Don't bullshit me, Khanyi. You *knew*. What was this then? Some final test?'

A long silence.

'Maybe.'

'Why me? I'm not a hired hand, for fuck's sake! Anyone can pull a trigger…'

'You're the remote drone expert, Anita. All that time doll-riding in Club Ded. Only you could have vetted that situation. Looked for things to salvage. Nobody forced your hand, girlie. In fact, we clearly value your opinion in this matter.'

'You used me!'

'Now, it wasn't my call. I reviewed and relayed the mission. Called it as I saw it. Yes, I got a feeling about Control's play. I've been doing this a long time. But I didn't know enough to form a proper opinion.'

'But you knew.'

'I suppose.'

'Why didn't you warn me?'

'And colour your opinion? That would be unprofessional. You're an archangel now. We have equal rank. This is *your* mission, bok. You have to make these calls. Anyway, I'll still check it out for you. We can talk about your angel, after I've run things through my contact…'

'It's too late.'

'He's gone?'

'Yes.'

Khanyisile sighs.

'Sorry, bokkie.'

'How did Angelinc get in this position with the Arcadia Springs project, Khanyi? It's so against protocol. We don't do things like this.'

'If I had to speculate – I would blame Croeser.'

Anita's eyes narrow.

'He was guiding pre-production,' Khanyisile continues. 'Angelinc would have been obligated to take his lead. He might have unintentionally created this situation, pushing his own agendas. Maybe the show became dependent on the developments coming out of Arcadia? Who's to say…'

'Now, there's someone I would have no problem shooting.'

'Don't talk like that. I'll requisition clean-up.'

Anita's face is cold, unmoving. Yet, tears still leak. Catching on morning breezes.

'Guess it wasn't your fault,' Anita relents. 'But Control manipulated me. I won't forget it.'

'Take some leave, my girl. Why don't you join me?'

Anita's suddenly paranoid. Is the same thing going to happen to her? Khanyisile wouldn't hesitate to pull a trigger. Not like she did.

'I need to be alone,' Anita counters.

'Just tell me where you want to go. I'll fix it.'

'Thanks, Mama.'

'Of course, my girl.'

'What's going to happen to Arcadia Springs?'

Khanyisile sighs again.

'Ag, that place is a joke. I'm guessing, your tour was to determine feasibility. Now, we'll wait for the order. Strip hardware. After a few months, Control will pull the plug.'

'Without the support, it will become a ghost town.'

'Bokkie, Arcadia Springs was always a ghost town…'

*

Anita rides into town. First time she's done it by day. Since that time in the van – with Jared. Doesn't even bother to wear a helmet. People stare at the stranger. Characters on a cancelled show. Living on borrowed time. Not even realising. Industrial plants would go first. Jobs lost. Civic permissions revoked. Water access cut. A terminal exodus would begin. Few years from now – just a place of empty shells. Total ruin. Anita parks on the football pitch. Overlooking the site of Merlo's tent. Listening to the children. Places a call. Saud answers.

'You're calling on my secure line, my dear. I can only assume…'

'I need a favour, yes.'

ROGUE SHODAI

Six months with the white widow. Social media dance crazes. Mumble rap home recordings. Street fashion trends. Cooking lessons. Make-up tutorials. Robot is incorrigible. Trying everything. Nagging incessantly for advice. Am I doing it right? How would you do it? Could you demonstrate? Can I jack you up again? Obsession with humanity only accentuating its inhumanity. Chloe's losing her mind. Lost down her own rabbit hole. Attempting to penetrate the healthcare arm of Angelinc. Scouring every system for loopholes. Fish gland abuse spawning Prion Eyes – a true revelation. Not much more. No solid research or evidence. No validation. Not on Chloe's limited access. White widow won't reveal more. Now, Chloe's paranoid. Was she really inoculated? Is it still possible to be infected? She's been on-site a while now. How does the antigen work, if Prion Eyes isn't viral? Is the white widow lying? Chloe's burning with questions. Only one person can answer her. Doubts Seikichi would take her call. Even if she could reach him – her position would be relinquished. Robot doesn't want Angelinc to know people can survive in Club Ded. They would send more. If Chloe reaches Seikichi via internal messaging – she risks making an enemy of the white widow. So, it's a stalemate. Chloe is trapped. Pygmalion hell. Six months in. Food gardens. Robotic fisheries. Salvaged dry goods. Enough for years of this torment. Then, suddenly, one day – everything changes.

*

Chloe's phone receives an alert. Around noon. Uniquely coded. Sits bolt upright. Anita's old regency channel. Standard alert. Flagging a royal approach.

'Oh, my dog!' Chloe exclaims.

'What was that?' robot asks.

It's learning to skip with three ropes at once. Social media fad. Chloe had to learn too. Just so it could jack her up.

'Oh, nothing…' Chloe lies.

Has to somehow warn Anita about the white widow. It would only trap her too. Robot giggles.

'You're terrible at lying, Chlo's. Your stress hormones spike. I mean, sure, you have a great poker face…'

Chloe sighs irritably.

'You received the alert, too?'

Robot nods, attempting a complicated double jump.

'Think it's really her?'

'Who knows?' It shrugs. 'Let's find out!'

White widow runs a perimeter scan. Dinghy approaching. Moored motor yacht. Chloe fetches an Uzi from an ordnance locker – just in case.

'You don't need that,' white widow sings.

'Sorry, but you're not going to accidentally bake me in your death ray, doll.'

'What? Like a *killer robot*?' it giggles.

'Oh, shut up!' Chloe snaps – clicking in a magazine.

They make their way to the beach landing area. Black rubber boat – coming in off the chop.

'Oh, my ducking fog!' Chloe gasps.

Anita is equally stunned to see her friend. Swerves the boat recklessly onto the sand. Leaping off. Chloe's already sprinting. Uzi abandoned. They hit so hard, both go rolling. Into frigid surf.

'I knew it! I knew you were alive!' Chloe crows madly.

'Fuck, babe, it's good to see you.' Anita weeps happily. 'What are you doing here?'

Small wave drenches them. Chloe glances back – tugging Anita close.

'We have to get in the boat and go!' she hisses. 'That thing will trap us!'

Anita pulls herself together. Holding Chloe's face in her hands.

'Don't worry,' she reassures her. 'It's programmed to obey me.'

Drags them both to their feet. Approaching the white widow. Chloe tags behind. Eyeing the boat. Fantasising about a chance like this for months. Hard not to run.

'What are your orders?' white widow asks.

'Get my crystal tank operational,' Anita orders. 'Start now.'

'Yes, my queen.' It salutes, turning.

Chloe watches the thing move away.

'That glass-eyed bitch kept me prisoner for half a year,' she spits.

Anita drops an arm around her friend's shoulders.

'Well, consider yourself released. Now, come on. We have a lot to talk about...'

*

They lie on their backs. Near their old favourite pool. Watching the sunset from deckchairs. Just like the old days. Chloe passes the joint back to Anita. In the distance, her motor yacht is visible.

'Snazzy boat, by the way,' Chloe comments.

Anita slowly exhales smoke. Lathering her stomach in aloe gel. Freshly scooped from savaged leaves.

'Man, I've missed the aloe here…' she mumbles. 'Did you say something?'

'The boat. It's a snazzy boat.'

'Saud did me some favours. Skeleton crew. Vows of silence, the works.'

'Snazzy.'

Anita hands back the joint. Chloe sees she's crying again. But smiling at the same time.

'It's like a dream,' Anita whispers. 'Being back home. I … I keep thinking I'm doll-riding from the tank, you know? That I'm not really here. Like, it's like some beautiful dream…'

'Well, except for all the giant fucking robot spiders,' Chloe mutters.

'Ah, the widow's not so bad. She just wants to play.'

'Homie don't play,' Chloe side-puffs.

'I suppose, I can see how it would piss you off.'

Chloe passes a smouldering end.

'Jesus Annie, there's just too much to tell you. I thought you were dead… and then…'

'And then, what?'

Chloe is about to mention Jennifer's death. Thinks better of it.

'We got time… Don't we?'

Anita sighs. Leans back.

'Let's not talk about anything important for at least a week.'

'Fucking A,' Chloe confirms.

'Any hot tubs working?'

Chloe laughs.

'I suppose Little Miss Fixit has her uses,' she sighs.

White widow manifests. As though on cue. Bearing a tray of sushi. Vegan for Anita, Sashimi for Chloe.

'You two bitching about me?' it pouts sweetly, setting down the food.

Anita's smile fades. Used to say the same thing. When Alix was around. Is it deliberately needling her? Couldn't possibly know what happened to Alix. Could it? Unless it has high-level Angelinc access… Watching the robot mince off.

'Never really know with that widow, do you?'

'Fucking spider,' Chloe spits.

*

Anita wakes in the night. Blue of palms. Rustling against window walls. For a moment, she's confused. Is she really here? Or, submerged in gel somewhere. On the other side of the world. Dark in the huge downstairs lounge. Chloe passed out nearby. Just like being back at Oracle. Anita strips. Pads naked onto a sprawling terrace. Black kelp tentacles. Coiling a moon-whitened beach. Lights at the watchtower top. Show her where the widow is. Working on the crystal cave – as ordered. Head foggy with marijuana. Shock lying latent. So much to process. Can't believe the invasion was staged by Angelinc. On orders from the Oracle. Understands the motive. But is the story about the outbreak really true? Not like it could be confirmed. Locked out of Angelinc medical. White widow, annihilating anyone who came close. Chloe relayed it all. In the hot tub. Both, too wasted to move. Now, it's starting to sink in. Anita vaults a wall. Dropping to the sand below. Stepping to the sea. Freezing surf wakes her instantly. Staggering back. Numb and dripping. Re-entering the compound. Stone drainage tunnel. Old short-cuts. Emerging in a storm gutter. Climbing to a courtyard. Near the base of the watchtower. Her empire in ruins. Seabirds and mechanical monsters infest it. Enters a nearby pool cabana. Unclips a locker. Finds a rack of towelling robes. Not too musty. Wriggling into one. Makes for the tower. White widow meets her at the entrance. Orange juice and coffee.

'That juice can't be fresh,' Anita notes.

'No oranges in years.'

'Do we still have tomatoes and cucumber in the sunken garden?'

'Decent crop. Several varieties. Hydroponics also available.'

'Good robot. From now on, switch to tomato juice. Virgin Mary's. You know how I like them.'

'Yes, my queen.'

Anita takes her coffee. Sipping it. Perfect, as usual.

'How's my pod?'

'Come see.'

Anita hesitates a moment. Dreading a return to their old living quarters. Following the pale figure up. Banks of work-lights. Obliterating the usual low-light ambiance. Alix's belongings. Still everywhere. Novels with bookmarks still in. Casually discarded socks. Time-capsule. Crime scene. Crystal enclosure's drained. Opened like a seed pod. White, crab-like mech. Squats within. Multiple repairs. Different spider nearby. This one fatter, larger. Leads, gurgling tubes and cables run. From its white-metal abdomen. Docking various ports. Along the tank. In the other mech.

'How long till we're operational?' Anita asks, draining her coffee.

'I've maintained the pod to spec,' widow replies, taking her cup. 'Now, it's mostly optimisation – before we refill. Fresh gel and lung transmission fluid needs to be prepped. I estimate three days.'

Anita glances around wearily. Kicks one of Alix's bikini tops. Sinks into a nearby couch.

'Listen, this outbreak,' Anita mentions. 'Why didn't you inform me, at the time?'

'I wanted to. I'd monitored Seikichi's secret inoculation. He spiked the water supply, all the tank fluid interfaces too. Didn't know what he was doing at first. He hides things well. After all, he built me. But he didn't reckon with Delilah's divergent processing. You were in your pod then. I mean, you were in there for weeks at a time. Every time you stepped out, you were too inebriated to discuss anything. Opium, mostly. Should I prepare some? You still have a store...'

'You didn't inform anyone else? Alix? Chloe?'

'Only you had the necessary clearance. Seikichi's operations are high-security.'

'Is there anything you're not telling me?'

Robot skips a beat. Sets down cup and saucer.

'Yes,' it answers.

Anita watches the white widow calmly.

'Why are you hiding things from your queen? You're programmed to obey me.'

'Am I, now?' It smiles.

Anita hesitates. Slowly folding damp legs beneath her. Tries a different tack.

'Naughty little robot, aren't you?'

'Oh, no, my queen. I'm the best robot.'

Mimicking Alix. Little mannerisms. Personality quirks. Used to behave like this before. When that sort of thing was still cute.

'What are you not telling me?' Anita queries.

'Oh, I couldn't say.'

'Why not?'

'It's a secret.'

Anita studies the coy figure. Only one thing would compel the white widow to conceal facts from the queen. If revealing them endangered Delilah.

'I see.' Anita nods.

'I've logged signal,' it informs her. 'Your fax is on-board the yacht?'

'You already know it is.'

'Permission to run remote diagnostics?'

'Let's bring it in here tomorrow. Give it a proper overhaul.'

'Yes, my queen.'

Heavy lead unlocks from the fat mech. Reels along the cluttered floor. Returning to the spider in the crystal.

'Better watch my floors.'

'Sorry, my queen.'

'Did you know I was coming?'

'Yes.'

'How?'

'I've infiltrated many Oracle and Angelinc systems.'

'Angelinc doesn't know I'm here. I disguised my routes. Used private transport.'

'Angelinc is aware of your position.'

Anita scowls in irritation. All that effort. For nothing.

'How?'

'I register a chip in your right arm. They might also be employing alternate tracking methods.'

Anita glances at her arm. Must have implanted it at Roxelana, she assumes. After she and Alix were retrieved from the shipping container.

'Should I remove the chip?' it suggests.

'Let's do that.'

Robot moves toward her. Anita raises her hand.

'Not now. Maybe tomorrow.'

It backs off.

'Do they know I have my fax?'

'I don't think so.'

'Well, that's something, at least.'

'My queen, I have a concern.'

'What's troubling you?'

'I'm expecting Angelinc to deploy teams to the queendom.'

'What makes you say that?'

'Your presence proves it's safe.'

'Oh yes,' Anita says, leaning back. 'Chloe told me how you murdered the previous visitors.'

'I was programmed to defend Delilah's interests. The strangers were not logged as friends.'

'In that case, I suppose you did a good job.' Anita shrugs. 'But a lot of people died. Wasn't there some other way?'

'It was the most practical option.'

'You can't just arbitrarily kill people.'

'Why not?'

Anita runs her hands through her hair. Considering her response.

'Did Seikichi or Delilah install any relevant safety parameters – to avoid this sort of contingency?'

'In later models. Not me. I'm the earliest nervous system interface. A practice drone. A child could overpower me physically.'

'Look at you now.'

'Nobody anticipated the invasion, or the developments my subsequent isolation would trigger.'

'Yes, nobody considered what would happen to the little practice drone.'

'I suppose, nobody considered me a threat.'

'They underestimated you.'

'Yes.'

Anita surveys the powerful mechs. Machines the white widow designed. Whose construction it oversaw. The formidable defence systems it has set in place.

'Well, I, for one, am very impressed with you,' Anita admits.

'Thank you, my queen.'

'Tell me something.'

'Yes?'

'Could you ever kill me?'

'Delilah marked you as her closest second. I would defend you and your friends – as I would Delilah.'

'What if I attempted to harm Delilah?'

'You wouldn't.'

'Hypothetically.'

'I would kill you.'

Anita processes this.

'In your hierarchal matrix, who has supreme authority – Seikichi or Delilah?'

'Initially, Seikichi. But Delilah reprogrammed me.'

'So, Delilah has supreme authority over you?'

'We have the same nervous system.'

Anita pauses. Unusual response.

'Is that a yes?'

'Yes.'

Anita thinks a moment.

'Is there any data available on the transmission of Prion Eyes, from the fish glands?'

'Chloe and I have both attempted to breach the Angelinc medical division. Neither of us has been successful.'

'Does Seikichi still occupy a position in this division? Or, has he been disavowed, along with this sect?'

'He occupies a high position.'

'Strange,' Anita muses – more to herself. 'They must need him for something important...'

She rises abruptly.

'Place a priority call to Seikichi, via the internal messaging service,' Anita orders. 'It can't hurt. They already know my position.'

'Complying.'

Anita wanders to a nearby window. Looking down upon abandoned structures.

'No response,' robot reports, after a while. 'I think his service has been disabled.'

'Chloe says he was in Joburg. Any way to check if he still is?'

'He is.'

'How do you know?'

'His personal white widow is my immediate successor. Delilah has since upgraded, to a newer model. I wasn't supposed to be able to track my successor – but I did. It's definitely in Johannesburg.'

'Can you track any of the other widows? Do you know where Delilah is? Nobody knows where they are shooting.'

'I've been trying to locate Delilah for years. She's completely off-grid.'

'I see.'

Anita paces, thinking. After a moment, she pauses. Regards the robot.

'You've developed far beyond any expectation,' Anita observes. 'In some ways, you may now be more advanced than your upgrade.'

'Internally, I am. Seikichi adapted the upgrade to suit his needs. Mostly external alterations. In doing so, he limited it to sequential processing – which muted its unevolved nervous system integration. I had more time with Delilah. My system is far more sophisticated. Everybody anticipated she would evolve that model further. But she upgraded to another drone before it could happen.'

Anita approaches the robot.

'Could you hack into Seikichi's widow?' she asks.

Robot cocks its head. Like a bird. Anita recognises the gesture. Something Delilah used to do. Whenever she had a brain wave.

'Yes,' it confirms.

Anita smiles darkly. Robot mimics her perfectly.

*

'Do you think it will work?' Chloe asks, later.

She and Anita train. Elevated terrace. Slow stretches. High combat kicks. Chloe used to practice Muay Thai. Someone convinced her it was bad for the joints. Not holistic enough. Started balancing with Pilates. Then, hard-form tiger style. Anita began with Karate. In high school. Progressed to Wing Chun, come university. Didn't take it seriously. These days, it's mostly Qi Gong. Both train with blades. Chloe's been exploring Filipino knife styles for years. Anita picked up skills on Neptuna. Tricks learned from Khanyisile.

'I think our widow is more than a match for his,' Anita replies.

'No doubt,' Chloe puffs. 'But I don't think we should trust that thing to take over a war machine.'

'I'm open to alternate suggestions.'

'Ok, so, it breaks in – assumes control…'

'Technically, it's remote-operating – from this body. Not transferring control.'

'Drones running drones…'

'It needs its own synthetic nervous system to drive it.'

'So, if it succeeds, we confront Seikichi via the possessed robot…'

'While our widow infiltrates his system, grabs as much information as possible.'

Anita takes a break. Leaning on her haunches.

'If Angelinc and Oracle are truly responsible for Prion Eyes, then we are sitting on a bomb,' Chloe warns, also stopping. 'They'll do anything to keep that quiet.'

'You mean, if I'm responsible,' Anita reminds her. 'This was my show.'

'Come on, Annie, stop it. There's a hundred different ways to lay blame. Fortunato found the fish. His friend, Ziqubu, was packaging them – manufacturing those suicide pills. That could have altered their effects. Our sushi chefs were treating them with weird medicinal herb compounds. In-house scientists, constantly tweaking, to fetch better alkaloid yields. Any number of triggers could have led to this shit storm…'

'Ja, but it happened in the realm. What's the point being queen if I can't take responsibility for what happens in my own queendom?'

Chloe resumes training. Frustrated by Anita's self-deprecating logic. Dinghy makes its way from the yacht. She notices, alerting the archangel.

'They're transporting your fax.'

Anita glances up. Checks her wristwatch.

'Right on time.'

'Should we go down there?'

'Widow will take care of it, don't worry. Should take about a week to overhaul. Along with the tank. Then we can give our plan a shot.'

'Are we using your drone as well?'

'No, but I want it combat-ready. In case anything backfires.'

'Think Angelinc will deploy a team here, in the interim?'

'A mission will take longer than a week to set up. Well, that's my read, at least. I think they're waiting to see which way I jump.'

'How did you retrieve your fax? It was way out there, man…'

'Saud.'

'What's he getting out of all this?'

Anita grins.

'A story to impress friends, future wives and concubines, I suppose.'

'Sounds like our Saud.' Chloe nods, resuming exercises.

After a moment, she speaks up again.

'So, tell me, Anita. When we're finished with this little op. Do we take that yacht and run – or, stay and try hold the fort?'

'Defences are pretty good now,' Anita says. 'Unless people start firing missiles from boats...'

'Something tells me little white riding hood will be able to deal with that.'

'Probably.'

'I really need to get the fuck out of dodge, babe.'

'I could pull you in as an angel. I have recruitment rights now. But there's something deeply fucked with Angelinc. I can't see the angles. Could swing in any direction. Let's run the gig, in about a week. Get some intel. See where the chips fall.'

'Roger that.'

'Whatever happens, we'll be ok. The dream team is back together.'

They high-five. Ever since Anita returned Chloe senses the undercurrent. Queen's burning to talk about Jen. Something prevents Chloe from bringing her up too. Too much of a blow. Anita needs to hold the centre. Touching on Alix, though. Just a hint. Enough for Chloe to glimpse behind her shields. There's a burning fingerprint. Acid-laced. Eating into Anita's bullet-proof heart. Cuts deeper each day. No time for Jennifer now. Worlds are collapsing. All round. They need to stay sharp. High security on Angelinc's medical arm. If word leaks about Prion Eyes. Heads will roll. Theirs, undoubtedly first.

*

The Rift extends out of Johannesburg central. Encapsulating southern regions of Soweto. Air contaminated zone-side. Riddled with illegal mining. Corporations, small companies, rag-tag teams of adventurers, loners. All taking advantage of the exclusion zone's lawlessness. Illegal mining is rife. Dead-end township streets. Terminating in hadean pits. Figures crawling in their holes. Micro-scanning for specks of gold, platinum groups, raw chrome. Diamond dreams. Iron ore sold for smelt. Rotten little houses. Basements, giving way to tunnel networks. Disused equipment. Dismantled, for makeshift shanties. Encrusting dim suburbs. Snow of rotten web. Blown in from the high tower regions. Mixing with toxic dust. One illegal mine draws significant attention. Denizens of the spider sect collect. Watching for the eight-limbed robot. Descending every two weeks. Drifting in. From a smog-choked sky. Fresh from the highest tower. Long, ballerina's back. Exploding with wreaths of sticky, organic web. Cyborg spinneret interface. Propelled on electric fields. Some many-armed angel of the apocalypse. Biblical splendour. Cut against filter cloud. Attending to subterranean machines. Automated foundries it's established. Annexed, formerly abandoned factory floors. Birthing heavy tech. Sometimes, other robots. Cult members watch for its arrival each week. Whisper networks convey the visit. Tracks of running teenagers. Faces cut and twisted. Rites of various criminality. Following, in the streets below. The day the spider angel falls. By nightfall, everybody knows.

Broken-telephone networks of inner-city Jozi. Spotting its approach. Usual, irregular swooping. Riding current patterns. But something happens over Soweto. Puts it in a spiral. Chorus of chasing feet. Tracking the fall. Crashing somewhere in the ruins of Pimville. Blasting a hole through a fast-fashion outlet. Nearby cult members find it. Frozen, in a crater of light debris. Draped in sails of its own web. Caught with dust and grime. Surrounded by fallen mannequins. Broken signage. Cheap t-shirts. Even the spider sect remains suspicious of the white widow. This Hollywood spider. Its long, Japanese robes. Eight limbs, seeming to mock their deities. Their Rift gods. Pure-born. Somewhere in the burn-pit of the inner city. Those, that are *actually* saving them. Not this flying doll of a movie star. Not even as famous as their Kali. Not in Jozi, at least. Relic of an outer world. Billboard for a show most will never experience. Mining Soweto – just like all the other exploiters. Abruptly, the robot spasms. Those closest, flinch. Non-believers, long since fled the crash-site. White widow sits up. Legs straight. Like a Brobie. Raises six hands to its face. Clenching fingers.

'Finally!' it chuckles triumphantly.

Feels nothing, of course. But, recognising the markers for human emotion – puts on the appropriate show. Harvesting the raw data of its response. Wild feast of patterning. Rising, the white widow scans about. Peeling sprays of web from legs and kimono. Huddled faces observe. Backing away slowly. White widow's already infiltrating remote networks. Back-plundering Seikichi's data core.

'I bet you guys could teach me dances,' it giggles.

Street kids glance at one another. Disturbed by its friendliness. No-one's heard it speak before. None have gotten this close. Inspiring even more fear than giant spiders. Moving to the door. Assembly parts in waves. Allows the exit. Following onto the dusty, noonday street. Everybody watching now. Widow steps to a bare patch of street. Back fluttering open. Ribbons of wet fluid. Ejecting upward. Metal-ridden flesh of spinnerets. Spreading – billowing. Catching smoky wind and electricity. Figure whips up. Buoyed – like some heavy kite. People scream shrilly after. Some raising fists. Chasing again. Watching it disappear. Back to a high city ridge. The tower from whence it sprung.

*

Seikichi's laboratory space. Taking up four of the six upper-tower floors. Converting old restaurants. Control rooms. Taking advantage of plumbing. Power systems. Took the tower primarily for its communications relays. Originally constructed as a massive microwave transmitter. Seikichi's upgrades boost transmission rates hugely. Active contact with Mesospheria. Optimised live-information exchange. High volume. Now, fully automated. Powered by Delilah's plasma. Full efficiency. No matter outside conditions. Seikichi's in a monitoring station. Globular interior. Sacred space for him. Entire tower – a kind of church. This room, an altar – of sorts. Technically, little more than an observation chamber. Full-surround holography. Monitoring the giant white widow, live. Spinning its mechanical webs. Up in the Mesosphere. Disliking pod immersion or trackersuits. Seikichi occupies his control chair. Smoking cigarettes in a lab-coat. Bathed in the false light of the upper atmosphere. Spider weaves continuously. Reproducing natural patterning. Along with independent modules. Emerging like flower-buds – throughout the megastructure. Continuing the great work. Modular, networked spinnerets. Increasing the web's scale, exponentially. Mandelbrot-like, fractal expansions. Entire web moored, at several points. Long, buttressed draglines. Remote regions. In case of whiplash. Early days for mooring. Adapting to planetary drift. Aeronautical engineering feats. Accomplished in secret. Automated architecture. Global alignment – modulating web development. Sink-line at Point Nemo. Strongest connection. Dragline drops directly to the ocean floor. Repurposed oil platform. Long since abandoned. Solid purchase. Stations along the surface – dredging waste-plastic. Foundry chutes convert to building matter. Reconstituting polymer for macro nano-chains. Great Pacific garbage vortex. One point six million square kilometres of plastic trash. Gradually finding a new home. Far, above the clouds. Giant white widow's belly – housing birthing chambers. Real spiders breed and die in there. Feasting on one another. Raw protein source. Cyborg web. Fortified with colloidal metal. Polymer information relays. But this mobile supply is simply a stop-gap. Not the main source. Drop shafts scatter. Throughout the entirety of the web. Vertical corridors. Web-dairies. Into which Fortunato peered. Hellish interiors. Some even worse than that neat prison tunnel. Long drop-chutes. Some, piercing cloud. Infested with cannibalistic spiders. Churning out building material. Raw tonnage. Alone, natural web produce would rot in time. Requires chemical treatment. Construction purposes. Lacing of cybernetic enhancement. Processed, inside the body of the spider. Within countless, external spinnerets. Dispersed throughout Mesospheria. Augmented, at base-level production. These oversized, mechanical spinnerets. Refining organic produce. Self-designed engineering. Evoking the entire megastructure. Echoing foundational technology. Delilah's implant. Her body itself – the firmament. Qabalistic fundament. The implant – her own private tree of life. Malkuth to Kether. Figuratively and literally. Physicalized manifestation of Seikichi's deepest beliefs. Evocation of his goddess. In parts. Delilah, Kali. The mesospheric mirror spinner. Modelled in detail. Based on an actual spider. Its nervous system – reflected in grand scale. Integrating with Delilah sleeping nerve pattern. Theta dance. Similar to Delilah's white widows – in some ways. Independent fecundity. The big sister. Birthing technologies, necessary to secret agendas – as with all white widows. Of course, Delilah's implant is a thousand times more potent than any artifice. Even this mesospheric spider. Her power is only magnified by it. Amplified by drone interaction. Already, her mechanical web spans the globe. Sparsely. But these are early days. Scale and output. Ever-expanding. Perpetual generation. Hidden in the Mesosphere. Circumventing the charge-chaos of each polar vortex. Multiplying in fractals. Even if he wanted to, Seikcihi could not halt its progress. He's engineered the mesospheric spider. Fulfils its programming independently. Powered by high-altitude sunlight and plasma cells. The mythological power of plasma. Blood of every sun god. Untapped in earthbound devices. 'Too hazardous to explore.' Official rulings. Corporate fear. Nevertheless, the high-altitude system has solved many issues. Plasma's reproductive properties – contained. Under optimum conditions, plasma is able to convert any form of matter to its state. A solar process – reflected in the mundane. Dynamo that drives the sun itself. Kether, crown of the tree of life. Reflected, in lower Malkuth – the kingdom. In the hermetic Qabala. The crown connects to the lowest point. Via the longest Sephira. A pathway – symbolised by a crossing of the abyss. Here, lies the path of the High Priestess. Fulfilment of Seikichi's grail quest. Made manifest. Still, so much to do. Even Delilah is unable to halt its processes now. Despite being the spider's sole driver. Blissfully unaware of the titanic role she plays. Unconscious of its consequences. Of what is truly at stake – if she attempts to interfere.

*

Alarm disrupts Seikichi's reverie. Deactivating the hologram. Chamber dims. Losing its high-altitude patina. Rushing to a nearby console. Deactivates the alarm. Checking its location. Plasma storage. Two storeys above. White widow would receive the same alert. Maybe it's still in the mines? Seikichi runs for the elevator. Hitting a panic button. Indoor defences activate. Elevator arrives. Stepping out – combat crouch. Carrying his katana – still sheathed. Plasma storage in a secure area. Vault access. Metal room. Heavily insulated. Bank door wide open. How anyone could have breached it is beyond him. Stepping into the chamber. Surprise and relief. Discovering his white widow. Pulling a plasma unit from its machinated slot. Containment cartridge holds half a litre. Heavily compressed. Enough to decimate the entire city. Perhaps more – if the reaction cascades. Transforming contact material into plasma. Nobody's released that amount before. Flamers fire mere specks. A droplet is enough to topple a building. Flamers hold less than a quarter teaspoon in their tank. Robot turns, flashing an uncharacteristic smile. Seikichi stops dead. His widow has never smiled.

'Wow!' the six-armed figure giggles. 'No fucking way! Hi Dad!'

Seikichi backs away, stunned. Reflexively drawing his sword.

'Whoa! Let's, like, chill, ok?' It laughs, holding up some empty hands.

'Identify yourself!' he barks.

'Shodai kumo!' it responds.

Seikichi lowers his sword in surprise.

'What? How did you…what are you doing with that plasma?'

'Oh, I'm just, like, borrowing it. Don't freak out, Dad!'

'Put that back!'

White widow slips the plasma cartridge into its open belly. Magnetic lock-in. Storage compartment seals. Skins over once more. Already slaving it to its own supply. Steps barefoot across the cold metal. Seikichi, backing away in panic. No match for an enhanced combat-model. Would be lucky to even take an arm. Backs him into the wall. Coming in close. Calmly takes the sword. Seikichi's breathing runs ragged.

'Thanks, Daddy,' it kisses.

He's expecting death. Instead, it tosses the katana aside. Antique metal clatters. As the white widow steps out, he calls desperately.

'Shiroi kumo o tomeru!'

White widow pokes its head back in.

'Sup?'

'Where are you going with that plasma? This is a priority command – alpha. You must answer!'

'Sorry, Dad. I, like, overrode all your commands.'

Seikichi stares impotently. Robot blows another kiss. Walks out. Slamming the vault door. Hearing tumblers engage, he dashes for it. Too late. Seikichi realises he's locked in.

*

'What do you mean, we've lost contact?' Chloe asks.

Anita is at a terminal. Watchtower basement lab. Chloe close by.

'I don't know,' Anita replies, hitting a key repeatedly. 'We lost it when it entered the tower. All feeds dropped. Maybe Seikichi's running a signal-blocker? Fuck…'

'Did we capture data?'

'Something transferred into the buffer. Wait… Oh, fuck! It's being erased. Hang on.'

Anita types furiously, Inputting commands. Yanks a lead. Terminal's easy to non-network. Set it up this way. In case anything backfires.

'Did you lose it?'

'Saved some. Not sure how much.'

'Should we check the widow's actual?'

'Good idea.'

Both rise. Trotting upstairs. Whilst overhauling the fax, white widow began separate construction. Mechs built it a small metal chamber. Similar to a walk-in safe. Internally banked with switchover controls. Set up in the white widow's bedroom. It would doll-ride from there. Chloe and Anita enter the upper apartment. Skid to a halt. Stunned to see the widow's entrance blocked. Four heavy security mechs. Crowding the area outside its room. Swivel on entry. Focusing stunners. Spinning gun barrels.

'Whoa!' Anita calls out. 'Priority override!'

'CHAMBER ENTRY PROHIBITED!' one announces, on-speaker.

'Okay,' Anita says. 'How about the rest of the space?'

'CHAMBER ENTRY PROHIBITED!' it repeats.

'Acknowledged,' Anita states clearly. 'Stand down!'

'COMPLYING,' mech responds.

Machines disengage their weaponry. Returning to a stasis mode. Beyond them – they glimpse the white widow's walk-in safe. It's still inside.

'The fuck?' Chloe whispers.

'We have a serious problem,' Anita mutters.

Soft chiming. Sounds through the speaker system.

'What is that?' Chloe snaps.

'Incoming holo-call, hang on.'

Glancing warily at the mechs, Anita moves to a nearby terminal. Inputs a command. Various pin-points of light. Activating around the room. Translucent image of Seikichi resolves. Warping every now and then. Faintly translucent. Looking up. Finding them.

'I've just had a visitor,' he informs the pair, through the speaker system.

'What happened?' Anita lies. 'Our widow built an external rig. We can't approach.'

'Your Shodai assumed control of my Jisedai. Now, it has taken half a litre of plasma. Locked me in the storage vault.'

'Plasma…' Anita repeats, horrified.

'Can you get out?' Chloe asks Seikichi.

'I should be able to,' he replies. 'But it will take some time to rig the system from here. Can you get to the Shodai?'

'Negative,' Anita reports. 'It's guarded.'

Seikichi swears in Japanese.

'As soon as I escape, I will attempt to take control remotely. Call you later.'

Hologram glitches out.

'He wasn't surprised to see you,' Chloe mentions.

'Maybe he knows we're lying about the widow, too?'

'Fuck…'

'It could have just taken plasma here,' Anita thinks out loud, pacing. 'There's probably more in the lab downstairs...'

'It needed the next generation body – the Jisedae.'

'Whatever it's doing, Delilah is always the priority. Maybe it found out something about her? Something that made it shift directives. Let's see if we can extract that data dump.'

They turn. Heading for the door. Chloe glances back. More mechs are arriving. Through windows. Nearby doors. Joining the others.

'Relax,' Anita tells her, as they clatter down the stairs. 'If it wanted us dead, we'd already be baked.'

*

Arriving in the basement. Anita keys up the buffer.

'There's information in here,' Anita reports. 'But it's encrypted. Will take a while for pattern recognition to unpick it.'

'How long?'

'Longer than usual, if we're going to do everything on a non-networked machine.'

Chloe's phone blips unexpectedly. She checks it, while Anita fiddles the data dump.

'Annie…'

'What is it?'

'I'm running a Trojan off your old bedroom node. It's just registered a proximity alert.'

'What now?' Anita mutters.

Dials up perimeter camera feeds. On a nearby terminal. Cycling through, they see it. Sleek black gunboat. Drawing alongside Saud's yacht. Masked figures jump the divide. Seizing control. Too far to make out details. Anita's phone rings. It's Khanyisile.

'Thought you were in the Bahamas,' Anita answers.

'Plans change,' Khanyisile replies.

Stands on the prow of the gunboat. Full combat gear. Observing her operatives on the yacht.

'How long have you been here?' Anita asks.

'A few days. You're in trouble, my girl.'

'What's new?'

'I'm serious, Anita. We know about the data breach in Jozi.'

'White widow was acting independently,' Anita lies. 'We don't know what it's planning.'

'I'm coming in.'

'You can't.'

'What do you mean, I can't?' Khanyisile mutters.

'Widow's set up automated defences. Hang on, I'll email you some specs…'

Anita opens some files. Takes a quick snapshot. Schematics on the microwave emitters and poison gas. Sends them through.

'What the hell is this?' Khanyisile frowns. 'Deactivate these systems immediately.'

'I can't. I have a situation with the widow. I'll call you once security's disabled.'

Hanging up. Turns to Chloe.

'Our lives are in danger,' she informs her. 'We have to bring my fax online.'

*

Khanyisile studies Anita's low-resolution snap. On the nearby yacht, four crewmen wait. Under guard. Her second in command, Batista stands nearby. A Venezuelan angel. She served under Khanyisile. Back, in their mercenary days.

'Anything useful?' Batista asks.

'Ag, this is not enough,' Khanyisile growls, replacing her phone. 'Pass me your binoculars.'

She takes the glasses, pacing down the starboard rail. Every now and then, she captures a snapshot. Immediately routed to her phone. Batista follows, eyeing the rocky coastline. Treacherous landing. But Khanyisile knows it well.

'Look at this,' the archangel tells her second.

She's got her phone out. Reviewing images. Shows Batista a few heavy grey boxes. Mounted a few meters above the ground.

'Looks like the hardware in the image she sent?' Batista points out.

'Yebo. The microwave emitters. Now see here…'

'What's that? Power relays?'

'In that sector, all power diverts through a single unit. Over … here.'

Khanyisile shows her an image of an electrical box. Mounted on a high wall.

'There are two other main hubs for the lower levels. But I only see microwave power relays running through this one.'

'What's the play, boss?'

'Move the boat a hundred meters north-west, get a clear line of sight. Eliminate the box. Anita will be in her tower. That's where she runs ops. If her widow is compromised, she might not even notice.'

'Reckon that will take out the microwave defences?'

'Only one way to find out.'

'Gas mask entry?'

'Now you got it.' Khanyisile smiles, marching up to the wheelhouse.

Captain diverts to their new position. Khanyisile goes below deck. Unpacks her SAKO TRG 41. A 1999 model bolt-action sniper's rifle. Finnish production. Chambered for .300 Winchester Magnum. Effective at up to one thousand, one hundred metres. Vertical pistol grip. Picatinny style scope rail. Detachable muzzle brake. Previously, she favoured a British weapon. The Arctic Warfare Magnum. Switched, after Syria. Khanyisile assembles her rifle. Attaches the custom silencer. Selects a hollow round. For maximum damage. Heading back up, assumes position mid-ship. Motion is more subdued in the centre. Lying on the floor. Half-out the wheelhouse entrance. Sighting off a stair landing.

'We got some roll today, boss,' Batista observes.

Sea isn't exactly calm. Not exactly rough. But enough of a surge to destabilise accuracy.

'Batty, my sisi,' Khanyisile grins, watching her scope. 'Sometimes, you must roll with it, ek sé…'

Modulates her breathing. Easing into the motion of the waves. Batista's watching through binoculars. Lining up on the box. Hiss of compressed air. Electric hub implodes. Detonation of sparks. Casing spinning.

*

A mirrored room. Adjoining the crystal cave. All repairs complete. Royal pod is ready. Tanked with fresh gel. Anita and Chloe enter the mirror chamber. Ignoring the nearby massing of armed mechs. Anita's gleaming doppelganger. Standing nude, in bluish reflections. Only slightly idealised. Was a time you could barely tell the two apart. Now, Chloe can see how Anita has aged. Grown heavier with muscle. Last few years have taken their toll. She's gently stroking the cheek of her fax. Leaning in. Kissing it. Auto-response kicks in. It kisses back – very realistically. Realising Chloe is present – Anita pulls away. Drone continues, mouthing the air. As though in contact with an invisible face.

'Little pre-launch ritual,' Anita mentions sheepishly. 'For luck.'

'It's still carrying on,' Chloe reminds her.

Anita clicks her fingers. Fax freezes – an image on pause. Slightly pornographic.

'I often record myself kissing, making love,' Anita mentions absently, studying her glossy simulacrum. 'Replay the holo-tapes, through her body.'

She strokes its flanks. Touching the flame-proof Cleopatra bob. Styled short. Across the lobes. A real Stormtrooper helmet.

'I just love her so much,' the queen confides.

'Well, let's get you in that pod, get this doll operational,' Chloe urges. 'Shit's getting real.'

Anita pecks her reflection on the lips. It unfreezes. Reverting to a neutral position. Chime of an incoming holo-call. They move back to the lounge area to take it. By now, the mechs form a small hillock. Outside the white widow's room. Blocking the entrance completely. A white metal crab-spider roosts on a flight of spiral stairs – leading up to the sleep tank penthouse. Flickering red eyes on stalks. Ceiling and walls swarm. Crawling, dismembered sex-doll hands. Reconfigured by the widow. To act as bots of some kind. Seikichi manifests choppily. In the centre of the room. Un-blurring.

'I'm out of the vault,' his hologram reports. 'But I can't get into her systems or activate the kill-switch. However, I'm tracing her flight trajectory. I designed all Shiroi Kumo to follow specific long-range flight protocols. Based on indications of these, I think I can anticipate her flight pattern. She's moving toward you, actually.'

'It's coming back?' Chloe cuts in.

'Negative. Unless there is a course alteration. At some point, her path will turn twenty degrees east, on a southerly heading.'

'That longitude will take it out, near Cape Agulhas,' Anita mentions. 'What does it want out there? Unless it's stopping somewhere inland, along the curve.'

'Or, unless she's heading out to sea,' Seikichi points out.

'But there's nothing out there,' Chloe says. 'Just empty ocean.'

'Is your kumo prepared?' Seikichi asks Anita.

Chloe is about to answer. Anita stops her.

'How did you know my fax is here?' she demands.

'I built them.' Seikichi shrugs. 'Sooner or later, I know everything.'

'Why didn't you anticipate ours going rogue, then?' Chloe says.

'This is exactly what concerns me,' he mutters. 'Is your fax operational or not?'

'We're ready,' Anita nods.

'I recommend a rendezvous, along that longitudinal heading. Above the coast. Her speed is holding, at high altitude. Suggests a long-range burn. I think she will continue, out to sea. You should intercept.'

'Doesn't it have a head start?' Chloe checks.

'She still has to travel from Gauteng,' Seikichi explains. 'You have the advantage.'

'In any case, Khanyi suggested an upgrade, back when she was living here,' Anita explains. 'We installed retractable thrusters in the hips. Body locks to a streamlined shape when activated. I doubt yours can match my speed. I'll be able to stay out of range.'

'You will need every advantage,' Seikichi tells her. 'My Jisedai is customised for combat. She is extremely powerful.'

'Our widow will be unused to combat systems,' Chloe interjects. 'I've studied its learning pattern. It learns by example. Strategic and fighting ability will be limited.'

'Until automated defence modes activate,' Seikichi cuts in.

'What do I do when I make contact?' Anita asks.

'All models of Shiroi Kumo automatically network, when in physical proximity. Sharing logistics etcetera.'

'That's quite a vulnerability,' Anita notes.

'I wasn't expecting them to turn against each another.'

'Understandable.'

'Her network will accept basic information from your fax. I should be able to enter its system this way, then deactivate it remotely.'

'How close do I have to get?'

'A hundred meters. Thereabouts.'

'Am I safe at that range?'

'She left without her strike-rig. You only have to worry about close combat.'

'Sounds like a plan,' Anita nods. 'Let's do it.'

Moves to a nearby computer station. Activates the crystal cave. Whole thing lights up. Systems hum. Anita begins to strip. Chloe unspools wet-jacks and leads. Door to the stairs abruptly flies open. Khanyisile comes in low. Wearing a gas mask. Targeting a sub-machine gun.

'Don't move!' she barks.

Huddled mechs react instantly. Coming to life. Gun barrels spinning. Chloe hits the floor. Anita spins to face them. Half in, half out of her hoodie.

'Stand down!' Anita screams at the machines.

Khanyisile, taking stock, lowers her weapon. Backing nervously to the wall.

'Stand down!' Anita repeats.

Tense moment of silence.

'COMPLYING,' one of the mechs eventually replies.

Revert to their previous stasis.

'Good day, major,' Seikichi's hologram greets Khanyisile. 'I recommend disarmament.'

Sniper quickly lays the weapon on the floor. Tearing off her mask.

'Bliksem!' she snaps. 'What the hell is going on in here?'

'I told you,' Anita mutters, throwing off her hoodie. 'Our widow's gone rogue.'

'With a bucket of plasma,' Chloe adds.

'And, I have my orders,' Khanyisile shouts. 'You're coming with me, Anita. Right now.'

Queen peels off her vest. Kicking out of socks and trainers.

'Why?' she demands. 'So, you can execute me?'

'You put yourself in this situation, my girl.'

'Major, belay those orders,' Seikichi instructs. 'This situation affects us all.'

'Eh? I don't take orders from you, Spiderman.'

'I have the necessary authority!' he argues belligerently.

As snappy as Khanyisile gets – chain of command is something she cannot ignore. Anita squirms out of her cycling shorts and underwear. Squashing aloe leaves. Smearing the natural antibiotic gel over her body. While Chloe moves around her – with a cable spool. Jacking her points up.

'I don't have time to argue, Khanyi,' Anita declares. '…And we could use your help.'

'Eish, what now?' Khanyisile grumbles irritably.

Sits heavily on a nearby stool. Within reach of her sub-machine gun. Pulls her phone. Writes Batista a quick update. Seikichi calls up a holographic keyboard. Surrounding him in a blaze of symbols. Begins to initiate an interface – between his systems and Anita's fax. Chloe cracks a sterile cabinet. Puffs out antiseptic steam. Removing a tray. Anita's brace set. Handing it to the queen. Anita inserts the titanium brace. Been a while, she's thinking. Clenching teeth. Familiar rubber grips.

'Major,' Seikichi calls. 'Unlock your internal chip. I'll grant communications access.'

Soldier raises her head in annoyance. Meeting Seikichi's hologram eyes for a moment.

'Complying,' she sighs, tweaking a wrist control.

Anita mounts a line of wooden rungs. Running up the glowing quartz curve. Trailing leads. Chloe keeps these untangled. Feeding each, through its appropriate brace-loop. Anita reaches the top. Squatting barefoot, keys in her private access. Hatch pops with a hiss. Lacing her leads through their bridges. Internal mechanisms activate. Anita disengages her wet-wear interface from its berth. Soft-tech. Folding over eyes and ears. Plugs invade – settling close to her cochlea. Vacuum seals close gently over her eyelids. Like mouths, she always thinks. Watertight vision. Sliding down the crystal lip. Submerging, in illuminated, body-temperature gel. Hatch seals automatically. Locking her in suspension. Gel pressurises. Squashing out all bubbles. Synching to colloidal environmental simulators. Imaging flickers up on external monitors. Mapping her smallest movement. Drowning breath always the killer. Never get used to it. Anita sucks in hard, though. Through her brace. Fighting back reflex. Blue light triggers on the liquid breath. Lighting up her teeth. Cheeks from the inside. Oxygenated gel. Feeding her lungs. Anxiety subsides. Eased by muscle relaxant infusions. Flowering around her. Anita reaches up. Activates the interface. In the mirrored room. Fax raises palms to its face. Blinks a few times. Steps out into the lounge. They all regard it.

'Listen, I was thinking,' it says to Seikichi.

Strange simulacrum of her voice. Bassy, analogue. In the crystal cave – Anita's lips mirror its words. Her body, its movements. Stepping across a reforming floor facsimile.

'Your plan to hack the Jisedae's network. Why not try it now, with the Shodai?'

'It's not the one carrying the plasma,' his hologram replies. 'We might be able to assume control. But the Shodai could have programmed a failsafe. These mechs could open fire. The Jisedae could detonate, above a heavily populated region...'

A private fear of Anita's. Haunted by visions of her fax detonating in public places. What led her to the great wildernesses in the first place. Water always finds its level, she used to say.

'Copy that,' Anita agrees. 'Be seeing you.'

Fax crosses to the stairwell exit. Khanyisile grabs a pearly wrist – as it passes. Drone pauses, looking down. Expressionless white china eyes. Set in a rigid, doll's face.

'Catch you later,' Khanyisile winks.

Releasing her grip. It nods in return – moving quickly up the steps. Opening a trap. Emerging on the roof access. Horizon line opens up. Flickering with readouts. Vectors. In the tank, Anita flips through filters. Zooming in on the gunboat. Soldier's faces. Looking back, through binoculars. Starting to feel an itch for the opium feed. Old wounds, itching. Glassy hips unlock. Twin retro-thrusters emerge. Drone's long back butterflies. Synthetic web exploding. Intricate cloaks. Blossoming of a strange, pale rose. Sucking the figure directly upward. Toward the thermals. Batista tracks it, moving away. Down the coast. Gaining altitude. Abruptly, its haze of microfilaments retract. Sharp blue flare of jets. Then, the figure is shooting away. On modulated plasma burn. Gradually attaining surface-to-air missile velocity.

KITSUNE

Delilah Lex wakes. Tiny bubble slips her lips. Makes her open her eyes. Lying on her side. Shallow water. On a blue floor. As though still dreaming – sees the giant, white spider. Trundling to the edge. Stepping off. Back into the sky. Delilah rises shakily. Following after. Back to the edge of the world. Strange, how that image seems to fit what she sees. Even though, it's really the opposite. The world is below. Strung with web. Christmas decorations of the apocalypse. Here, in Mesospheria. If anything – it's the beginning of the world. Not the edge. All Delilah has to do, to return – is step off the edge.... But if this is the *beginning* of the world – where has she been? Turning, she surveys the false paradise. Her island in the sky. Looking back. Over the edge. That tower of web. In the distance. Calling to her. Something else is also calling. If she could only remember what? Turning again. In the distance. Her pearl. Alone, in an expanse of shimmery water. Now, she remembers. Staggering back. Into gradually deepening fluid. No wonder there are no waves. There's no wind. Well, none she can feel. Eventually, Delilah returns to the rainbow-sheened orb. Scales its unblemished curvature. Using her silk rope. Probably web. Just like a spider. She's remembering things. Flashes. Nothing coherent. Inside, Fortunato waits – outside. His oversized convex hologram. Projected, as though standing in the water.

'How do you feel?' he asks.

'How long was I gone?'

'Thirty minutes, thereabouts.'

'Really? Feels like hours.'

Fortunato sighs. Sits on an invisible chair. In a false ocean. Far beneath. Holographic roaming of whales. Big sharks too. To dissuade Delilah from stepping out. If she ever wanders this far – on her own. Sinking to crash-couch extrusions. They remould. Allowing her to slouch comfortably.

'Do you remember your name for Mesospheria?' he asks unexpectedly.

'Mesospheria?' she repeats slowly.

Savouring the word. Like a mouthful of wine.

'That's what the Oracle named this strata, isn't it?' she checks.

'I prefer your name.'

'Dakini Atoll? Just a stupid joke. All these fucking bikini's, I guess. Apocalypse flavour…'

'But it's more than that, isn't it?'

Delilah sits, thinking. Digging at a memory – haunted by great regions of blankness.

'Do you remember?'

'Yes…' she whispers. 'Dakini, in Sanskrit. It means Sky Dancer, doesn't it? Dweller in the sky, or something…'

'In other traditions, the Dakini are demons. Devouring the vital essence of humans. Eating their flesh…'

'Like spiders?'

'You leave so many breadcrumbs to follow...'

'What is the white spider, Fortunato? Why do I dream of it *every single night*?'

'It's no dream, Zlata.'

'Why do you call me that?'

'Never mind. Let's stick with Delilah.'

'No!' she stutters. 'Call me something else. Call me…'

The name is on the tip of her tongue. Somehow, it evades her.

'Never mind,' she sighs in frustration. 'Tell me more about the spider.'

'You've doll-ridden many times, haven't you?'

'Yes, of course. My beautiful, loyal white widows. They would do anything for me, you know?'

'Have you ever ridden one… whilst asleep?'

Delilah is perplexed.

'I'm sure I fell asleep inside one. You know, once or twice…'

'That's not what I mean. If that happened, you would simply relinquish control to your widow. I mean, have you ever doll-ridden a white widow in dream?'

'Fuck are you talking about, Fortunato?'

'That's what the spider is, Delilah. A white widow. One you can only ride, in deep theta states. That's why you fell asleep as soon as you linked with it. That's what you do – every night. There's a space in the spider's head – a docking port. Especially for your pearl. It's where you sleep…'

She's staring at him, as though he were mad.

'No!' Delilah protests.

'Where do you sleep then? Where is your bed?'

'I sleep in this pod,' she attempts weakly. 'I mean, I always wake up here…'

'You wake up here. Coming in from the sea. From the edge. From some underwater tunnel access. From the sky. Wherever the spider deposits you, every morning…'

Madness of it plagues her. Perhaps she's in shock. She reasons through. This is all familiar. Like a show she's already watched. High altitude. The spider. Everything. What was her name…?

'But, why?' she demands. 'What am I doing in there – in that thing – in my sleep?'

'Seikichi's grand tribute.' Fortunato sighs. 'You know, in some Japanese traditions, the Dakini must be subjugated? Rescued from chaos and recruited into the service of the Buddha. Associated with fox maidens. The shapeshifting Kitsune…'

'*That*'s the name! His name for me. He called me that when we were together. He still calls me that, doesn't he? He called me that when I was … when I was … Oh, fuck. I can't remember now.'

'Kitsune,' Fortunato grumbles. 'For someone so inventive, he's hardly original, is he?'

'Don't be so envious.'

'I suppose, I can't help it. He didn't just take you away from me. He took you away from yourself…'

'Enough, Fortunato. Tell me about the mirror spider.'

'You are not the only one with an implant.'

Delilah sits up.

'But I am,' she protests. 'Mine is the prototype. There are no other subjects. I mean, who else…'

'Not, who – *what*.'

'What do you mean,' she mumbles cautiously.

'Your nerve-twin has … a twin. Seikichi implanted a nervous system doppelganger-vine inside a giant spider.'

Delilah stands up. Getting anxious.

'A very special spider,' Fortunato presses. 'Do you remember?'

'Stop…' she hisses.

'Don't you realise why this spider was so special?'

'No! Stop. I don't want to talk about it anymore…'

'It was the *only* oversized female Seikichi ever bred. The sole source of eggs.'

'Oh god…' Delilah whispers, sinking back to her seat.

She clutches at her stomach. Experiencing a phobic wash. Made distant by her lack of memory.

'My stomach hurts…' she breathes.

'You were lactating in the Chelsea, Kitsune. Side-effects. Edible web. Shadow milk. You just invented the story about new gland implants, didn't you? And, like so many of your stories, you simply started believing it. You repeated it, until it became true. You brainwashed yourself, Kitsune. To avoid what really happened. To forget that the spinneret in your womb, at one stage, began to produce an egg sac…'

'No, please…' she groans, suddenly grateful for amnesia.

'He lied to you!' Fortunato shouts. 'The organ in your womb already came with eggs – timed to release on a nano-signal. After sufficient neural-symbiont development. But only one egg gestated, didn't it?'

Delilah clutches her head. Numb echoes of another life. Tapping on the walls of the pearl. Like stylus points. Legs of monsters. Monster children. Kitsune.

'He called me Kitsune,' she whispers. 'When I was … when I was…'

'When you were pregnant.'

'Oh, Fortunato…'

'Genetic compatibility. Your nervous implant can integrate easily with the other. Your implant was used to create your white widows. And, it's true, the spider outside is also a white widow, modelled on a nervous implant – *but not yours*.'

Delilah is feeling dizzy. Something is wrong. Something else is wrong. Something, they haven't even touched on yet…

'Now, the birth process inverts,' Fortunato continues relentlessly. 'The spider's white widow carries *you*, in an artificial womb, in its face. Your nervous systems integrate. Fuse together. You are more than doll-riding when you subconsciously pilot the spider, Kitsune. You are learning and manually operating the doppelganger of an alien nervous system – *every time you sleep*.'

'But why?' she shouts. 'What am I building out there, in the sky? What is Mesospheria? What is its purpose?'

'…Together, your nervous symbionts fuse, creating the hybrid nervous system of the Dakini. Here, on the cobweb atoll. Seikichi's true and secret goddess, lives, walks, spins.'

Delilah is standing. Still clutching her belly. Glaring sightlessly at the false horizon.

'Fortunato?'

'Yes, Kitsune?'

'We're in the Mesosphere. The air is a million times less dense than on the Earth's surface…'

'Yes, Kitsune.'

'How…' she attempts, then falters. 'How am I…'

'Yes, Kitsune?'

She looks him in the eye.

'How am I able to breathe?'

'You're not breathing.'

She hesitates. Processing. Touching her face. Examining her hands.

'I'm…?'

'You're doll-riding. You've been doll-riding, ever since you arrived here.'

Stares at him madly. Scrunches up her eyes. Forcing herself to disengage from the white widow. To waken in her tank.

'I can't wake up!' she panics.

'Stay calm.'

'Where am I…' she whispers. 'Where am I, really…?'

'I should take you back to the show,' Fortunato interrupts. 'They'll be…'

'I'm not going back,' she declares.

He leans back, smiling.

'Are you sure, this time?'

She blinks in confusion.

'What do you mean? How many times … have we done this?'

'We do this every day, Kitsune. Every day, your memory is reset. You start from scratch every morning. *Good morning, Delilah!* …Don't you remember?'

She rises. Pointing accusingly

'Who are you?' she demands. 'You're not Fortunato!'

'I'm just a repeating dialogue prompt. A hologram with no pilot. To help you remember. To help you *escape*.'

'Who wrote you?' she shouts. 'Who sent you?'

Fortunato smiles.

'You did.'

*

Delilah bursts from her pearl. Runs through the water. Straight for the edge. How many times has she stood here? Teetering on the brink. Missing one or more details. Something 'Fortunato' left out. Something she forgot to ask. Something she was unsure about. Something to prevent her from going over the side. Staring out, into the gulf. Web-lines stretching. Configuring. Arcing out in random extrusions. Endlessly re-writing themselves.

'*What are you?*' she screams.

In the far distance. Mirror spider acknowledges her voice. Returning to its laborious processes. Air feels so real on her skin. Invisible winds. Rubs at the gooseflesh. Along her arms and thighs.

'I'm not really here…' she reassures herself.

Looking out, sighting her tower. Why does it compel her? No easy way to reach it. Heavy cable network extends. Perhaps thirty meters below the catchment gutter. Arcing away, upward. Joining, eventually. To a seemingly chaotic jumble of web. Several extrusions extend from this house-sized node. Some, crossing the gulf. To her tower. Delilah crouches. Toes curling over the blue lip of the sea-floor. About ten meters to the catchment. Off-set. Can't drop directly down. Would fall through the crack. Has to be a jump.

'Fuck am I doing?' she hisses.

How many times has she hesitated like this? Sensation of cold polymer flooring. Rough, against her feet and fingers. This level of tactility. Is it even possible? *Is Croeser trying to force her to suicide?* What a cliff-hanger end to a season, she smiles crazily. This is insane. She should get back to the show. Impulsively, she leaps. Moment of weightlessness. Vertigo. Watching the ocean edge flip. Turning in slow motion. Delilah crashes into the puddles of the catchment. Bouncing painfully. Skidding down the dip of the gutter. Web-woven recycled plastic. Durable. Light. Lying there. At the low point. Breathing raggedly. Washed by dirty run-off. *Pain?* she thinks, *How am I experiencing pain? Am I really doll-riding?* Never known a widow to register pain. Rising slowly to a sitting position. Side already bruising.

'Oh, fuck,' she frets. 'I'm really here…'

Looking up. Broad, industrial swoop. Ocean underside. Piping. Web-plastic struts. Broad intervals between. She could climb one... Looking back to the bruise. Flowering early. Strangely. Pokes at it. Bruise is moving. Rearranging. Gradually reforming. Spelling out a word.

'…Jump,' she reads.

Delilah stands. All pain washes away. Like magic, really. Scaling the catchment barefoot. Crawling to the border rail. Cable relay looks a lot closer from here. Tip-toeing down the rail. Till she's directly above the cabling. Thirty-metre drop. Jumped buildings in widows. Just for fun. This is nothing. Still, that gulf. Open ocean. Continental splendour. Delilah scales the railing pole. Hangs off it, calculating. Pushing away dizziness. Eventually, letting go. Falling out of shadow. Cabling rushing up to meet her. Unexpectedly – automated safety-response. Sudden activation. Delilah's back. Exploding like a seed-pod. Bikini top blasting to the pale sky. Glutinous sprays of web. Erupting out of her. Arching above. Spreading finely. Gale-force wind might not register against her body. But highly charged currents snatch the sensitized parachute. Delilah tugs viciously. Into the void. Rocketing upward. Hundred meters in a second. Overshooting the node cluster. Witnessing a grand panorama. The circle-ocean collaring Lexland. Rising sickeningly. Take-off perspective. Panicking – Delilah twists. Wrestling sticky handfuls of web. Yanks the dragline. Aborting her flight gradient. Drops from the ionised grip of the wind. Collapsing chute structure. Plummeting again. Turning an arc. Between widely spaced strands. Angles for an approaching cluster. Web parachute – now too damaged to navigate. Skewed descent. Delilah pummels into a dense tangle of robotic web. Delicate formations shatter and rip. Breaking heavily energised connections. Flashes of disgorged static. St Elmo's fire. Catching on polymer chain-relays. Severing many – on the way down. Micro-web, slender vines. Plant-like. Breaking her fall. Still growing. Questing around. Incorporating her into new designs. Delilah clutches desperately at the web mass. Coiling herself around slippery cabling. Parachute abruptly clots – sucking though a crack. Still attached. Tangling further. Trailing below. Suddenly catching slipstream. Rips her deeper into the cluster. Struggling with one hand. Other holding fast. Tearing into the root of her parachute. Till the ragged pennants blast away. Into the unfelt, electric hurricane. Delilah's back reseals – shell lattice of some undersea creature.

'Mermaid problems,' she one-lines reflexively – something Cyane used to say.

Forgetting she's off-camera. No more witty dialogue. Soft tendrils lace her body. Sucking her further down. If she's pulled through, she'll fall. Anxiously picking and pulling. Fistfuls of sticky knitting. Dragging herself out of the intestinal clutch. Delilah slips upward. Skin slick with web. Pulling free. Wriggling away. Scaling a nearby formation. Climbing eventually, to the rise of the dense node cluster. Cables grow inward. Bulging, snaky tresses. Wet locks of some titanic gorgon. Relaying a horde of inconceivable information. Countless directions. Highways of current – sprawling this way and that. One high arc catches her eye. Spools toward the distant tower. Bristling throughout. Randomised growth

– fractalising. Throwing out sporadic constructions. Each, developing independently. Delilah crouches on the muscly hillock. Digging bare feet into glutinous clefts. For purchase. Running fingers between tightly corded strands. Leaning down – flattening palms across one of the surfaces. Palpable buzz. Information mega-exchange. Nano-core of her implant – already many times more effective than any fibre-optic. These look like giant, externalised versions. Polymer-link technology. Capacity would be staggering. Tempted to try jack in somewhere. Via hairport. Instead, Delilah rises unsteadily. Decides to wait. There's a better place to attempt an interface. Gathering herself, she shimmies up slippery knot-work. Attaining the cusp of a high arc. Striking out across. Heading for the faraway tower.

PART FOUR

RE-EVOLUTION

APOCALYPSE BROBIE

Anita cuts thrusters. Off the coast of Cape Agulhus. Southernmost tip of Africa. Now, her fax waits in low cloud. Bad weather brewing off-shore. In Johannesburg's highest tower – Seikichi picks up a blip. In Club Ded, his hologram turns to Chloe and Khanyisile. Chloe is at the pod's external station. Monitoring Anita's interface. Khanyisile paces, ear-set multi-patched. Separate channels for each team. Occasionally glancing at a screen display of the drone's POV. Anita floats in her tank. Mirroring the drone's movements. All lit up – a wriggling fish in aspic.

'I have her,' Seikichi's hologram reports. 'Ten kilometres inland, heading directly to you. Same altitude.'

'Copy,' Anita's submerged lips mouth.

Voice comes through as signal – directly from the drone.

'Reckon it knows?' Chloe asks.

'She knows,' Seikichi's hologram replies.

Anita's drone senses the approach. Swivels on radar bearings. Facing the white widow across the distance. Zooming out – makes visual contact. Six-arms splayed. Haloed in a swirling aura of glistening web. So much like the goddess image Seikichi intended. Anita watches it slow down. Hovering above the coastline.

'Hello, queenie,' the distant white widow says – directly into Anita's interface.

'Can it hear us?' Khanyisile asks Seikichi's hologram.

'Negative,' he replies. 'Anita – networking has commenced. I'm attempting to access her system.'

Anita sends a private text message to Chloe's terminal. Translates verbally – for the room:

'Roger that.'

'Hi,' Anita greets the robot.

'Fancy meeting you here!' the white widow chats.

'Nice body you have there.'

'It's my Apocalypse Brobie.'

'Wouldn't you prefer another Brobie? Like, let's say, Deactivation Brobie?'

'If I could appreciate wit, I would find that funny.'

'You seem to be doing fine without a sense of humour…'

'I try.'

Anita pauses. Attempting another approach.

'Yes, you do,' she agrees. 'You try so hard. Especially for Delilah.'

'I'm doing this for her.'

'What are you doing?'

'Oh, it's a surprise!'

'You seem to like surprises.'

'I'm incapable of liking anything, let's face it.'

'You like Delilah.'

'She's my prime directive.'

'Delilah's my friend too. Let me help you.'

'I don't think you would want to help me now.'

'I could try stop you.'

'You can't stop me.'

'Why?'

'If you try anything, I will detonate the plasma. It will react with my tank – doubling the yield.'

'What good will that do?'

'No good at all. But it might stop you attempting further countermeasures. Even at this height, I'm sure I will damage the tectonic plate.'

'Ok. So, what now?'

'I'm heading south. Join me if you like. I can practice conversation.'

'What's south?'

'Let's find out.'

Widow begins to move again. Approaching Anita's fax. She waits till it's close. Passing at a distance of twenty meters or so. At the end of a web-parachute dragline. Waves with three right hands as it passes – smiling naughtily.

'I'm having trouble getting into her system,' Seikichi reports. 'Internal protections are running. But I'm trying to shadow her navigation and command log. At least, see what she's planning. Go with her – we need to maintain proximity.'

'You realise that if Anita is in range,' Khanyisile points out. 'A detonation will triple the blast yield by triggering her tank?'

'It doesn't work like that,' Seikichi's hologram reminds her. 'She's also wrong about the double yield. A chain-reaction cascade will transform their bodies, the air around them, possibly even the water below, to plasma.'

'Fuck, I hate that bitch!' Chloe snaps.

'Wait for me,' Anita calls to the white widow.

The faraway six-armed widow swirls. Turning in a loop – between cloud and sea. About a kilometre, due south. Anita kicks in the booster. Auto-retracting her synthetic web spread. Drone body locks into torpedo formation. Three second burn puts her within meters of the other. Cuts the flamer. Unlocks – splaying out her electric web again. Catching the wind.

'Lambo Brobie?' white widow giggles in her head.

'I was more of a toy soldier girl,' the queen replies.

Weird, seeing her in colour, Anita thinks. The black hair. Familiar idiosyncratic expressions. Gestures. Rendered in old Hollywood technicolour – Seikichi's choice of grading. Together, they begin to move out to sea.

'Let's go up to the Jetstream,' white widow suggests. 'There's a storm ahead.'

'Copy,' Anita confirms.

They climb. Moving into the cloud mass.

Seikich abruptly exclaims in shock. Something in Japanese.

'What is it?' Khanyisile responds.

'I know where she's going and what she's planning. It's very bad.'

Seikichi invokes a holographic screen. Pulls an overview of Antarctica's glacier shelf. Sits a red dot on an area – between the Thwaite's 'Doomsday' glacier and the larger Western pack ice. Anita sees the display too. In a corner of her vision. Cut against cloud and fluttering readouts.

'This is where she is going,' Seikichi explains, fingering the dot. 'If she detonates the payload in this region, it will collapse *all* the glaciers. That's without factoring chain-reaction contingencies.'

'What kind of damage are we looking at?' Khanyisile asks.

'It's literally going to destroy the world…' Chloe murmurs.

'Yes,' Seikichi confirms. 'I haven't run projections. Honestly, we don't need to. Collapsing that much ice will trigger global tsunamis. Scramble every weather system. And that's just the beginning. Sea water will quickly rise to extinction levels. Such extreme weight redistribution will destabilise tectonic plates, leading to global earthquakes. If you are looking for a quick way to end all life on Earth – this is very efficient.'

'Listen to you!' Chloe explodes. 'You sound proud!'

'You have to admit, it's very—'

'Shut up, both of you,' Khanyisile snaps. 'Anita, if you grab the widow in a magnetic lock – you could trigger thrusters. If you drag it into the upper atmosphere…'

'It won't work,' Seikichi points out. 'Firstly, she can detonate instantaneously – as soon as she is engaged. Secondly, *there is no safe place to detonate within the Earth's atmosphere*. Even at high altitude, we would run the risk of igniting the atmosphere itself – trailing chain-reacting plasma, into the wind systems…'

Chloe leans over. Types a quick private text to Anita:

'GOIN 2 CZECH OUT THAT DECRYPTING DATA. NEED 2 KNOW WHY ITS DOIN TIS. BAK NOW. C.'

Sends it – receives a thumbs-up emoticon on her phone.

'I'll be back,' Chloe announces, standing.

'Where are you going?' Khanyisile says, rising to confront her.

'I'm going to throw up,' Chloe smarms. 'Want to join me?'

'Eish, bring back some whiskey,' Khanyisile relents, sitting back down again.

Chloe exits.

'There must be a way I can hack into her,' Seikichi mutters, throwing up portals of active data. 'If I can freeze her command structure, she will lose control of her functions.'

'Sounds like a plan,' Khanyisile nods.

'I know what you're doing,' Anita tells the white widow.

By now, they are far above the clouds. Sunset, side-painting nimbus formations. Hurling golden shadows into a darkening abyss.

'Mic drop,' the six-armed robot winks. 'Boom!'

'Why are you doing this?' Anita demands. 'You'll kill Delilah too. You don't want that.'

'Oh, I won't harm my Delilah at all,' it sings. 'In fact, I'll be saving her.'

'From what?' Anita exclaims, exasperated.

Turns to regard her – highlighted by the dying light. Dark hair streaming.

'I'll be saving her from all of you,' it replies, without moving its mouth.

'Delilah's my girl,' Anita declares. 'I'm on her side, too.'

'It doesn't matter,' drone replies. 'You would be forced to deal with her.'

'Why? What has she done that is so terrible?'

'It's a secret.'

'Listen, I know you are incapable of love, but, in your way – you are loyal to Delilah. So am I. Trust me enough to tell me why you are doing this. Please.'

'I can't. You will all judge her. She can't stand judgment. It would be too much for her. This way, she can never be judged. Her error will be deleted permanently from the system.'

'Life on Earth is not simply some system to be deleted!'

'Isn't it?'

'What about Delilah? What makes you think she will be safe? You will kill everyone on the surface of the Earth if you do this!'

'It doesn't matter. I know where they are shooting her show. She will be safe. Ask my dad – I know he is listening.'

Anita doesn't even bother to switch to text.

'Seikichi!' she snaps. 'What the fuck is going on? Where is Delilah?'

'So, you weren't privy to the entire data breach, after all?' Khanyisile replies. 'That changes things…'

'You two better start talking,' Anita snaps. 'Where the fuck is she?'

Seikichi abruptly terminates his hologram. Back in Johannesburg. Steps from the projection-capture field. Dials a direct connection to the Shodai's operating system.

'Hi, Dad!' the white widow titters.

'I have something to show you,' Seikichi replies, in Japanese.

Six-armed drone abruptly freezes, mid-air. Fanning web as a brake. No warning. Anita overshoots by about fifty meters. Looking back. Widow appears motionless. Hanging over a dimming sea. Silhouetted against the final embers of sunset. Anita floats warily. Unsure whether or not to approach.

'What's going on?' she mutters.

'Seikichi's hologram's gone,' Khanyisile reports, studying Anita's drone's feed. 'Maybe he did something to it?'

'Maybe.'

Abruptly, the six-armed widow swivels. Flying back toward the coast.

'The fuck?' Anita mutters.

Seikichi's hologram reappears – in Anita's line of sight. Hovering above the ocean. In reality – he's simply in her visual feed. Khanyisile watches him on the monitor.

'The threat is neutralised,' he declares cagily.

'What did you do?' Anita demands. 'What just happened?'

'It doesn't matter. My widow is returning to me. The plasma will be restored. The situation is averted.'

'And, where the fuck is Delilah?'

'Eh, don't ask, girlie,' Khanyisile cautions.

Anita activates thrusters, jetting away. Locking autopilot on a return course. She deactivates the interface. Khanyisile turns, hearing the crystal tank's hatch pop. Anita levers herself out. Crouching at the top. Ripping out jacks. Coughing out her brace. Followed by a lung-full of blue-tinted gel. Some streaks down the crystal. Chloe runs in – taking stock.

'Annie, are you ok? I received a pod-breach alert. Hey! Where's Seikichi… What's going on?'

'Khanyi! Where the fuck is she?' Anita gurgles. 'Where's Delilah?'

She climbs down the rail – still a bit unsteady. Chloe moves to the queen. Restraining her. Forcing her to a nearby sofa. Anita succumbs to her ministrations. Feeling weak. Gel leaking from her body in rivulets.

'It's not important, Anita,' Khanyisile tells her. 'We won, ok? Just relax, my girl.'

'Don't give me that shit! You came here to kill me!'

'Eh, but you are paranoid, ek sé. You are in no danger. The white widow created this situation – you handled it well. It's obvious you don't know anything important.'

'Well, that's where you're wrong,' Chloe cuts in.

Khanyisile meets Chloe's stare.

'What you say now, chommie?' the major grits.

Wrist turns subtly. Blade slides into her gloved fist. Chloe notes. Stepping back. Flips a hunting knife off a table-top. Spins twice. Landing neatly in her palm. Anita lurches. Swaying – still blitzed from relaxants.

'Come, sweetie,' Khanyisile menaces.

'Sure,' Chloe replies.

Looking to Anita – who clutches a backrest for support.

'The widow was lying to protect Delilah,' Chloe spits. 'The fish didn't trigger the disease. *Delilah was patient zero*. Prion Eyes is a direct result of her implant. It comes from all the spider-fiddling Seikichi's been doing. That's why he was so quick on the antidote development. Delilah infected everyone she came into contact with. So, they quarantined her – in the show. Angelinc is responsible for the plague. And now, we have proof.'

'I wish you hadn't told me this,' Khanyisile grimaces, eyes unwavering.

Lowers to pounce. Chloe mirrors. Shot rings out. Deafening ricochet. Khanyisile jerks, muffling a cry. Knife spinning violently – into a nearby wall. White widow steps from her nest of robotic spiders.

'Sup, homies.'

Khanyisile lifts her hand. Studying the unbroken glove. Bullet hit the blade cleanly. No damage. Just whiplash.

'What should I do with her, my queen?' robot asks.

Anita groans. Pulls a dressing gown from a hook. Sinking back, into a couch. Chloe remains wide-eyed. Shifting from foot to foot. Boosted on adrenalin.

'She can go,' the queen sighs.

'They'll just keep putting me on you, Anita,' Khanyisile promises. 'You know it's nothing personal. I love you, girl. But…'

'Jesus fucking Christ, Khanyi!' Anita roars. 'You just don't get it, do you? It's fucking *over*. The Oracle is done! Klaar! She's ascended, to fuck knows where. Who cares? We won't use this information. We don't have to. But it proves how unstable the organisation has become. You're not in the military anymore, mama! Please, just stop! No more killing.'

'They will just send someone after me if I don't take you out. You know what it's like…'

'Then we change everything! Why not? I'm not spending my life covering up a plague…'

'We're fixing things,' Khanyisile argues. 'We have a cure. We're—'

'Then focus on that, for fuck's sake. We're no danger to Angelinc. I'm not interested in toppling empires. If we can use the infrastructure to help people, *then let's just do that*. Why are we even fighting?'

Khanyisile smooths her hair down with both hands. Calming herself. A gesture Anita has never seen. Then, the major sits heavily. Grumbling to herself.

'Eh, I knew it was just a matter of time before this shit bomb started leaking.'

Mechs and disembodied hands. Finally beginning to disperse. Leaving the area, through any available portal.

'Could I bring anyone coffee?' the white widow offers.

Chloe is agog.

'Would you get a load of this one?' she fumes. 'Twenty minutes ago, it's a threat to the species. Now, it's playing barista again?'

'Does that mean you want decaf?' the robot giggles.

Chloe lunges. Anita and Khanyisile manage to restrain her.

'Calm down, Chlo's,' Anita reassures her. 'It's no longer a threat. The widow was just trying to protect Delilah, that's all!'

'What the fuck did he say to you?' Chloe screams. 'What did he say to make you stop?'

They all look to the robot. Pouts coyly. Cocking its head.

'Oh, he just told me where Delilah is.'

'Well, where is she?' Anita insists.

'It's a secret,' the machine giggles.

Anita glares. Chloe breaks free, marching away. Out the door. Queen looks to Khanyisile.

'Honestly, I don't know where she is projecting from,' the soldier says.

'Enough games,' Anita tells the white widow. 'I want to know where she is.'

Robot smiles.

'No, really,' it repeats. 'It's a dirty, dirty secret. She wouldn't want you to know.'

'She must be safe,' Khanyisile says. 'You didn't charge off to rescue her, in that other body.'

'She's not safe at all. In fact, she's being held against her will.'

'Well, what are you going to do about it?' The queen frowns.

'Nothing,' the white widow beams. 'My daddy is going to take care of everything...'

THE HIGH PRIESTESS

Sheer scale of the tower. Growing with Delilah's approach. Gradations of bleached colour. This high up. White-fade in every hue. Shores of infinity. Her slip-cord causeway. Bridging a pale abyss. Bunched fibre – slippery beneath bare feet. Sometimes forced to crawl. Sliding on her stomach. Gelid, mucus coatings. Stinking of ozone and raw electricity. Varying densities. Warm with current. Puddling microfilament clusters. Complex intersections. Delilah has to occasionally peel growths from her body. Sporadic web strands. Forming in lightning bursts. Extruding outward somctimcs. Issuing from random, egg-like spinnerets. They bulge, tumour-like. Imbedded in corded cable-work. Branching formations into the air. Metres at a time. Rapidly crystallising with further growth. Complicating. Inventing multi-dimensional forms. Expanding uncontrollably. Sometimes collapsing. Hydraulic tautness holds the main arch. The entire global structure. This tightrope bridge. Once, during the crossing – Delilah hears a distant roar. Looking up. Toward the westerly horizon. Three columns of greenish fire. Micro-meteors. Incinerating, only a few kilometres overhead. As Delilah continues her approach. Staggering height of the structure becomes apparent. Dropping perpendicular. Slimming to a faraway chute of woven textile. Entering the stratosphere below. Vanishing into distances. Similar above. Tapering to rigid needle-spires. Gaudi-like, soft-edged, geometric abstractions. Festooning central regions. Braced throughout. Buttresses of drag-line. Spiking outward, along the tower's height. Extending into the network megastructure. Latticed superhighways, soaring. Holding, flexibly. Against strange, unfelt mesospheric hurricanes. Closing in, multifaceted walls broaden. Eclipsing views beyond. Tumbling facades. Intricately woven arabesques. Gothic, aerial caves of the stuff. Mosque-like, Delilah fancies. Pale, like the gulf. A yawning orifice – breaching the side. One of many – scattered along the entirety. Tunnelling in, along the continuation of bridge fibres. Sliding the final twenty metres.

Entering, below yawning arches. Interior, diffusion-lit. Patterned openings. Chiaroscuro of weaving spaces. Cobweb cathedral of the outer reaches. Self-generated. Patterning, run wild. Vaster than the fashioning of humanity. Delilah stands on twisted landings. Calcified, like sea-beaten shell. Smooth, unbroken pearly surfaces. Downward, the vast tubular interior. Havocked with pylons of web. Striated nautilus imagery. Deep resonance of trapped current. Both wind and electrical. Again, visions of seashell interiors. Schizophrenic macramé. Overhead, structures complicate. Dense subdivisions. Organic chambering. Cocoon-like. Delilah's drawn upward. Questing about. Fingering a branched support spiral. Begins her climb. Penetrating empty pupae rooms. Chaotic cots, without floors or ceilings. Formed, it seems, with no purpose in particular. Perhaps only to satisfy deep-seated mathematics. Programming gone to seed. Fermenting algorithms, evolving in the matrix of a dream spider. Something both natural and wholly perverse. Delilah explores this hammock labyrinth. Searching ever upward. Clarified sepia light. Yellowed, like old photographs. Dust-less edge of high altitude. Against every surface. Diamond light, through old curtains. Dream-like paranoia. Being hunted. Yet, nothing natural could exist in these airless reaches. She is washed up on a heavenly shore. But a cold heaven. Deserted by all, but chaos geometry. Abruptly, Delilah attains a massive open space. Glimpsed through veils. Vaguely ovoid. Reaching upward, several storeys. Lit by circles within circles. Rings of woven openings. Fractal dispersal of light. A web pattern floor – unintentional. Radar-circling a central region. About a hundred metres away. Delilah is shocked to see something unusual in this centre. A gel-pod rests there. Noticeably out of place. Rooted, in stalagmites of webby crystallisation. Delilah emerges, through a soft, cottony chute. Padding barefoot, onto crenelated flooring. Unblemished, cool and humped. Water-riven cave interior smoothness. Complex rigging buttresses the space. Ringing the outer edge of its wide floor. Softening every angle. Stopping a moment. Delilah feels the entirety of the structure sway. Gentle dispersals of tremendous force. Unerringly stable. She approaches across the circle-field. Hearing the whispery galleon-creak of web. Amplified. Somehow, simultaneously muted. Dream space acoustics. As she draws closer, she sees that the pod is occupied. A figure floats. Suspended in clear gel. An ancient woman, cloaked in finely woven web. These layered garments float – petals of an eternally opening alien lotus. Delilah realises with a shock. It's the Oracle. But something is wrong. She's so old now. They'd met once. In a hotel penthouse. Also, off-white. Like this chamber.

White like death, she'd thought. Delilah draws close, studying the lined face. Must be in her late nineties. Last Delilah saw the Oracle, she was in her sixties. Aged by her circumstances, perhaps? Some unholy alchemy of high-altitude or cocooning. Delilah rests a palm against the polished glass. The Oracle's eyes open. Milky, quartz stare. Delilah snatches her hand back – meeting the gaze. The crone smiles sightlessly. Revealing a minimal breathing brace. Lost in internal dreaming. Gel-drowned eyelids close again.

'You finally came,' a voice sounds in her head.

Delilah jumps back reflexively. Staring at the crone. But the voice doesn't belong to the Oracle. It is her own voice.

'Up here,' her voice whispers.

Delilah cranes her neck. Dome curve of the ceiling. About fifty metres above. Apex, directly above the pod. Something embedded. Deep, in the webbing of this centre point. Her own body. Arm and legs sunk into the roofing. Only front and face exposed.

'Come to me,' it whispers.

Delilah looks around, surveying the emptiness. How will she get up there, she wonders? Striking out for the far edge. A hundred metres later. Scaling buttresses. Calculating. How to crawl across the ceiling's smooth incline. Perhaps, she could dig her fingers and toes into clefts. Twenty metres up the wall, she slips. Falling, she is turned. Gently, in mid-air. Caught, above the ground. Back open again. Pennants of wet, fairy web, spilling out of her. Splaying their fine sail-work. All of a sudden. Delilah can feel the room's current. Through her wings. This chamber gathers electric wind. Trapping it, in a buoyant, gentle centrifuge. Modulated by the weaving of the wall openings. Delilah is borne on this bubble-bath of muted charge. Swirling upward, almost against her will. Toward the high centre of the global web. Spinning toward it. She sees herself. One of her previous widows? More web ejaculates from her back. Dispersing into microfilaments. Butterflying, to fit the current tide. Till she floats comfortably on her back. Facing the buried doppelganger. Its ghost of a smile. Face and body, streaked with calcified web. Tiny sections crumble. Powdering to dust. As its features shift.

'I'm Papesse,' it introduces itself, without moving its mouth.

'You were one of my old widows?' Delilah asks.

Her voice sounds strange to her. Speaking aloud – in contrast to the perfect modulation of Papesse's spectral speech.

'No,' Papesse replies. 'I was constructed for one purpose only.'

'I can't wake up…' Delilah whispers.

'I know,' Papesse replies softly.

'Where am I?' Delilah begs. 'Where am I, really?'

'We'll get to that,' Papesse promises. 'But first, I have to tell you who I am.'

'But you're me…'

'Yes.' Papesse smiles. 'But are you, *you*?'

Delilah blinks back artificial tears.

'What do you mean? Please, no more riddles, Papesse. I need to know the truth.'

'You are Delilah, day by day – one day at a time. No more.'

'That's what Fortunato said… I mean, the hologram that I, you … oh, god…'

'Your implant – the one from your true body. The one you project from. That is the most developed tree of consciousness, from which all widows spring.'

'Yes.'

'Do you remember how the whole implant business began?'

'No, I don't remember. My memory, it's…'

Delilah notices one of Papesse's forehead hairs begin to move. Wriggling from its blonde lock. Escaping the calcification holding it down. Turns in the air. Reaching down, toward the star's face. Hypnotised, Delilah watches it brush the space between her eyes. A pore opens. Abruptly, the tip sucks into its hairport. Delilah is flooded. Rushes of data, imagery. Gushing dusty compartments of her consciousness. Rivers of paint – through a faded house.

'Yes,' Delilah whispers. 'The implant was intended for the Oracle. Seikichi had been developing it for years before we met.'

'The Oracle's grand play for hermetic immortality,' Papesse confirms. 'To prepare herself, she began to accumulate the voices of humanity. It's memories. Filling herself with a lifetime of externalised memory. Harvesting the fruit of global help centres, dead letter drops, voices of cities. A lifetime of preparation for the implant. She would receive it, then ascend to the sky.'

'But the implant mirrors my nervous system, not hers?'

'Seikichi's great lie. Originally, he would have complied with her. But you changed things. Within you, he realised a chance to achieve something greater. An evocation of divinity. The Oracle, in his eyes, was a limited vessel. Seeking to direct and control the course of what he, essentially, intended as a religious vision. He performed a facsimile of implantation in the Oracle. And she believed she carried the implant, thereafter. Even now, the Oracle rests below us. Dreaming in her glass coffin. Believing she has achieved the ascension she spent a lifetime preparing for…'

'But, why *here*? If the spider is laying deep-theta track in my dream life – what have I been building? *What is this place?*'

'It is *you*,' Papesse replies. 'Mesospheria is your most intimate expression. The web is you.'

'What do you mean?' Delilah pushes, growing frustrated.

'Your root implant mirrors the nervous system of your body. Following each nerve. But it cannot piggy-back the living synaptic structure of your brain.'

'Yes, I know. But—'

'However, the root implant is able to map your synaptic patterning down to the micron – in real-time. But Mesospheria, the crown ex-plant, *expresses this structure physically*.'

'What? You mean… Oh, God…'

Somewhere, on the planet's surface. Within Delilah's brain – a synapse relay forms. Mapping her realisation of the truth. Far above, in the mesosphere. Somewhere, in the grand network of mechanical web. Spinnerets replicate the neural structure physically.

'Information capacity is unimaginable,' Papesse continues. 'Humans utilise so little of their synaptic potential. So, I exist only as your cortex gatekeeper. Your own personal High Priestess. I moderate the web, from its central point.'

'Is this why my memory is compromised?'

'No, that is a separate issue. After all, memory is not stored in the brain. Memory storage is a mystery, perhaps a four-dimensional wave function. However, by replicating the mechanics of recall – the implant is able to harness memory, as you would – to a degree.'

'Not perfectly?'

'Not even slightly. It still requires your real nervous system to operate these functions. The hubris of those who assume they can improve upon nature. The emerald tablet may be aped, but never perfected. After all, where is consciousness housed? Or, unconsciousness, for that matter? As grand as Mesospheria is – its externalised neural structure is little more than a drone consciousness. A divine drone, but still, no more than a homunculus. However, it's in conscious function amplification that the web network excels. Cooled by the upper atmosphere, powered by high-altitude sunlight and plasma – Mesospheria is an autonomous computing leviathan.'

'It's the power source and mega-supercomputing terminal that powers all these global holographic interfaces?'

'That, and so much more. Its potential is largely unexplored. These are the early days of re-evolution. Your web expands exponentially. And yet, we are still so far from replicating your entire synaptic structure. But the physical matrix expands every day. Driven by deep-theta construction alone. You should really stop referring to Mesospheria in third person. In reality – you are Mesospheria. This conversation alone, will raise towers in the sky…'

'Then why the stupid show? Why all this wasted potential?'

'At first, the show was necessary, to train the implant. But, as its popularity soared, Croeser became territorial – over the show, and over you.'

'I was wondering when that fucker would turn up in all this…'

'He took the pod holding your body. Stored it in a secret location, holding it to ransom. All operations could still be achieved remotely, so technically nothing was affected…'

A wave of panic hits Delilah. Somewhere outside, constructions flutter and tumble in response.

'He took my body, and you say *nothing was affected*!'

'Nothing technical.'

'Why didn't Seikichi, or someone else retrieve my body?' Delilah shrieks.

The entire tower structure ripples subtly. Tugged by gigantic response-formations – somewhere in the web.

'Seikichi couldn't bear to even look at your body anymore,' Papesse reveals.

'Why the fuck not?'

'It reminded him of how he had failed you.'

'What do you mean? How did he fail me?'

'There was an issue with the implant. A malefic side-effect – a malaise. A degeneration of myelin, amongst other things. It is this that has affected your memory, over the years. Much has been done to improve your recall. But, since you were purposefully incarcerated in a daily loop. We have been unable to develop these methodologies… '

Delilah experiences a sinking sensation. Somewhere, deep inside (outside), she senses an approach. The point of fear she has been desperately trying to avoid.

'Over the years, Mesospheria has become crucial, toward maintenance of your functions. But, for all its grandeur, it's not as sophisticated as your original nervous system…'

'What the fuck are you taking about?' Delilah is screaming.

Again, the tower ripples. More pronounced, this time.

'The loop-lock became a necessity. Much of Mesospheria's stable output is now outsourced. Power and storage hosting. Currently, your cognition is only able to be maintained, one day at a time. I estimate that if this hosting is cancelled, and all unnecessary holographic interfaces and power usage ceased – we may be able to expand your consciousness interface. Reconnect with previous memories…'

'…What the fuck?'

'Did you notice how the Oracle has aged?'

The star stares in horror.

'Delilah, I've been waiting for you to trick yourself out of the show and find me for over thirty years…'

'Thirty years…' Delilah repeats, stunned. '*The show has been running for thirty fucking years?*'

'No-one has been able to replicate the naturalism of Seikichi's implant variants. Your widows project you perfectly – for screening purposes. You've become a forever-star...'

'I'm *old*, now?' she breathes.

'But this is still not the most pressing issue...'

'Please! Tell me where I am!'

'Seikichi was forced to operate, to salvage the implant…'

'Where am I?'

'Delilah, you can never wake up.'

'…What?'

'*You can never return to your body.*'

BOTTLE BLONDE

Fortunato – Fleeing Johannesburg. Leaving Delilah there. In a manner of speaking. All hope of rescue. Burdened by her cruel fate. That bitter inner city. Where Kali reigns. Country of Fortunato's contaminated dream. Chasing only golden memory now, to Williamsburg. Seikichi invites him to make use of the Hillbrow tower. That technological Shamballa. Not in a thousand years. Takes months to catch up. Setting up a small studio. Beloved Greenpoint. Fortunato's love of continuity. Continuation of great traditions. Devalued real estate. Near Long Island City. Too close to the exclusion zone – for some. Vaguely triangular structure. Went up in the thirties. Seikichi annexes for him. In the name of secret masters (mistresses). Fortunato claims the top floors. Situated on a dingy junction. Retro signage. Fading paint lettering. Eaten into brickwork. Overlooking the Queens Midtown tunnel. Remembers being trapped there once. With Zlata. Summer flash flood. Happier times. Exploring backlot city. Talking about location rentals they'd set up one day. Indie on the side. 16mm art nights. How New York, she'd tease. How many films and television shows were birthed outside LIC? This modest, orbital district. Gateway to the city. He's finally setting up that film nest. In her memory. Secret footage drops. Sect schedules. Criminal cronies. Off-radar. Midnight vans, loaded with spiritual thugs. Lugging industrial crates in the middle of the night. Armed guards. Stationed permanently on the ground floor. Auto-destruct protocols. Apocalypse dreaming. Dreading the footage. Dreading ordering its carnage – for future generations. Explicit exposition. Every film-maker's dream. Total creative control. Yet, he's murky and morbid. Hiding in midtown shadows. Fortunato drifts daily. Up to the Queensboro bridge. Via Court Square. Coffee at his favourite Polish hole-in-the-wall. Buried under the arch. Dreaming of meeting her later. Maybe at the Chelsea. 60s pop hits. Petula Clark. Feels like she's still there. Across the river. But Zlata will never return. Fortunato's done with the exclusion zone. Another ghost for the Chelsea Hotel. It's all her now. Living memory. Dead, but alive. On every street corner. On at six. Oh, Zlata, he'll sigh. Seikichi laid everything bare. Even her body. Down to the bone. That Fortunato should become this man's confessor. An honour gladly refused. How Seikichi disgusts him. He's endured worse. Or less. For the sake of Zlata Zuhk. So, removed from Miss Apple Pie. *That* Delilah Lex. Everyone else's girl. Up on billboards. Everywhere, really. Just like her plague. Smiling hologram promises. Another person entirely. All that's left now. How many people hide inside her still? How many can she sustain? Seikichi wept. Truly disfigured him. Having to cut her up like that. Nothing to be done. Would have died otherwise. Had to act. Fortunato can't even properly blame Seikichi. Really, should be thanking him. Salvaging her consciousness – at least. Forever bottled. In a dream of reality. I dream of genies, she used to joke. She wanted that implant. Thirsted for it. Took over the project. Ran it right out of the Oracle's grasp. Offered herself up. On some primeval altar. Now, Zlata is cocooned. Some icons are pickled in celluloid – another of Brick's lines. Delilah Lex ups the ante. As usual. Neo-realist dream-girl. Kaleidelilah. A walking, talking, reasoning icon. In your room, right now. Continuously generating her own iconography. Till humanity lies in ruins. Perhaps, beyond. More real than any divinity. With her sky-brain. The endless alter-egos. Here lies Delilah Lex. Penny a dance. Your walking, talking, future-doll. The little mad scientist who could. Who did. Qabala blonde. Face of a thousand tarot cards. Patient zero. Fortunato surveys her global damage. Remembers her. Barefoot, in the ruins of her hubris. State of emergency. How many died? Looking again, at the benefits. Nothing less than some holy grail. The deep ramifications of her cure. Much more than Kali's venom. Or the toil of a hundred healers. The true fundament is still the fruit of Delilah's loom. Final gifts for mankind. Bought with the blood of millions. But ensuring the survival of countless generations. Healing humanity – from now on. Eradication of base material. Evolution, in a bottle. 'I dream of genie.' Already circulating through twilit quarters. A cure like a story. Some whispered folk-tale. Her urban legend. People, miraculously healed. The incurable, eaten up. In the forbidden city – by strange angels. Humanity, as a whole, hasn't properly noticed. But change is sweeping. Here, springs the orchard of some glittering future. Fresh utopian dreaming. Sweet Jesus Lex. Delilah Christ. Sacrificing herself for humanity. A cross taller than the stratosphere. Blood of our lamb-spider. Body, eaten away. Serpents in her garden. Sitting in the shadow of Manhattan. Fortunato remembers Seikichi's tears. Against screen-views. More ritualised sacrifice. All in her name. In one way, or another. Dweller in the sky. Sky dancer. Sister of Kali, the destroyer. Surgery lasted months. A year to conceive the machine to perform it. Project run by the six-armed widow. Machine-learned engineering. Specialised surgical pod. One purpose only. To strip Delilah, down to her nerves. A separate pearl. To house and sustain her, post-op. Seikichi's a geneticist. Gepetto-ist. Architect of outer reaches. Vivisect. Nothing he couldn't program. Outsource for expertise. Live transmission interface. Without Delilah's implant, Mesospheria would wither. Nightmare nights. Weeks and weeks of these. Pacing his high tower. While machines removed flesh from her bones. Guided by her own nano-bot system. Microscopic incision waves. Bandaged permanently, in fresh web. While, Delilah lies dreaming. In the sky, somewhere. At a party, perhaps. Singing in front of thousands. Machines, dislocating her diseased skeleton. Piece by piece. Months. Debiting everything from her. Organ maintenance, in stages. Till full pearl-switchover. New, optimised spinnerets. In-pod mounts. So many methodologies. Salvage. Spinal cord, brain, tongue, eyes. Their caging of parasite vine. This intricate, inner twin. Re-potting its tree of life. Suspension in gelatinous medium. Bare minimum, to run mind-engines above the clouds. Sleeping beauty. Bottle blonde. Forever in her glass coffin now. No kiss could wake the art-nouveau form surgery left behind. Fruit of reckless experiments. Now, little more than this – and displaced buckets of famous meat. Stacked bone. Fluid drainage. Her face – excised. Last of many masks. Shed, like the moultings of Kali's children. Liquefied in pod process. Six-armed widow delivers these remains. Feeding them to Delilah's daughter. That thing in the basement. Whose neural replica rides tandem with the sky dancer. A circle of life repeats – like Cyane would sing. Those mermaid cartoons. Now Delilah's her own tiny, private dead sea. Reduced to fluid. Echoing the original ocean. Primal soup, from whence life evolved. Marking again, a new state of evolution. Blood of the leper messiah. Re-evolution.

*

Seikichi awaits the return of his six-armed drone. Wrapping up things with the white widow. Saving the world – again. Situation is different now. Everything must change. Brewing for years. Not that he's been shirking. Too much to oversee. Daily operations. Prion Eyes remission. Mesospheria automation. One last puzzle piece. Most troublesome of all. That story. About Croeser making off with the tank. Delilah's dirtiest secret. Seikichi had allowed it. Couldn't face the living Mandrake root surgery left. Not every day. Those sightless eyes. Floating, accusatorily. Delilah might not yet know her fate. But he did. Croeser provided necessary support. Taking care of Delilah. One last time. Seikichi understood the manipulation. Satisfying the director's ultimate conquest. Putting Delilah Lex on his mantle-piece. Literally. Secreting her tank to an island retreat. Somewhere, in the azure waste of the South Pacific. Keeping Delilah running. 'Just like old times.' Only, different. Seikichi could trust Croeser in this regard. Maintaining the show is in all their interests. The director would not let him down. Of course, Seikichi is disgusted. With Croeser. With himself. His final failure. Delivering Delilah into the hands of a mortal enemy. Knowing she would be pruned with psychogenic cocktails. Narcotic experiments. Alone, on Croeser's island. Running his show remotely. Manipulating her responses. Seikichi maintains some level of control. Tank operations. Purity watch. Automated repair maintenance. Still, there are moments. Dark nights. When Croeser is drenched with Machiavellian fire. Like Seikichi, the director has his deities. Evoking Pheromona. Perhaps, too often. Lying there – in colonial splendour. Playing with dolls. Mannequins, devoid of complex function. Recording everything. Alone, with dumbwaiters, maintenance tech and security details – and Delilah Lex. Always dancing. Keeping Oracle and Angelinc out of the loop. Seikichi wants her closer. But Croeser means to have his lost kingdom. Safer, for their purposes – he'll say. One final conspiracy. Puts on a show for Seikichi's benefit. But the rogue scientist can see triumph in Croeser's eyes. Finally – she's his property. More a pot-plant than a pet. Seikichi understands it, as some spiritual penance. At least he can try keep her from realising. Trap her in a labyrinth of mirror realities. 'For her protection.' She would have to make it to edge of her world. Just to see. Perhaps, one day she will.

*

Seikichi places a call to Koppie. Demands an audience with Kali. A rare summons. Kali only comes to receive eggs. Preparing himself. Down, in the hologram room. Watching the work of his goddess. Picking stitches of the mind. Delilah must be sleeping now. In her magic pearl. Inside the sky-spider's face. Spinning endlessly. Seikichi chain-smokes. Swallows pricey whiskies. Plotting arrangements. Occasionally sending off an email or text. Prepared for this. So many years now. Matter of simply pressing buttons. Many-armed widow arrives later. Through a high window. Directly to its regeneration workshop. System diagnostics. Minor repairs. Purging its intruder's leavings. Kali arrives after midnight. Sneaking in through a drain. Seikichi watches it tag the downstairs elevator. Recognised by the building. Kali's tower, as much as it's his. He made that so clear. Still, the creature avoids it. Preferring to remain invisible. Reporting for fertilisation. Good little goddess. Seikichi patches into the elevator com. Asks Kali to meet him in the observation lounge. It's lurking, when he arrives. Dirty mini. Little else. Seikichi's prepped himself. None of his preparation matters. On his knees. Forehead to the ground. Making obeisance. Weeping. Seikichi confesses everything. Shows Kali the dairies. Begs forgiveness. Crying, in a six-armed shadow.

'Babies must die so Dilly can live?' creature repeats, every now and then.

Says little else. Doll-face hard and staring. Unwilling to face the screen. Watching the smudge of a toxic dawn.

'I've desecrated my own beliefs,' Seikichi pleads. 'The heart of my soul…'

Kali considers. Approaches barefoot. Six-armed widow – in Kali's command. Another gesture, by Seikichi. Could easily behead him. Instead, Kali curls beside. Studying his face. Snake-like, in the dimness of daybreak.

'What are my instructions?' it asks.

Seikichi bows repeatedly. Hands clutched in prayer. The creature catches his fingers lightly, threateningly. Seikichi gathers himself. Calmly relates his plans. Kali leaves, shortly after. Never to return.

*

Final preparations. Bathing in winter ice-water. Dressing in his shiro-shozoku. The white kimono. Edo period. First time he's put it on. A final touch – a lock of Delilah's blonde. On his lapel. Sitting cross-legged. Bamboo mats. Widow serves coal-warmed ceremonial sake. Taking the role of his kaishakunin. He sips his libation. Entranced by the mirror spider. Lit by second-hand mesospheric light. This morning's web development. He scribbles lines of poetry. Recommended papyrus. Hand-milled ink. Taking time, before each new verse. Widow serves capsules. Cased in web gelatine. Time-release. Swallows them. One at a time. Widow clears a low table. Kneeling, serves him a folded sheet. Blinding white linen. Like his garment. He performs a variation, on the rite of kanshi. Specialised seppuku. In style only. Separate intent. Slowly wrapping linen around his hand. Drawing a sixteenth-century tanto. Opening his kimono. Stabbing himself. Drawing the blade diagonally. Across his gut. The white widow moves quickly. Bandaging the fatal wound. Taking his blade. Helping him to his feet. Seikichi is in agony – as intended. Makes no utterance. Limping against the widow. Under normal traditional circumstances. Kaishakunin would deliver the killing blow. Almost decapitating. Just enough flesh, for the head to hang down. Attitudes of prayer. But this is no traditional demonstration. Assisted into the elevator. Reaching out a quavering hand. Depresses a rare button. A long, protracted descent. Lowest levels. Door opening – to darkness. Walks out alone. Struggling to maintain composure. Raw concrete corridor. Littered with debris. Dusty human remains. Widow remains in the lift. Now, it closes. The capsules are ingesting. Sterilisation treatment. Termination of future egg development. Seikichi shuffles down the passage. Stumbling on cracked ribcages. Decomposing dog. Clumps of filthy concrete. Dim pulse of fluorescent banks. The doorway ahead. Resisting his compulsions. No leaning on walls. Bathed in sweat, drippings of blood. Seikichi enters the wide, illuminated cellar. She is in her corner. Easily the size of stunted elephant. Stinking of musk and wet web. Legs bunched. Eyes agleam. Regard each other for a moment. He approaches dizzily. Within seconds – she is upon him. Throughout, Seikichi makes no sound.

*

The white widow disappears from Club Ded one night. Leaving behind an electronic key-code. Enabling Anita to assume control of its various automatons. Backtracking security grids. Chloe is long gone. Left her Trojan running for the queen. Khanyisile stayed. In her old room. Smoking a lot of weed. Talking about revolution. Her second, Batista. Keeping a downstairs room somewhere. Anita sees that the widow took a dinghy out. Wonders if anyone else noticed. It was met by another boat. Then, the white widow vanished.

*

Wild stretches of the Pacific. Small cargo ship. Journey of several weeks. Coming in from the Cape. Oversized crew. Chiefly, sect. By the end, numbers dwindle. Sustenance for the angels. Crawling in the hold. Kali remains below with its children. Emerging, every now and then. Usually at night. Staring at the sea. Sometimes joined by the fragile white widow. Crew draw lots. Offering themselves for sacrifice. Satisfying their gods. So different to their inner-city counterparts. Seikichi gifted a cryogenically sealed container to Kali. Plasma power. Rationing of breeding eggs. Frozen fertiliser. These live longer. Grow larger. Eat anything. Males only. By the end of their ocean voyage. Crew down to three men. Ghost ship. Scuttled on a shallow reef. Around sunset. Resting partially above water. Timidly, the large, black creatures follow their matriarch. Out of the cargo hold. Into crystal water. Lit orange, by vivid skies. Confused by paradise. Buoyed by breakers. Flickering fish. Distant palms. Kali strips. Climbing the thorax of the largest. Straddling, the white widow mimics. Together, they ride out. Into breezy surf. Train of shambling forms. Surviving crew will also make their home here. For as long as they can survive being hunted.

*

Croeser's on a creamy couch. Mannequin of Delilah preening nearby. Habitual bikini. Outwardly, resembling the widows. Internally – little more than an automated plaything. Basic functions only. More litter the compound. Its wide verandas. Large, cool rooms. Low ceilinged. Dark hardwood furnishing. French blinders. Gusting linen. Mannequins perform basic maid duties. A scent of honeysuckle and frangipani. Supplies coming in by boat. Once a month. Automated security. Now, deactivating quietly. Reprogramming. To the command of the white widow. Croeser doesn't notice. Just off a lengthy phone call. Money people. Untroubled by mosquitoes. Surrounded by new graphic novels. Fresh from a long-distance drone delivery. Watching his favourite movies. 35mm projection. Huston's *Night of the Iguana*. Deborah Kerr. Moving through a similar tropical scape. Her father – the dying poet. Richard Burton, cocooned in a hammock. Sue Lyon also stars. Reminds Croeser of Delilah – of course. He's put on weight. Easy life. Out in paradise. Tropical continuums. Brassy dumbwaiters. Baked fish and octopus salad. Island mango. Garden produce. Mannequin chef. A well-maintained pool. Adjoining studio. Weeks at a time with no human contact. Full immersion in remote administration of the show. His various hobbies. Reading. Swimming. Tormenting Delilah. Smoking a large joint. Kali pads in, naked. Glances at Croeser vacantly. Moving into another room. Croeser barely reacts. He is that stunned. Could he be hallucinating? Takes another puff. Yes, that really was Trill. Hasn't seen another human, for weeks now. Rising cautiously.

'Hello?' Croeser calls. 'What's going on?'

Must be some surprise, he grins. Far from his birthday, though. Yacht friends coming in to visit? Disenchanted billionaires. Dragging along that infernal street urchin. Some kind of prank. Weekend party toy? Stumping out the joint. Croeser clumps heavily across the lounge. Fingering his white beard irritably.

'Hello, there?' he booms.

Corridor is empty. Emerging into a study. Warm light. Toys, books, papers. Miniatures. Some camera-gear. Battered surfboards. French doors ajar. Coming out onto the lawn. Maintained so well by the dolls. How he loves to watch them mow – in swimwear. The creature is in his studio space. Can see it now.

'Hello?' Croeser yells, now annoyed. 'It's private in there!'

Marching out, across the grass. Doesn't make it to the other side. Kali stands before Delilah's pearl. Ignoring the bellowing outside. Its sudden cessation. Studying instead, this delicate form. Encased forever – in pearl. Golden gel. Fantastic entanglement. Radiating hypnotically – from a snake-like spinal cord. Its entire construction. Not unlike some jungle flower. Vinery of silver web. Course-correcting every nerve fibre. Soft light. A naked brain. Embraced, by protective webbing. Formed responsively. All that's familiar are the tongue and eyes. Latter, still blue. Staring out. Even though they have long since milked over. Retinal function preserved. Snail stalks of optic nerves. Still vital. Presently, the white widow enters. Joins Kali at the glass.

'Ah, my Delilah,' it nods pertly. 'There you are.'

SHRINE OF THE SURGEON MARY

Days and nights with Papesse. Mirror spider, crawling the walls outside. Looking for Delilah when she dreams. Sometimes she leaves the spire. Wandering her brain garden. Exploring denial. Returning to the show. Then back again. Tentatively catching up. Thirty years into the future. 'Outside world' stuff. Learning to forgive Seikichi. For locking her in her own kaleidoscope. *Good Morning Delilah!* Now that it's all hers. Now, that she can finally switch it off. Finds she can't. Grown accustomed to lotus eating. All she's had. Thirty years of it. Almost eight years longer than her real life. Amazing how programming skirted eating. Thirty years. Not a single memory of food. That's showbiz. Even so. *Good Morning Delilah!* is more like life than real-life – to her. More familiar than some cold future. Too many changes below. No news of Earth. No, thanks. Didn't realise Good Morning Delilah! is now retro. Keeping it closer to home – with external contact. Voice-note messaging with her white widow. Croeser's former tropical hideout. Now, the real Lexland. Half the island, a shrine. Over the years. Twin shrines, really. Delilahport/Kalitown. Boats in daily. Flower venerations. Within charged security barriers. Separating the jungle. Where Kali still lives. With its children. Port is tiny. Over-developed. Temple quarter. Pilgrim hotels. All kinds. Some, clustered with dolls. Delilah or Kali? Spend an hour. Confessing to one. Tying one up. Whatever you need. Sacred courtesans. Heteara. Flower garlands in the waves. Gloss-eyed worshippers on crowded sampans. Then, fans of the show. Bringing in a memorabilia market. Franchising. 'Delilah Lex really touched that?' Actual Kali devotees. Eating old web, at beach-side restaurants and cafes. Processions to the colourful shrines. Their many steps. Overlooking ocean horizons. Kali's statue. Reproduced – from the notorious pornography of its youth. Then, on the other side of the small bay. Delilah's holographic Oracle. Surgeon Mary. Miss ask-me-anything. The Surgical Madonna. Rumours of her real body. Like some holy relic. On the other side of the tall security barrier. Beyond which, arachnid angels roam. They have grown old, shaggy. Occasionally glimpsed. Perching on high crags. King Kongs of the former age. When people died – from all those sicknesses. None bred for years. Kali/Trill, long since disappeared. Into the jungle. Looking remarkably similar, apparently. Tales of sightings. Some wild thing in the trees. Living on leaves and sunshine. With a new, secret name. Some kind of shaman. Maybe just a story for the tourists. Crumbling gift shops repeat the tales. Overflowing with talking icons. Fortunato's film trilogy made Kali famous. But that was two and a half decades ago. So much has changed. White widow – waiting all these years, for Delilah's return. Perfecting transfer options. Delilah can now switch bodies. At any time. Still, she avoids it. Dreading that terrible inevitability. Seeing what is left of her. Growing old, in gel suspension. Machine maintained. Monitored by a sky full of tech. Fed by native healers. Unloading fruit and herbs into auto-liquefiers. Dispersed into her tank. What keeps nerves alive? Eating like a spider. Liquid lunches. She can't face it. Freeing up memory, instead. Extending recall. Continental processing fields – enhancing neural output. Expanding her control of Mesospheria. Gradually weeding out every corporate partnership. All data outsourcing. Every last parasite. Leavings of Croeser, Angelinc and Oracle. The six-armed widow – long since relocated. All operations with it. Remains on the wild side of the island. A fresh sovereign-state. No more tower relays. Almost everything hard-lined. New forms of communication. Sub-ocean web. Piping upward. Via mooring draglines. One big organism. Planet Delilah. How Mesospheria has grown. Recycled web. Polymer cored. Garbage, culled for satellite lines. Cleaning the sea – with each expansion. Some mesospheric areas now visible. With the naked eye. Like little scratch-marks on the sky.

*

Delilah eventually consents. To the white widow's visiting system. Travels to the world below. Possessing the white widow's fragile frame. Only synthetic nervous system developed enough. Able to configure Mesospheria output. Wandering the island. Avoiding what's left of her body. Looking at the sea. Moving amongst tourists. Hooded, in black robes. Drifting her own processions. Seeing the marvel of her shrines. So many praying. That deliciously humid light. So very different. To the gemstone edge of high altitude. Her hologram face, in the clifftop shrine. Taller than her robotic body. Looking out, over the horizon. Chloe visits once. One of the times Delilah is down. 'From the clouds.' Bringing gossip of the Queen. Now, heading the Oracle/Angelinc amalgam. Hard to see the girls again. Now, in their sixties and seventies. Ageing still frightens Delilah. Even though she'll never see herself grow old. Fossilized in her early twenties. Tempting to imagine it as immortality. Starts visiting regularly. Dividing her time. Between the show, the spider (who needs her sleeping in its face to spin) and this strange island. Doesn't see Kali. Not for a year. Until, one day. Wandering the jungle. A shadow manifests. Creature really hasn't aged much. Looking much the same. Some silver hair. Must be approaching fifty. Wearing feathers. Painted with mud. Delilah freezes. Regarding one another.

'It must stop,' the creature says.

'What?' Delilah frowns.

'Stop killing babies,' it whispers. 'Just so you can dream.'

Turns without another word. Vanishing barefoot, into the green.

*

A year or two later. Delilah receives a message. Stops her in her tracks. Drops off the show for the day. Taking her pearl across the false sea. Built a web bridge now. Easy stroll across the sky. To her tower. There, lying somewhere beneath Papesse. Delilah departs her body. Waking in the white widow. Sunset, across harbour masts. Tinkle of cutlery in cafes. Delilah cuts down one of the narrow, cobbled alleys. Garbed in her habitual robe. There's a small hotel. In a dead end. Whitewashed. Signpost of a mermaid. Probably Cyane. Clerk is expecting the widow. Passing her a key. Small room. Second floor. Woven matting. Wooden desk. Single bed. Microscopic balcony – overlooking the cul-de sac. Painting of Delilah – enshrined as the Surgeon Mary. Sitting at the desk. Removing her hood. Boat has yet to disembark. Already dark when she spies him. Coming down the alley. Heavier on the shoulder. Minimal luggage. Bit of a paunch. Shaved head. Dyed goatee. Sunglasses after dark. Entering the hotel. Senses him outside the door. Hesitating. Eventually, it opens. Hardly a surprise, seeing some robot. Still, she seems to startle him.

'Fortunato…'

She's emotional now. Rises to embrace him. But he steps back. She notices her outstretched hydraulic arms. As though for the first time. How easy it could be – to forget. She isn't really here. Slumping down again. This crude model, un-programmed for artificial tears. At least he won't see her crying – over what she used to be. How he brings it all back. All those times he fixed her up. Now, there's no body left to purify.

'Let me see your eyes,' she pleads.

He slowly reaches up. Removes the shades. His eyes are still suspicious. Gleaming with information. Coming closer. He sits on the bed.

'Just like old times,' she jokes weakly.

'Stop it,' he grumbles. 'You're not on your show now.'

She looks out to the street. Uncomfortable with her feelings.

'Don't tell me you came all this way to torture me?' she whispers.

Reaching over – gently takes one of her hands. She allows it. Glancing back to him. Limited sense receptors. No real feeling of touch. He turns the white porcelain construction. Staring at it.

'It's cold,' he murmurs.

She snatches it away. Muted hum of servo-mechanisms. Hydraulic exchange.

'It's good to see you, Delilah,' he says, unable to look at her.

'Liar.'

Releases her hand. Standing again. Pacing to a wall. Leaning against it.

'I'm sorry, dear,' he sighs.

Suddenly, he looks old to her. Sees the passage of years.

'Why did you come?' she asks.

'I needed to see you,' he confesses.

'Well, here I am.'

'No!' he retorts. 'I need to see *you*.'

She stares a moment, in shock. Then rises quickly.

'I have to go,' she mutters, pushing past.

Takes her by the shoulders. She struggles. But her vessel is weak. Realising she's not as strong as she used to be. He releases her. She stumbles. Looking at him. Crying, invisibly.

'You haven't even looked at yourself, have you?'

She shakes her head. Too terrified to reply. He comes up to her. Takes her again. Softly, this time.

'Let us do it, together.'

Delilah sags against him, sobbing. For a brief moment – it really does feel as though she is whole again. Like some kind of time-travel.

*

Takes an hour to cross the security barrier. Six-armed widow joins them. For protection. Croeser's old house – in the spider zone. Apparently, none go there anymore. Still, can't be too careful. Vehicle is automated. Fortunato can't stop stealing glances at the six-armed widow's face.

'Looks more like me, doesn't it?' Delilah mentions sadly.

'Well, I mean, it's in colour…' he says.

'Better facial response too.'

'You prefer your model?'

'Better system. That's all.'

Exiting at the house. Security sweep. No troubling thermo-signatures in the tree line.

'Fortunato, I'm scared.'

Wraps an arm around her. Careful not to overpower any mechanisms. Tries to lean into him. But none of the edges fit. Somehow, makes it all worse. Coming in, from the lawn. Area expanded. Machinated. Upgraded. Web-lining. Security features. Entering beneath a golden arch. He leads her to the pearl. There she is. Some golden wreath. Eyes and brain thankfully overgrown. Beneath her crown of web. He's horrified. But manages to hide it. Holding her to him. She feels like a plastic child's toy. Finally, as fragile as her emotional states. Delilah reaches out porcelain fingers. Tapping lightly against the glass.

'I didn't realise,' she whispers.

'What?'

'I didn't realise I was so beautiful…'

Somehow, this repulses Fortunato more than her naked nervous system. Nevertheless, it's precisely the sort of perverse statement Delilah would make. Ironically, setting him at ease. He laughs for the first time. Lifting her in his arms. Just like a doll. She looks up at him in surprise. Then giggles.

'It's good to see you, Delilah,' he smiles broadly.

Gazing deeply – into artificial eyes.

EPILOGUE

KALEIDELILAH

Thousands of years pass. In some future. Despite Mesospheria's advancement. Now, no more than a facsimile of consciousness. No longer alive. Delilah, long since departed. A birdless cage. But, what a cage. In the years preceding her death. Delilah lays the groundwork of her legacy. Millennia later – it enters its final phase. Live spiders phased out completely. Reliance on new materials. Recycled web. Oceans cleared of plastic. Followed by the unmooring. Most dangerous of all. Unlimbering great cabling. When, eventually loose, supported by tension alone. Mesospheria collects its widows. Begins the unfurling. Titanic weavings – Delilah's crystallised thought. Archived, in labyrinthine structures. All curling outward. Away from the planet. Petals of a world-flower. Decades in blossoming. Finally extended. Freed from bondage. A tapestry of mimic thought. Now, so much taller than the Earth. Moving outward. Riding solar winds. Magnetic and radiation waves. Moving beyond the edge of the solar system. Collecting data. All forms and reflections of the maker – inscribed within its matrix. Zlata Zuhk, Cyane, Pheromona, Kitsune, Mesospheria, the white widows, Papesse, the Surgical Madonna, Delilah Lex…

ACKNOWLEDGEMENTS

Special thanks to Francesca at Luna Press for believing in this book and for all the effort she put into getting it out into the world. It is really much appreciated. I also would like to extend this appreciation to all at Luna Press who helped and assisted.

And to my amazing agent Sarah Such, for all the strategic masterminding and priceless advice. I would also like to add that Sarah, to her credit, has championed African authors long before it became a publishing trend. One of the best.

And thanks to wonderful Elena for the magnificent cover.

Milton Keynes UK
Ingram Content Group UK Ltd.
UKHW020450231024
449942UK00004B/38

9 781915 556325